Dear Friends:

In my novel, *Summer Rental*, three l............................se
lives all seem to be on the brink of . . . so................................
a monthlong vacation in Ebbtide, a broken-down summer rental on the
beach at the Outer Banks. They arrive expecting a halcyon reunion, but then
Madison, a stranger with a secret past, moves in to share the rent, and they
meet Ty, the hunky-yet-mysterious surfer who lives over the garage, and their
vacation suddenly becomes much more than any of them bargained for.

If a delicious beach read is an essential component for your own vacation getaway, I hope you'll find what you're looking for within these covers.
And just in case you need a checklist, here's my own list of summer-rental
essentials—conveniently available at Costco!

- ☐ skin-care products
- ☐ hair-care products
- ☐ cases of bottled water, soft drinks,
  beer, wine
- ☐ margarita mix!
- ☐ lemons and limes
- ☐ fresh berries and fruit for smoothies
- ☐ blender for smoothies/frozen
  margaritas
- ☐ picnic fixings
- ☐ frozen shrimp
- ☐ hot dogs

- ☐ hamburgers
- ☐ popsicles
- ☐ ice cream
- ☐ rotisserie chicken
- ☐ reading glasses

*Beach Reading:*
- ☐ latest Mary Kay Andrews
  novel (natch!)
- ☐ magazines
- ☐ aspirin

Just add water (preferably from the beach) and stir.

I had an absolute blast writing *Summer Rental* and I hope you have
equally as much fun reading it.

Enjoy!

*Mary Kay Andrews*

Praise for *Summer Rental*

"Mary Kay Andrews spins a beach-blanket sizzler around three lifelong friends . . . a warm-weather treat that has a lot going for it, not least the sunny forecast that summer love can blossom into a four-season commitment."

—*Publishers Weekly*

"Andrews writes another charmer with a picturesque Southern setting and winsome female characters."                                                           —*Booklist*

"[R]eaders of *Summer Rental* will stay glued to their sandy beach chairs waiting to see what happens next."          —*The Christian Science Monitor*

"Secrets are shared, a mystery woman appears, love may be in the air."

—*People* magazine

"[T]his is prime beach-read material."     —*Daily Record* (Gannett newspapers)

"*Summer Rental* is like a great day at the beach. You don't want it to end. Enjoy a vacation any time of the year with the ever-delightful Mary Kay Andrews."          —Susan Elizabeth Phillips, author of *Call Me Irresistable*

"The bright and breezy plot of *Summer Rental* delivers just the right combination of sexy romance and warm friendship."          —*Chicago Tribune*

"*Summer Rental* is just a delight to savor. The lively cast of characters is complex, genuine, and strong, and the interplay between the long-term friends is heartwarming."          —*Times Record News* (Texas)

"You will relate to the women and their relationships as you laze through the pages . . . and you will smile, chuckle, and maybe even get a little misty eyed."

—*Examiner.com*

## ALSO BY MARY KAY ANDREWS

*The Fixer Upper*

*Deep Dish*

*Savannah Breeze*

*Blue Christmas*

*Hissy Fit*

*Little Bitty Lies*

*Savannah Blues*

# Summer Rental

# Mary Kay Andrews

St. Martin's Griffin
New York

This is a work of fiction. All of the characters, organizations, and events portrayed in this novel are either products of the author's imagination or are used fictitiously.

SUMMER RENTAL. Copyright © 2011 by Whodunnit, Inc. All rights reserved. Printed in the United States of America. For information, address St. Martin's Press, 175 Fifth Avenue, New York, N.Y. 10010.

www.stmartins.com

THE LIBRARY OF CONGRESS HAS CATALOGED THE HARDCOVER EDITION AS FOLLOWS:

Andrews, Mary Kay, 1954–
    Summer rental / Mary Kay Andrews.—1st ed.
        p. cm.
    ISBN 978-0-312-64269-3
    1. Women—Fiction. 2. Female friendship—Fiction. 3. Summer—Fiction.
    4. Vacations—Fiction. 5. Outer Banks (N.C.)—Fiction. I. Title.
    PS3570.R587S78 2011
    813'.54—dc22

                                                2011004404

ISBN 978-1-250-02196-0 (Costco Edition)

First St. Martin's Griffin Edition: May 2012

10   9   8   7   6   5   4   3   2   1

*Dedicated with love to Molly Hogan Abel,*
*who actually* did *hang the moon and the stars*

# Acknowledgments

The author wishes to express heartfelt thanks to all those who patiently answered her questions, offered her advice and/or Diet Coke, or just put up with her whining and complaining during the writing and research of this novel. Any errors or misstatements of fact are my own and not theirs.

Huge thanks go to the Weymouth Center for the Arts and Humanities of Southern Pines, North Carolina, where large portions of this novel were plotted, and to my precious, invaluable writer buddies, Diane Chamberlain, Margaret Maron, Katy Munger, Sarah Shaber, Alexandra Sokoloff, and Bren Witchger, who trounced me at Scrabble and Balderdash and helped in more ways than I can say. Thanks to Anne Needham for helping me with foreclosure info; to Beth Fleishman, who helped me scout Nags Head; Frank Jones, who told me about day-trading; Sascha Springer, my source on location scouts; and Bobbie Murray of Pelican Cottages of Nags Head, who rented me the adorable Windswept cottage and connected me with longtime Nags Head residents Jean and Edward Griffin and Nancy and Peter Rascoe.

To my editor, the amazing Jennifer Enderlin, I offer everlasting gratitude for whipping me, and the girls of Ebbtide, into shape. Many thanks also to the team at St. Martin's Press, including but not limited to the fabulous Sally Richardson, Matthew Shear, Matthew Baldacci, John Karle, John Murphy, and Dori Weintraub. The best damn agent in the whole world, Stuart Krichevsky, guided and presided, and was, as always, a beacon of light when things got funky, so huge thanks to him and the girls of SKLA.

Family might be listed last, but they come first in my heart, and in my thanks—to Tom, Andy, Katie, Mark, and yes, Molly, all my love, now and always.

# 1

It was not an auspicious beginning for a vacation, let alone for a new life. The rain chased her all the way down the East Coast, slashing at the windshield, pounding her car from every angle. Between the backwash from a continuous stream of eighteen-wheelers blowing past her at eighty miles an hour (in contrast to her own sedate fifty-five mph) and violent gusts of wind from the storm, it was all she could do to stay on the roadway.

It was her own fault, Ellis decided. She should have stuck to her original plan. She should have gotten up at a sensible hour, at least waiting until daylight to start the drive from Philadelphia to North Carolina. Instead, on some insane impulse, she'd simply locked up the town house and driven off shortly after midnight.

It was a most un-Ellis-like decision. But then, her old life, back there in Philly, was gone. And somewhere, on that long drive south, she had subconsciously decided that the seeds of a new life must be waiting, at the beach. In August.

Ellis took a deep breath and rolled her shoulders, first forward, and then backwards, trying to work out the kinks from six hours of driving. She reached for the commuter mug of coffee in the Accord's cup holder and took a long sip, hoping it would clear the fatigue fog.

An hour later, she saw the sign: Nags Head, 132 miles. She smiled. The rain had slowed to a light drizzle. She should arrive at the house, which was called Ebbtide, by around seven.

Her smile faded. What had she been thinking? Check-in was at 2 P.M., according to the renter's agreement she'd signed.

She composed a mental e-mail to herself: To: EllisSullivan@hotmail.com. From: EllisSullivan@hotmail.com. Subject: Failure to plan = plan to fail.

But the memo would have to wait. The highway rose and she found herself on a long, gently arching bridge. One more damned bridge. Surely it was the last. The Chesapeake Bay Bridge had nearly done her in. She felt her jaw clench tightly. Her fingertips clamped the steering wheel, and her heart raced. A bead of sweat trickled down her back.

Nags Head was on the Outer Banks of North Carolina. She'd studied her guidebooks, maps, and AAA Triptik for weeks now. She knew the island's geography, even its topography, intimately. But she'd refused to allow herself to focus on the bridge issue. Because the fact was, as the girls knew all too well, bridges—even wimpy little bridges like the Sam Varnedoe that separated Whitemarsh and Wilmington islands back home in Savannah—scared the living bejeezus out of Ellis Sullivan.

She kept her eyes straight ahead, not daring to look right or left at the water flowing under the bridge. When she'd finally crossed the bridge, her hands were clammy, her T-shirt sweat-soaked.

Now she was on the Outer Banks proper. Signs for the little towns flashed by: Corolla, Duck, Southern Shores, Kitty Hawk, Avalon Beach. The sun rose, and she was somehow shocked at how densely developed the beachfront was here. She'd expected to see clumps of sea oats silhouetted against sparkling blue water; sailboats bobbing at anchor; great, gray shingled houses staring moodily out to sea; the occasional lighthouse. The reality was that, so far, what she'd seen of the storied Outer Banks could just as well have been the Jersey shore, Myrtle Beach, Fort Lauderdale, or any other East Coast tourist resort—meaning miles and miles of hotels and motels, restaurants, and strip shopping centers lining both sides of the road, and a shoreline packed with cheek-to-jowl condo complexes and huge, pastel-painted beach houses.

She followed Route 12 south, and when the GPS computerized voice instructed her to turn left and then right, she knew she was getting close. Virginia Dare Trail was the beach road. Here, at least, there was a little bit of elbow room between the houses. Once or twice she actually caught a glimpse of sand dunes and sea oat plumes. Finally, the well-modulated woman's voice announced cheerily, "Arrive at destination, on left."

Ellis slowed the car and stared. A long crushed-shell drive led through a weedy patch of sand. There was a mailbox at the curb, with a sun-bleached cedar sign in the cutout shape of a whale. EBBTIDE was painted on the sign in faded white letters. The driveway ended at what looked like a two-story garage. The wood-shingled structure was a weathered grayish-brownish affair. Through a set of open wooden garage doors, she spotted a beat-up tan Bronco with a red surfboard strapped to the rooftop rack.

To the side of the garage, a rambling three-story wood-frame house arose from a set of wooden stairs. Stretched across the front of the house was a long, open porch. A row of rocking chairs marched across the porch, and a gaudy striped beach towel was draped carelessly across a railing. From the sandy side yard, a wooden walkway led up and over a towering sand dune.

On an impulse, she pulled the car into the next driveway. Here, there was no house at all, only the charred remains of a concrete-block foundation, along with some blackened timbers. A black-and-orange NO TRESPASSING sign was posted on a block wall. Ellis put the Accord in park and got out of the car, her cramped legs and back screaming in protest. The air was already hot and muggy. She did a couple of deep knee bends, scanning the yard next door for any signs of life. Had the earlier renters already checked out? Or did the Bronco in the garage belong to somebody who was still enjoying a last hour or two on the beach before it was time to head home?

She strolled over to the mailbox and peered up at the house. Their house, at least for the month of August. Ellis intended to make every hour of this month count.

"Ebbtide," she said aloud, satisfied that the exterior of the house, at least, seemed to match the photo she'd spotted in the Vacation Rentals by Owner listing. Of course, that photo had also shown an inviting green lawn dotted with billowing blue hydrangeas and a hot-pink bicycle built for two with a charming wicker basket leaning up against a rose-covered picket fence. None of these were in evidence now. In fact, the only thing in evidence in what passed for a yard, besides a bumper crop of weeds, was a busted-up Styrofoam cooler full of empty malt liquor cans and a sodden heap of yellowing newspapers, still in their plastic wrappers.

She glanced down at her watch. She had half a day to kill until check-in. Being Ellis, she'd already planned to arrive hours before the others. The extra time would give her a chance to go to the grocery store, prepare their first night's dinner, get the house situated. Linens were not included in the house rental, so she'd brought enough sheets and towels for everybody, just in case. And yes, she would have first crack at choosing her bedroom, but since she *had* done all the legwork finding the house and planning this trip, would anybody really mind?

Well, maybe Willa would mind. She was only older than the others by twenty months, but really, she could be so pushy and bossy. It would be just like Willa to accuse Ellis of hogging the best bedroom. Which she had no intention of doing. She just didn't want a bedroom facing the street and a lot of noise. She was a light sleeper—and she had a lot of thinking to do. And anyway, as the only single woman in the group, she was used to her own space. Too used to it, she thought wryly.

She was dying to see Ebbtide up close. She glanced up and down the road. There was no sign of traffic. Just another sleepy summer morning at the beach. Maybe it wouldn't hurt to walk up the driveway of the burnt-out house to see what she could see. Technically, she knew, it was trespassing. But it wasn't like she was looting the place. What was left to loot?

Quickly, before she lost her nerve, Ellis trotted up the crushed oyster-shell drive. Another wooden boardwalk and a set of stairs leading up and over the sand dune, just like the one at Ebbtide, seemed to have survived the fire that had taken this house. She trod the steps quickly, not wanting to be seen from the road.

There was a shed-roofed deck at the top of the dunes. At one time it would have been an amazing place to sit and sip a cocktail and enjoy the ocean breezes. But not now. Some of the decking had rotted out, and the railings missed pickets in several places. A couple of broken plastic lawn chairs lay sprawled on their side, but it was the view that captured Ellis's attention. From here she could see the Nags Head she'd imagined. The dunes, covered with sea oats, beach plums, and shrubs whose names she didn't know, sloped down to meet a wide, white beach. The tide was out, and the Atlantic Ocean sparkled gray-blue below. Here and there, people walked along the shore, stooping to pick up shells.

"Perfect!" Ellis exclaimed. Just then, she heard the slap of a wooden screen door. Turning, she saw movement from the second-floor apartment over the garage at Ebbtide. That apartment had a small wooden deck wrapping around the sides and back of it. As she watched, a man walked out onto the deck. She could see him clearly—good Lord—he was in his underwear.

The man was barefoot, deeply tanned, with unkempt sun-bleached brownish hair. A pair of baggy white boxer briefs hung low on his slim hips. He turned, faced the water, yawned and stretched. And then, while Ellis watched, slack-jawed with amazement and disgust, he quite casually proceeded to pee off the edge of the deck.

He took his own good time about it too. Ellis was rooted to the spot where she stood, her face crimson with embarrassment. When he was finally finished, he stretched and turned. And that's when he spotted her, a lone figure in hot pink capris and a white T-shirt, her long dark hair blowing in the breeze coming off the beach.

The man gave her a nonchalant smile. His teeth were white and even, and from here she could see the golden stubble of a days-old beard. He waved casually. "Hey," he called. "How ya doin'?"

Ellis managed a strangled "Hey." And then she fled down the stairs as fast as her flip-flop-shod feet would take her.

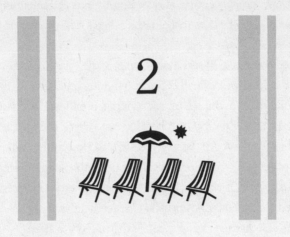

# 2

Ellis jumped in the Accord and backed out onto the roadway so quickly she nearly mowed over the Ebbtide mailbox. That's what she got for trespassing, she thought. A bird's-eye view of a pervert. She checked over her shoulder, back towards that garage apartment, to see if the man would reemerge from the deck to see where she'd gone. But there was no sign of him now.

Hopefully, she thought, he was the owner of that Bronco parked in the garage. Hopefully, he would be checking out of Ebbtide any time now, and he would be long gone by her check-in. Hopefully.

But what was she going to do with herself until then? There was an outlet mall down the road, but it probably didn't open until ten. And she needed to get groceries, but she didn't want her refrigerated goods to sit in her hot car for the hours until check-in.

She drove aimlessly down the road until she came to a restaurant whose marquee promised BREAKFAST SERVED ALL DAY—EVERY DAY. The parking lot was full. She even spotted a couple of UPS trucks, which, her father had told her years ago, meant the joint must be half decent.

The hostess showed her to a table near the window, and Ellis ordered scrambled eggs, turkey sausage, and an English muffin. Unbuttered. No coffee. She was wide awake now. Instead, she asked for ice water and grapefruit juice.

When the food came, she ate slowly, willing the time to pass quickly. The restaurant was noisy with small children laughing and running between the tables and the excited chatter of vacationing families and friends. When she'd finished eating, Ellis took out her iPhone to check her e-mails.

The iPhone was new. All those years she'd worked at the bank, the Black-Berry clipped securely to the outside of her pocketbook had been her lifeline to her workday world. It was the first thing she touched every morning, weekends included—even before she brushed her teeth and showered—and it was the last thing she checked at night, before drifting off to sleep.

But two weeks ago, an e-mail on that BlackBerry had summoned her to a meeting with Phyllis K. Stone in human resources. Around the company, Ms. Stone was known as "the grim reaper" or "Stonehenge." But she'd always been perfectly nice to Ellis on the rare occasions they'd had dealings. On that particular day, Ellis had assumed she was going to be given her new health-care packet. But the packet which Ms. Stone silently slid across her desk to Ellis had nothing to do with deductibles or co-pays. BancAtlantic, her employer for the past eleven years, was, Ms. Stone said blandly, being swallowed up—no, *acquired* was the exact word—by CityGroup, Inc.

"Obviously, CityGroup has its own marketing department," Ms. Stone went on. "And because their concern at this time is in cost savings and maximum efficiency as well as financial stability for our stockholders, the executive committee has decided that BancAtlantic's marketing group will be extraneous."

Ellis wasn't sure she understood what Ms. Stone was saying. "Extraneous? Does that mean I'll be transferred over to the CityGroup side?"

Ms. Stone slid the packet a millimeter closer to Ellis. "I'm afraid not."

Ellis felt her mouth go dry and her palms begin to sweat. She liked her job, liked the people she worked with, loved the lifestyle it afforded her: the town house in a good neighborhood, business travel with a generous expense account, a new car every three years. "Then," she said, her voice quavering a little, "I'll be offered another position within the bank? I mean, it's not like I was born into marketing. My degree is in finance, and before I joined Banc-Atlantic..."

Ms. Stone's lips pursed slightly. Her fuchsia lipstick had feathered into the deep creases in her upper lip. She had a mustache too. Ellis wondered why she didn't wax it, or at least get it bleached.

Now Ms. Stone was tapping the file folder again. It had a glossy photograph of BancAtlantic's granite-and-chrome headquarters building on it, and the words TRANSITIONS FOR TOMORROW were superimposed across the photo.

There was a clattering outside the window of Ms. Stone's seventh-floor office. Ellis looked up and saw a window-washing apparatus glide slowly past. But the men on the apparatus were not window washers. They wore dark jumpsuits, and they were wrestling with a huge chrome logo, consisting of eight-foot-high letters: CG, in flowing script.

It occurred to Ellis that the bank's new owners were not waiting until tomorrow for transitions.

"This is your separation package," Ms. Stone said quietly. "You'll find it's quite generous. You'll have your pension, of course. Your buyout will give you two weeks' salary for every year of your service with the institution."

"Institution?" Ellis said dully.

"BancAtlantic," Ms. Stone reminded her. "Although," she said, glancing down at the wristwatch strapped to her unnaturally narrow wrist, "as of three minutes ago, BancAtlantic ceased to exist. We're CityGroup now. It's an exciting time, isn't it?"

Somehow, Ellis thought, she would not have chosen "exciting" as the adjective to describe this moment. She finally reached over and picked up the file folder which Ms. Stone had been inching towards her. She rifled through the contents. It contained legal forms and memos, and just looking at the fine print of the documents made a vein in her forehead throb. She had to get back to her office, read the documents, and try to process everything.

She stood up. "How long?" she asked. "I've got a big project I've been working on, and the report should be done by next week."

Ms. Stone blinked. Ellis could have sworn she hadn't seen the woman blink before. Ever.

"Oh," Ms. Stone said. "I thought you understood. Your termination is immediate."

"Like, right now?"

"I'm afraid so," Ms. Stone said, holding out her hand, palm up, expectantly.

Ellis Sullivan was not normally a woman given to sarcasm. But somehow, the occasion seemed to cry out for . . . something.

"What?" Ellis said hotly. "It's not enough you just *fired* me? You took my job, my career, eleven years of my life? And for that I get, what? Twenty-two weeks of pay? Are you *freakin'* kidding me? What do you want now, lady? A kidney? My spleen maybe?"

Ms. Stone's mustachioed upper lip twitched. "That's entirely uncalled for," she said, her voice tight. "This is purely a professional business decision made by the executive committee. Please don't try to make it personal."

"Not personal?" Ellis cried, fighting back tears.

"Not in the least," Ms. Stone said. She stood up now. She was a good six inches shorter than Ellis. She was holding out her hand again. "I'm going to have to ask for your employee security badge."

Ellis ripped the laminated badge from the beaded silk cord that hung around her neck, and flung it right in Ms. Stone's face. The woman blinked again, and then ducked, but the badge glanced off her chin before falling onto the desktop.

"The cord's mine," Ellis said. "It's not company property."

"Fine," Ms. Stone said. "Understood. And now I'll need your BlackBerry. The company's BlackBerry, that is."

Ellis winced. "I don't have it with me," she admitted. "It's in my office. I'll drop it off here after I clean out my desk."

Ms. Stone smirked. "Your desk has already been cleaned out." She crossed to the door and opened it. A security guard in an unfamiliar charcoal gray uniform stood in the hallway, clutching a large cardboard carton. Sticking out of the top of the carton was a goofy red-plush stuffed bear wearing a T-shirt with the BancAtlantic logo stitched in green script. Ellis had won the bear two years ago at the department's Christmas party. Her Louis Vuitton pocketbook, the one she'd splurged on after her last promotion, was draped across the security guard's arm.

Ms. Stone jerked her head in the direction of the pocketbook. Ellis took it from the guard, reached inside, and unclipped the BlackBerry.

Ms. Stone ducked, but all the fight had suddenly drained from Ellis. She put the BlackBerry on the edge of the desk, turned and followed the waiting security guard down the hall and into the elevator.

There she held out her arms for the carton. "I can take it from here. Don't worry. I won't come running back upstairs with an Uzi or anything."

The guard shrugged. "Sorry. I've gotta escort you all the way out of the building. It's policy."

She punched the "B" button on the control panel, and they rode the elevator down to the basement parking garage in silence. The guard followed her to the Accord. She opened the trunk and he put the carton inside it, handing her a slip of paper that had been lying on top of the contents.

"It's an inventory of everything from your office," he said apologetically. "If you could just initial it, you know?"

She scrawled her initials at the bottom of the page without even looking at the list and handed it back to him.

He nodded. "This really sucks, man. I hate this part."

"Not your first termination of the day?"

"You're my eleventh," he said gloomily. "After lunch, we've got commercial loan. The whole stinkin' department."

Ellis nodded. It was no consolation to know that the rest of her company was being disassembled and discarded, one department at a time. "See ya," she said, knowing she wouldn't.

She hadn't known what to do with herself for the first two days after what she'd come to think of as T-day. The first morning, she'd gotten up at her usual 6 A.M. and groped in the dark for her BlackBerry. After a brief moment of panic, she'd remembered that the bank had repossessed it, along with her former identity. Then, groaning, she settled back into the bed, realizing she really had no pressing need to get up.

What followed was a week of bereavement. She went two days without bathing, lived in grungy yoga pants and sweatshirts, subsisted on a steady diet of cold cereal and daytime television because she couldn't bear leaving the town house. Anyway, where would she go? After seven straight days of therapy courtesy of Dr. Phil reruns, she'd forced herself to go out and buy the iPhone. She even bought a perky pink rubber jacket for the thing.

Since she'd never had any e-mail address other than her BancAtlantic one, she set herself up with a Hotmail account and e-mailed everybody she could think of that she had a new e-mail. There had been the inevitable flurry of replies from friends wanting to know what was up.

She couldn't stand the idea of anybody pitying her, especially since she already had enough self-pity to go around, so she made up a peppy reply: "Midlife career adjustment! Time to stop and smell the roses! Details to follow."

But there were no details. Not yet. This trip with the girls, which she'd been plotting since April, when they'd all been together down in Savannah for Julia's mother's funeral, was the only thing that had kept her going since she'd lost her job. A small, insistent voice in the back of her head kept telling her she should have canceled the trip, should have saved her money, should have put herself right back out there on the job market.

And she'd replied to that small, insistent voice. Shut. The. Hell. Up.

It was almost August. No way was she canceling this beach trip.

So here she was, sitting in a restaurant in Nags Head, North Carolina, and two weeks' worth of her severance package had already been eaten up. She didn't care. In the past five years, she'd taken exactly one week of vacation per year, spending Christmas with her mother and aunt at the condo down in Sarasota, listening to her mother bicker with Aunt Claudia.

In April, Ellis had sat next to Julia in the front row of Blessed Sacrament Church in Savannah. Dorie sat on the other side of Julia, and Willa sat beside Dorie. Booker, Julia's boyfriend of many years, couldn't make the trip from London. All four of the girls clutched each other's hands as a young priest none of them recognized, Father Tranh, said the Mass of Christian Burial for Catherine Donohue Capelli. Later, back at the Capelli house, after all the funeral-goers had finally cleared out, the girls had taken off their funeral dresses, climbed into pajamas, and sprawled out on the double bed in Julia's old bedroom, just like they'd done all those Friday nights in the old days. Only this time, instead of sipping Pabst Blue Ribbon stolen from Mr. Capelli's beer fridge in the garage, they'd gotten shit-faced on a pitcher of cosmos.

And that's when they'd hatched the plan. No more catching up at funerals. Ellis's father had died two years earlier, and Mr. Capelli had been gone, what? Six years? No more of that, Julia had declared, waving the empty pitcher in the air.

"We're gonna go away together," she announced. "To the beach. All of us." She'd looked over at Dorie, the newlywed of the group, and added, meaningfully, "Just us girls."

The group had elected Ellis, the planner, the organizer, ruthlessly efficient Ellis, to put the trip together. And that's what she'd done. And now here she was, jobless, but with the whole month of August to spend in a summer rental with her best friends. Plus Willa, Dorie's sister, who'd invited herself along.

She felt positively giddy at the prospect. The amber-hued summers of her girlhood had been the sweetest of her life. She and Dorie and Julia had been inseparable, spending weeks at a time at Julia's grandmother's rambling cottage on Tybee Island, lazing around the beach during the day, spending hours getting ready to go out in the evenings.

Dorie always trailed a wake of would-be boyfriends, so they'd traveled in a pack, cruising the beach road in Julia's mother's big Fleetwood Caddy. It hadn't mattered that Ellis didn't have her own boyfriend. The Caddy was white with a moonroof and the fifth tire mounted on the trunk, a total pimp car, which they all thought screamingly hysterical—that Julia's churchgoing mother drove a pimpmobile. They loved the Fleetwood because it could fit six or seven people on its big leather bench seats. They'd roll the windows down and blast their favorite song, screaming the tagline—"WHOOMP, There It Is!"—over and over again, and the Fleetwood would rock with the heavy bass beat.

They'd dance at a club whose name Ellis had long since forgotten, but she could still remember the boy she'd met and danced with all night long the last summer weekend before her sophomore year of college. His name was Nick, and he went to Boston College, and she'd gladly let him grope her while they swayed to "I Swear," and she'd allowed herself to fantasize that it was Nick who was promising—by the moon and the stars above—to love her forever. Then school had started, and he'd e-mailed a couple of times, and then nothing.

Ellis looked down at the iPhone. She opened an e-mail window and typed in the address:

Mr.Culpepper@Ebbtide.com.

Dear Mr. Culpepper. I realize that my group's check-in time for Ebbtide technically isn't until 2 p.m. today, but I find myself in the area earlier than planned, and wonder if it would be possible to have access to the house any earlier. Say around noon? I'd be totally grateful. Sincerely, Ellis Sullivan.

She pushed the send button and a moment later heard the soft whooshing noise that notified her the message had been sent. Not for the first time, she pictured Mr. Culpepper as a wizened but kindly old duffer. She imagined him in a faded but starched Hawaiian shirt, with knobby knees protruding below madras Bermuda shorts, and wearing high black socks and beat-up sandals. His face would be weathered, his head nearly bald. He would take an instant liking to her and the girls, calling them "sweetheart" and "dearie."

She couldn't wait to meet Mr. Culpepper in person.

# 3

Maryn drove south, switching between the interstate and winding back roads, with no specific destination in mind. Away. That was the only place she knew she was going. Away from her home, what little family she had left. Away from Biggie; that one really hurt. But there was nothing she could do about that. She could still see Biggie's melting brown eyes watching as she rushed around the house, throwing her things in a duffle bag. He'd followed her from room to room, and then, when she was about to leave, he'd met her at the back door, his red leather leash in his mouth, convinced they were going to the dog park.

It broke her heart to leave Biggie behind. She told herself the aging golden retriever would be all right. He would never harm Biggie, not even to get back at her. He adored Biggie, had raised him from a puppy. Biggie had been there before her, and he would be there after her. Wouldn't he? Anyway, the main thing was that she had to get away. From him. And that meant leaving Biggie behind.

Thinking of him, she twisted the diamond solitaire on her ring finger. She'd wanted to fling it at him so many times, tell him yes, he'd bought her with it, but he'd gotten the deal of a lifetime. She'd almost left it behind, along with her other belongings. But at the last second, she decided she would keep wearing it, a reminder—as if she needed one—of how easily and cheaply she'd sold herself to the devil.

Maryn glanced down at her arm. Her sleeve hid them, but she could still feel the bracelet of ugly purple bruises on her left forearm. Another reminder of the real Don Shackleford. The bruises would fade, she knew, but she doubted she would ever forget his icy rage, the way he'd so easily clamped a hand around her arm—squeezing until she'd cried out in agony, his expression never changing as he told her exactly what he'd do to her if he ever caught her snooping around in his private business again.

"I'll bury you," he'd said, a strange light coming into his pale blue eyes. "Someplace where you'll never be found. Nobody will even know you're missing until it's too late. Not Adam, not your mother, nobody will know what happened, where Maryn has gone." He'd smiled at the thought of that. A moment later, he'd released her arm, but not before bending his head to her forearm and tenderly kissing the angry red welts he'd left there.

By the time she heard his Escalade roar out of the driveway, she'd already started planning her escape.

She locked the front door and ran to her bedroom. When she retrieved the money from the Ugg boots at the back of her closet, she was startled to discover that she'd amassed nearly six thousand dollars. Her seed money was twenty-seven hundred dollars in winnings from an April trip to Atlantic City, money she'd won at blackjack, and which she'd told Don she'd spent on clothes and shoes. Lying to him came easily to her and didn't seem wrong. The rest of the money was added in spurts: a twenty picked up from the wad of bills Don tossed on his dresser at night, a hundred saved back from the money she told him she needed for a new jacket, five hundred dollars realized when she exchanged the ridiculously expensive (and ugly) watch he'd given her for her birthday for a more suitable model.

Maryn couldn't say why she'd been squirreling away those twenties and fifties. Was it really for that Hermès Kelly bag she'd been eyeing, or was it more the vague memory of her mother's cynical advice, delivered with a cigarette dangling from colorless lips? "A woman always needs to have her own money. Always. Get-outta-town money."

Thank God for the one good piece of advice her mama had given her. The packing hadn't taken long. Twenty minutes? She'd changed blouses, putting on a long-sleeved silk top to hide the bruises on her arm. So here she was, back on the road. Again.

How long had she been driving? Her eyes burned with exhaustion, her arms and shoulders ached. She should stop soon. Stop for sleep. For food, although her stomach roiled at the thought of eating.

She'd crossed the Virginia line, saw that she was in North Carolina now. The sun was coming up. She flipped the Dior sunglasses down over her eyes and squinted at a billboard advertising a place called The Buccaneer, a motel on Nags Head.

Nags Head. Her parents had taken her to Nags Head the summer after her father was transferred to Fort Bragg, in Fayetteville, North Carolina. She'd been what, twelve? They'd stayed in a tiny motel, right on the beach, and her father took her fishing on the pier, just the two of them. The motel had a pool and a little coffee shop, and they'd eaten out every night, a real treat. One night they'd played putt-putt golf, another time they rode bumper cars in an amusement park.

Had that been the last happy summer? The divorce came a year later. Just as she was settling into her new school. Not that she'd made many friends there. She'd been a goofy-looking kid, all knees and elbows, with hair the color of dirty dishwater and a head too big for her body. Maryn had been appalled when she became the first girl in her sixth-grade class to need a bra. Her mother, of course, had celebrated this fact by buying Maryn the tightest-fitting tank top she could find. "If you got it, flaunt it," Mama told her. To avoid a fight, Maryn wore the tank, but topped it with a baggy shirt the minute she left the house for school.

She'd just started cracking the social code of her new school when Mama loaded her into the faded blue Buick that May and announced they were going to visit Aunt Patsy in New Jersey. "If you think I'm stayin' in this godforsaken excuse of a town while your daddy parades around with that whore girlfriend of his, you've got another think coming," Mama said, throwing the car into reverse and slamming into the mailbox at the end of the driveway. She didn't even stop to look at her crumpled rear fender.

Visit? How about move in with her mother's older sister, Aunt Patsy, a part-time hairdresser and full-time alcoholic? By fall, Maryn had emerged from puberty and entered junior high, two inches taller, wearing a B cup, tight-fitting new acid-washed Jordache jeans, and a glamorous blond hairdo courtesy of Aunt Patsy. Also by fall, Maryn's mother had joined Aunt Patsy at the hair salon—and the liquor store.

Maryn's first few weeks of junior high had been a triumph. A petite brunette named Brooke sat in front of her in homeroom and took pity on the new girl, inviting her to sit at the cool girls' table at lunch. She'd gotten invited to sleepovers and skating parties and spent hours on the phone with Brooke every night, rehashing who-likes-who, with her mother and aunt relishing every second of Maryn's newfound popularity.

In October, she'd gotten invited to her first boy-girl function: a Halloween party. The invitation threw her mother and Aunt Patsy into a frenzy of sewing and thrift-store shopping. On the appointed night, Maryn slithered into Heather Palumbo's basement rec room dressed in a towering black wig and a flowing, long-sleeved black sheath with a deeply plunging neckline. Her face had been whitened with pancake makeup, her eyes rimmed and outlined with stark black liner, her lips lacquered bloodred, matching her inch-long fake red fingernails.

All these years later, Maryn could still remember the impact her entry had on the party. Brooke and Heather and Colleen, dressed in '50s-era poodle skirts, bobby socks, and letter sweaters, gathered in a circle around her, staring at her as though she'd just been beamed down from another planet. "What are you supposed to be?" Colleen demanded, hands on hips.

"You know," Maryn said, taken aback. "Elvira. Mistress of the Dark. Like from TV?"

"You look," Heather sneered, "like a prostitute."

Maryn's cheeks burned with shame. She'd slipped upstairs to try to call her mother and ask her to come pick her up early, but Mama and Patsy had dropped her off and headed straight to Harlow's, their favorite bar.

When Maryn got back to the basement, she'd found that the girls had turned on her. The boys, however, had been a different story. They'd swarmed around her, laughing and talking too loud, bringing her Cokes and asking her to dance. In what seemed like an instant, she'd simultaneously become both the belle of the ball and the school skank—depending on your gender.

If Brooke and Colleen quit calling, Alex and Nathan and Jordan (an eighth-grader) took up the slack. At first, Maryn was devastated at the loss of Brooke's friendship. But her mother and aunt reveled in her sudden status as a femme fatale.

"You don't need those silly little bitches," Aunt Patsy advised. "Every single one of them is jealous of you because you're cuter and the boys like you better than them." As the weeks and months passed, and it became clear that she held a surprising new power over the opposite sex, Maryn decided she liked boys just fine.

Not that she didn't miss having a best girlfriend. When Aunt Patsy lost her job at the Stylesetter Salon at the beginning of Maryn's sophomore year of high school, forcing them to move to a smaller rental house in a different school district, Maryn made a conscious decision to reinvent herself.

Before school started that year, Maryn hung out at the mall, studying what the other girls were wearing. She bought button-fly Levi's 501 jeans and pastel Gap tees, quit bleaching her hair, and toned down her makeup.

And for what? Despite her best efforts, Maryn found herself frozen out of the cliques and circles in her new school. So when Wesley Bates, the cute, dumb jock who was her chemistry lab partner, asked her out for the third Saturday in a row, Maryn had finally agreed to go, even though she'd heard through the school grapevine that Wesley was supposedly dating a girl named Janelle Rivenbark.

One date. She'd gone out with Wes exactly once, but to Janelle Rivenbark and her coven, that had been more than enough to seal her fate. The next Monday, she'd found hate notes stuffed into her locker. Every night, there were

5eaoig

crank phone calls and hang ups. Bags of flaming dog poop were left on her doorstep, her mother's car was egged, her aunt's yard festooned with toilet paper on a weekly basis.

"Screw 'em," her mother advised, and finally, Maryn had come to the same conclusion. From that point on, Maryn made her own rules. She was never without at least one boyfriend and wasn't shy about stealing a boy, especially if his previous girlfriend was friends with Janelle Rivenbark.

All the while, her mama and Aunt Patsy cheered her on, living vicariously through her romantic conquests. No matter how late she came in on a Friday or Saturday night, her mother waited up, eager to rehash the night's events.

Thinking of her mother now made Maryn wince. When had they last talked—three, four months ago? Maryn's eyelids drooped, then fluttered. She had to get off the road. She hit the button to open her window, let in some fresh air. Nags Head, she decided. She would stop in Nags Head. It was far enough away from New Jersey. Far enough away from him.

# 4

Ty Bazemore went around to the back of the house and tried the door-knob. Good. It was locked. God knows, there was nothing really valuable in the house, but it was better to make sure about stuff like this.

He unlocked the door and stepped inside the kitchen. "Christ!" he muttered, looking around. The place was a disaster. Dirty pots and pans were piled in a sink full of sludgy gray water. Every dish in the house seemed to be piled on the countertop. The trash can in the corner was overflowing with empty beer cans and wine bottles, and there was a distinct fishy smell.

He peered down into a pot that had been left on the stove top. Yup. It was full of shrimp peels, and it had been there a day or two. He picked up the pot and went to dump it out, and for the first time, noticed the slurping sound his flip-flops were making on the linoleum floor.

He looked down and lifted his right heel slightly. The flip-flop stuck to the floor.

"Fuckin' college punks," he said aloud.

He should have known better. The e-mail address for their reservation had been Cooter@Gamecocks.com. The VRBO and Craigslist ads clearly stated that rental of the house was restricted to adults. But Cooter and company had paid for a week in advance, and the American Express card they'd paid with had gone through with no problem. He'd had a bad feeling about it from the start, but, hey, thirty-four hundred dollars was nothing to sneeze at, not these days.

So when the caravan of cars had pulled into the driveway—first a stripped-down Jeep, then two pickup trucks and a lime green VW bug convertible carrying four half-drunk chicks—he'd made up his mind to ignore them. He'd watched with a sinking heart, though, as sixteen college kids piled into the house. And that was just the first night.

The ad specifically stated that the house slept a maximum of ten people—which wasn't totally accurate, since two of those people would have to be willing to bed down on the butt-sprung living room sleeper sofa he'd picked up off a curb back in March.

With a sigh, Ty went out to the back porch and dragged in the big-wheeled garbage can. He grabbed his janitor's bucket and mop and the battered Food Lion grocery cart some other little college pricks had left at the back door earlier in the summer, which now contained his cleaning supplies.

Not for the first time, Ty pondered the irony of his situation. Maybe his old man had been right. Maybe, if he'd stayed in law school, he'd be sitting pretty at some white-shoe law firm in Manhattan.

Maybe he'd still be with Kendra too. Nah, probably not. But maybe he'd have a fatty mutual fund, maybe he'd be driving a Jag, wintering in Cabo, or at least Key West. Maybe he shouldn't have sunk every last dime and mortgaged himself to the hilt trying to save Ebbtide. *Told you not to buy that dump.*

Maybe, if he'd listened to his old man, he wouldn't be living in a tiny garage apartment, staring at a computer screen all night 'til he was glassy-eyed and brain-dead. Maybe he wouldn't be cleaning toilets by day and worrying that the next phone call or e-mail would mean the end of all of it.

The clock was ticking. He had less than six weeks left to save Ebbtide. Otherwise, come September 15, the house would be auctioned off on the steps of the Dare County courthouse. He'd be out on the streets, jobless, homeless. And his old man would stand there, shaking his head. Kendra, his ex, and

Ryan, her new husband, aka Fuckface, would be right there with his old man, oozing phony sympathy. They might not say it, but they'd all be thinking it. *Told you so.*

Ty looked out the kitchen window. If he leaned out, he could see the waves rolling in on the beach. They had some size to them this morning. His stomach growled loudly. If he got this pigsty cleaned up, in say, three hours, he'd have just enough time to make it to Abigail's before they ran out of the Saturday lunch special: mahi-mahi tacos.

He pulled the grocery cart into the combined living/dining room at the front of the house and his eyes widened at the degree of destruction his tenants had wrought there. Armchairs, tables, and lamps were upended. The battered wooden floor wore a thick carpet of beach sand, and the sofa cushions were lined up end to end in front of the fireplace, where a trio of untwisted wire coat hangers suggested an impromptu wienie roast. Which would have been fine, if the fireplace damper had been opened, which it hadn't. Fingers of greasy black soot marred the white mantel, which Ty had repainted in June. His grandfather's huge, framed navigational map of Currituck Sound, which had hung over said mantel, was askew on its hanger, its glass shattered. Tufts of stuffing poked out of one of the sofa cushions, which had a baseball-sized hole burnt into it. The unmistakable odor of stale beer and cheap weed lingered in the air.

"Christ," he repeated. He yanked his iPhone from the pocket of his baggy board shorts and scrolled over to the last e-mail he'd gotten from his good buddy, ol' Cooter.

He typed rapidly, his fingertips flying over the tiny keyboard.

"Hey Cooter," he wrote. "Kiss your $500 security deposit goodbye. Asshole. Sincerely, Mr. Culpepper, manager, Ebbtide.com."

When he got the notification that the message had been sent, he looked down at his incoming message box and sighed. Another e-mail from another pain in the ass. The PITAs were the reason he always communicated with his tenants by e-mail and never gave out his phone number. As far as they knew, Mr. Culpepper was a cranky old bastard who resided somewhere in the Internet. They didn't need to know that their landlord was actually the guy who lived over the garage, just a door knock away if the toilet didn't flush or you couldn't figure out how to use the remote control.

This particular PITA's name was Ellis Sullivan. He'd been peppering Ty with nit-picking questions for weeks now. From the tenor of the questions—should he bring his own linens, were there beach chairs, bicycles, a grill—Ty decided Ellis was undoubtedly gay. Straight guys, like ol' Cooter, just wanted to know the location of the nearest liquor store.

Ellis Sullivan and his friends were supposed to check in later today. The later the better, as far as Ty was concerned. God knew how long it would take to clean up the kitchen and living room. His shoulders sagged as he realized he hadn't even taken a look upstairs yet.

He was headed for the stairs when he became aware of a faint gurgling sound. It was coming from the bathroom tucked under the stairs. Funny, the door was closed and it didn't want to budge. He braced one leg against the doorjamb and yanked hard. The door flew open, and a torrent of foul-smelling water rushed out into the hallway.

"Shiiiit," Ty said. And he meant that literally.

Ellis took her time finishing breakfast. She checked her e-mails repeatedly, finding nothing new except for sale offers from Bloomingdale's and more e-mails from old friends at the bank, who'd also had unpleasant termination sessions with Stonehenge.

In the days following her downsizing (which was how she preferred to think of it), Ellis had been consumed with the injustice of her situation. She'd spent hours, days really, commiserating with her former colleagues. She'd joined a "I got jobbed by BancAtlantic" Facebook group and chatboard and had even attended a meet-up at a bar in the suburbs, where everybody had gotten sloppy drunk and teary-eyed about their dire situations.

No more, though, Ellis had resolved. She'd been a saver her whole life. Her father had left her a little inheritance, so her town house was paid for. Her car was paid off, and she'd wisely decided years ago against investing her pension funds in her own bank's stock. She was by no means wealthy, but she had a little cushion, and she refused to panic. Or so she told herself.

So she scrolled down the messages in her in-box, looking in vain for a reply to her message to Mr. Culpepper.

Finding none, she got out the printout of the VRBO ad for Ebbtide. Strange, the only thing it lacked was a contact number.

She frowned and tapped out a follow-up e-mail, reminding Mr. Culpepper of her request for an early check-in, and suggesting that he call her on her cell phone, to let her know the house was ready.

Finally, there was nothing else to do but kill some time at the outlet mall. But first, she'd just take a spin past the house, to see if the previous guests had checked out.

She cruised down Virginia Dare Trail, slowing as she came to the house, but there was a line of cars directly behind her, so she pulled into the driveway at Ebbtide.

Damn! The Bronco hadn't moved from the garage. But the broken cooler and beer bottles had been picked up since her last drive-by, and now a large wheeled garbage can overflowing with trash had been parked in the weedy area beside the mailbox. She craned her neck to try to see if there was any activity around the house.

She checked her e-mail in-box one more time. Nothing. Reluctantly, she decided to head for the outlets.

At one, Ty loaded the last load of damp towels into the dryer. Straightening, he looked out the window of the ground-floor laundry room just in time to see the same silver Accord slowly cruise past. This was the Accord's third pass in the past hour. What was up with that? It couldn't be one of the assholes from the bank, right? It was Saturday, for God's sake. Not that he had time to worry about it too much. As bad as the first floor of the house had been, the second floor was worse. Much worse.

It was a horror show, is what it was. The bathrooms held piles of wet, mildewed towels, and somebody had barfed in the shower stall. He'd found what looked like a dog turd in the closet in one of the front bedrooms. How the hell had they snuck a dog past him? And it must have been a friggin' Great Dane from the looks of things. The twin-bed mattresses from the back bedroom had been dragged out to the sleeping porch and piled on the floor, where last night's rain had given them a good soaking. Trash was strewn everywhere, and the wood-slat shades in two of the bedrooms looked like somebody had taken a baseball bat to them.

Ty had never worked as hard, or as feverishly. He had to replace the ruined twin-bed mattresses with a double bed he'd dragged out of the attic. The window shades were a total loss, so he rigged up some faded flowery curtains he found on a shelf at the back of the locked owner's closet on the ground floor. He shoveled and mopped and scoured and plunged until his back and legs ached, and his hands were rubbed raw from all the bleach and disinfectant.

Check-in time was only minutes away. He knew that without looking at his watch, because he'd received three more e-mails from friggin' Ellis Sullivan, wanting to know why he couldn't have access to the house, like, now. He hadn't bothered to answer. He was too busy staving off disaster.

And now he heard the tap of a car horn from the driveway. Not a blast, really, just a tap. He darted to the window and looked out. Christ! The silver Accord was parked in the driveway, blocking him in. And somebody was walking towards the door. No. It couldn't be. But it was. Oh yeah. It was totally the dark-headed chick who'd caught him whizzing off his deck this morning. Ty Bazemore was having himself quite a day, all right.

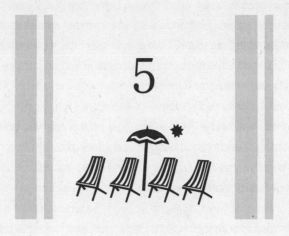

# 5

On her third pass by Ebbtide, Ellis decided it was time to take action. She'd wasted half a day already. After all, it was five after two, so these people were now, officially, encroaching on her time. She pulled into the driveway and stared daggers at the Bronco, which was still parked in the garage. She gave two polite taps on the Accord's horn. But the tap brought nobody scurrying out of Ebbtide. She glanced down again at her iPhone, but there was still no reply from Mr. Culpepper.

She parked and walked briskly towards the house and up the front steps. She hesitated a moment before stepping onto the porch—her mother hadn't raised her to be the sort of person who just went barging up to somebody else's house. Even fifteen years of living up north couldn't change that.

"Hello?" she called softly. All was quiet. She took a good look around. The porch was broad, and although the clapboard frame of the house was brownish gray and unpainted, the trim was painted white. The porch railing had built-in benches that raked outwards, and a clothesline with bleached-out wooden clothespins was looped between the posts, just under the rafters. Four white rocking chairs were upended, two on either side of the front door. There was a galvanized tin pail half-filled with water sitting right beside the steps. PROPERTY OF EBBTIDE was painted on it in bright blue letters. She made her footsteps on the weathered gray porch boards loud and deliberate—sort of an early warning signal that she'd arrived.

The hinges of the rusted screen door squeaked loudly when she pulled it open. There was no doorbell, so she knocked briskly on the periwinkle blue door. And then she knocked, and banged, and knocked some more. She walked over to the window, and cupping her hands, peered into the darkened room. The place looked neat enough, but there was no sign of life.

Just then, her cell phone dinged softly, notifying her that she had an e-mail. She pulled it from the pocket of her capris and looked at the in-box.

To: EllisSullivan@hotmail.com
From: Mr.Culpepper@Ebbtide.com
Subject: Check-in: Sorry, it is our policy not to allow early check-ins. After 2 pm, you'll find the key to the front door in an envelope under the front doormat. Be advised there is a $25 fee for replacement keys. Enjoy your stay.

"Prick," Ellis muttered under her breath. She found the key, unlocked the door, and stepped inside.

It took a moment for her eyes to adjust to the darkened room. She found a light switch by the door and flipped it on. A ceiling fan hummed to life overhead.

"Hmm," she said, looking around. "Not too bad." She was in a large combined living/dining area. The walls were varnished knotty pine that had grown dark with age. The wood floors were still damp from a recent mopping, and the familiar smell of Murphy Oil soap hung in the air. Ellis smiled. Her grandmother always mopped her wood floors with Murphy soap. She decided this was a good omen.

The place was not fancy, but then she'd seen that in the photographs on the website. There was a faded oval rag rug on the living room floor, a large, lumpy sofa, and a couple of '80s-era armchairs facing a soot-blackened fire-place. The walls were dotted with what somebody considered beach-appropriate art—paint-by-number scenes depicting lighthouses, fishing boats, tropical birds, and waving palm trees.

A nicely framed nautical chart hung over the mantel, but its glass was badly cracked. Ellis leaned in and examined it with interest. She loved the names of the rivers and sounds. Pasquotank, Croatan, Ocracoke, Currituck, and her favorite, Mattamuskeet. But then, Ellis adored anything with names and numbers and places: maps, graphs, charts. As a child, she'd traded a doll—an expensive Madame Alexander dressed as Princess Diana, sent to her by her godmother in Atlanta—for her older brother Baylor's light-up globe. Baylor had turned around and given the doll to his little fourth-grade girl-friend.

Reluctantly, Ellis turned away from the chart. She had a car to unload and a house to set up.

The dining area held a long, scrubbed pine table and was surrounded by eight mismatched white-painted wooden chairs. A hideous plastic flower arrangement in a fish-shaped ceramic bowl was centered on a plastic doily in the middle of the table. It looked like somebody's granny had just gotten up to fetch another cup of tea.

A smallish kitchen opened off the dining area. It was clean, yes, but it had definitely seen better days. Here, the board walls were enameled white. The cupboards were painted white, with green glass knobs, and the counters were yellow linoleum with aluminum trim. Instead of upper cupboards there was a pair of shelf units with scalloped trim nailed to the wall on either side of a kitchen window that looked out onto the sand dunes. A small stack of chipped plates, two plastic cereal bowls, and some plastic convenience store go-cups were lined up along the shelves. In the middle of the room stood a large wooden table with a chipped turquoise enamel top. The floors were of cracked and faded yellow-and-white checkerboard linoleum tiles. There was a four-burner electric stove with curious push-button controls and a white refrigera-tor with rust spots around the corners of the doors.

Ellis opened the refrigerator, which was empty except for a box of baking soda, and then she peeked inside the freezer, which held two miserly alumi-num ice cube trays, but no automatic ice maker. She congratulated herself for picking up a five-pound bag of ice to keep the groceries she'd bought cold until check-in time. She noticed, to her chagrin, that there was no dishwasher. How had she missed this during all the hours she'd spent poring over the pictures and description of the house?

Never mind, she told herself. It was only for a month, and after all, four women—not to mention Dorie's husband, Stephen—were sharing this house. Everybody would pitch in and make do. It would be like Girl Scout camp, Ellis told herself. But with air-conditioning and indoor plumbing.

Finally, August had come. The month they'd all been planning for was becoming a reality. Ellis could not wait for the fun to begin. As she left the kitchen, she did an impromptu skip-step.

Ty tipped the Corona bottle to his lips and sucked down the last drop of icy beer. He wandered around the corner of the porch to check on his new ten-ant's whereabouts. Whoa! The silver Honda was pulled up directly in front of the house now, and as he watched, a woman in pink pants and a tight white T-shirt hurried towards the house, her arms full of grocery sacks. Her dark hair fanned out behind her in the breeze.

No. It couldn't be. Could it? "Ellis, dude," he whispered. "You're not gay. You're a girl."

In fact, she was *the* girl. The one from this morning. He'd really only got-ten a glimpse of her this morning, but now, as he leaned up against the side of his apartment, watching as she ferried endless suitcases, boxes, and bags into the house, her sandals flapping madly, he liked what he saw. Her figure was what his mother would have called "sturdy," with a high, round butt that probably wouldn't be considered fashionable, but which Ty found fascinating. She had her hair pulled back with some kind of a headband, and her oval face was bright pink in the blazing afternoon sun.

Intriguing. But no, he told himself sternly. This Ellis person might have a cute butt, but she'd already proven herself a major pain in his ass, a distraction he totally didn't need right now. His cell phone beeped. He picked it up and read the alert. Hodarthe, a pharmaceutical company out of Topeka, was announcing that the FDA had approved a promising new cholesterol-busting drug. Maybe it was time to dump some of his Pfizer stock. Or maybe it was too late. He needed to do some quick research.

Ellis Sullivan was leaning into the trunk of the Honda, her head obscured from view. He allowed himself one last, lingering gaze, and turned to go back to work.

Ellis had just finished emptying the first bag of groceries when she happened to look down at the counter where she'd stacked the rolls of paper towels, toilet paper, and coffee. Ants! A small army of the tiny ones her grandmother called sugar ants made a thin black line leading from the window sill to the back of the sink. Gak! She grabbed a paper towel, wet it, and frantically wiped at the counters. She flung the under-sink cupboard door open, looking for bug spray, but all she found was a damp sponge and a plastic jug of drain cleaner.

Ellis ran to the laundry room and then the linen closet, opening and closing doors, but there was no sign of bug spray. She shuddered. She'd hated bugs her whole life, and although she loved Savannah and the South, she never once missed its bugs after she moved to Philly. She fought the impulse to run out to the car and drive over to the first store to buy an arsenal of Raid, Black Flag, or whatever. They were only harmless little sugar ants, she told herself. But if they'd been roaches, she *so* would have been out of there.

She made herself return to the kitchen. She soaked a paper towel with drain cleaner and dabbed it on the windowsill. That oughta put a hurt on the little bastards, she thought grimly. At least until she could get some proper bug spray. She put away the rest of the groceries, lining up the cans of Diet Coke, the white wine, skim milk, half-and-half, and bottled water in the fridge. She found an empty cupboard and decided it would be the liquor cabinet. Vodka, gin, rum, scotch, and oh yes, whiskey for Julia, who'd become a die-hard Jack Daniel's fan at the tender age of fourteen, when she'd begun snitching it from her father's liquor cabinet, refilling the bottle with water. She'd bought mixers too: tonic water, 7-Up, grapefruit juice, and cranberry juice for Dorie, who liked Cape Cods. Funny, she couldn't remember what Willa liked to drink. Dorie's sister Willa was two years older than the rest of them, which meant that she was the girls' go-to source for liquor when they were teenagers, since her boyfriend Ricky was legal. Of course, Willa always charged them five bucks extra, which Ellis thought was pretty pissy of her. But then, that was Willa for you. Even way back then, she had an angle or an agenda—and it was all Willa, all the time.

Finally, Ellis got the kitchen just the way she wanted it. There was a fugly amateur seascape hanging on the wall beside the stove. She took it down and put it on top of the fridge and replaced it with the whiteboard she'd bought at the office-supply store. She'd spent a happy forty-five minutes ruling off the Kaper chart, carefully listing the assigned chores, the days of the week, and everybody's names with color-coded Sharpies. It was truly a work of art.

She stood back and admired her handiwork. Now, she thought, it was time to head upstairs and get the bedrooms organized.

But when she'd lugged her big wheeled suitcase upstairs and opened the first bedroom door, her heart sank.

The room was painted white, with battleship-gray painted board floors. It was large and square, and two big windows gave a glorious view of the impossibly blue summer sky. But it was nearly empty. A lonely little double bed was shoved into a corner, covered with a limp and faded pink-and-blue floral quilted spread. A pair of wafer-thin pillows sat at the head of the bed, and there was an olive-drab army blanket folded at the foot of it. There was no nightstand, no lamps or mirror, no chairs or even a luggage rack. A rickety-looking three-drawer pine dresser was against the wall opposite the bed. There was a miniscule closet with no coat hangers, not even a wire one. A small window beside the dresser held a rusty air conditioner.

"A window unit!" Ellis cried. The room was hot and stuffy. She walked out into the hallway and opened up the other two bedroom doors. They were furnished just as sparsely, and yes, each had a dinky little air conditioner stuck into a window.

She switched on the air conditioners in each room. They were loud and they rattled the windows, but within a few minutes, she could feel the temperatures begin to drop and her own boiling blood pressure start to simmer down.

Wait until she got hold of Mr. Culpepper! Nothing upstairs was as it had been described on the Ebbtide website. Her room should have had a queen-sized bed—not the crappy little double bed that was in there now. Julia's room, which was painted baby blue, should have had a double bed, but it held only a narrow twin. And Willa's room, the daffodil yellow one, held yet another double bed. Ellis winced, anticipating what Willa's reaction would be to that. Willa had reluctantly agreed to pay an extra two hundred bucks if the girls would let her have the room with the king-sized bed, since that's what she and her husband were used to sleeping in at home. Arthur wasn't coming along, of course, but Willa had insisted she couldn't possibly sleep in anything less than a king.

Once she'd turned on all the air conditioners, Ellis trudged up the narrow staircase to the third floor. The stairs were steep, and the walls so close that she didn't see how anybody could get a full-sized suitcase up them. She had to stop to catch her breath when at last she'd reached the third floor. It was even hotter up here, she discovered.

She found herself on a small landing. Unlike the second floor, the walls up here were unpainted board. They smelled faintly piney. There were three doors. She opened the first and found the tiny bathroom, with its claw-foot tub and funny high-backed commode. She could only shake her head when she saw that the tub had no shower. Dorie wasn't the type to complain, that was her sister Willa's specialty, but even sweet Dorie wouldn't be happy about not having a shower.

Ellis tugged at the door on the facing wall. It was swollen from the heat and humidity, but she finally managed to yank it open, only to discover an unfinished attic space. The high-ceilinged room was stifling and full of dusty cardboard boxes, trunks, and dust-covered bits of furniture. Maybe, Ellis thought idly, between sneezes, she could find some spare end tables and chairs to make their bedrooms more habitable. Later.

She opened the third door to find the bedroom. Tucked up under the eaves of the house, it had a low, sloping ceiling, but a dormer window opposite the bed ran the length of the room, and Ellis could see an amazing view of the ocean below. The waves were rolling in, and children darted in and out of the water. She yanked the window open and a breeze wafted in, carrying the smell of saltwater with it. There was another window, high in the wall above the bed, and if she stood on her tiptoes, she could see out to the street.

The room was just as sparsely furnished as the others, the bed was a double, with a sad, thin mattress. There was no overhead fan as in the downstairs bedrooms, but there was a pair of nightstands, each with a twee little white milk-glass lamp. Instead of a closet, a white, mirrored chifforobe stood in a corner of the room. And the air-conditioning unit was stuck into a hole that had been cut in the wall right beside the bed, which meant that whoever slept on that side would have it blasting in her ear all night long. The sad thing was, this was the best bedroom in the house. Ellis was glad Dorie and Stephen would have it. Not particularly glad about the Stephen part. After all, they'd agreed, way back in April, at Julia's mama's funeral, that this would be strictly a chick trip.

But Dorie and Stephen had been married only a year. Since they both taught school, August was the last month they'd have for vacation. Nobody, not even Julia, had the heart to say no to Dorie. Anyway, Stephen really was very nice. He liked to cook, and he was quiet, and he'd probably spend most of his time at the beach reading, Dorie had promised. So they'd relented and agreed, just this once, that Stephen could be one of the girls.

At least, Ellis thought, Stephen wouldn't be in their hair downstairs. They wouldn't have to worry about running into him in their underwear, or keep having to put the toilet seat down on the second floor.

But she was definitely still going to give Mr. Culpepper an earful! It was probably too late to get out of the house now, since he had half the month's rent, but she was already calculating how much of a discount she was going to ask for, considering the crappy beds, the window air-conditioning units, and—oh yes, the ants.

There it was again, the nagging, insistent itch she could not scratch. Money. Would she have enough? What would happen when this month was over? And how long would it be before her money ran out?

# 6

Ellis heard the crunch of gravel outside. Then a series of short, loud blasts from a car horn. She stood on tiptoes and looked out the window over the bed. A dark red minivan had pulled into the driveway, and a familiar blonde was leaning halfway out the passenger window, hollering at the top of her lungs.

"Whoo-hoo! We're here!"

Ellis flew down the two flights of stairs, out the front door and off the porch, launching herself in the direction of the van.

"Oh my God!" Ellis cried, falling into Julia's outstretched arms. "You're here. August is here. I can't believe we're all finally here."

She held Julia at arm's length and looked at her critically. "And you're so much blonder. I love it, but when did you decide to go platinum?"

Before Julia could answer, Dorie had gotten out of the minivan, and then the three of them were hugging and shrieking and babbling and jumping up and down so hard that it sounded like a sorority chapter meeting.

"Excuse me," Dorie said, finally pulling away. "I can't wait to see the house and catch up. But y'all have got to excuse me. I had an iced tea an hour ago, and my eyeballs are positively floating."

"Go on," Ellis said, laughing. "You never could hold your water. Julia and I will start unloading."

She walked to the back of the minivan and groped around for the catch on the tailgate. "Where are the others?" she asked Julia. "Are Willa and Stephen driving up separately? Dorie didn't mention that when I talked to her the day before yesterday."

Julia raised one elegant eyebrow. "There's quite a lot Dorie hasn't mentioned. To either of us. They aren't coming, sweetie."

"At all?" Ellis said, bewildered. "What happened?"

"The bitch bailed on us! Dorie said Willa just rang her up last night, right before she was to pick her up, and announced that she couldn't go."

"Just like that?"

Julia shrugged, and the strap of her orange tank top slid off one sunbrowned shoulder. "Willa told Dorie something had come up with one of the kids. Isn't that just like her? She horns in on our trip, and because we don't want to hurt Dorie's feelings, we agree that she can come, plan around her, go to the expense of renting the bigger house with the extra bedroom, then she just up and cancels. You want to know what I think?"

"What?"

"I don't think she ever really intended to come," Julia said. "She was just up to her same old games again, pushing Dorie's buttons, testing to see if Dorie would cave in and invite her. Willa's never had any real friends of her own. Why would she? The woman's a raving bitch."

"But what about Stephen?" Ellis pressed. "Is he coming later? I know Dorie said he's been working really hard all summer, trying to get his master's thesis finished before school starts up again."

Julia grabbed a battered leather suitcase from the back of the van and set it on the driveway. "Stephen's quite another puzzle. When she picked me up at the airport this morning, all Dorie would tell me was basically the same thing: 'Stephen's working so hard on his thesis, he has to meet with his advisor, he needs absolute quiet, he's heartbroken that he can't come after all.' Blah, blah, blah."

"You don't believe her? Why would she make up something like that? Dorie wouldn't lie. Not to us."

They heard the slap of the screen door and Julia glanced back at the house. "Shh. She's coming. I'm not saying she's lying exactly. But she's not telling us the whole story. This is not our Dorie. Not at all."

"Did Julia tell you the bad news?" Dorie asked, approaching the van. "I know you guys must hate me. Stephen feels awful about not coming. He was so looking forward to the beach. But he's just frantic with worry about his thesis. And Willa . . ." Her voice trailed off. "Annabeth, her youngest, was supposed to be at sailing camp this week. But she gets these terrible headaches. And she's only six. They got her glasses, but . . ."

"Willa is Willa," Julia said dryly. "You don't have to apologize for her, Dorie. She's been like this her whole life."

Dorie's cheeks flushed bright red. "I know she can be a pill sometimes, you guys."

Ellis gave her a quick hug. "We all have our moments. We understand. Anyway, I'm just really bummed for you, having to spend the month without Stephen. We're all going to miss him."

Julia, standing directly behind Dorie, crossed her eyes and grimaced. The last statement was an outright lie, and they both knew it. They'd had a spirited e-mail exchange as soon as Dorie had brought up the possibility of having Stephen join them at the beach.

"No way!" Julia had written. "This is our time together. Remember? No effin' boys. Anyway, if Booker finds out, the next thing you know, he'll want to come. And then it'll be couples. And that's not what this month is about."

Booker and Julia had lived together for years, first in New York, and then, for the past six years, in London. Booker was a photographer, and Julia was a model. Ellis didn't quite understand their relationship. Sometimes, the way Julia talked about Booker, you had to wonder what had kept them together all this time.

Ellis hadn't liked to conspire against Dorie behind her back, but for once, she was in total agreement with Julia. She liked Stephen, although they'd only met twice before Dorie's wedding a year ago. He was attractive and thoughtful and obviously wild for Dorie. As for Dorie, she was long overdue for a good man. But just this once, couldn't they leave men out of it? Especially since Ellis was so obviously without a man—and had been for more years than she cared to admit.

That had never been the case with Dorie. With her strawberry blond hair, freckles, and kittenish green eyes, not to mention her voluptuous curves, Dorie was the man magnet of the group. She had been since third grade, when every single boy at Blessed Sacrament School wanted to be her valentine. Nobody could remember a time when Dorie had been without a boyfriend. And it wasn't like she even tried. She was just Dorie.

Once, when she was a freshman at the University of Georgia, she'd started dating a doctor. An honest-to-God physician. A gynecologist, if you could believe it. Howard had been gaga for Dorie. He'd given her a pair of two-carat diamond stud earrings—which she didn't dare show her mother—taken her on a spring break trip to Vegas, let her drive his Mercedes all the way to Savannah and back just so she could hang out with her girlfriends for Saint Patrick's Day.

The fling had lasted nearly a year. And then Dorie, who was only twenty, after all, got tired of playing doctor with a thirty-year-old who wanted her to quit her sorority and instead spend weekends hanging out with him at the country club. It wasn't until *years* later that she got up the nerve to admit where she'd actually met Howard.

They'd all gone back to the Dunaways' house after Willa's bachelorette party; they'd been doing tequila shooters at Spanky's down on River Street. It was their own version of Truth or Dare. Of course, nobody else had a story near as cool as Dorie's.

"I went to the student health clinic, you know, to get on the pill, because Bo and I were getting pretty serious, and I thought only sluts used condoms, but I was terrified of getting knocked up," Dorie had said, giggling nervously. "And anyway, who do you think gave me my first pelvic exam? Howard! And he was really so sweet, so gentle, you know? Afterwards, he called me into his office, and he gave me this very serious talk about the dangers of STDs and all that. I almost died, I was so embarrassed! Then he handed me my prescription and a package with, like, six months' worth of Ortho-Novum, and he'd written his home phone number on the back of the prescription."

Howard had been one of the nicer guys in Dorie's constantly changing constellation of boyfriends. A lot of them had been rats. So when she'd started talking about "the new guy at school"—meaning, Our Lady of Angels, the Catholic girls' high school they'd all attended, and where Dorie taught English—nobody really thought much of it. Stephen was the girls' soccer coach, and he taught history. He was lanky and dark haired, with a deliciously dry sense of humor. He wasn't from Savannah, he'd grown up in Omaha. And he was Catholic, so Dorie's mother approved. He and Dorie dated for two years before he finally talked her into getting married.

Dr. Dunaway—Dorie's mom (she had a Ph.D. in English and always insisted that everybody call her "Doctor" instead of "Mrs.")—had been so relieved that Dorie was finally settling down, she'd even helped Dorie pay for the wedding.

"I still can't believe how cheap that woman is," Julia had complained at the reception, where the alcohol had consisted of jug wine and a keg of Natty Lite. "Remember how she used to make Dorie and Willa use their allowances to buy their own shampoo and tampons?"

So Stephen was nice, but he was still a man, and this *was* supposed to have been a chick trip. Ellis was glad he'd bowed out at the last minute. And she felt guilty for being glad.

"Come on, you guys," Ellis exclaimed, refusing to look Julia in the eyes for fear of laughing. "It's hot as hell out here. Let's get this stuff inside. I want to show you the house."

"Screw the house," Julia said dramatically, throwing a garment bag over her shoulder. "I don't know about you two, but I'm here for the beach. We've had a hideous winter in England, and no spring to speak of. Just rain and more rain. So no offense, Ellis, but right now the only thing I want you to show me is the ice, the bourbon, and the beach. In that exact order."

"You got it," Ellis said, grabbing a tote bag. "And don't worry, Dorie. I even bought you your own bottle of tequila. And I brought my blender from home, just in case, which was a good thing, 'cuz there wasn't one here."

Dorie wrinkled her nose. "Actually? Right now I'd settle for another big ol' iced tea."

Julia stopped in her tracks. "Seriously? Iced tea? Eudora Dunaway is turning down a margarita? Alert the media!"

Dorie gave Julia a playful kick in the pants. "Hey! You make me sound like a falling-down drunk. It just so happens that I had a serious case of tequila poisoning after a friend's Cinco de Mayo party, and I haven't been able to look at the stuff ever since."

"S-u-u-u-r-e," Julia said. "Dorie is breaking up with Jose Cuervo. You hear that, Ellis?"

Ellis heard, and she saw the barely disguised suspicion in Julia's eyes, and she thought—just maybe—Julia was onto something. Something about Dorie was . . . off.

# 7

To: Mr.Culpepper@Ebbtide.com
From: EllisSullivan@hotmail.com
Subject: WTF? Fleas!
Mr. Culpepper, you need to get an exterminator over here ASAP. This place is crawling with fleas. Also ants and mildew. And the kitchen faucet drips. Constantly. And the mattresses suck, bigtime. Your website specifically stated that our house would have a "fully stocked kitchen." In my mind, a fully stocked kitchen includes items such as a stove with more than one working burner and such basics as saucepans, silverware, and dishes. I do not consider five cracked, chipped, and mismatched plates and a collection of plastic NASCAR go-cups to be "serving-ware for eight." As this is my third e-mail in the past two days, I'd appreciate it if you would take care of these things, IMMEDIATELY.

Ellis tapped the "send" button and scratched her right knee absentmindedly. Both of her ankles, her calves, and the backs of her knees were dotted with angry red flea bites. She had flea bites underneath her breasts, and flea bites on the back of her neck.

Julia had only a couple of bites, on her ankles, and Dorie didn't have a single one. But the fleas must have made Ellis's bedroom their home office, because that first morning at Ebbtide she woke up scratching like a maniac. She'd stared down at the white sheet on her bed, and had been horrified to see a semimicroscopic insect hopping around. "Fleas!" she'd screeched.

She'd stripped her bed of all the linens, taken every stitch of clothing out of her suitcases, even picked up the throw rug on the floor, and washed and bleached the daylights out of everything. But the fleas didn't care.

When she'd gone downstairs that first morning, Julia and Dorie were already sitting at the kitchen table, sipping coffee.

"Ellis," Julia said, pointing at the Kaper chart on the kitchen wall. "You're not really serious about this thing—right?"

Ellis got herself a glass of orange juice and settled at the kitchen table. "Well, now that Stephen and Willa aren't coming, I guess I'll have to redo it, but I still don't think it'll be too much trouble, not if everybody pitches in."

Julia stood and pointed at the first line of the chart with her half-eaten piece of toast. She read aloud in a high-pitched schoolmarm voice: "Monday: Julia cooks breakfast. Dorie does dishes. Willa sweeps sand from floors. Stephen takes out trash. Ellis does laundry."

Dorie pressed her napkin to her lips to suppress a giggle, but after Ellis glared at her, she looked down innocently at her cereal bowl.

"Ellis, honey," Julia said, nibbling at her toast. "I'm sorry. It's ludicrous. It really is. This chart thing . . . what did they call it back in Girl Scouts?"

"A Kaper chart," Ellis said quietly.

"Oh yes, Kaper." Julia nodded. "Excellent for eight-year-olds who have to be reminded to scrub their teeth and gather wood for the campfire. But for the love of God! We're grown women here. I'm thirty-five years old. I don't need a chart to tell me to hang up a wet towel."

Ellis felt her face go pink. "I just thought . . . well, I thought it might help the month go smoother, if things were sort of organized. Unlike you guys, I'm used to living alone and doing everything myself. I thought the chart would be kind of fun, but obviously I was wrong." She pulled the whiteboard off the wall and walked rapidly out of the room, her back stiff. A moment later, she was back, but only to pick up her empty juice glass, rinse it out, and place it on the drainboard. Then she stalked out of the room. Dorie and Julia heard the screen door open and then slam shut.

"Shit." Julia tossed the toast crust onto her plate. "I'd forgotten how prickly our girl can be. But really, Dorie, it had to be said."

Dorie picked up both their plates and coffee cups and put them into the sink full of soapy water. "It could have been said nicer. Ellis isn't like you, Julia. She didn't grow up fighting and fussing with a bunch of brothers. You really hurt her feelings. And after all the work she did putting this together for all of us. It wouldn't hurt to go along with her. At least for the first week or so."

Julia sighed. "Now you're gonna make me play nice, aren't you?"

Dorie grinned. "Either that, or you pick up your Tinkertoys and go home."

Dorie walked out to the front porch, with Julia trailing reluctantly behind. They stopped at the front door and peeked out. The whiteboard was poking out of the top of the trash can at the edge of the driveway, and its creator, Ellis, was sitting on one of the porch chairs, rocking rapidly to and fro, staring off into space. It was a gorgeous summer morning, sunny, not too humid, with banks of high, puffy white clouds overhead.

It was the second day of August, and already they'd started to bicker.

"Come on, Ellis," Dorie coaxed. "Don't be mad. Julia didn't mean anything by it." She turned and glared at Julia. "Did you, Julia?"

"Julia's a bitch," Julia whispered loudly, poking her head out the door. She tiptoed onto the porch and stood behind Ellis's chair. "And just for that, Julia's going to have to clean the latrines for the whole month, right, Dorie?"

Dorie sat down on the rocker next to Ellis's. "Absolutely. *And* she gets no s'mores. Ever."

Julia knelt down on the floor on the other side of Ellis. She wrapped her arms around her friend's waist and laid her head on Ellis's lap. "Julia's sorry," she said in a little tiny mouse voice. "She loves Ellie-Belly and doesn't ever want to hurt her friend's feelings."

Ellis suppressed a smile. She patted Julia's head and then gave it a sharp thump. "Get up, you nutjob. And don't think you're going to get out of cooking my dinner tonight, either."

Julia groaned. "Thank God. My knees are killing me." She flopped down into the other rocking chair. "So what should we do today? Our first whole day at the beach? Bike ride? Shopping? Hang gliding over at Jockey's Ridge? I saw a brochure for the most marvelous-looking school where they actually teach you to hang glide. Remember that time we all went bungee jumping at Myrtle Beach?"

"You and Dorie went bungee jumping," Ellis corrected. "I couldn't even watch. I was petrified you'd be killed, and I'd have to explain to your mothers what happened."

"Nah, you were just scared if we got killed you'd have to go home alone and drive over the Talmadge bridge all by yourself," Julia taunted.

"True," Ellis admitted.

"Why don't we just hang at the beach here?" Dorie asked.

The others turned to look at her in surprise. Dorie had never been one to pass up an adventure.

"What?" she said innocently, catching their meaning. "Why do we have to do anything at all? I'm just enjoying being here, spending time with you guys. Anyway, hang gliding is expensive. You forget, I'm living on a schoolteacher's salary. A private school too—which doesn't pay diddly, I might add."

Ellis jumped to her feet. "Dorie's right," she said. "This is perfect beach weather. I'm gonna go put on my suit. If nothing else, maybe the saltwater will heal my flea bites."

Julia looked at Ellis's outstretched legs. "Eww! Disgusting! Have you contacted our landlord?"

"Mr. Culpepper? Repeatedly," Ellis said. "I sent him another e-mail just before I came downstairs. If I don't hear from him by lunchtime, I'm going to just find an exterminator in the phone book and tell Culpepper I'm going to deduct it from the rest of our rent. And I told him how unhappy we are about the mildew and the ants."

"And the crappy mattresses, I hope," Julia added. "I haven't slept on a bed that lumpy since I went hosteling in Belgium after high school. We're paying enough rent for this dump that we should at least be able to expect a decent bed."

"About the rent," Dorie said hesitantly. "I really think Willa should offer to go ahead and pay her share, even though she did cancel."

"Did she offer to reimuburse us?" Julia asked.

"Not yet," Dorie admitted.

"Well, I wouldn't hold my breath waiting for her to offer," Julia said. "Even though good old Arthur is swimming in dough. It wouldn't occur to darling Willa that the rest of us might be out-of-pocket because of her."

"I could ask her," Dorie volunteered. "But you know Willa."

"We do," Ellis said briskly. "So we won't count on her chipping in. If she does, that would be great; if not, no biggie. Like I said, I'm seriously thinking of renegotiating our lease on Ebbtide. The place is totally not what he advertised."

"I think it's kinda sweet," Dorie said. "Did you know, in the daylight, you can look through the cracks in the floorboards in that bathroom under the stairs and see little fiddler crabs crawling around in the sand under the house?"

"Sweet Jesus!" Julia said. "I am never using that bathroom again."

"Oh, Julia, quit being so damned British," Dorie said impishly. "You grew up in Savannah, Georgia, just like the rest of us. It's not like you never saw a fiddler crab before. Or a cockroach or an ant."

Julia stuck her tongue out at Dorie. "Screw you. I might have grown up living around creepy-crawlies, but that doesn't mean I want to live with 'em as a grown-up."

Ty had been watching the waves off and on since sunrise. They weren't really that big, but it was a break—he'd been sitting at his computer for the past twenty-four hours, researching cholesterol and statin fighters in every online medical journal he could find. He was no scientist—hell, he'd barely passed high school chemistry—but this new drug Hodarthe had come up with sounded like it could be a winner.

He'd done well the previous day with a start-up company in California that was doing interesting things using recycled glass in commercial concrete applications, so he had some funds, and he was poised to take a position with Hodarthe. But damned if he hadn't just received *another* e-mail from Ellis Sullivan.

He chuckled to himself as he reread her latest missive. "WTF? Fleas!" Little old Ellis was turning out to be a real ballbuster. He found himself scratching at a phantom flea bite even as he read. She was right, though. He *did* have to do something about the fleas. If they got too out of hand, he'd never get rid of 'em, and they might just chase away Ellis and her girlfriends. He couldn't afford to lose a month's rent.

Much as he hated to, he picked up the phone and called an old high school buddy, Frank, who had gone into his father's pest control business over in Elizabeth City. After some idle chatter about prospects for Carolina football (sorry) and the economy (way sorrier), Frank promised to head over to Ebbtide for a little bug-bombing session that afternoon. They even worked out a trade: Frank would provide pest control services for three months in return for a week's vacation at Ebbtide.

Ty didn't have to tell Frank money was tight; Frank knew about the jam he'd gotten himself into. Hell, everybody on the Outer Banks knew that Ty Bazemore was in a world of hurt. The first foreclosure notice for Ebbtide had been published in the newspaper in July, and every week since, the notice had run in the paper's legal ads, rubbing salt into his already wounded ego. Six weeks. That's how much time he had to pull off a miracle. Until then, he needed to keep his tenants happy and, somehow, raise enough money to catch up on six months' worth of missed house payments and back taxes.

But it wouldn't do to let Ellis Sullivan get the upper hand. So he fired off a missive of his own.

To: EllisSullivan@hotmail.com
From: Mr.Culpepper@Ebbtide.com
Subject: Alleged fleas.

Ms. Sullivan, if the house has fleas, you must have brought them with you. Likewise the ants. I've never had complaints before, about bugs or the mattresses. But Frank from Bug-Off Pest Control will be out today, after 2 pm. You'll have to vacate the premises for at least two hours, unless you enjoy inhaling toxic fumes. If you don't like my dishes, there's a Walmart in Kitty Hawk. I'll send somebody to take a look at the faucet. Happy?

Through the open door, he could hear the waves rolling into shore. He could stand it no more. He got up and strolled out to the porch.

The women of Ebbtide had pitched camp on a stretch of sand directly below. They had a jaunty striped pink-and-yellow umbrella, three lounge chairs, and a large cooler. The brunette, Ellis, and a tall, elegant blonde were playing Pro Kadima, inexpertly slapping the little rubber ball around, dashing back and forth in the sand, laughing hysterically.

The blonde was a knockout, with long, slender bronzed legs and a bright orange bikini that left little to the imagination.

The third woman was a petite strawberry blonde. She was stretched out in her chair, a pair of sunglasses perched on her little snub nose, reading a magazine. Even the loose-fitting sleeveless cover-up she wore over her swimsuit couldn't disguise a body that was luscious—and that was a word Ty didn't just throw around. Her pale, freckled skin was already turning pink, and it wasn't yet noon.

But it was Ellis, pain-in-the-ass Ellis, he couldn't keep his eyes off of. She'd knotted her long hair in a goofy ponytail on top of her head, emphasizing the graceful curve of her long neck. Her modest, black one-piece bathing suit should not have been alluring, but somehow it was—the high cut legs showed off her great butt, the scoop neckline revealed a promising amount of creamy cleavage. And when she ran, as she was doing now, looking like a total klutz, the suit rode up in the back and down in the front, giving him a rewarding view.

Ellis Sullivan was not by any means the hottest thing he'd ever seen on this stretch of beach. That honor, he thought, ironically, would have to go to Kendra, whom he'd first spotted the summer they were fifteen, as she did a slow, taunting stroll past him while he painted his grandmother's Adirondack chairs on this same deck. He found himself scowling at the memory of that day.

Dorie had promised herself she'd go for a swim at exactly 11 A.M. She ran and dove into the waves, letting them take her out and under, again and again. The water was wonderful. She floated on her back and looked up at the clouds, trying to force herself to empty her cluttered mind and think of . . . absolutely nothing.

But the worries lapped at her as surely as the warm waves. Damn Willa for backing out on them! Dorie had budgeted this vacation down to the last nickel, counting on splitting expenses four ways. And now? Her budget was blown to hell. She had just barely enough money to pay for her share of the rent, let alone kick in her share for groceries. And then there was Stephen. It was all just too sad, too awful. He would have loved this place. The thought came to her unbidden, as did the unexpected wave, washing over her face. She stood up, sputtering and choking, the saltwater burning her eyes and throat.

She was running back to her chair when she spotted him—a man, standing on the second-floor deck of the garage right beside their house.

The other girls were opening beers when she got back. She opted for an icy bottle of water instead, and as she was toweling off, she glanced up and saw the man again. He hadn't moved.

"Hey," she said, running a comb through her tangled hair. "Who's that guy?"

"What guy?" Julia said, not bothering to look around. She twisted the cap from her beer and took a long drink. "Probably one of your old boyfriends."

"Wrong," Dorie said. "I've never dated anybody from North Carolina. I had a boyfriend who went to Wake Forest, but that doesn't count because he was from Charleston."

"Where is this guy?" Ellis asked, standing up.

"Right there." Dorie pointed towards the garage apartment. "He's totally been staring at us for the past ten minutes."

Ellis put on her sunglasses and looked.

"It's him!" she exclaimed.

Now Julia was looking too. "Him who?"

"That's the guy," Ellis exclaimed. "Remember? I told you, he was standing right there, peeing off that porch, yesterday morning when I got here."

"Gross," Dorie said.

"He doesn't look gross to me," Julia said. "He looks kind of, um, yummy to me. He's all tan and ripped. My God, look at those pecs!"

"Julia!" Ellis and Dorie exclaimed in unison.

"Excuse me," Julia said. "Can I help it if I've had my fill of looking at flabby white Englishmen in the past few years? Have you two ever seen European men at the beach? They all wear those nasty little Speedos with their schlongs waving around."

"Banana hammocks," Dorie said, giggling. "Disgusting. Booker doesn't wear one, does he?"

"Booker?" Julia said with a derisive snort. "Hah! Booker hates the beach. He always says if he wants to get sun poisoning or skin cancer, he'll do it someplace with air-conditioning and decent cable reception."

"Stephen loves the beach," Dorie said wistfully. "He'll drive out to Tybee in the middle of the winter, just so he can walk barefoot in the sand."

"It's just too bad he couldn't come after all," Julia said sympathetically. "Have you talked to him since we got here?"

Dorie's eyes filled with tears. "No. . . ."

Ellis shot Julia a warning look. Julia shrugged.

"Oh look," Julia said, turning back towards the dunes. "The guy! He sees us looking at him." She gave him a coquettish wave. "And he doesn't even care. Oh my God. He's waving back. Who the hell is he?"

"That's what I intend to find out," Ellis said.

# 8

Ellis marched herself right up the stairway over the dune, stopping only to slide her feet into a pair of flip-flops she'd left at the edge of the steps.

"Hey!" she called, standing at the covered deck at the top of the dunes, her hands at her hips. "Hey, you!"

"Who, me?" Ty called, leaning down over the porch railing. He could just barely see a bit of her nipples from this vantage point.

"Yes, you," Ellis retorted. "What the hell do you think you're doing?"

"Just taking in the scenery," Ty said innocently. "How about yourself?"

"My friends and I *were* relaxing on the beach," Ellis said. "Until we became aware that we were being spied on by some pervert."

"What makes you think I'm a pervert?"

"Yesterday I caught you pissing off that same deck. Today you're up there staring at us. What's your name, anyway?"

He was taken off guard by her question, and before he knew it, he was actually telling her. "My name is Ty Bazemore. Why do you ask?"

She nodded, seeming to memorize it. "Ty Bazemore. Is that it? Not Tyson, or Tyler?"

"Just Ty," he said. "What's your name?"

"None of your business," she said. "What are you doing up there on that porch?"

"I happen to live here," he said indignantly.

"Does Mr. Culpepper know you're staying up there?"

He managed to suppress a smile. "Culpepper knows all about me."

"Don't you have anything better to do with your time?" she asked.

"Come to think of it," he said, looking down at his watch, "I do." He started to go back inside, but then he thought of something.

She was halfway down the beach stairs.

"Hey," he called. "Why do you want to know my name?"

"So I can Google you," she called back, not bothering to turn around. "And I intend to run the tag on that Bronco too, Ty Bazemore."

"The perv's name is Ty," Ellis reported when she got back to the girls. "He claims he rents the garage apartment from Mr. Culpepper."

"What makes you think he's a perv?" Julia asked, thumbing through *Vogue*.

"He was peeing off that deck!" Ellis said. "Right there in front of God and everybody."

"That doesn't make him a pervert," Julia said, dog-earing one of the pages. "It just makes him a guy. My brothers used to pee off the second-floor porch at the house at Isle of Hope when they were kids. It was like a contest. Peeing for distance, they called it."

"My brother did the same kind of stuff. And sometimes, when Stephen's in the backyard mowing the grass, he'll pee behind the garage," Dorie volunteered. "He doesn't think I know. I think it's kinda funny. Didn't your brother ever do anything like that?"

"Baylor wouldn't have dared. My mother would have had a cat-fit," Ellis said. "I don't care what you guys say, I'm keeping an eye on Ty Bazemore."

"Mmmm," Julia purred suggestively. "I'll help."

"Me too," Dorie said. "He's adorable. He'd make the perfect summer fling for you, Ellis."

"As if," Ellis said.

. . .

At lunchtime, the girls trooped back up the dunes to the house.

"I'm starved," Julia announced. She was leafing through a thick booklet advertising local shops and restaurants. "Where shall we go for lunch? Seafood, right? The fish we get in England is crap. It's the one big thing I miss about living in Savannah. Do you guys remember my mom's fried grouper sandwiches?"

"I remember her she-crab bisque," Ellis said. Unlike her own mother, who was strictly a meat and potatoes, canned peas, and cherry Jell-O kind of cook, Catherine Capelli had been a fabulous cook. "And I'd give anything for another plate of her spaghetti with the Italian sausage that she'd make in the wintertime."

"And those little yeast rolls she'd make, dripping with garlic butter," Dorie put in. "And all the different kinds of cookies she'd bake every year at Christmas. She'd fix a huge plate for each of us to take home to our families. It's a miracle we all didn't end up fat little piggies after eating your mama's cooking all those years, Julia."

"She could cook, there was no denying that," Julia said lightly. "But you still haven't told me where you want to go have lunch." She rifled the pages of the booklet. "Awful Arthur's? Barefoot Bernie's? Dirty Dick's?"

Ellis picked up a manila folder she'd left on top of the microwave. "Let's see. I've got coupons for Mako Mike's and Freaky Freddie's. Buy one entrée, get a second free."

"You guys go," Dorie said. "Maybe I'll just fix myself a peanut-butter-and-jelly sandwich."

"Peanut butter and jelly? At the beach? Are you nuts?" Julia said.

"I prefer to think of it as being thrifty," Dorie replied. "I mean, c'mon, Ellis, aren't you the tiniest bit worried about your situation? I know you'll get another great job, but I just think I'd be crazy worried if I were you."

"I've got some irons in the fire," Ellis said blithely. "But I'll be all right. As long as I'm sensible about my spending, which I usually am anyway." She opened the refrigerator door, secretly relieved at the twenty dollar bill she'd save by eating lunch at home. "Look, I stopped at the seafood place up the street when I got in yesterday and picked up some shrimp. They claimed it was right off the boat. And I brought a can of Old Bay seasoning. We can steam some shrimp in beer."

"What else have you got in there?" Dorie asked, leaning in to look. She held up a head of romaine lettuce, a cucumber, and a tomato. "Great. I'll throw a salad together while the shrimp are cooking."

"Oh, all right," Julia relented. "We'll stay in for lunch. But tonight, we're going out for dinner so I can get my fried grouper fix. And it's my treat, so don't even try to argue."

They took turns showering, and when lunch was ready, they sat companionably around the enamel-topped kitchen table. They discussed plans for the afternoon, while Ellis checked her e-mail.

"Hey," she announced. "Old man Culpepper finally answered my e-mail. A pest-control guy is coming over to spray the house at two. But he says we've got to stay out of the house for a couple of hours afterwards."

"Suits me," Julia said. "I've got a new book, and the beach is calling me back."

"Guess I've had enough sun for one day," Dorie said, holding out her sunburnt arm.

"Me too," Ellis agreed. "I saw a movie theater up the street. Why don't we catch a matinee?"

"A chick flick!" Dorie's green eyes lit up. "I'll bring my biggest pocketbook and we'll sneak in our own Diet Cokes like we did in junior high. And we can stop and buy a giant box of candy at the Dollar Store."

"Well . . ." Ellis said. "You know they always have those big signs that say 'outside food and drink prohibited'. . . ."

Julia set her beer bottle down on the countertop. "Who cares? They just put those signs up so you'll have to buy their five-dollar Cokes and seven-dollar tubs of popcorn. Nobody pays any attention to those signs."

"I do," Ellis said stubbornly. "What if we got caught? How embarrassing would that be?"

"Who's going to catch you?" Julia wanted to know. "It's not like they have ushers in movie theaters anymore. And even if they did, what do you think is going to happen if they catch you sneaking in your own stuff? Huh? You think they're gonna revoke your driver's license? Seize your jujubes as contraband?"

"Never mind her, Ellis," Dorie said. "I'll carry the Cokes and Milk Duds in my purse." She paused then, remembering that her redrawn budget had no room for movies—let alone seven-dollar boxes of popcorn.

Ellis noticed Dorie's sudden look of concern. She opened the manila folder again. "I went online and downloaded some Movie Lover's passes. If we get there before 1:30, our tickets are only two bucks. And there's one for each of us."

Julia rolled her eyes. "What is with you two with the coupons and early-bird specials? We're on vacation. We've all worked hard and we deserve to be good to ourselves. If you're that hard up for money, just say so." She grabbed her pocketbook.

Ellis saw Dorie bite her lip and look away. "Thanks anyway. We'll pay our own way," she said, her voice deliberately even. "And if you don't want to be seen with a couple of coupon-clippers, we'll understand."

"Oh. Sorry. I didn't mean . . . well, you know." Julia hastily craned her neck to look out the kitchen window. "It's kind of clouding up out there. So if you've got a spare coupon, I guess I could go. Anyway, I figure I laid down a pretty good base coat this morning."

"You're half Italian," Dorie pointed out. "You were born with a base coat. Unlike me, with this darned red hair and freckles. I swear, I think I get sunburn from my night-light."

Ty saw the women load up into the red minivan and head off down Virginia Dare Trail. It was only a little after one. He waited five minutes, and then another five, just to make sure they weren't doubling back. Then he picked up his toolbox and key ring and, whistling, headed over to Ebbtide.

He stood on the porch, hesitant. Beach towels were draped over the rocking chairs, and three bathing suits—the orange bikini, a lime green flowered one-piece, and the black one-piece, were pinned to the clothesline. Three pairs of flip-flops were neatly lined up by the front door. He fit the key in the lock but still didn't turn it. It didn't feel right, somehow. But it was his house, damn it. He was the landlord. Ellis Sullivan had been nagging about a dripping faucet and fleas and ants. So he had a legitimate reason to be in the house.

Then why did he feel so creepy?

Because some neurotic chick accused him of spying on her and her friends? When did it become a crime to stand on his own deck and enjoy the sight of a pretty woman? It was a public beach, wasn't it? It wasn't like he'd taken a pair of binoculars to peep into some unsuspecting woman's bedroom.

He squared his shoulders, unlocked the door, and marched inside. He went directly towards the kitchen. He could hear the faucet dripping from the hallway.

The kitchen looked a hell of a lot better than the last time he'd been in it. The floor was swept, the counters and stove top sparkled, and damp plates and glasses were neatly stacked in the dish drainer, a clean dish towel draped across them. He could smell the Old Bay seasoning they'd used to cook shrimp, but there were also faint undernotes of flowery perfume and coconut-scented suntan lotion.

Ty put his toolbox on the counter. He opened the cupboard under the sink and shut off the water. Then he dug out a pair of Channellocks from the toolbox and went to work. A washer. It just needed a washer. He was putting his tools away when he noticed the dishes stacked on the open shelves. Or what there were of them. He could have sworn there had been dishes for eight when he'd gotten the house ready back before Easter. Now, there were, as Ellis Sullivan had claimed, only five dinner plates. Five chipped, cracked plates. Three cereal bowls, none of them matching. What had happened to all the china he'd stocked the house with back in the spring? He opened one of two drawers. The silverware was pretty skimpy too. There were no knives to speak of. In the cupboard, he found a couple of small saucepans, none with a lid, and the world's smallest cast-iron skillet.

And what about the range? He turned all the burners to high and held the palm of his hand over them. Only the smallest eye, at the back of the stove, worked.

His shoulders slumped. His old man had taught him how to do basic plumbing and rudimentary electrical repairs, but he didn't have any idea how to fix this stove. It had been in the house since his grandmother lived here, at least since the 1970s. It was unlikely he'd find somebody who could fix it, since you probably couldn't even buy replacement parts for the thing anymore.

He was standing there, staring at the half-broken stove, when the doorbell rang.

"Ty Bazemore!"

He wouldn't have recognized Frank Patterson if he hadn't been wearing a BUG-OFF PEST CONTROL uniform shirt, with the name FRANK embroidered in script above the left breast. They'd gone to high school together, where Patterson quarterbacked for the football team and Ty had played tight end.

"Dude!" Ty said, pumping his old teammate's hand. "How the hell are you?"

They stood in the living room, chatting awkwardly. "You're lookin' good, Frank," Ty said. "Bug busting must agree with you."

"It's a living," Frank said. "How 'bout you? Are those your boards I saw out in that garage?"

"Yeah," Ty said. "I'm still surfing. When I get time, which I haven't lately." Finally, they got down to business.

"Fleas, huh?" Frank said, giving the living room an appraising look.

Ty's face darkened. "Friggin' college kids snuck a dog in here last week."

"You don't live here?"

Ty laughed. "No, man, I can't afford to live here. I live over the garage, in what used to be the maid's apartment. I rent out the house."

"Pretty cool old place," Frank said, running a hand over the wood-paneled wall. "It's one of the original ones, right?"

Ty shrugged. "This isn't one of the original thirteen, the ones they call the 'unpainted aristocracy.' My grandmother's aunt bought it in the 1920s. We've still got the original bill of sale. She paid eight thousand dollars back then."

"My dad used to have the pest control contract on the one right next door," Frank said. "The Lunsfords. Nice folks. Clark and Margaret? Maybe you knew them? After the last hurricane hit it so bad, they sold it to some people from Virginia."

"Haven't met the new owners," Ty said. "But Mrs. Lunsford, Miss Marga-ret, we called her, she was one of my grandmother's running buddies. They were classmates at Saint Mary's, back in the day."

"What was your grandmother's name?" Frank asked. "Not Bazemore, right?"

"No," Ty said. "This house belonged to my mom's family. She was a Culpep-per. Edwina and Garrett Culpepper. My granddad died about ten years ago. And then Nanny, she passed two years ago. Everybody called her Winnie."

"I remember hearing your mom passed, some years back, right?"

"That's right," Ty said. "She died the year after Granddad. Hard to believe it's been that long."

Frank nodded his head in mute agreement. He picked up his canister of chemicals and, pointing a long-necked wand, began walking around the pe-rimeter of the room, spraying as he talked.

"Your grandmother left you the house, huh? That's pretty awesome. House like this, right on the ocean. I mean, it's none of my business, but it's worth some bank, right?"

"It would be if it were fixed up," Ty agreed. "Anyway, Nanny left the house to my mom's only brother, my uncle, who lives in South Dakota. His wife hates the beach, and they never had any kids. He was gonna sell it, so I got the bright idea that I should buy it from them. You know, the place was a gold mine—or so I thought."

"Awesome."

"Place is a dump," Ty said, gloomily. "A giant money pit. That's the real reason my uncle was so glad to unload it. My grandmother never wanted to modernize anything. Wanted to leave things like they were when she was a little girl and they'd come up here from Charlotte and spend the whole sum-mer. There's no central heat or air. Granddad finally put in window units, back in the '80s. No insulation, of course. In some places, you can see daylight through these old floorboards. I about froze my ass living here this past win-ter. In Nanny's day, they closed the house up every October and didn't open it back up until Good Friday. The plumbing sucks, too. Only two full bathrooms for this whole big house and only one indoor shower. And the taxes? The county thinks this dump is worth two million dollars! Don't get me started."

"Crazy," Frank agreed, moving into the dining area and then into the kitchen.

"Hey, look at this," he chuckled, looking down the room. "This is some old school, here."

"And not in a good way," Ty said, leaning on the doorframe. "That stove is shot. I just got new tenants for the whole month. Three women! Been here a day, and they're already bitching about the place."

"You need a new stove?" Frank asked casually.

"Yeah," Ty said, bending down to scratch his ankle. "I need a lot of new stuff for this house. But I can't afford shit."

"Reason I ask," Frank said, "is we just replaced all the appliances over at our place. We put the fridge out in the garage, you know, for beer and stuff. But the stove, it's just sitting on the back porch, gathering dust. My wife's kinda into cooking. Wouldn't let up until we got all new stainless-steel fridge and stove and dishwasher. The old stove's fine, she just had her heart set on stainless steel. You know how they get."

"Yeah," Ty said. "I guess."

"You and Kendra still together?" Frank asked, shooting him a curious look before squatting down and directing the pesticide to the kick plate under the counters. Frank knew Kendra from high school, of course. Everybody on the Outer Banks knew the Wilcox family. Kendra's father Boomer had been chairman of the Dare County Commission, and her grandfather had been a superior court judge. Kendra was the fourth generation of lawyer Wilcoxes.

"Nah," Ty said. "We split up a while ago."

"Sorry, man," Frank said. He opened the kitchen door. "You want me to hit the porch out here?"

"Everything," Ty said, following him out. "The place is crawling with fleas. And it all happened in, like, a week."

"Yeah," Frank said, walking up and down the length of the porch, "the little bastards run amok this time of year. You can't let them get ahead of you. I'm not trying to sell you nothin', but seriously, you might wanna think about signing a contract. Save you some money over the long run."

"I'll think about it," Ty said, but his voice said he wouldn't.

Frank stood and faced the ocean. A faint breeze ruffled the sea oats, and the plum-colored skies promised rain. Just beyond where the waves broke, he spotted a dolphin.

"I can see why you'd want to keep this house," Frank said, leaning on the porch rail. "My wife and kids are gonna go nuts about this place. Fall, huh?"

"I'm wide open in October," Ty said. "Unless the bank takes it back before then. You just name the weekend."

"Fishing oughtta start picking up about midmonth," Frank said. "My youngest one? That little girl flat loves to fish. She's her daddy's girl all the way."

"My granddaddy showed me how to bait a hook right out there," Ty said, pointing to the ocean. "I was probably about five. He used to catch the hell out of the red drum in the fall."

"October," Frank repeated. He looked over at Ty, who was still gazing at the place where he'd caught his first fish. Raindrops, big fat ones, began plopping on the sun-bleached walkway over the dunes. People on the beach started gathering up chairs and towels.

"Listen, Ty," Frank said suddenly. "You think you want that stove, we could run over to my place and throw it in the back of the truck. Might as well haul the old one outta here and drop it at the dump."

Ty held out his hand and the men shook. "You got a deal."

# 9

To: Mr.Culpepper@Ebbtide.com
From: EllisSullivan@hotmail.com
Subject: Thanks!

Dear Mr. Culpepper. I take back all the nasty stuff I said about you. The fleas and ants are gone. The new stove is a huge improvement, and I'm sure you'll notice a savings on your water bill since the leaky faucet has been fixed. Also, the new (old) dishes are very sweet. My friends and I just love china with pink roses. Dorie, who is one of our group, says she thinks her grandmother had that exact same china pattern. So again, thanks! Ellis. P.S. What can you tell us about the guy who lives in the garage apartment here? He seems to keep very odd hours—we've noticed the light stays on over there all night long. He's not a serial killer, right? (Just kidding. Mostly.)

------------------------------------------------------------------------

To: EllisSullivan@hotmail.com
From: Mr.Culpepper@Ebbtide.com
Subject: Garage guy

Dear Ellis: Ty Bazemore is harmless. He tells me he makes a living day trading, but maybe that's just a cover story for an international white-slaver. (Just kidding. Mostly.)

"Hey, you guys," Ellis said, putting her iPhone back into the protective plastic pocket of her beach bag. "Mr. Culpepper says that guy above the garage is a day trader. That's why he stays up all night."

"Interesting," Julia said. "I wonder if he literally stays up all night?"

"Julia!" Ellis said, not really shocked.

"Mmm," Dorie said drowsily. She was stretched out facedown on her canvas-covered chaise. Her fingers trailed in the sand, and her body was slick with suntan lotion and perspiration. "What time is it? I think I can only take fifteen more minutes on my stomach."

"It's three o'clock," Julia said, propping herself on one elbow to assess her friend's tanning progress. "You've only been like that for fifteen minutes, and you already look like a boiled lobster. I swear, Dorie, you are the whitest white girl I have ever known."

"Mmm," Dorie said. Moments later, she was softly snoring.

"Such a party animal," Julia said. "Come on, Ellis. I'm bored. Walk down the beach with me, okay?"

Ellis glanced down at their sleeping friend. "Should we just leave her like that? She is getting pretty burnt."

Julia took a beach towel from her bag and gently draped it over Dorie's motionless body. "She'll be fine," Julia said. She slung her beach bag over her shoulder. "Let's walk down to that ice cream shack near the pier. I'm starved."

Ellis pulled her cover-up over her bathing suit, tucked some money into the pocket, and, as a second thought, added her phone.

Julia, who never missed anything, rolled her eyes. "Another thing I don't miss about living in the States! You people and your mania for your mobiles. Do you ever go anywhere without that thing? Can't you just relax? At least while we're together?"

Four days of living in close quarters with Julia had taught Ellis to shrug off her friend's caustic comments. "What about you?" she countered. "Don't you supermodels have to keep in touch with your agencies to find out about bookings or whatever you call it?"

"I am so *not* a supermodel," Julia said. "Anyway, I told the agency I was taking the month off." She picked up the pace, and with her long lean legs had soon left Ellis a couple yards behind.

"Wait up," Ellis called, nearly sprinting to catch up with her friend. "I thought this used to be your busy time," she said.

"Things change," Julia said. "Anyway, I'm on vacay."

Ellis followed Julia up towards the boardwalk crossover and was walking as fast as she could, but even though she wore flip-flops the flour-fine sand scorched her feet.

"I thought I was doing a pretty good job of relaxing. As for worrying— well, I can't help it. I'm thirty-four years old. I've had some kind of a job since I was fourteen years old. I've been in banking since Daddy helped me get my first job at Savannah Bank when I was seventeen. Now, well, I just don't know what's going to happen next."

"Nobody knows what's going to happen next, ever," Julia said, gesturing wildly with her hands. "That's my whole point, Ellis. You've got no control over anything, so why not just sit back and take life as it comes?"

Now it was Ellis's turn to roll her eyes. "That's fine for you to say. I mean, I know you're not an heiress or anything, but at least you've got a nice inheritance to live on. And work that you can do anytime, anywhere. You've been all over the world. And let's face it, you've got Booker. Me? I've lived in three places in my life: Savannah, Charlotte, and Philly. And I've got me. And Mama. Daddy left her just enough to live on, if she's really careful. And she's not. It'll be me taking care of her eventually, not my brother. So yes, I worry. I guess if I had your life, I wouldn't have to worry. But I don't. So I worry a lot. But I'm trying not to let it ruin this month for us."

Julia walked on, three or four steps ahead of Ellis, who couldn't catch up with her friend's long-legged gait, no matter how hard she tried.

Ellis was already regretting her outburst. It was tacky to talk about Julia's money that way. It wasn't like Julia went around flaunting the fact that she was semirich or the fact that Ellis and Dorie were semipoor.

When they got to the paved road, Ellis trotted until she was right beside Julia. "You're mad at me, aren't you?"

"Nope," Julia said. "I'm not going to get mad at you for saying what you're thinking. At least, I hope I won't. It's just that you don't really have a clue what my life is like."

"I don't?"

"Not really," Julia said. They'd reached the open-air ice cream shop. It was a concrete block affair, painted with circus-bright red-and-yellow stripes. A dozen people stood in line in front of them, waiting to order, and the picnic tables, located in the shade of the shop's overhang, were full. Rock music blared from speakers mounted on wooden columns. Ellis and Julia crowded close together, seeking refuge from the searing ninety-plus heat.

The song was Bruce Springsteen's "Dancing in the Dark." Without thinking, they started swaying their upper bodies to the music.

"What's this song remind you of?" Julia asked, reading the chalkboard menu.

"Me?" Beneath two days' tan, Ellis blushed.

"I knew it!" Julia cackled. "Ellis and Mikey Cavanaugh, gettin' jiggy at my fifteenth-birthday party."

"Would you please shut up?" Ellis said. "People can hear you."

"So what?" Julia twirled around, juking right and left, humming the song that had been their junior high anthem. "Oh, you were so hot for Mikey Cavanaugh back then. My mother saw you making out with him behind the garage, you know. She was gonna call your mama and tell her, but Daddy told her to mind her own business. Oooh, Ellis, you were a bad little girl back in the day."

"Shut up," Ellis said, going pink with the delicious memory of kissing the cutest boy at the party.

"Take your order?" The girl behind the counter was Hispanic, and she wore a pained expression and a ridiculous paper cap made to look like an ice cream cone. "Ma'am?" she said loudly, to the oblivious Julia.

Ellis jostled Julia's arm. "Come on. It's your turn."

"Oh. Yeah. Let me see. All right. Do you have gelato?"

"Julia! This is Nags Head, not Rome," Ellis said. "It's ice cream, all right?" She leaned into the counter. "She'll have a single scoop of Rocky Road in a cup, and I'll have a single coffee chocolate chip in a sugar cone. And two large cups of ice water, please."

Before Julia could stop her, Ellis handed over a five-dollar bill, and plunked the change in a tip jar displayed prominently on the counter.

By mutual agreement, they perched at the end of a picnic bench at a table where a young mother busily spooned ice cream into her sandy toddler's wailing mouth.

"I can't believe you remembered about the Rocky Road, and the cup, no cone, after all these years," Julia said, dipping the tiny plastic spoon into the ice cream.

"And I can't believe you still won't let me live Mikey Cavanaugh down—twenty years later," Ellis said. "Did your mother really see us together, or are you just saying that to torture me?"

"She really did!" Julia nodded vigorously. "You know, until the day she died, she still thought you were a bad influence on me."

"Me?" Ellis hooted. "I was the voice of reason. The sane one. If it weren't for me, you would have gone to jail or hell, long ago."

"I know," Julia said. "Ellis Sullivan, designated driver for life. Mama always thought I was the angel and you were the devil, and I wasn't going to tell her any different. And you know, when you got out of college and got engaged, Mama told me she was glad, because you were finally going to settle down with that nice boy. She didn't even really mind that he was Jewish, and a Yankee."

Ellis sighed. "Bless her heart, your mama never did have a clue."

"You ever hear from him?" Julia asked, tilting her head. The three of them, Julia, Dorie, and Ellis, had all pledged, long ago, to never again speak the name of Ellis's ex-husband. "He's dead to us," Dorie had proclaimed at the end of the three-month-long marriage.

And his name, which was Ben Greene, and the wedding and marriage, as far as her friends knew, seemed to have miraculously faded from Ellis's memory. It was such an un-Ellis-like thing to have happened that she could almost persuade herself that it hadn't. Almost.

"I haven't heard from him in years," Ellis said, which was technically true. "Last I heard, he'd gotten remarried. I think they have a baby."

Through the magic of Google, where she'd found *Greene Acres,* his second wife's chatty blog, Ellis knew exactly where Ben was living (Winnetka, Illinois), what he was doing (running his family's furniture-import business), and the name of his new wife (Sherry). She knew they had two shelties (Lulu and Lucky) and a two-year-old son named Sam (after Ben's favorite uncle).

And she would have died if anybody, *especially* Ben, knew just how often she read *Greene Acres.*

"Well, thank God for small favors," Julia said vehemently. "He's somebody else's problem and not yours. Sweet Jesus! Can you imagine having a baby with ears like his? You'd have to put a sidecar on the baby buggy just to accommodate 'em."

On the contrary, Ellis had seen photos of little Sam, and she thought he was the most adorable toddler she'd ever laid eyes on. He had huge, soulful blue eyes, a thick fringe of pale hair, and a perfect, cupid-bow's mouth, which he must have gotten from his mother, because everybody in Ben's family had nearly nonexistent upper lips.

"Ellis?" Julia was looking at her strangely.

"His ears weren't that big," Ellis said. "You just never liked him from the get-go."

"And was I wrong? Did you have to file papers on him even before you'd finished writing the thank-you notes for the wedding presents?"

"You were right," Ellis said, wadding up her paper napkin and crushing it on top of her unfinished ice cream cone. She tossed both, underhand, into the metal trash basket, and took a long drink of ice water. "I hated you for it at the time, but you were oh, so right."

Everybody but Ellis had known just how wrong Ben was for her. And the day Ben realized it too, just three months into the marriage, he'd calmly, coldly announced, at dinner, two days before her birthday, that the whole thing had been a regrettable mistake. That was the exact word he'd used, too. Regrettable. There'd been no fight, no ugly scene, just Ben, in his pale-yellow golf shirt, pushing back from the table, setting his fork at the edge of his dinner plate, saying, his eyes serious but dry, "I'm sorry, Ellis, but we both know this will never work."

Pressed by his tearful—well, hysterical, really—bride, Ben had finally uttered the words that had stilled the tears and broken Ellis's heart for good. "I'm just not in love with you. I thought I was, I wanted to be, but I'm not."

Before the night was out, Ben had packed his clothes, his books, his CDs, and moved out of their apartment. And before Ellis could even really comprehend what was happening, the divorce was final and the marriage was almost, but not completely, forgotten.

Nobody but Ellis knew how she still grieved for what was gone. Her marriage was the first thing she'd ever really failed at. Afterwards, she'd packed away all the wedding china, silver, and crystal, which she could no longer bear to look at, and simply thrown all her energy and talent into her job, winning promotions, rave job evaluations, and raises. But the loneliness never subsided. She missed living with a man, having somebody to eat dinner with and buy shirts for. She missed having somebody waiting at the airport baggage claim when she came home from a business trip, and she missed slow, delicious Saturday morning lovemaking. Oh God, had it really been ten years since she'd had sex? More. Eleven and a half years, if you didn't count some heavy petting with a man she had dated in the year immediately following her divorce, when she'd been desperate to prove to herself just how over Ben she was.

Julia stood up abruptly. "Come on, we better get back to Dorie. I don't want to have to be giving her oatmeal baths like we did that summer at Myrtle Beach."

Ellis grimaced. "What were we thinking, slathering ourselves with that nasty baby oil and iodine mess? It's a wonder we don't all have skin cancer. "

"We weren't thinking. We were drinking," Julia reminded her. They strolled back across the street and over the dune to the beach below.

"Listen," Julia said suddenly. "What do you think is really going on with Dorie?"

"Dorie? Nothing. Why? What do you think is going on?"

"It hasn't struck you that we've been here over three days now and she hasn't once called Stephen?"

"Nooo," Ellis said. "I guess she hasn't. But maybe she's just letting him alone so he can concentrate on his thesis."

"Nuh-uh," Julia said. "He hasn't called her, either. I know, because her room's right next to mine."

"Maybe they had a fight. Maybe she's pissed he decided he was too busy to come. I don't know, Julia. But I don't think it's any of our business, whatever it is."

"This isn't Dorie," Julia said stubbornly. "Something really bad has happened to her. Listen, at the movie the other day? She cried all the way through it."

Ellis's brow wrinkled. "It was a comedy! Nobody cries at a Ben Stiller movie."

"She got up twice to go to the bathroom," Julia said. "Didn't want us to see her bawling her eyes out. Something is going on with them, Ellis. I can sense it."

"Then do me a favor, Julia," Ellis whirled and grabbed Julia's wrist to make her point. "Leave her alone. I mean it. If she wants to tell us, she will. If she and Stephen are going through a rough time, the best thing we can do for her is just be here for her. You hear me?"

"Of course," Julia said. "You act like I'm some kind of bully or something. I've known Dorie as long as you have. I love her as much as you do. I want her to be happy, that's all."

They were almost back at the beach. Something had been bothering Ellis. "Listen, Julia," she said, slowing down so her friend would have to also. "Since we're on the subject of happiness . . . What's going on with you and Booker?"

Julia stopped walking and made an elaborate gesture of adjusting the oversized silk scarf she'd casually knotted around her waist. "Nothing," she said. "Same old, same old."

"You lie like a rug," Ellis said. "Now come on, out with it. You're not breaking up, right?"

"Not exactly," Julia said. "It's gotten complicated. And you know how I hate complications. Really, I don't know why he wants to mess with a good thing. But that's Booker. He never has been able to leave well enough alone."

"What's he done now?" Ellis asked.

"Oh Gawwd," Julia said. "What hasn't he done? Well, for starters, he's gone and taken a real job."

"In England?"

"No, and that's the problem," Julia said, frowning. "He's head of the photo department at some magazine publishing company you never heard of in Washington. I mean, can you imagine? Booker, in a coat and tie? Actually punching a clock? It boggles the mind."

"In DC?" Ellis said, her voice only an octave below a squeal. "But, Julia, that's great. DC's only a hop and a jump from Philly! You know, if I manage to find another job and stay in Philly. But whatever, right? I mean, you'll be back in the States, that's all we care about."

"I wouldn't start buying Amtrak stock just yet," Julia said. She was walking, no, almost running now.

"What?" Ellis was out of breath from trying to catch up. "Hey, slow down. Julia!"

"Who says I want to move back to the States?" Julia turned and snapped. "Who says I want to give up my career for Booker? Who says I have to get married and start pumping out a baby a year like my poor mother? She basically lived in those fugly maternity clothes for seven years, all before she was twenty-five, and I never remember a time when she did anything for herself, her whole life. I'm only thirty-five, for God's sake! I like my life just the way it is. All right?"

Ellis blinked. What would be wrong with having a life like that, like the one Julia's mother had—with babies and a loving husband, and yes, spit-up and drool and even stretch marks? Julia said she couldn't remember her mother having any time alone—Ellis had practically lived at the Capellis' during her teenage years, and she couldn't ever remember seeing Catherine Capelli when she wasn't singing or laughing or telling a joke—surrounded by her noisy, adoring family.

"Nobody's saying you have to do any of that," Ellis said quietly.

"That's what you think," Julia said, her shoulders sagging. "Look, we're at the beach. Can we not talk about this right now? I'm going for a swim."

Ellis stood on the tide line, the place where the burning sand met the wet sand. It was strewn with broken shells and dried seaweed. She stepped out of her sandals and dug her toes into the cool sand. Her hand closed around the cell phone in the pocket of her cover-up. She had résumés out at a couple different places. A former colleague had sent her a promising lead about a job at a start-up financial services company in Pittsburgh.

Pittsburgh. She didn't know a soul in Pittsburgh. Starting over in a new town? At a new company, a new job? Unbidden, she pictured herself, alone, in a new apartment, studying a stack of takeout menus, with an empty evening, an empty weekend, stretching out before her, in appalling, *regrettable* aloneness.

Worry, Ellis thought, hell yes. Worry didn't begin to cover what she was feeling right now.

# 10

It wasn't until her stomach rumbled that Maryn realized how hungry she was. She pulled the car into the next strip shopping center she passed. The place was called The Picky Pelican. Stupid name for a restaurant. But she was really, really hungry.

And she was desperate to talk to Adam. Her one friend. Funny, when you thought about it. Adam Kuykendall was the least likely candidate for a best friend that Maryn could think of. Short and stocky, with thinning blond hair, geeky glasses, and a scraggly soul patch on his chin, Adam and Maryn had bonded as soon as she'd started work at Prescott and Associates, a midsized family-owned insurance agency in Cherry Hill.

The other women in the office wanted nothing to do with Maryn, giving her disapproving sideways glances, pointedly excluding her from their lunchtime cliques and after-work drink outings. Most were older, married, with kids, even grandkids. Adam was the only male nonagent in the whole office.

So they were both outsiders. At first, Maryn had just assumed he was gay. But he was surprisingly good company, and he'd won her over her first week at work with his wickedly cutting comments about their bitchy female coworkers. Within a week of meeting, they'd established their rituals—lunch from the Italian deli around the corner, Friday night happy hour, Sunday movie matinees—chick flicks for her, slasher movies for him.

And then Don came into her life eighteen months ago. And everything changed.

She had to talk to Adam right away, warn him. Don knows. I'm gone. I'm afraid. Afraid he'll come after me. Afraid he'll come after you. Be careful. I'm gone.

Adam would have to wait, though. She yawned, got out of the car, locked it, and looked around, automatically tensing at the sight of a black SUV and, quickly, rebuking herself. This SUV was an Explorer, not an Escalade. Don Shackleford did not know where she was. Yet.

Inside the restaurant, all the tables were full. There was one seat vacant, at the counter, between a guy who looked like a construction worker and a young woman her age, with a sunburnt nose, who looked to have just walked in off the beach.

The restaurant smelled like hamburgers and French fries. Maryn's stomach growled again. She needed food, a bed, a new name, new identity, new life. But for now, a seat at the counter at The Picky Pelican would have to do.

# 11

Dorie sat alone at the luncheonette counter. Even though it was nearly two, the place was still mobbed with a late lunch crowd. "Here ya go, hon," the waitress said, as she carefully poured the chocolate shake from the stainless-steel shaker into the tall, frosted glass and then placed it on the fluted white-paper place mat. "Wait," the waitress said. She turned to the back bar and returned with a can of whipped cream in one hand and a maraschino cherry in the other. "There now," the waitress said, plopping the cherry atop the mound of whipped cream.

"Thank you so much," Dorie said, shooting the waitress a smile. "This looks awesome."

She plunged the straw into the shake and took a deep sip. The sensation of the ice-cold chocolate sent a chill down her sunburnt back, but that didn't slow her down. When she'd woken up back at the beach, Ellis and Julia were gone, and she was starving. Again. She'd washed the sand off at the outside shower, slipped into her cover-up, and gone in search of something to eat. The little luncheonette was called The Picky Pelican. It sat in the middle of a strip shopping center only a few blocks from Ebbtide, and it reminded her of Clary's Soda Fountain, back home.

So she'd found the seat at the counter, but when the waitress brought the menu, nothing really appealed to her. Except a chocolate milk shake.

Dorie tried to take her time finishing the shake. She'd felt a little guilty, leaving without telling the girls where she was going, but then, hadn't they gone off without her while she was sleeping on her lounge chair?

She pulled a magazine out of her beach bag and flicked idly through the pages.

"Ah-hem." A woman in expensive-looking designer sunglasses cleared her throat.

Dorie looked up from her magazine. "Hello," she said.

"Would you mind if I sat here?" The woman gestured at the empty stool beside Dorie's. It was the only vacant one at the counter.

"Not at all," Dorie said.

"Thanks." The woman sat down and silently picked up a menu. She was attractive, maybe a little younger than Dorie, and with her tailored black slacks, black sling-back stiletto heels, and clingy silk leopard-print blouse, she looked distinctly out of place amongst the T-shirts-and-shorts-wearing beach crowd in the restaurant. Dorie went back to her magazine, forcing herself to take tiny sips of her milk shake. What she really wanted was a second shake. But this one cost nearly four bucks, and she'd have to leave a buck tip, and that was five bucks that she hadn't budgeted on spending. Five bucks she really shouldn't spend.

She looked down at her cell phone, and for the tenth time that day, tried to force herself to call her sister. Willa had plenty of money. Arthur was rich, and Willa hadn't worked a day since she'd married. It was rotten of her to cancel at the last minute, and even rottener not to offer to pay her share anyway. Back when she'd invited herself to come along with the others, she'd even hinted to Dorie that she'd be happy to pay for both their shares. Of course, she'd never mentioned the offer again.

She shouldn't have come, Dorie thought glumly. When Willa had canceled, she should have stayed home too. She had no business spending all this money for a month at the beach. Especially now.

The waitress came over, and the woman next to her ordered a club sandwich and an iced tea. Dorie's stomach growled. Suddenly she felt she would *kill* for a club sandwich. Even though she'd had a grilled-cheese sandwich for lunch back at the house, not to mention a mound of potato chips.

Dorie turned back to her magazine and tried to concentrate on an article offering "Ten Tips to Save Money Now." The article was a joke, advising readers to cut corners by giving up their Starbucks and doing their own nails. Dorie didn't go to Starbucks. And she hadn't had a professional manicure in years.

A few moments later, the waitress was back with the woman's food. "Can I get you anything else?" she heard the waitress ask.

"Um, well," the blond woman said, her voice low. "I'm looking for a motel room around here. Nothing fancy. It doesn't have to be on the beach or anything. Just something clean and cheap, maybe with a little kitchenette. Would you have any suggestions?"

"Cheap?" the waitress laughed. "Honey, this is high season at Nags Head. I guess that would depend on what you call cheap. My cousin and her kids stayed at a little place over on the inlet. Joint didn't even have a pool. And they had to give close to two hundred bucks a night."

"Oh." The blonde's voice sounded tired, defeated even.

"You might want to drive on down the road, check someplace like Elizabeth City. I think they got a Motel 6 over there."

"Thanks," the blonde said. The waitress drifted away.

"Excuse me."

Dorie looked up from her magazine.

"Could you pass the pepper, please?" Maryn pointed at the pepper shaker directly in front of Dorie.

"Here you go," Dorie said, sliding the shaker over.

Maryn deconstructed her club sandwich, carefully removing each layer of bread, and with a knife, scraping off the excess mayonnaise before sprinkling the thin slices of bloodred tomato with an avalanche of pepper.

She caught Dorie watching her with interest. "I wish, just once, they'd ask before slathering mayo all over everything," she said.

"I know," Dorie agreed. "I'm the same way with mustard. A little goes a long way, if you ask me. But that sure is a pretty tomato."

"Um-hmm," the blonde said, restacking her sandwich. "We don't get tomatoes this nice until really late in the season back home. But there's nothing like a Jersey tomato."

Dorie laughed. "You haven't tasted one out of my daddy's garden. He grows these huge ones, he calls 'em Mortgage Lifters, I could eat 'em 'til I'm sick."

"Are you from around here?" the blonde asked.

"Nope," Dorie said. "I'm from Savannah, Georgia. How 'bout you?"

"Jersey," Maryn said, deliberately vague. She took a delicate bite of her sandwich and dabbed with her napkin at a bit of mayo on her lip.

"My friends and I are here for the whole month," Dorie volunteered.

"Oh?" the blonde put the sandwich down. "At a motel? Isn't that pretty expensive?"

"We've got a house," Dorie said proudly. "Right on the beach. There are three of us, and we share expenses, so it works out to be way cheaper than a motel. Of course," she added ruefully, "it's more expensive than we'd planned, because my sister canceled on us at the last minute."

"A house," Maryn said thoughtfully. "How do you go about finding something like that?"

Dorie laughed. "Ellis, one of my girlfriends? She's a planning freak. She put this whole trip together. I think she found it on VRBO. Or maybe Craigslist."

"VRBO?"

"Vacation Rentals by Owner. It's like an international website for rental houses all over the world."

"Never heard of that before," Maryn admitted. "Maybe I should check it out. I'm looking for a place to stay around here for a couple weeks."

"Good luck on that. I think things get booked up around here pretty early. Ellis booked our house months ago. Of course, that's when we were planning to have five people instead of only three."

"This was sort of a last-minute decision," Maryn said, shrugging. "Guess I'll maybe look for a place in Elizabeth City. Although the idea of a Motel 6, that's kinda grim. I was hoping to find something on the beach."

Maryn returned her attention to her sandwich.

And Dorie had an idea. Her bedroom—the one she and Stephen were to have shared on the top floor, was lonely. She'd felt isolated with Ellis and Julia on the second floor, so she'd moved down to the room that would have been Willa's.

She eyed the blonde warily. She was expensively dressed, well groomed. Was it crazy, this idea taking root? She'd been obsessed with money worries since arriving at Nags Head. Maybe, just maybe, it wasn't such a crazy idea.

Dorie cleared her throat. "Um, don't take this the wrong way, okay?"

The blonde turned and raised her sunglasses. Her eyes were a clear cornflower blue. "Yes?"

"Look," Dorie said, blushing a little. "I had an idea. You're looking for a place to stay at the beach, and as it happens, we've got an extra bedroom and bath. . . ."

"Oh," the blonde said. "Well, I don't know. . . ."

"It's pretty private," Dorie went on. "You'd have the top floor of the house. My husband and I were going to stay there, but he couldn't come at the last minute, and then my sister canceled too, so we've got all this extra space."

The blonde stared at her, as though she were inspecting a head of cabbage at the supermarket. Dorie felt herself blushing again. What the hell was she doing? Inviting a total stranger to move in with them? The girls would think she'd gone nuts.

"I could use the kitchen?" the blonde asked.

"Uh, yeah. I mean, of course," Dorie stuttered. "You can have access to the whole house. We're pretty casual, it's just the three of us. I'm a schoolteacher, and my friend Julia is a model. And Ellis works at a bank. Or, actually, she used to work at a bank."

"How much?" Maryn asked.

Now it was Dorie's turn to stare back. The blonde's clothes looked expensive. And her jewelry looked even more expensive. She wore a huge diamond solitaire on her right ring finger and a diamond tennis bracelet on her left wrist. The handbag she balanced on her lap was white ostrich skin, the size of a small dog. The zipper pull bore a Prada nameplate. And the gold letters on the sleek tortoiseshell sunglasses perched on her head spelled out DIOR. Dorie was no expert, but the pocketbook and the sunglasses looked like the real thing to her.

She did the math in her head, adding an extra five hundred-dollar cushion, and named the price.

"Hmm," the blonde said. "I wasn't thinking anywhere near that much."

"It's the nicest bedroom in the house," Dorie pointed out. "With beach access. And off-street parking."

"Is there a garage?" Maryn asked eagerly.

"Yeees," Dorie said, though she had no idea if the garage guy would be willing to let somebody else park in it. Maybe if they offered to throw some of this woman's cash his way, he'd agree to share.

"Does it have a private entrance?"

Dorie bit her lip. There was an outside spiral staircase leading up to the third floor, but it was narrow and scary-looking, and none of the girls had even thought to try going up it. Still, it was technically a private entrance. And this woman was anxious to have a room with a garage and a private entrance. And she obviously had the money to pay for both.

"It has a private entrance," Dorie said, nodding for emphasis. "But if you want to park in the garage, that'll be an extra hundred bucks a week."

The blonde took a sip of her iced tea. She put her glass down on the counter, and twisted the diamond solitaire ring for a moment. Dorie found herself holding her breath.

"Fine," she said finally. "I'll take it."

Dorie grinned. "Great. But we'll want the rent in cash. In advance."

Maryn shook her head. "I'd prefer to pay half now, half at the end of the month. In case I have a change of plans."

"Deal," Dorie said, putting out her hand. "By the way, my name is Dorie Dunaway."

The blonde hesitated, and then took Dorie's hand. "I'm Madison. Madison Venable. When can I move in?"

Dorie looked down at her watch. "How's four o'clock? I'll want to let my friends know you're coming and make sure your space in the garage is empty."

"That'll work," Madison said. "I've got some things to take care of this afternoon, then I'll be over."

"The house is called Ebbtide," Dorie said, putting her money on the counter beside her empty glass. "It's three blocks north of here, on the beach road, which is Virginia Dare. There's a sign at the entrance to the driveway, and you'll see my red van."

# 12

Julia and Ellis were sitting on the front porch, painting each other's toenails a ridiculous shade of neon green. "There you are!" Ellis cried, as Dorie flopped down onto a rocking chair beside her. "Where'd you disappear to?"

"I woke up and you guys were gone," Dorie said accusingly.

"We went for ice cream," Julia said. "We didn't think you'd care."

Dorie laughed. "That's what I did too, only it was a milk shake." She licked her lips. "Yummy. I don't know when the last time was that I had a real milk shake made with real chocolate syrup and ice cream and the works. Not to mention whipped cream and a cherry."

"Sounds divine," Julia said. She held the bottle of nail polish aloft. "It's called Lime-a-Lishus. Want to be next?"

"No thanks," Dorie said. "I did my toes right before I left home."

"We were just talking about what to do about dinner," Ellis said. "It's your turn tonight. Got any thoughts?"

"Not yet," Dorie said, sitting on the edge of the rocking chair so that it leaned into the girls. "Listen, you guys, I just did something kinda crazy."

"What? You picked up a guy along with your milk shake?" Julia laughed. "Now that's our old Dorie!"

"Lord no!" Dorie said. "Here's the thing. I kinda rented out the top floor of this house to a woman I just met."

"Sure you did," Ellis said lazily, flexing her toes and admiring her daring new look.

"For reals," Dorie said, sitting up straight. "I totally did. Her name's Madison, she dresses like she's got plenty of bucks, and I overheard her asking the waitress about renting a motel room with a kitchenette. She was sitting next to me at the restaurant, and we kind of struck up a conversation. So I offered her the room that was going to be mine and Stephen's. And she took it. She's going to pay us six hundred dollars more than Willa would have. So what do you guys think?"

Julia put the bottle of nail polish on the floor. "I think," she said slowly, "that you have lost your freaking mind. You can't be serious, Dorie. Do you mean to tell me you just invited a total stranger to live with us for the next month? Don't you think that's something you might have run by Ellis and me?"

Dorie bit her lip. "Yeah, I guess. But the money will more than make up for what Willa would have paid. I just thought, I mean, it's sort of my fault Willa let us all down. She's my sister, and I'm the one who talked you guys into letting her come. I should have known she would pull a stunt like that. I just figured it was my responsibility to fix things. So I did."

Ellis took Dorie's hand. "You're really worried about the money part, I know. But honey, you're not responsible for what Willa did. And Julia and I aren't mad at you about it. That's just Willa."

"I am worried about the money," Dorie cried. "I mean, Ellis, you're out of work, and Julia's not working as much as she used to, so I think money's tight for all of us. . . ."

"Who says I'm not working?" Julia said, bristling. "What the hell is that supposed to mean?"

"Nothing," Dorie said, backpedaling.

"Julia!" Ellis said sharply. "Cut the crap. You just told me yourself that you're not working as much. And anyway, you know Dorie didn't mean it like that. The truth is, money is kinda tight for all of us. But Dorie, you really should have talked to us about this before you offered to rent out your room."

"I know," Dorie said, sniffling. "God, I'm such a screwup. But, it all happened so fast. And it just seemed like a good idea at the time."

"What do you even know about this girl?" Julia asked.

Dorie hesitated. "She's from New Jersey, and on vacation, sort of a spur-of-the-moment beach trip . . . and, oh yeah, she hates it when they put too much mayo on a sandwich."

"Oh, she's a mayo hater, is she? Say no more! That seals the deal for me." Julia rolled her eyes.

Dorie bit her lip. "I guess I could tell Madison we've changed our minds. . . ." Her voice trailed off. "She's coming over at four. I'll tell her then."

"Well. . . ." Ellis cleared her throat. "It is a lot of money."

"And the room's just sitting there, empty," Dorie reminded them. "It's not like she'd be rooming with us. Not even on the same floor as the rest of us."

"But she's a stranger, Dorie," Julia said. "You don't really know anything about her. Maybe she's a pathological liar. Maybe she's really from Arkansas. And maybe she actually adores mayo and can't stand ketchup. Who knows? She could walk down those stairs one night and murder us all in our beds, as we're sleeping."

"But, why would she do something like that?" Dorie asked, digging in her heels. Julia's bossiness was starting to wear thin with her. The more Julia protested Madison's coming, the more Dorie thought it was a good idea. "Anyway, if you're that worried about her, we could all get locks on the bedroom doors."

"Surely, that's not necessary," Ellis said, her voice trailing off.

Dorie studied Ellis, knowing she was the swing vote on the matter of Madison.

"Just meet her, please?" Dorie said, keeping her eyes on Ellis. "You'll see, she's perfectly nice. And the setup is perfect. Madison could come and go by that outside stairway around back. That's what she wanted, a separate entrance. And she wanted to make sure she could use the kitchen, and of course, I told her that would be fine. You guys, she seems like somebody we could trust. She agreed to pay cash—half up front, half at the end of the month. I watched her drive off. She's got a new-looking Volvo SUV. And she's got some major-league diamonds. And, I mean, she was wearing Dior sunglasses and carrying a Prada bag. I guess they were the real thing, I don't really know a lot about that kind of stuff. . . ."

"I do," Julia said quickly. "I can spot bootleg Prada from a mile away."

"Okay, when she comes over, you can totally check out all that stuff," Dorie said. "What do you say?"

"It couldn't hurt to meet her," Ellis said. "Right, Julia?"

"Whatever," Julia said, mustering a stern look. "But when this homicidal maniac slashes you to pieces with a butcher knife, don't say I didn't warn you."

"Then it's settled," Dorie said happily. "Unless you guys get just a really weird vibe, Madison is in. Now, I'll just run upstairs and leave some clean towels in the bathroom. It's the least I can do, since she's taking up Willa's slack."

"I'll give you a hand," Ellis volunteered.

"There's just one more thing," Dorie added. "Madison wants to be able to keep her car in the garage. I told her we'd have to charge her a hundred dollars more a week, and she didn't bat an eyelash."

"We don't have access to the garage," Ellis said. "Garage boy keeps his Bronco there."

"There's room for two cars," Dorie said. "Maybe Ty Bazemore wouldn't mind. Maybe you could ask Mr. Culpepper for permission."

"Maybe," Ellis said, sounding noncommittal. "I'll check and see."

# 13

Maryn watched Dorie's red van pull out of the parking lot. Had she done something totally crazy? She'd just agreed to rent a room in a house full of women—total strangers—sight unseen. Why? Something about this girl made her feel safe. Dorie seemed like somebody she could trust. And Maryn couldn't remember the last time she had trusted another woman she wasn't related to.

She told herself the new plan made perfect sense. This way her name wouldn't show up on any hotel or motel register. She wouldn't be using a credit card. She'd be hidden away in a private home, in a place he'd never look, her car parked in a garage, hidden from prying eyes.

Maryn pulled her cell phone from her handbag and checked for messages. Four missed calls from Don. She deleted them with a tap of her fingertip, wishing the task were as easy in the real world as it was in the digital one. She wondered idly if she should call Adam, tell him how right he'd been about Don. She wished she could tell him, wished they could talk. Adam was the only one she could trust. But it wasn't safe. Not for him, not for her.

Maryn nibbled nervously at her cuticle. What should she do? Call the police? Call the old man, R.G. Prescott himself? And tell him what? "I used to work for you, and my husband, Don Shackleford, is your accountant, and incidentally, he's ripped you off to the tune of a couple million dollars, have a nice day?"

No. She had no real proof. She hadn't worked for the insurance company in months. Shortly after their marriage, Don had insisted she quit—he had plenty of money, they didn't need her penny-ante salary, and anyway, she had plenty to do at home, the three-thousand-square-foot town house they were renting while the new house was under construction. She'd kept up the friendship with Adam after leaving the company, but she was careful not to mention Adam to Don, who thought Adam was a loser—and anyway, why couldn't she make friends with the wives of some of his golf buddies?

Adam had called on her cell phone last Friday, and it was obvious that something was wrong. "We need to talk," he'd said, his voice low, insisting they meet at a coffee shop miles away from Cherry Hill.

She'd laughed when he walked in fifteen minutes late, wearing oversized sunglasses and a baseball cap pulled low over his face. "What, you're incognito?"

"This is serious, Maryn," Adam had said. "Listen. We had outside auditors show up at the office today. They wouldn't tell anybody what they were looking for, but I know for a fact that something's funny with half a dozen of our accounts."

She shrugged. "What's that got to do with me? I haven't worked there in months. And anyway, I just handled claims processing."

"This isn't about you," Adam said. "It's about your husband."

"Don?" She still didn't get it.

Adam smirked. "How do you think he got so rich? How many other CPAs do you know who live like him? The houses, new cars, trips to Vegas, Palm Beach, Bermuda? How much do you think it costs to belong to a country club like yours?" He gestured towards Maryn's engagement ring. "Robby Prescott is old money, third generation, and his wife doesn't have a ring like that."

"That's crazy," Maryn said heatedly. She got up to leave. "Don doesn't have to steal. He owns investment property, an office building on the south side, some self-storage companies. Just because you don't like him doesn't mean he's a crook."

Adam grabbed her sleeve, and her coffee spilled all over the table, splashing on her favorite Armani skirt. "Listen to me," he insisted. "The guy is dirty. There's money missing, or at least unaccounted for. Like, two million dollars."

"You're talking about my husband," Maryn said, her voice cold. "Now let go. And don't call me again. Ever."

Her anger lasted all of a day. And then she started to wonder. Just where did all Don's money come from? Why was he so secretive about his business affairs? He was generous with her, but she had no checking account of her own, not even a debit card, only credit cards, and she never saw a bill or bank statement. Everything was sent directly to his office. If she needed cash, she asked, and Don gave. "I'm your own personal ATM," he told her more than once, graphically demonstrating just what he expected from her in return for his generosity.

And exactly twenty-four hours after her meeting with Adam, Maryn had started to look for answers. And what she found was much, much more than she bargained for. The truth hadn't set her free at all, she thought now. It had sent her running for her life.

She put the phone away and dismissed any thought of asking anybody for help. Who would believe her? For now, she had more pressing matters to attend to. Her designer clothes—big-city career pieces—made her stand out like a sore thumb in a beach town. And the few pieces of clothing she'd hurriedly thrown into her duffle were just as unsuited to her current situation.

There was an outlet mall just down the road. She'd pick up a new wardrobe for the new person she'd just invented on the spot, a few minutes ago. Madison would need some shorts and T-shirts, a pair of Levi's, some flip-flops. And her own clothes—Maryn's clothes, the ones with all those expensive designer tags that she'd once lusted over? There was a Goodwill donation bin in the parking lot of the mall. That would be the end of Maryn. And the beginning of Madison.

"Here she comes," Dorie said, as the Volvo bumped along down the driveway.

"Nice car," Julia said, eyeing it. "Wonder where she stole it?"

"Be nice," Dorie warned, jumping up from the rocking chair she'd been perched on.

She waited until Madison had parked the car in front of the driveway, and then walked slowly down to meet her.

"Hi, Madison," Dorie said, smiling. "I'm so glad you're here. Did you have any trouble finding us?"

"Not at all," Madison said, unloading her duffle bag and laptop case from the trunk.

"Here," Dorie said, tugging at the strap of the duffle bag, "Let me help you carry your stuff in."

"No!" Madison jerked the duffle bag away. "I mean, no thanks. I can manage by myself."

"All right," Dorie said. "Come on up to the porch. We're just having some iced tea. The girls are dying to meet you."

"If it's all right with you," Madison said, "I've had a long day. I'd just as soon see my room first, and get settled in. Maybe we could handle the introductions later?"

Dorie's cheeks flushed hot pink. "Actually, I was a little bit premature in offering to rent the room without everybody having met you first. "

Madison's smile was tight. "They want to check me out, make sure I'm not some kind of freak, right?"

"I'm so sorry. It's just that I did this all on my own, without consulting anybody," Dorie said apologetically. "I'm not usually this impulsive. But I'm sure it'll be fine, as soon as they meet you."

Madison let out a long sigh of annoyance. "Let's get it over with then."

"Girls," Dorie said, "this is Madison."

Ellis stood up and held out her hand. "Madison, hi. I'm Ellis Sullivan."

Julia stayed in her rocking chair. She looked Madison up and down and finally put down her glass of iced tea. "Hello," she said. "I'm Julia."

"Hi there," Madison said warily. She clutched her pocketbook and looked around the porch. "This looks very nice. Thanks for agreeing to let me horn in on your getaway."

"We're glad to have you," Ellis said. She gestured towards the rocking chair she'd just abandoned. "Join us, won't you? I just made a pitcher of iced tea."

"Thank you," Madison said. She put the duffle bag and laptop on the floor beside the rocking chair and took the glass of iced tea Ellis poured.

An uneasy silence fell over the porch, punctuated only by the rhythmic sound of Julia's chair, rocking back and forth on the worn wooden floorboards.

"I guess Dorie told you about all of us," Ellis said, anxious to break the ice.

"Not really," Madison said. "She just said you all were old friends. From Savannah?"

"Actually, I'm the only one still living in Savannah," Dorie said, jumping in. "I teach English at a Catholic girls' high school. Ellis lives in Philadelphia, and she's in banking."

"Was in banking," Ellis said. "I've just been downsized."

"And Julia lives in London. When she's not traveling. She's a model. You've probably seen her in magazines. Sumptuesse shampoo? That was Julia," Dorie said. "She was the face of Sumptuesse."

"But not lately," Julia said wryly. "What about you, Madison? What brings you to Nags Head?"

Madison had been waiting for it, and she was ready with an answer that was mostly true.

"I'm running away from home," she said glibly, with a toss of her head. "Man troubles."

"So sorry," Dorie said, reaching out and awkwardly patting Madison's hand.

"I'll get over it," Madison said, her smile tight.

"Where's home?" Julia said, pressing on.

"Good question," Madison said smoothly. "I've bounced around a lot. Jersey most recently. But that's about to change. I'm examining my options."

"I know what that's like," Ellis said, nodding her head in agreement. "Time for reinvention, right? I'm not even sure I'll go back into banking."

"What?" Dorie said, looking confused. "You never told us you're planning a career change. What would you do?"

Ellis shrugged. "Who knows? Maybe I'll take up skydiving. Or run away and join the circus."

"Right," Julia said. "And I'll take up brain surgery."

"Ellis is afraid of heights," Dorie said, seeing Madison's questioning look. "And Julia can't stand the sight of blood. She flunked high school biology because she refused to dissect her fetal pig."

Madison yawned and set down her iced tea glass. "Sorry," she said. "I hope I'm not being rude, but I really am tired after a day of driving." She glanced over at Dorie. "If that's all right?"

"Of course," Dorie exclaimed, looking over at the other two women. "Right?"

Julia shrugged. Ellis stood up again. "Welcome to Ebbtide," she said warmly.

"Come on, Madison," Dorie said. "I'll show you your room. Or would you like to see the rest of the house first?"

"I'll take the tour later, if you don't mind," Madison said.

"All right," Dorie said, trying not to look surprised. "Sure. Well, your entrance is around the back of the house. I'll show you the way."

"Thanks," Madison said.

Dorie picked her way carefully up the three flights of stairs, clinging tightly to the metal rail. The paint was rusted and peeling and stuck to the damp palms of her hand. Madison was only a few steps behind, and while Dorie could feel herself winded after just the first floor, the other woman's step was light, her breathing unaffected.

She and Ellis had made quick work of getting the room ready for their guest. The room, which had been empty, was stifling, so they switched on the air-conditioning unit to try and cool it down. Then, while Ellis made up the bed with clean linens, Dorie had dragged a small oak dresser, nightstand, and ancient green desk lamp from the attic storage space. They'd damp mopped the floor and swept the cobwebs from the windowsills. It had taken both of them to force open the warped door to the outside-stair landing. It obviously hadn't been used in quite a while.

Dorie opened the door and stepped aside to let Madison enter the room first, keeping her fingers crossed that the room would meet her approval.

It took Madison only a moment to look around. She set her duffle bag on the bed and stood her laptop case on the dresser. She walked over and looked out the front window. From here she had a clear view of the street. A double window faced the ocean.

"It's fine," she said briskly.

"I'm glad," Dorie said. She pointed through the bedroom door to the stair landing. "Your bathroom is right there. You have a set of clean towels. There's a laundry room off the kitchen."

"What about the key?" Madison asked.

"The key?"

"To the door," Madison said impatiently. "Doors, that is."

"Oh." Dorie looked at the exterior door they'd just come through. It had an old-fashioned keyhole. The bedroom door had a thumb-latch lock, but nothing else. "We don't have a key to the outside stairway," Dorie admitted. "I guess maybe we could ask Mr. Culpepper about getting one."

"Yes," Madison said. "I'll need a key."

"I don't think there is a lock for your bedroom door," Dorie said, gesturing towards it. "But you don't need to worry about that. Since you've got the whole top floor, nobody else will be coming up here."

"I'd feel better about having a lock," Madison said.

"Really? I mean, we do have locks on the downstairs doors," Dorie said, "and I'll get you a key made for those. But half the time we don't even remember to lock up. It's the beach, and I guess that's not something we worry about."

"I worry about it," Madison said firmly, her hand on the door to the inside-stair landing. "I'm used to living in the city. I won't sleep until I have a lock and a key—to both these doors. I'll be happy to pay to get a locksmith in."

Her eyes flickered to the hallway, a clear signal to Dorie that she was dismissed.

"All right," Dorie said finally, getting the hint. "I'll let you get some rest. And I'll get Ellis to ask Mr. Culpepper about the locks."

"Thank you," Madison said, giving Dorie a tight smile. "I'd appreciate that." She picked up the Prada bag, took out a thick, white envelope and handed it to Dorie. "My rent," she said. "I just assumed your friends wouldn't want to take a check."

Dorie's face colored. "Well, uh, we hadn't really discussed that...."

Madison started to close the door.

"Oh!" Dorie said, poking her head back inside. "I nearly forgot. We take turns cooking, and tonight's my night. It's nothing fancy, just rotisserie chicken from Harris Teeter and Caesar salad. But we'd love it if you'd join us for dinner. We usually eat between seven and eight."

"That's very sweet," Madison said. "But I'll probably take a rain check. That club sandwich I had this afternoon will tide me over 'til morning."

"Well . . . if you change your mind, or want to join us in a glass of wine or something," Dorie said, heading down the stairs. "Just come on down."

"I'll do that." Madison closed the door, and Dorie heard the thumb latch click into place.


Julia and Ellis were sitting on the sofa in the living room when Dorie got downstairs.

"Well?" Ellis asked expectantly. "Did she like the room?"

"More importantly, did she pay the rent?" Julia asked.

Dorie sat down in one of the faded chintz armchairs by the fireplace. "She liked the room fine, as far as I could tell. Madison's just, well . . . reserved, I guess you'd say." She held up the envelope of cash. "And yes, she gave me the rent money. In cash." She stared accusingly at Julia. "She was sure you guys wouldn't take her check."

"Cash is king," Julia said lightly. "Is she coming downstairs for dinner?" Julia craned her neck in the direction of the stairs, as though Madison might be coming down at any moment.

"Not right now," Dorie said. "She said she's pretty tired. I get the feeling she might have just driven into town today."

"She's got New Jersey tags on that Volvo she's driving," Julia reported. "And I think you're right about her having money, Dorie. That is not a cheap car. Those XC70s run around forty-seven thousand dollars, and that's just for the basics. Hers is loaded, got the onboard nav screen and the works."

"How do you suddenly happen to know so much about cars?" Ellis asked. "You haven't owned one in years, right?"

"Oh, Booker's turned into a total gearhead," Julia said airily. "That's the car he's been lusting after for months now."

Dorie had opened the envelope and was silently counting the money. "You guys," she said, looking from Julia to Ellis. "There's three thousand dollars here. All in fifty-dollar bills."

Ellis peered over Dorie's shoulder at the cash. "Didn't you say she only wanted to pay half in advance and half at the end of the month?"

"Let me see that," Julia said, putting out her hand for the money. She fanned the bills out across her bare, tanned legs. "Holy mother," Julia said. "Dorie's right. And these are all brand-new bills. What do you make of that?"

"Maybe she knocked over a bank on the way over here?" Ellis said, giggling uneasily at her own joke.

"She did ask if we could get a new lock put on that door to the outside staircase. And get the key to her room," Dorie said reluctantly. "And she wants a key to the front door too. She said she was willing to pay to have a locksmith come in. Maybe that's why the extra money."

"What the hell?" Julia said angrily. "Does she think we're a bunch of thieves or something?"

"She said she's used to living in the city, and that she won't sleep at night until she feels secure," Dorie said. She looked over at Ellis. "Maybe you could ask Mr. Culpepper if it's all right to get the locks put on? Tell him we'll pay for it?"

"I can do that," Ellis said. "But I really don't want to let him know we're subletting that third floor room. He's already charging us an extra fifty dollars a week to use the garage. I'm afraid if he figures out what we're doing, he'll hit us up for even more money."

"You're right," Julia said. "Just don't even mention Madison. Just blame it on one of us. Tell him we're paranoid or something."

"That's not far from the truth," Ellis said. "I'm really not a scaredy-cat, but maybe when we get the locksmith in, should we ask him to put locks on our bedroom doors too?"

"Why would we do that?" Dorie asked. She took the bills from Julia, and stuffed them back into the cash envelope.

"Because," Julia said slowly. "We've just invited a stranger into our midst, and we actually know virtually nothing about her. Did you guys notice how evasive she was when I asked her about herself? If she's that interested in locking us out, maybe we need to start thinking about doing the same for ourselves."

"Oh, Julia," Dorie said, flushing. "That's not fair! I mean, I know you were pissed that I rented the room out, but honestly, I think I know a little bit about people. Madison seems perfectly nice. Perfectly normal. She's just a little shy. And she wants her privacy. What's so scary about that?"

"Nothing scary to me," Julia said. "But if she can drive a car that costs nearly fifty thousand dollars and carry a two-thousand-dollar pocketbook, which, by the way, is the real deal, doesn't it seem a little odd to you that she wants to rent a crappy bedroom in a fairly crappy house? And that she's willing to pay all this money to do it—sight unseen?"

"I'm sorry, but I've got to agree with Julia, it really does seem odd to me," Ellis said.

"And I for one intend to keep my eyes and ears open around the woman," Julia added. "There's a lot more I'd like to know about this Madison."

"I really don't care why she wants to live here," Dorie said. "All I care about is that now I don't have to call my sister and grovel and beg her to pay her share for the house. So you guys can go ahead and lock your doors and play detective all you want. Just don't chase her off. Okay?"

# 14

The cable was out. When they turned on the television after dinner, the screen was as gray and fuzzy as a discarded sweater.

Ellis reached for her iPhone. "I'm e-mailing Mr. Culpepper. Honestly, we get one thing fixed, and something else breaks down."

"Why don't you just call him?" Dorie asked.

"I don't have his phone number," Ellis said, typing away. "And he's pretty cagey about letting me know where he lives, or believe me, I'd be camped out on his doorstep until he got everything here squared away."

Julia poured herself another glass of wine and leaned back in her chair. "Don't get your panties in a wad on my account. I could care less about watching television. Especially in the summertime."

Ellis loaded up the dinner plates and silverware and dumped them into the deep sink she'd filled with soapy water before sitting down to dinner. This part of the summer, she noted happily, was going just as planned, especially now that they had Madison, and her money, contributing to their financial well-being. Madison had been there three days now, and turned down all their invitations to join them for dinner, explaining that she didn't really "do" dinner.

She was, as Dorie had said, shy around them, spending most of her time in her room, with an occasional walk on the beach. The day after she'd moved in, she'd brought a bike home, and now, when she left the house, it was usually on her bike. Despite Julia's dire predictions, nothing out of the ordinary had happened since Madison's arrival.

She was odd, a loner, evasive when asked for personal information. Ellis had suggested that Madison was suffering from a broken heart, and Dorie seconded the emotion. "That ring of hers," Julia had commented, "would go a long way towards healing my broken heart."

"Come on, Ellis," Dorie called now from the dining room. "Leave the dishes 'til later. I'm glad the television's on the fritz. Let's do something together. There's a bunch of jigsaw puzzles here. Let's work on one of those."

"Suits me," Ellis said.

"Ugh, jigsaw puzzles," Julia said, making a face. "Why don't we just put on our Supp-Hose and eat some stewed prunes while we're at it? Come on, you guys, we've got to figure out something livelier than that. We're not dead yet, are we?"

"I brought some DVDs," Ellis started. "Or we could play a board game. What's over there, Dorie?"

"Mmm, let's see. Uno, Monopoly, Trivial Pursuit. Oh, I know, cards. Let's play five hundred, like we used to do at the beach at home."

"Yeah," Ellis said, getting up from the table. "Five hundred. Shuffle the cards, Julia. And I'll make some popcorn."

"Open another bottle of wine, while you're at it," Julia ordered. "And not that cheap crap, either. I put a nice bottle of pinot grigio in the fridge before dinner."

Ty read the latest e-mail from Ellis Sullivan and laughed despite himself. Maybe she wasn't wrapped quite as tightly as he'd thought.

To: Mr.Culpepper@Ebbtide.com
From: EllisSullivan@hotmail.com
Subject: Cable's out
Dear Mr. Culpepper, Hate to pout, but our cable is out.—Ellis

Of course her cable was out. His cable was out too. He had a pile of past-due notices on his desk, and the disconnect warning was on the very top. He toyed with the idea of trying to bypass the cable box. A buddy had shown him how to do this back in his college days. But with his luck, he'd get caught and get his ass slammed in jail.

To: EllisSullivan@hotmail.com

From: Mr.Culpepper@Ebbtide.com

Subject: Cable

Dear Ellis: Please don't have a hissy. I've called Comcast, but the line is busy.

Pleased with himself for this small accomplishment, he pushed the send button. And then he forwarded her latest missive to the file where he had kept all the rest of her e-mails. It was getting to be quite a collection.

Without television and the Nationals game he'd planned to watch, the evening stretched out before him seemed as empty and depressing as the silent television screen perched on the plastic milk crate in the corner of his living room.

He went to the fridge, got a beer, and walked out onto the deck. He slumped down onto a chair and stared out at the water. Must have been a good sunset, he mused, looking at the orange-and-purple-streaked sky. He'd missed it, of course, because he'd been online, searching for a way out of his predicament. That's how he spent most of his time these days, looking for a way out of the hole he'd dug himself into. It was a hell of a note. He'd risked everything buying this place, desperately wanting to live on the ocean again. Now he had it—Ebbtide, perched right on the edge of the Outer Banks, and he might as well have been living in a cave for all the good it did him. He hadn't surfed, hadn't gone for a morning swim, hadn't even caught a decent sunset—not in weeks.

There had to be a way out. But how?

He took a long pull on the beer bottle. He heard laughter and music coming from the direction of Ebbtide. If he stood at the far end of the deck, he could see into the dining room, bathed in the golden yellow light of the chandelier.

The three women were sitting around the table, playing cards. There was a wine bottle on the table, and half-filled glasses. The tall one, Julia, was talking rapid-fire, waving her hands for emphasis. The cute little strawberry blonde was giggling helplessly, running her fingers through her hair. Ellis, he noticed, seemed to be the scorekeeper. She was arguing, and smiling, and writing something on a pad of paper. Suddenly she looked up. Ty ducked instinctively. Had she seen him watching him? Nah. One of the women said something, and Ellis pelted her with a piece of popcorn, and now they were having a full-on popcorn fight, and their shrieks of laughter floated over the dune and out to sea.

The cards and the golden light and the silvery peals of laughter reminded him of summers past. The whole family was staying at Ebbtide, and his mother and grandmother were having a meeting of what they called "the swill sisters." He'd been, what? Six? His father had to explain that these ladies were not really his mom's sisters, but just a few old friends his mom had known since she was a girl, nearly his age.

His grandmother had spent the day of the swill sisters meeting feverishly baking little cookies and making egg-salad, pimento-cheese, and chicken-salad sandwiches, all cut into tiny, crustless triangles. His mother had fluffed and fussed and swept and scrubbed the old pine floors to a fine, dull gleam. A flowery tablecloth had been spread across the battered dining room table, and from the big cedar chest that sat in the hall under the stairs, a set of gold-rimmed, rose-strewn dishes and delicate pink wineglasses he'd never seen before were produced.

At six o'clock, his grandmother had banished them. "No boys allowed," she'd said, laughingly pushing them out the door. So he and his dad had walked down the road to the pizza parlor, where they'd slowly eaten a large pie and watched the Braves game on the television mounted on the wall over the bar. His dad had beer, and he'd given Ty a sip, warning him not to tell "the womenfolk."

When they'd walked back home, the sandy driveway was still filled with cars, so he'd waited by the kitchen door, and his father had tiptoed into the house, emerging a moment later with a paper napkin filled with the little cookies and cakes, and a can of root beer for Ty.

"Contraband," his dad had called it in a conspiratorial whisper. They took their stolen treats and went to the garage apartment. Back then, they still called the apartment Tillie's house, because it was where his grandmother's maid, Tillie, and her three children lived every summer when they came down to the beach from his grandmother's big house in Edenton.

Ty had only a vague memory of Tillie, a slight, stoop-shouldered black lady who colored her hair bright red, chewed gum nonstop, and wore what looked to him like a white nurse's uniform. He did remember how Tillie put ice in her coffee in the morning, and how she liked to boss his mother around. But Tillie had quit coming to the beach in the '80s, because, as his father reported, she wanted to be paid a living wage, "and your grandmother, bless her heart, is tight as a tick."

So Tillie's house had become a place to store unused furniture and an overflow of houseguests. The night of the swill sisters meeting, his father dragged two rickety wooden chairs out to the deck, and they'd sat there and gorged on desserts. They could see his grandmother and his mother and a gaggle of women, arrayed around the gussied-up dining room table. Music was playing, and some of the ladies were playing a card game, and everybody was laughing and having a real party.

Ty had been mesmerized by the glimpse of his mother and his usually dignified grandmother, acting like the girls in his class at school. "What are they talking about?" he'd asked his father, who was leaning with his back against the deck railing. "What's so funny?"

"Who, them?" Ty's father glanced in the direction of the big house and shrugged. "Son, there ain't no telling what's on a woman's mind. You get a bunch of hens together like that, and all bets are off. They might be talking about shoes or clothes. Or they might be talking about whoever's not there tonight. Probably they're talking about how sorry somebody's husband is. Doesn't really matter. 'Cause even if you and me were right in there with 'em, we probably wouldn't understand what's so funny. Not in a million years."

. . .

"Rummy!" Ellis shouted jubilantly, slapping the cards faceup on the table.

"Oh no, not again," Dorie said. She fanned her own cards for the others to see. "You caught me holding a handful of aces and kings. Again." She ticked her fingertips across the cards. "That gives me, like, minus sixty."

"I'm at forty," Julia reported, laying down her own cards. "Where's that put us, Ellis?"

"Hmmm. I'm at 485. Julia, you're at 410. And Dorie, honey, you're at 220."

"I'm hopeless," Dorie said, yawning. "And tired. It's what, nearly midnight? I think I'm gonna take myself off to bed."

"Not yet," Ellis protested. "It's still early. And you could still have a comeback. Come on, Dorie, don't go to bed yet. Not when we're having so much fun. Hey, what about some ice cream? I've got Fudgsicles in the freezer."

"Chocolate?" Dorie raised an eyebrow. "Well, why didn't you say so? I may suck at cards, but I'm grrreeatttt at chocolate."

"You didn't always suck at cards," Julia observed. "You used to whip us all single-handed. I never saw anybody who could memorize cards like you, Dorie."

Dorie pushed her hair back from her face. "My mind's not in it," she said lightly. "I'm having a blonde spell. A strawberry-blonde spell."

"What *is* on your mind?" Julia asked. Ellis shot her a warning look, but Julia never took her own eyes from Dorie.

"Oh, you know," Dorie said. "Money. Work. The usual stuff. Never mind me. I'll be better once Ellis hands out those Fudgsicles she's bribing me with."

"Dorie?" Julia slid her chair over so that it was beside her friend's. "Come on, girlfriend. We know something is upsetting you."

"Julia!" Ellis said. "You promised."

Julia shrugged. "I lied. Now, come on, Dorie. Out with it."

Dorie's face paled. She swept all the cards on the table into a pile, and busied herself rebuilding the deck. "I'm that obvious?" she asked, looking from Julia to Ellis.

"No poker face at all," Ellis said, taking a seat on Dorie's other side. "But you don't have to talk about it if you don't want to."

"It's Stephen, isn't it?" Julia broke in, ignoring Ellis's glare.

"Oh God," Dorie whispered. "Yes. Stephen . . ." A single tear slid down her face. She bit her lip. "Stephen and I . . . God. I can't believe this is happening. I can't even make myself say it."

Julia filled a glass with the last of the pinot grigio and slid it in front of Dorie. "Here. Drink up."

"No," Dorie gently pushed the glass away. "I can do this. I can. I have to. Starting tonight." She took a deep breath, and suddenly the words came pouring out.

"I lied to you all. I did. And I'm sorry. The truth is, Stephen finished his thesis weeks ago. He didn't come to the beach with me . . . because . . . we're getting a divorce. And he moved out two weeks ago. And now I've got to sell the house. I couldn't tell you. I haven't told anybody. Especially Willa. Oh God, what will Willa say? And my mom? This will absolutely kill her. How am I going to tell her? And the school? I know one of us has to quit Our Lady of Angels. We can't both work there. Not now. But I don't know what to do. I can't think. Not even about the simplest stuff. I can't even decide what kind of cereal to eat for breakfast, or what to wear in the morning. It's like my brain is frozen. And I shouldn't have come to the beach. I should have stayed home and figured everything out, but I wanted to come. I wanted to get in my car and run away. Just keep driving. All I could think about was, 'I am going to the beach. And I am not going to deal with this. When I'm at the beach, none of this will matter.' So, I came."

The torrent of words stopped as suddenly as it had started. Dorie's shoulders slumped. She wiped ineffectively at the tears that were now streaming down her face. "Oh, God. What a mess."

"Oh, Dorie," Ellis said, throwing her arms around her friend. "I am so sorry." She was crying too. "Oh, sweetie, I don't know what to say." She felt utterly helpless in the face of Dorie's pain.

"I know, right?" Dorie said, her voice shaky. "Mr. and Mrs. Perfect are getting a divorce. How screwed up is this?"

Julia took a long sip of Dorie's untouched glass of wine. "I knew it. As soon as I laid eyes on you at the airport, I knew it was something like this. I kept hoping it wasn't, you know, this. But I just knew in my heart that it was."

"You're a witch," Dorie said, dabbing at her eyes with a paper napkin. "You always were."

"Not really," Julia said. "You're just so incredibly easy to read. You haven't called him, he hasn't called you. You've been weepy and mopey. And you can't play cards for shit."

"I'm sorry," Dorie said, sniffing. "I hate being Debbie Downer."

"Do you want to talk about it?" Ellis asked.

"No. I mean, yeah, I can talk about it. If you guys don't mind the popcorn getting all soggy. I don't even know where to start."

"Let me guess," Julia said. "I bet Mr. Perfect has himself a girlfriend. Am I right?"

"Julia," Ellis said, through gritted teeth. "Before this night is out, I am going to strangle you. I really am."

Dorie's laugh was shaky. "Let her alone, Ellis. Maybe she's not as witchy as I thought. You're only half right, Julia. Stephen does have somebody else. But it's not a girl. It's a guy."

"What?" Ellis cried.

"No way!" Julia said. "You're telling us Stephen is gay?"

Dorie was crying again, and the words were streaming as fast as the tears. "I'm such an idiot. How could I not have known? I mean, I knew *something* was wrong, but I never dreamed it was this. Easter break, we were supposed to go to Destin with another couple from school, and a day before we were supposed to leave, Stephen announced that he wasn't going. He said he didn't care if I went, in fact, he wanted me to go, but he said he'd had a rough semester, and he just wanted to go off hiking, by himself, up in the mountains. I told myself it was because he doesn't really like my girlfriend's husband, Brad. I mean, Brad can be hard to take sometimes. He's a marathoner, and he never shuts up about running and his times and all that. So I let Stephen go off hiking. And when he got back, I thought he'd be in a better mood. But he wasn't. He got moodier. And that's not Stephen. Not normally. Normally, he is Mr. Happy-Go-Lucky. Which is why I fell for him. And we had fights. Not a lot, and not about anything important, but you know, the whole two years we dated, we never, ever fought."

Julia guffawed. "Well, that should have been a warning signal right there. Booker and I fight every day of our lives."

"But we didn't," Dorie said. "My mom and my dad, you know, before they got divorced, they fought like cats and dogs. Willa and Nash and I, we were so glad when they finally split up. You never saw kids so happy about a divorce. And I told myself when I got married, I would never fight like they did. Because if two people are right for each other, and they love each other, they don't have to fight, you know?"

"My parents used to fight now and then," Julia said thoughtfully. "Not like Booker and me, but yeah, they'd get into it every once in a while. But then Daddy would buy Mama flowers and a piece of jewelry, or she'd make his favorite cannoli, and they'd make up like nothing happened. And they were married for like, forty years."

Ellis thought about her own parents. Lawrence Sullivan had been a patient, quiet man who doted on Ellis's mother. She couldn't remember him ever disagreeing with her mother, at least not in front of her and Baylor. Fighting would not have been his style.

"Your daddy and mama were pretty special," Ellis told Julia. "Like Ward and June Cleaver."

"Or Doris Day and Rock Hudson," Dorie said sadly. "Only Rock Hudson turned out to be gay. Just like Stephen."

Dorie looked up and saw Julia watching her. She sighed. "Now you're gonna ask me how the sex was, right?"

Julia grinned. "I was scheming a way to get you away from Ellis, 'cuz I knew Ellis would never let me ask."

"Who says?" Ellis retorted. "I'm not that big a prude. Am I? I mean, I know it's totally none of our business, but still. We are your best friends. . . ."

"C'mon, pretty please?" Julia pleaded. "You don't have to give me all the hot and steamy details. Just big picture, you know?"

Dorie rolled her eyes. "The sex was fine," she said, exasperated. "It was never even an issue. I got married at thirty-three, for God's sake! And while a lady doesn't like to get a reputation, I think you know I wasn't exactly celibate before I met Stephen. You think I would have married him if we weren't good together in bed?"

Julia considered this. "So . . . there was nothing kinky?"

"No," Dorie snapped. "And I didn't catch him dressing up in my panties, or hanging out at the men's room at the park, or trolling the squares in downtown Savannah after midnight. I'm telling you, and you can believe me or not, but up until two months ago, I thought I had a marriage that was rock solid."

She blinked furiously at the tears welling up in her eyes. "I loved Stephen. And I believed he loved me. And now, it's all gone to crap."

"Don't cry any more," Julia begged. "I'm sorry I brought it up. It's Ellis's fault for letting me, right? Let's all be pissed off at Ellis. And Stephen, too. May he rot in gay hell."

# 15

Ellis went out to the kitchen and got the box of Fudgsicles and a roll of paper towels, which she solemnly handed around to Dorie and Julia.

Dorie licked the ice cream bar in silence, while Julia attacked hers, biting off the top and demolishing it in minutes. Ellis licked and chewed and wiped frantically at the ice cream dripping down onto her hands.

"Better?" she asked Dorie.

"A little," Dorie said, sniffling.

"There's not enough chocolate in the world to fix this kind of thing," Julia said. "Dorie, Ellis is going to kill me for asking, but I can't help it. How ... I mean ... how did you find out about Stephen?"

"Jesus, Julia!" Ellis said. "Would you please let her alone?"

"It's all right, Ellis," Dorie said. "It's like a car wreck. You know it's terrible, but you just can't help looking, right? I didn't catch him with another man, if that's what you're wondering. It was just a bunch of little things. I thought he was stressed about getting his master's, so I didn't pay much attention. And then, he quit his soccer team. You guys met Stephen, right? He lived and died for soccer, not just coaching the girls at school, but playing. But he just quit the team. And the thing is, he didn't tell me he'd quit. He'd leave the house, and I just assumed he was going to practice, but it turns out he wasn't."

"He was going to meet his boyfriend?" Julia asked.

"No," Dorie said. "He swears he wasn't. He says now he just sort of drove around. He'd go to the mall and sit in his car, or drive out to Tybee and back."

"Why'd he quit soccer?" Ellis asked gently.

Dorie's face turned pink. "The guy . . . his name is Matt? He's on the team too. He's always been out. But not in a swishy, flamer kind of way. Stephen said . . ." She gulped and looked down at her hands. She'd twisted the paper ice cream wrapper into a cylinder, and now she was shredding it. "He said he realized months ago that he was, I guess, attracted to Matt. And it really scared him. And disgusted him."

"Oh, poor Dorie," Ellis said with a sigh.

"Stephen swears he never meant for anything to happen," Dorie went on. "That's why he quit the team. He thought if he didn't see Matt, didn't talk to him, it would be all right."

"But it wasn't, was it?" Julia asked.

"As soon as school was out in May, Stephen flew out to Omaha to be with his dad. Henry had a stroke while Stephen was there. He's alive, but he's on a ventilator, and now, they've told the family it's just a matter of time."

"God. On top of everything else," Julia muttered. "So, what happened?"

"When he came back home, he wouldn't talk about his dad," Dorie said. "He started drinking, you know, not a lot, but more than usual. Scotch, too. He never really drank hard liquor before. Neither of us did. And then, one night, right before the Fourth of July, he just . . . he just . . ." She faltered, and started crying again. This time Julia tore off a paper towel from the roll and handed it to Dorie.

"Blow," she ordered. Dorie nodded and did as she was told. Ellis took a paper towel and dabbed at her own eyes. "Gotta remember to add Kleenex to the grocery list this week," she said absent-mindedly.

Dorie took another deep breath and launched back into her story. "He just went for a drive, and he didn't come back. Not that night. I was going crazy! He wouldn't answer his cell phone, and I called everybody we knew asking if they'd seen him. I even called the emergency rooms at Saint Joe's and Memorial to see if he'd been in an accident."

"You must have been terrified," Ellis said. "I don't even know what I'd have done if I were you."

"I'd have been so pissed," Julia said.

"I was terrified, and then when he came home and he was all right, I was really pissed. We had the biggest fight ever. I was standing in the kitchen, in my nightgown, and, you guys, I was screaming. I mean screaming at him. And Stephen, he just broke down crying. And that's when he told me. That he'd gone to a bar, and Matt was there, and he was drinking, and . . . he just . . . went home with Matt. And he didn't call me because he didn't want to lie to me."

Dorie took another deep breath. Her eyes were red from crying, and her nose was running. Ellis and Julia were crying too.

"So that's it?" Ellis asked. "He's gay, and you're getting divorced? End of story?"

"End of story," Dorie agreed. "End of Mr. and Mrs. Perfect. End of every-friggin'-thing."

"Is that what you want? Have you thought about going to counseling?" Ellis asked.

"Counseling!" Julia hooted. "She just told you the man is gay. What good is marriage counseling when it comes to something like that?"

"I don't know," Ellis said helplessly. "Maybe, maybe Stephen really isn't totally gay. It was only one time, right? Maybe this is just . . . like a phase. Dorie said he's been under a lot of stress, with finishing his thesis, and his dad being so sick. Maybe if they got counseling, if they could talk things out with a therapist . . . I just think there has to be another way."

"Well, that's just dumb," Julia said, shaking her head. "What, you think this is like that column in your mom's *Ladies' Home Journal*—CAN THIS MAR-RIAGE BE SAVED?"

"I hate to say it, but Julia's right," Dorie said. "Don't you see? I'm screwed. Stephen says he loves me, and I believe him, I really do. But he's not *in* love with me. There's somebody else. How do I compete with that? If it were a woman, I'd do something. Cut my hair, dye it, lose weight, get a boob job...."

"A boob job?" Julia exclaimed, slapping the tabletop for emphasis. "You're a friggin' 32D, Dorie. You've worn a D cup since, like, kindergarten." It was only a slight exaggeration. "You're so skinny everywhere else, if you got any bigger, you couldn't stand upright."

"I know," Ellis chimed in. "Remember, Dorie? In seventh grade, when we were just getting our training bras, you were already in an underwire."

"Double-D Dunaway," Julia crowed. "Nope, the only way you compete with this Matt guy, as far as I can see, is if you manage to grow a penis."

Dorie started to giggle. Ellis started too. In a moment, the three of them were all laughing so hard, tears were running down their faces. They laughed until they were crying and then laughing again.

"You guys, hush," Dorie said, waving her hands and pointing towards the ceiling. "You'll wake up Madison."

"What's she gonna do?" Julia demanded. "Call the cops on us?"

"I'm so sorry, Dorie," Ellis said, pressing her hand to her own chest. "It's not funny, not really."

"It's a friggin' tragedy," Julia agreed, snorting pinot out her nose.

That got them all started laughing again—the giggle fits from hell.

Until Dorie's green eyes widened. "Oh no," she said, gasping for air between guffaws.

"What?" Julia demanded.

"I think," Dorie said, haltingly. "I think I just peed my pants."

Which sent Ellis into peals of merry laughter. "You guys, do you remember Patti Shaffhausen from second grade at Blessed Sacrament? Miss Raterman's class? She used to wet her pants, like, every other day. And because I sat in back of her, Miss Raterman would make me go to the girls' bathroom and help her get cleaned up. Remember, we used to call her Pee-Pants Patti?"

"Oh my God," Dorie said. "Pee-Pants Patti Shaffhausen! You won't believe this, but Patti Shaffhausen is my dentist. She and her husband live on the same street in Ardsley Park as Willa. And he's a urologist."

"Stop!" Julia begged. Now it was her turn to clutch at her chest. "Stop, or I'm gonna pee my pants."

"Guys," Dorie said. "It's not just the laughing. I pee my pants—just a little—like, every day. I'm pregnant, guys."

# 16

That's not funny, Dorie," Julia said.

"But it's true."

Ellis and Julia both chose that moment to take large gulps of wine.

"Is this what you call a pregnant pause?" Dorie said finally, her grin lopsided.

"When?" Ellis asked, when she could catch her breath. "I mean, when are you due?"

"I'm three months pregnant. The baby's due in February. I'm hoping for Valentine's Day." Dorie turned to Julia, her green eyes flashing. "And before you ask, yes, I do intend to keep the baby. I don't know what else is going to happen in my life, but the one thing I do know is that I am going to have this baby."

Julia bristled. "I wasn't going to suggest . . ."

"Good," Dorie said, her voice becoming uncharacteristically firm. "I know you don't go to church anymore, Julia, but I do. I'm not one of those crazy bomb-flinging right-to-lifers, but for me, I just don't believe in abortion. End of discussion!"

"I can't believe you still buy into all that Catholic voodoo," Julia muttered.

"I do," Dorie said. "Well, most of it anyway. I guess I'm gonna have to figure out the divorce part, though."

Ellis flung her arms around Dorie. "Oh my God! A baby. This is amazing! I can't believe it. We're gonna have a baby, y'all." She looked over Dorie's head at Julia, who sat back in her chair, arms folded across her chest. "She's pregnant! Bet you didn't see that coming, Witch Julia."

"Nope," Julia agreed. "I totally didn't see that one coming."

"I can't believe you didn't guess, Julia," Dorie said. "I've been running into the bathroom every five minutes, it feels like, and feeding my face every minute of the day. I can hardly stay awake, I'm so sleepy all the time."

"But you've been drinking wine with the rest of us," Julia said accusingly.

"Nope," Dorie laughed. "You guys have been so busy sucking down the wine and margaritas, you didn't even notice me dumping my glass in the sink. I haven't had a drink since the dipstick turned blue back in June."

"What does Stephen think about all this?" Julia asked.

Dorie gazed down at her belly. Her voice, when she answered, was very small. "He doesn't know yet. You guys are the first ones I've told."

"I don't understand," Ellis said finally. "You found out you're pregnant in June. Way before you and Stephen split up. Why didn't you tell him about the baby when you found out?"

"I just . . . didn't," Dorie said. "We weren't trying to get pregnant. Not at all. This was all my fault. A slipup. We'd talked about a baby, and he said he wanted kids, eventually. But somehow, when I found out about the baby, right after Stephen's dad had a stroke, it just seemed like a terrible time to announce that I was pregnant. I knew he'd be worried about money, and I just didn't want to pile on another responsibility."

"For God's sake, Dorie," Julia said. "That is so like you. How can this be all your fault? Unless you impregnated yourself with a turkey baster when Stephen wasn't looking. You're the one who's got to carry this baby for nine months, along with everything else, and you're worried about poor old Stephen having too much responsibility. He doesn't deserve you, Dorie. He never did."

Dorie pressed her fingertips over her eyelids. "A month ago, I would have said you were all wrong about Stephen. Now? I just don't know what to think. One minute I hate his guts. I want to scream and rant and rave and kick him in the nuts and grab him and shake the crap out of him and ask him why on earth he ever married me if he thought there was even a remote possibility he was gay. I mean, how *could* he? How *dare* he? And then, I start thinking how painful all this must be for Stephen."

"Go with the kicking-in-the-nuts reaction," Julia said dryly.

"Damn," Dorie said, standing up abruptly. "Now I've gotta pee again. You see what I'm like? I'm a mess. Guess I'll run upstairs and change my shorts while I'm at it. I don't want you guys to start calling me Pee-Pants Dorie."

When Dorie was out of earshot, Julia poured herself another glass of wine, and after a moment's hesitation, topped off Ellis's glass too.

Ellis took a sip of the wine. She felt inexplicable tears welling up. Were they for what her best friend was facing, or were they, selfishly, for herself— unmarried and still childless at thirty-five, a state she'd never envisioned for herself?

Her brother Baylor was five years older, and as a child, Ellis had always longed for a baby sister to play with—even after her mother patiently explained that Ellis was "the caboose," as she called her. She'd been a funny little girl, the kind who still played with dolls when all her other friends had long since abandoned them. She'd always baby-sat as a teenager, and still did, occasionally, for friends back in Philly. All their children called her "Aunt Ellie." Was that all she'd ever be, Aunt Ellie?

"Wow," Ellis whispered, hoping Julia would assume her tears were for Dorie instead of herself. "I don't believe this. A baby."

"Me neither," Julia said. "What are we gonna do?"

"We're going to throw her a fabulous baby shower," Ellis declared. "Can't you just be happy for her? You heard Dorie. She wants this baby. She'll make a wonderful mother."

"A single mom," Julia said glumly. "I don't believe she ever envisioned doing it all by herself. And speaking of mothers, I do not want to be around when she drops this little bomb on her mom."

Ellis winced. "Ow. Yeah. I'm sure old Phyllis will have plenty to say on this topic."

"She'll figure out a way to make this all Dorie's fault," Julia predicted. "You wait and see. She'll blame Dorie for turning Stephen queer."

"Julia!" Ellis laughed ruefully. But she couldn't argue with what her friend said, because it was too true. Phyllis Dunaway had a talent for finding fault with her youngest daughter. She might have been a big-deal college English professor, but as a wife and mother, Dr. Dunaway was, to Ellis's way of thinking, a big dud. For years, she'd bullied Dorie's dad, Gabe, a sweet and slightly nebbishy college professor whose specialty was *Beowulf.* It had been Phyllis's idea to name all three Dunaway children after American writers—Willa for Willa Cather, Nash for Ogden Nash, and Dorie, the baby, who had been burdened with the unwieldy and unlikely name of Eudora, for Eudora Welty.

"What about Gabe?" Julia asked. "Does Dorie ever see her dad these days?"

Dorie and the girls had just started seventh grade at OLA when the Dunaways announced they were splitting up. Not long after, Gabe Dunaway moved an hour away, to Statesboro, to take a job teaching English at the college there.

Ellis shrugged. "I think he sends birthday cards and Christmas gifts. But he remarried a couple years ago, and you know how her mom is. Dorie doesn't dare mention his name, even after all these years. She couldn't even invite him to the wedding, since Phyllis was paying for it."

"What an evil shrew," Julia said. "It's amazing to me that Dorie turned out as well-adjusted as she did, especially considering all those years of verbal abuse Phyllis subjected her to. God, my mother hated her. Did you know, that time when we were sophomores and Phyllis threw Dorie out of the house because she found out Dorie was sneaking around dating that boy who got kicked out of Savannah High for selling weed, my mom actually tried to talk my dad into asking Phyllis to let Dorie live with us?"

"No!" Ellis said. "That's so funny. When that happened, I begged my mom to adopt Dorie. I was so clueless, I didn't understand you couldn't adopt somebody whose parents were still living. God bless Mama, she actually got up 've to call Phyllis and suggest that Dorie wasn't really the tramp of the ⌐⌐ ⌐. Phyllis never spoke to my mom again. Mama and I have had our own moments, God knows, but I'll never forget how proud of her I was when she stuck up for Dorie that time."

"If Phyllis had been my mother, I think I would have taken an axe to her years ago," Julia said. "Like it was Dorie's fault that she was so pretty. I think Phyllis hated the fact that Dorie looked like her dad's side of the family. Remember how she used to call Dorie 'her pretty little flake'?"

"And Dorie wasn't dumb," Ellis agreed. "Maybe she didn't have a 4.0 GPA like Willa, but she made decent grades."

"Didn't matter," Julia said. "Willa was always the smart, successful one according to Phyllis. So Willa went to law school and made partner when she was only in her thirties? Whoopie-shit. And now she's not even practicing law. And what about good old Nash, the only son, the golden boy who could never do wrong? What's he doing these days? I'm almost afraid to ask Dorie."

"Nash," said Ellis succinctly, "is still Nash. Still writing poetry, although as far as I know, he's never had a word published. Last I heard, he was living rent-free in Dorie's grandma's old house on Forty-eighth Street. And you'll love this part: he drives a big ol' '70s hearse, and he gives these ghost tours of haunted houses downtown."

"You're kidding me," Julia said. "For real?"

Ellis slapped her right hand over her heart. "As God is my witness. Last time I was home, I saw him handing out flyers on Bay Street. You should have seen him," she said, giggling. "He was wearing this zip-front jumpsuit, and an army surplus gas mask, and he had what looked like an old vacuum cleaner canister strapped on his back. He gave me his business card. At first I thought maybe he was hitting on me, then I figured out he just wanted me to cough up eighty-five dollars for his stinkin' tour. Can you believe it? Julia, he's even got a website."

"Ghostdusters.com," Dorie said, padding barefoot into the dining room. She'd changed into a pair of drawstring cotton pajama pants and a Hello Kitty tank top, her hair caught in a ponytail on top of her head. She looked all of thirteen. "Could you die? All that fancy education, and he's squatting in

Granny's house and hustling tourists with these ridiculous stories about talking tombstones in Colonial Cemetery and headless duels in Monterey Square."

Ellis blushed guiltily. "It sounds like it could be a pretty successful business, though."

"Yeah, maybe if he wanted to work at it, it could be, but you know Nash. Work really is a four-letter word as far as he's concerned. Hey, is anybody else hungry? I'm thinking about fixing myself a grilled cheese sandwich."

"We just ate four hours ago," Julia reminded her. "Not to mention popcorn and Fudgsicles."

"I'm eating for two now," Dorie said. "At least now that you guys know, I can stop sneaking around and binging on cereal and scrambled eggs when you're not looking."

"If I ate like that I'd blow up like a balloon," Ellis said. "I still can't believe you're three months pregnant, walking around looking like a stick."

Dorie pulled up her tank top and pooched out her tummy. "A stick? Look at this gut! There's a baby in there, for real." She turned around and wiggled her butt at her friends. "And look at this ass. It's like, two axe handles wide, as my daddy would say."

Julia gave Dorie's butt an affectionate slap. "Who are you kidding? You've still got the tiniest hiney on the planet, Dorie. For now anyway. Come on. I'll fix you your grilled cheese, little mama."

The three of them trooped into the kitchen. Dorie and Ellis perched at the kitchen table while Julia melted butter in a frying pan and assembled Dorie's sandwich.

When the sandwich was golden brown, with melted cheddar cheese oozing out the sides, Julia flipped it onto a plate and slid it in front of Dorie, along with a glass of milk.

"Oh, bliss," Dorie said, taking a bite and rolling her eyes. "Stephen always says the best sandwich in the world is the one somebody else makes for you."

"About Stephen," Ellis said slowly. "Dorie, you really are going to have to tell him about the baby. Have you even talked to him since he moved out?"

Dorie chewed slowly. She took another bite of grilled cheese and then another. When the sandwich was half eaten, she pushed the plate away.

"I can't," she said. "I can't talk to him. I can't hear his voice. I can't see him. Not yet. He calls, but I don't answer. I know he drives past the house. I've seen his car cruise past half a dozen times. He doesn't have the balls to stop and ring the doorbell. Which is good, 'cuz I don't think I could answer the door if he did."

"Do you even know where he's living?" Julia asked.

"At Matt's, I suppose," Dorie said. "He's got a big old Victorian in Midtown. We went to a party there last fall."

"You're going to have to talk to Stephen, Dorie, and sooner would be better than later. You know what a small town Savannah is," Julia said. "You're gonna start showing sooner or later. And you know how people talk. You need to figure out the next step."

"I can't," Dorie wailed. "I don't know what to say to him. Anway, I don't know what the next step is. I don't know how to get a divorce."

"I do," Ellis said lightly. "It's not that hard, really. Look at me, I got mine at twenty-three. If this is really what you want, Dorie, I'll give you my lawyer's name. He was one of Baylor's fraternity brothers. He's still in Savannah, I know, because he sends me a Christmas card every year. Guess he thinks that now I'm in my thirties, I'll start throwing some divorce work his way."

Dorie tore off a chunk of the grilled cheese sandwich and nibbled at it. "I never, ever thought I would be thinking about getting a divorce. After my parents split up, I swore when I fell in love, it would be forever. You guys know how many men I went with over the years. I never even considered marrying any of them. Not until I met Stephen. That's why I waited so long to say yes. I wanted to be sure." She propped her feet up on the kitchen table. "The only thing I know for sure now is that nothing is for sure. And look at me—I'm barefoot and pregnant in the kitchen. And oh yeah, my baby daddy has a boyfriend." She sniffed loudly.

"How could you know?" Ellis said sympathetically. "I mean, you guys lived together for a year. We all thought it was the real deal."

"Yeah, he fooled even me," Julia agreed. "And you know I never liked any other guy you dated before. My gaydar is usually pretty accurate." She glanced over at Dorie. "I really am sorry, honey. Do you want to talk about something else?"

"It's okay," Dorie said, trying to smile through her tears. "Don't mind me. I'm just hormonal. I cry all the time. I cried this morning when I realized we were out of Frosted Flakes."

"I'll get another box," Julia said. "Promise."

"Are you sure you still feel like talking?" Ellis asked. "It's getting late, and I know you must be emotionally exhausted."

"No, I'm all right," Dorie said, brushing bread crumbs from her tank top. "It feels good to finally talk to somebody about all this. I've had all these secrets bottled up inside me. It just felt like I was going to explode if I didn't tell somebody about the baby."

"You didn't want to tell Willa?" Ellis asked. "I mean, she's your only sister."

Dorie shook her head. "Willa! I love her, but bless her heart, you guys know how she is. She's so bossy. She'd tell me I'd chosen the wrong obstetrician, the wrong hospital. The wrong man, for sure. She'd be dragging me to La Leche meetings and I don't know what all. And she'd for sure rat me out to Mama. And I can't handle any of that right now. I need time to process, to figure it all out." She sniffed. "I need this time at the beach with you guys, I really do. I need August like I never needed it before."

"You got it," Julia said. "We're here, and we got your back."

Ellis went to the sink and began rinsing out the wine glasses. "Listen, Dorie," she began, "when does school start back?"

Dorie grimaced. "Don't remind me. The week after Labor Day. Teachers report back the Thursday before, for preplanning."

"That's only a little over three weeks," Julia pointed out. "Are you sure you're up to going back to work at Our Lady of Angels? Especially with Stephen working there too?"

"I've got to," Dorie said dully. "I signed a contract. Anyway, I need the money, and I'm gonna need the medical benefits, at least until after the baby comes."

"Doesn't Stephen have the same medical benefits?" Ellis asked. "Wouldn't you be covered under his policy, assuming you didn't go back to OLA?"

"I don't know," Dorie admitted. "But it doesn't matter. I'm not quitting my job. I love teaching the girls, I really do. The money's not great, but that's not the point."

"It will be, if you're going to be a single mother," Julia said. "Don't forget, you'll have to pay for day care, and a hundred other things. And what about a place to live? What will you do about the house? Do you think Stephen will let you keep it?"

Dorie clapped her hands over her ears. She rocked back and forth in her chair. "I don't know, I don't know, I don't know," she singsonged. "I just freakin' don't know. I only know I hate Stephen. Hate. Hate. Hate."

"I hate him too," Ellis said, yawning.

"I hate him more than both of you," Julia declared. "I know. Let's fire up the van, drive over to his place, and key his car."

"No," Ellis said, taking up the challenge. "Let's egg his house and TP it."

"Or key the car, egg the car, and TP his house *and* his car," Dorie countered, getting into the spirit of things. "Remember when we did that to Amber Peek, senior year, after she started spreading rumors that Julia was pregnant right before Christmas break?"

"I just remember my daddy made me pay for a whole new paint job for that piece-of-crap Tercel of hers when we got caught," Ellis said.

"It was worth it though," Dorie said. "Amber Peek. That lying bitch."

They were both looking at Julia now, waiting for her to chime in with her own diatribe against her mortal enemy, Amber Peek.

"Good old Amber," Julia said. "She was a bitch, and a sneak, and I'm glad you guys screwed up her car. But she wasn't lying. Not that time. I really was pregnant, you know."

# 17

Ellis and Dorie sat back in their chairs, too stunned to speak.

"Don't look at me like that," Julia said shakily. "I wanted to tell you. But my mother was so mortified...so...ashamed. She made me swear I'd keep it a secret. I almost told you, that night after her funeral, back at the house, but I couldn't do it. Not in her house. Not after I promised."

Finally Ellis picked up the discarded deck of cards. She began laying out a hand of solitaire.

"Why tell us now?" she asked.

"I need to," Julia said. "I've needed to tell you for a long time. But I was afraid of what you'd think of me."

"Oh, Julia," Dorie said softly. "Julia."

Ellis wrinkled her brow. "But...you didn't even have a boyfriend your senior year."

Julia grinned the old Julia grin. "Not one you guys knew about. You wouldn't have approved. He was an army Ranger, stationed at the air base at Hunter. We met at an oyster roast. He asked me out, I went. He was cute, even with those awful haircuts they made the guys get, and I could tell he was totally smitten."

"Did he have a name?" Ellis asked, annoyed, all these years later, that Julia had managed to conceal such a huge secret.

"Jack," Julia said. "His name was Jack, he was twenty years old, and the thing I liked best about him was that he was a good half-a-head taller than me—which sealed the deal. I mean, I was six feet tall, so there weren't a lot of guys out there that I could look up to. We went out exactly four times before we had sex."

"He forced you!" Dorie cried. "Raped you?"

"Nope," Julia said. "He was nice. Horny, but nice. I wanted to. I was eighteen years old, and I'd decided I didn't want to be a virgin anymore. After all," she said, nodding at Dorie, "you'd already done the deed, the summer before we were seniors. And as far as I knew, Ellis might never pop her cherry. So I just decided to go for it."

"And?" Ellis said, trying to decide how she felt about being regarded as a potential nun.

"He was sweet," Julia said, her face softening at the memory. "Although I don't think he had a hell of a lot more experience than I did. There were no fireworks—but then again, no nightmares, either. Anway, you know that crap we used to hear about how nobody ever gets knocked up the first time they do it? Turns out, it really is crap."

"You had unprotected sex, with an army Ranger?" Dorie said, her eyes widening. "You could have gotten AIDS. Or syphilis."

"It wasn't totally unprotected. He had a Trojan, although as it turned out, it must have been a really old Trojan. I didn't get an STD. I just got pregnant."

"Oh. My. God." Ellis swept the cards into a pile. "Julia, how did you manage to keep it secret? We never had a clue. Ever. Not even when Amber Peek started running her mouth."

"The baby?" Dorie guessed. "At Christmas, when you had your appendix out? That's what really happened?"

"It's not what you're thinking," Julia said. "When I missed my first period, I didn't think anything of it. You guys remember, I never had normal periods. But when I skipped my second one, I knew. But I just couldn't bring myself to tell my parents. It would have killed them. As it turned out, I didn't have to. The last day before Christmas break, right after my chemistry final, I'd gone to the bathroom. My stomach was killing me. I was so damned ignorant, I just thought that was part of being pregnant. I didn't tell you guys, I didn't tell anybody. I was bleeding. There was so much blood, I was terrified. I remember, I bought a Kotex from the vending machine in the bathroom, and I went straight home."

"You were hemorrhaging?" Ellis asked.

"The bleeding slowed down after a while, but I had these godawful cramps," Julia said. "I was curled up in bed and Mama just happened to walk by my bedroom door. She heard me moaning and crying, came in, and I was in so much pain, I couldn't even speak. But I had a fever, like 102 degrees, and then she saw the blood on my sheets, and she freaked out.

"Loaded me in her Cadillac and carried me straight to the emergency room at Saint Joseph's, where the doctor, who just happened to be a woman in Mama's Bunco club, had to break the news that her daughter, still dressed in her Catholic girl's school uniform, was not suffering from a ruptured appendix, as Mama insisted, but rather, that I had an ectopic pregnancy."

"You could have died," Dorie said solemnly.

"Right at that moment, I wished I had," Julia said. "If you'd seen the look on Mama's face when I had to admit that yes, I really was pregnant. It was like she'd been punched in the stomach."

"What . . . what did they do?" Dorie asked. "I'm sorry, I know this is hideous to ask, but I can't not."

"It's all right," Julia said, shrugging. "After all, I made you bare your soul, didn't I? Anyway, they did laparoscopic surgery. Right before they sent me home from the hospital, the doctor, Mama's friend, came in to see me. She told me the embryo had attached itself to the wall of my fallopian tube, which caused the tube to rupture, and that it never would have been a viable pregnancy. She also gave me a prescription for the pill, bless her heart."

"What about your parents?" Ellis asked. "How were they with it?"

"As far as Daddy knew, I really did have my appendix out," Julia said. "In the car on the way home from the hospital, Mama just told me she was disappointed in me. Jesus! Disappointed! Talk about a guilt trip. It was ten times worse than being screamed at or punished."

Dorie shuddered. "I don't want to think about how Phyllis would have handled that when I was eighteen. I don't even want to think about how she'll handle my pregnancy now, and I'm thirty-five and haven't lived at home in fifteen years."

"Mama said that it was Our Lady of Angels who intervened on my behalf and saved my life. I really could have bled out and died, probably would have if she hadn't barged into my room. Mama pointed out that she wasn't even supposed to be home that afternoon, she was supposed to go Christmas shopping, but something made her decide to cancel and stay home. Every year after that, right up until she got too sick to leave the house, she went to Mass in the chapel at OLA on December twelfth, the anniversary of the day I went to the hospital, to leave a wreath of flowers on the statue of Our Lady."

"Your mama was a saint," Dorie said, shaking her head. "I hope you know that."

"I do," Julia said, her lower lip trembling. "You don't know how much I miss her."

Ellis raised her wine glass in a toast. "To Catherine Capelli. God rest her soul. And to hell with Amber Peek!"

Julia raised her own glass, and Dorie, lacking one, raised her Fudgsicle stick.

Later, after they'd pushed a sleepy Dorie off to bed, Julia and Ellis went back to the kitchen to clean up. By unspoken agreement, Julia put away the dishes and Ellis swept the floors. "I'm turning in," Julia said finally, draping the dish towel over the back of the kitchen door. "All this emotional upheaval just wears me out."

"Can you stand one more question? I swear, after this, I won't bring it up again," Ellis said.

"I think I know what you're gonna ask. Jack, right?"

"Well, yeah," Ellis said. "Did you ever tell him? Or even see him again?"

"No, and no. He got shipped off to paratrooper school at the end of October, right around the time I missed my first period. He wrote me a couple times, and I wrote back once, but we were just kids. He wanted me to come see him, but I had school, and anyway, in my case, absence didn't make the heart grow fonder. As for telling him about the pregnancy—no, I never did. I couldn't even really admit it to myself, let alone him. I was all about denial."

Ellis touched Julia's shoulder lightly. "That was a hell of a secret to keep all these years. Does Booker even know?"

"No," Julia said sharply. "I told you, aside from my mother—and that bitch Amber Peek, who only found out because her cousin happened to be in the emergency room with a broken wrist the night I was there—nobody knew."

"Will you tell him now, since you've told us?"

Julia sighed. "Probably. He wouldn't care so much about the pregnancy thing, Booker's been around. The thing is, he wants kids. And I'm not even sure I can have a baby."

"Oh yeah," Ellis said, her eyes widening. "What does your gynecologist say?"

"I've never really asked," Julia admitted. "At the time, they told me lots of women get pregnant and have babies after having an ectopic pregnancy, even with only one good tube, like I have. All these years, it's never really been an issue. I had a great career, I'd seen my mother drowning in babies and diapers, and I told myself that was never gonna happen to me."

"But now?"

"Who knows?" Julia said lightly. "Anyway, I really am going to bed now. G'night, Ellie-Belly."

When Julia was gone, Ellis wandered aimlessly around the house. She put the deck of cards back in their box, pushed chairs under the dining room table, straightened sofa cushions. She tried the television again, but the cable was still out. She got out her phone for the first time in hours, checking to see if she had any e-mails or missed calls.

Nothing. She'd halfway been hoping for an e-mail from Mr. Culpepper. She smiled at the memory of his last message, and wondered again just how old Mr. Culpepper might be. Not that it mattered.

It was late, well past midnight, but she was oddly restless. The bookshelves by the fireplace were full of paperbacks. She trailed her fingertips across their spines—mostly romances, mysteries, and thrillers. She chose a battered Kathleen Woodiwiss paperback, *The Flame and the Flower,* smiling at the memory of how she and Julia had swiped Julia's mother's copy of the same book. They'd been what, thirteen? They'd taken the book out to the Capellis' boathouse and read it by flashlight, giggling over the smutty parts.

Ellis went upstairs and put on her pajamas. The air in the room was hot and still. She turned on the ceiling fan and dialed down the thermostat on the window air-conditioning unit. She climbed into bed, and switched on the old-fashioned white hobnail glass lamp on her bedside table. Its shade was yellowed and coated with dust, and the bulb threw off a tiny, tired glow of orangish light. Not that it mattered. She was too keyed up to settle down with a book. She turned off the light and willed herself to sleep.

Eventually, she closed her eyes and drifted into a dream. She was in a hospital nursery, full of dozens and dozens of beautiful, pink, pudgy babies. In her dream, she leaned over a pink bassinet and saw an infant with Dorie's strawberry blond hair, freckles, and green eyes. The next bassinet held a long, slender baby with Julia's perfect cheekbones and dark, almond eyes. And next to that was another infant—with familiar marble blue eyes, protruding ears, and the Greene thin upper lip. The little boy opened his mouth and screamed—well, yowled—as she leaned in closer to look. Ellis's dream self scurried away, and in the next bassinet, she saw the most beautiful baby of all: a little boy with a thick shock of dark hair like her mother's, and her father's calm, steady gaze. The baby was sucking his thumb, and when he saw dream-Ellis, he looked up and winked.

The wink startled Ellis awake. She sat straight up in bed, and for a moment, wondered if the dream meant anything. Eventually she decided maybe it just meant she shouldn't drink so much wine late at night. She yawned and wished she could sleep again, but the loud hum of the air conditioner and the responding rattle of the window glass now had her wide awake. And hungry.

She went downstairs and out to the kitchen, opening cupboards and the refrigerator, trying to decide what she was hungry for, and settling for a chunk of cheddar cheese. She ate half, and then pitched the rest into the trash. Not really hungry, not really sleepy. What a mood she was in. She turned off the kitchen light, intending to go back to bed, but when she glanced out the window, she saw the full moon and reconsidered. She was at the beach, wasn't she? Might as well enjoy it.

It was still hot out, but a breeze rustled the sea oats on the dunes, and she smelled a hint of beach rosemary mixed with the salt air. The worn boards of the walkway were cool to the soles of her bare feet. When she reached the landing at the top of the walk, she was startled. Somebody was sitting in one of the beach chairs. Suddenly remembering how she was dressed, she started to back away, but it was too late.

The garage guy turned around in his chair, a cigar clamped between his lips. The lit end glowed in the deep purple darkness. He looked her up and down, and then turned back towards the ocean.

It pissed Ellis off, him dismissing her like that. Did he think she'd turn tail and run, like the last time? She had as much right to be here as him. Pajamas or no.

"Hey," she said, defiantly sinking down into the chair next to his.

He grunted an acknowledgment and continued staring off at the twin moons, one hanging low in the summer sky, the other reflected in the ocean.

Ellis settled back into the beach chair. She wished she'd thrown a robe or something over the thin cotton tank top and baggy pink boxer shorts with their silly design of flying cupcakes. She crossed her arms over her chest, hoping Ty Bazemore hadn't noticed her bralessness. Or the cupcakes.

The beach below was totally deserted. It was high tide, and the waves rolled lazily in over the spot where the three women had earlier spread out their umbrella and chairs. Ellis stared up at the stars and tried to relax. This was August, damn it. The month she'd been planning for and anticipating ever since Julia's mother's funeral. She had earned this vacation.

But there was a lot to think about. Dorie and Stephen. Dorie and the baby. Julia's big secret. And what about her own life? She felt guilty worrying about herself when her best friend's life was in such turmoil, but the truth was inescapable. She felt stuck. A lifetime of planning and living by the rules had netted her a nest egg, a paid-off car and house—the safety net her father had always emphasized—and a life as dull and colorless as the sand beneath her toes. She was being strangled by that damned safety net. She would get another job, maybe move to another town if necessary, but would her life really be any different? She'd spoken glibly of reinvention to Madison, their odd new housemate, but that had just been talk, hadn't it?

She glanced over at Ty Bazemore. His eyes met hers.

"How's it going?" he asked.

"Not so good," she blurted, instantly regretting her own candor.

He raised an eyebrow.

"Can't sleep," she said lamely. "Those window units make a terrible racket. And," she rushed on, "I lost my job. And I don't know what I want to do next. I don't know if I should stay in Philly, or cut my losses and move on. But I don't know if I could sell my town house in this market. And anyway, where would I go? Back to Savannah? I love my mother, but she drives me nuts sometimes."

Ellis clamped both hands over her mouth. Had she really just dumped her whole life out in the open for this total stranger, the guy who lived in the garage and peed off the deck?

"Sorry," she said, feeling her face flush. "TMI."

"Huh?"

"You know. Too much information. Don't mind me. Guess I'm a little wired tonight."

"What do you do?" Ty asked.

"Huh?"

"Back in Philly," Ty said. "What kind of job did you get fired from?"

"Not fired," Ellis corrected. "Downsized. My bank got taken over by a bigger bank."

"But you don't work there anymore."

"True."

"And leaving wasn't your idea."

"No. I loved my job. Or so I thought."

"You thought?"

Ellis shrugged. "It's really a long story. But the bottom line is, it turns out bank marketing was not the stuff of fairy tales."

He laughed. "But you still got fired."

Ellis frowned. Who did this jerk think he was? "It was a downsizing," she repeated. "My department was redundant. It's really a very generous severance package. Anyway, what kind of work do you do?"

Ty considered a moment before answering. She already knew the answer to her own question, because Mr. Culpepper had told her. But he wasn't supposed to know that, was he?

"I do a little day trading," he said.

"How's that going?"

"It's up and down. Like the market. I do all right."

He really was infuriatingly smug.

"Got any good stock tips for me?" she asked.

"Buy low. Sell high."

"Gee, thanks," Ellis said sarcastically. "Let me write that one down."

"Sorry," Ty said. "I'm kinda in a mood myself. But that was unnecessary. No, I don't have any stock tips. You wouldn't want one of mine anyway." He tapped the cigar ash into the sand, and decided to change the subject.

"This your first time on the Outer Banks?"

"Yeah," she said. "I grew up in Savannah. Which is kinda on the beach. But it's totally different here. The dunes and all. It's beautiful, in a wild kind of way."

"You should have seen it when I was a kid," Ty said. "Most of these houses weren't here. It was mostly dunes and beach. You know, there are still wild ponies on the beach up in Corolla. It was an awesome place to grow up. Never put on a pair of shoes from the time school let out in June 'til the time we went back in September."

"You grew up here?"

He'd said too much. "Around here," Ty said vaguely. "I went to high school in Manteo. I practically lived on the beach. Got my first surfboard when I was ten."

"So," Ellis said, giving him a winning smile, "so, what's the deal with you? Are you hiding a wife and children in this little garage apartment?"

"Nothing like that," Ty said. "No kids, not married. Currently."

Ellis tucked away the word "currently" for further thought.

"And have you always been a day trader?"

"No, that's kind of a recent thing," he said. "I was in law school, but I dropped out. I've always been interested in real estate and investing, so I decided to give it a shot. Of course, I would pick the worst time since the Depression to dabble in the stock market."

"Tell me about it," Ellis said. "Banking's not so hot either. But you must do okay with the market, right?"

He flipped the lid on his cigar lighter and stared out at the water. "I've picked some winners, but seems like I've picked more dogs lately. To tell you the truth, I've been picking up some bartending shifts at a place down in Kitty Hawk to pay the bills. Cadillac Jack's. You ever hear of it?"

"No," she said. "We haven't really been going out at night much."

"You guys should come in and check it out. I'm actually working tomorrow night."

"Maybe we will," Ellis said, sounding uncertain.

"Been up to Jockey's Ridge yet?" Ty asked.

"Not yet," Ellis admitted. "We've been lazy bums, just kinda hanging around on the beach. But we've got the whole month, right?"

"Lucky you." Ty gave her a questioning glance. "So, seems like the three of you have been friends for a while, right?"

She grinned. "Only our whole lives. We met in grade school, in Savannah. I was the new kid, since I went to public school until third grade. Dorie and Julia have been friends since kindergarten. And we've just stayed close, even after all these years. Of course, we don't get to see each other that often. Dorie still lives in Savannah, but Julia lives in London. She's a model. And of course, I'm in Philly. Or I was." She frowned then. "Dorie's older sister, Willa, was supposed to come with us, but she blew us off at the last minute. Willa can be a real pain in the butt, so we didn't really mind that much."

"What about the new girl?" Ty asked. He'd seen her riding her bike up and down the beach road, but never with the other girls.

"Oh. Madison?" She gave Ty a furtive look. "Do me a favor, okay, don't mention her to Mr. Culpepper. We don't want him to jack up the rent any more."

"My lips are sealed," Ty said, clamping them together to keep them from twitching in amusement. "So, she's not one of your regular posse?"

"Not hardly," Ellis said. "Dorie met her in a restaurant, and they got talking, and Madison mentioned that she was looking for a motel room. Dorie's been pretty worried about money, and one thing led to another, and she offered to rent her a room at Ebbtide."

"Just like that?" Ty raised an eyebrow. "Seems kinda risky to me, inviting a stranger to live with you. What do y'all know about her?"

"She's been living in New Jersey, but she just broke up with her boyfriend. Or so we gathered. Madison says she's 'in transition.' She's sort of odd. She keeps strictly to herself, usually won't even eat with us. But she pays her share of the bills—with cash, so I guess it's working out okay."

"Yeah," Ty said cautiously. "It must be pretty expensive, taking that big house for a whole month. How much is old man Culpepper getting for the place, anyhow?"

"Too much," Ellis said. "The place could be nice, you know? It's a gorgeous old house, but the furniture's really ratty, and the house itself could use a lot of maintenance. I've had to really keep after Mr. Culpepper to take care of stuff like the stove and a leaking faucet. And don't even ask about the flea situation." She shuddered and held out an ankle. "Look—it looks like I've had the measles."

Ty considered her ankle. It was a pretty ankle. Ellis had nice ankles, and good legs, and the outfit she was wearing—a tight-fitting tank top and some kinda girly boxer shorts with ridiculous cupcakes printed all over them—was an excellent look for her. It didn't hurt that she was obviously braless, another look Ty was highly in favor of.

She caught him taking in more than her ankles, and quickly tucked her feet primly under her chair, all the while blushing furiously.

"Mind if I ask you something?" Ty said quickly, hoping she'd forgive his ogling.

"Depends on what it is."

"What is it about women? I mean, the three of you are scattered all over the place—but you still take the trouble to rent a house and spend a whole month together. What's up with that? I mean, I have buddies, old friends, but I can't imagine any of us spending a weekend away together, let alone a month."

Ellis shrugged. "Why wouldn't we want to spend time together? These are my best friends in the whole world. We've been through a lot together. You know, all that teenage drama, and then college, and family stuff. Dorie's parents had a nasty divorce when we were in middle school, and then I lost my dad a few years ago, and both Julia's parents are dead now. And don't get me started on the men stuff."

She hesitated, and then plunged ahead. "I don't know if I could have gotten through my divorce if it weren't for Dorie and Julia. It was an awful time for me, but they were totally there for me. Julia took the train down from a magazine shoot she'd been doing in New York and actually moved in with me for two weeks. I was a pathetic mess. I eventually took a leave of absence from work, but Julia refused to let me wallow in my misery. She made me eat, get my hair cut and colored, and go back to work. And Dorie—she's a schoolteacher, so she couldn't just drop everything, but she called me every night and every morning, for months, just to see how I was doing."

Ty raised an eyebrow. "You're divorced?"

She blushed again. She really was good at it, too.

"It was a long time ago. I got married right out of college. I was young and dumb. It lasted all of three months. Crazy, huh?"

"What happened?"

Ellis gave it some thought. "We worked at the same bank. He was different from the guys I'd dated back home. He was the same age as me, but he seemed older, you know, very sure of himself, and he gave me this big rush. I didn't really know him. He didn't really know me. I guess I was in love with the idea of being in love with him. And then, after the big wedding, when we were actually living together, away from our families and friends and everybody, it turned out he wasn't such a nice guy. In fact, it turned out he was a total shit."

Ty frowned. "What, he hit you or something?"

"Nothing as dramatic as that," Ellis said. "One night at dinner, he just announced the 'marriage thing' wasn't working, and that he'd discovered he didn't actually love me."

"That must have sucked."

She turned and leveled a gaze at him. "Why am I telling you all of this? I never, ever talk about my divorce, except to the girls. And here I am, spilling my guts to you."

"And you don't even like me," Ty said helpfully.

"You didn't make a very good first impression," she reminded him.

"Hey!" he protested. "I didn't know you were spying on me. You could have let me know you were standing there or something, you know."

"Do you always parade around in your drawers and pee in public?" Ellis asked. "What if somebody else had seen you? Like a child? You could get arrested for public indecency."

"It was early. Nobody ever gets to that part of the beach that time of day. And anyway, somebody would really have to work at seeing me from the beach, what with the dunes and the sea oats and everything."

"*We* see you from that part of the beach," she said pointedly.

"And I haven't hardly walked out on the deck in my boxers at all lately, either," Ty said. "Anyway, can I help it if you and your gorgeous friends choose to run around in your skimpy bathing suits right outside my deck? I mean, it would be un-American if I didn't appreciate the natural beauty right there on the beach."

"Humph," she humphed. But the corners of her lips twitched slightly. She concluded that up close like this, Ty Bazemore wasn't nearly as repulsive. In fact, he was alarmingly attractive, with his rumpled hair and cleft chin. She'd always been a sucker for a cleft chin.

"I'll just bet you do enjoy looking at Dorie and Julia," she said lightly. "I mean, Julia's a model, and as for Dorie, well, no matter what she does to try to hide it, she's always had the kind of looks that draws men like flies."

He raised an eyebrow. "Yeah, they're okay," he said. "Especially the curvy little redhead. But actually, since you mention it, you're pretty killer in a bathing suit yourself, Ellis Sullivan. Especially that black one-piece."

She gaped at him, blushing furiously.

He grinned innocently. "Hey, don't look at me like that. It's a simple observation. A compliment. No need to call the vice squad."

This conversation was taking a decidedly personal turn, Ellis decided. She fought the urge to cut and run. Ty Bazemore had just told her he liked her black bathing suit. She should stay and flirt. She remembered how to flirt, didn't she?

In the meantime, he was still looking at her, lazily taking in those stupid cupcake boxers and her flimsy tanktop. Panic set in again. She yawned widely and stood to go.

"Bedtime," she said. "Well, good night."

"So soon?" he said, standing up lazily. "What's your hurry?"

"No hurry," she said lightly, starting back up the boardwalk towards the house. "It's been a long day and I'm tired, that's all."

"I scared you with that compliment, didn't I?" he called. "Funny, you didn't strike me as a wussy."

That stopped her in her tracks. Wussy? Who was he calling a wussy?

She marched right back to the deck, stopping when she was inches away from him. "You take that back," she said, her fists clenched. "I killed a rattlesnake in my backyard with a shovel when I was ten. My daddy was standing right there but he was terrified of snakes. He barfed when he saw what I'd done. I was the only girl at our neighborhood pool who would backward dive off the high dive. I was the quarterback on my college coed flag-football team, and I broke my nose and played the next day anyway. I am *not* a wussy."

It was all true—all except for the high-dive part. But *he* didn't know that.

"You're scared of me though," Ty said, looking her right in the eyes.

"Am not."

"Prove it."

Her eyes narrowed. "How?"

"Like this," he said, pulling her towards him and sliding his arms around her waist. His mouth was an inch from hers, her eyes half closed. "You're afraid to kiss me," he taunted, his lips barely grazing hers.

"Am not," she said, her breath catching as she said it.

"Prove it."

She sighed impatiently, wrapped her arms around his neck, tilted her face to his and kissed him softly. Her lips were full and warm with promise. Gently, he pulled her closer, gathering the soft fabric of her shorts into his hands. With his tongue, he teased her lips apart. She melted into his chest. For a moment. And then, without warning, she wriggled out of his arms.

"Told ya I wasn't a wussy," she said, and then Ellis Sullivan, flying cupcake boxers and all, was scampering up the walkway in the bright moonlight. He slowly followed, pausing to take a last look at the water, and when he got to the deck of his own place, he looked over at Ebbtide, just in time to see the next-to-last light in the house blink off.

# 18

Julia was nearly asleep when she heard her cell phone vibrating on the rickety wooden nightstand. She fumbled for it in the dark, and sighed when she saw the screen.

"Hey," she said, sitting up in bed.

"Hey, baby," Booker said softly. "You missing me?"

"Yeahhh," she said slowly, smiling as she pictured him. He'd be sitting there in his favorite ratty gray high school gym shorts and a bleached-out T-shirt. His wiry gray-streaked hair would be standing on end, because he ran his fingers through it when he was bored, and the horn-rimmed glasses would have slid down on his nose. Most likely he'd be drinking his favorite late-night treat—Dr Pepper. "Come to think of it, I am."

Julia Capelli had been a nineteen-year-old college dropout, bumming around Europe for a year, picking up modeling assignments wherever she could, when she met Booker Calloway in a grotty pub in Brighton.

He was a fashion photographer, and she'd been hired for a low-budget teenybopper catalog shoot. She'd been drinking with a couple of the other girls, and he'd stopped at their table to buy them all drinks and hit on Geenie, the busty redhead in their bunch. He was already thirty then, sexy as hell with his long, dark hair, gold-flecked hazel eyes, and ever-present Nikons slung bandolier-style across his chest. He was a confirmed expatriate who'd grown up in California and who swore he'd never go back.

Booker completely ignored Julia that night, but the next day, after the shoot, he'd pulled her aside to offer her some advice—"get yourself to a tanning bed, for Chrissake"—and to offer to take some better head shots for her book. They'd done a couple more shoots together, and after that, Booker was acting as her de facto agent, and then one day, she'd realized that they were essentially working—and living—together, full time.

It seemed to Julia that their couplehood had just gradually evolved. And why not? He was smart, successful, a thoughtful and kind lover, a level-headed presence in the crazy world they both inhabited. Everybody loved Booker, even her mother, who'd been fully prepared to hate the totally inappropriate older man who'd seduced her daughter into staying in England instead of coming home to the States, college, her family, a normal life. Within five minutes of meeting him, Catherine Capelli was totally won over. The only thing her mother didn't like about Booker was that her headstrong daughter steadfastly refused to marry him.

Booker never let her forget that one of the last things her mother told her before her death was that she should "marry that nice man, Sugar, before he gets away."

"I could come down there Saturday morning," he was saying now. "My meetings in DC are over Friday night. It's not that long a drive, I could head back here Monday morning. What do you say?"

She sighed again. "Book, we've already been over this. This is a chick trip. No boys allowed. Anyway, it's barely been a week. I need some time to sort things out. We have an agreement, remember?"

"You have an agreement," he grumbled. "I didn't have much choice in the matter, did I?"

She chuckled ruefully. "Not much. Now, can we talk about something else? How's it going up there? Do you like the people you're working with?"

"They're all right, a pretty tight-knit bunch. I'd forgotten how bureaucratic a magazine can be. They've got policies and procedures for everything. And it's gonna take a while to get up to speed with their software."

"You can do it," she reassured him. "And anyway, they're making it worth your while, remember?"

"Damned straight they are. Hey, guess what? I think I found us a house today."

She flopped back down onto her back. "Oh, Book. I don't know. I told you..."

"Julia, just hear me out," he said, his voice pleading. "You'll love it. It's in Alexandria. Right on the metro line. Built in 1918, what's that style house you always talk about, the ones with all the built-in china cabinets and bookcases and stuff?"

"Craftsman?"

"Yeah, that's it. The real estate agent said it's the best example of Craftsman architecture in the whole neighborhood. It's got a big, wide porch across the front, and these great windows that give the most amazing light. And hardwood floors. Three fireplaces. Living room, den, and master bedroom. Four bedrooms. Only two baths, but there's this funny little trunk room just off the master that would make a great master bath. The kitchen needs a total redo, but the agent thinks we can get the house for way less than asking price, because the owner's already taken a job in LA, and he's desperate to unload the place. Hey, I took a bunch of shots with my cell phone. I'll send 'em right now. Wait until you see this place, Julia."

She squeezed her eyes shut. He was like a kid describing a new bike. And he hadn't heard a damned thing she'd been telling him for the past six weeks.

"Oh, Book," she said finally. "It sounds wonderful. Really. But I don't need a house. I don't need to live in DC. I don't need to get married. I love you. I do. But I can't do this."

Silence. "I just... I mean, I guess I don't get it. You say you love me. You know I love you. I thought the new job, moving back to the States, would be a good thing. I'll have real security for the first time. No more crazy freelancing, running all over the globe, running down assignments. We can have our own house. A real home. No more shitty flats in London."

"I love that shitty flat," Julia put in, picturing it in her mind's eye: the orange Arne Jacobsen Egg Chair she'd picked up at a car-boot sale in suburban London, the white leather Conran sofa she'd bought with her first earnings from a magazine job, the bits and bobs of silver and china picked up at the Bermondsey Market, all arranged against walls she'd painted and layered with pictures and photographs picked up at junk markets and antique stalls in every city she'd ever visited.

Now, faced with the possibility of giving up her home for the past ten years, she realized she'd been nesting without even realizing it.

"Ok, well, maybe we keep the flat for when you're over there for modeling gigs."

She cringed at the mention of her career. "Booker, denial is not just a river in Egypt. I'm not getting modeling gigs these days. Not the kind I used to get. I'm thirty-five. I'm not cover-girl material anymore, except for maybe *Modern Maturity*. Last month I did a catalog shoot for Lands' End, for God's sake. Next thing you know, I'll be the spokesmodel for Depends."

"What are you talking about?" he demanded. "Julia, that's nuts. You forget how many years I was in the business. You've got more work than you can handle. Yeah, I realize it's not *Elle* or *Vogue,* but you're also not exactly ready for the glue factory just yet. You are still a sensational-looking girl, and you can have a career in modeling for as long as you want."

"Maybe I don't want a career in modeling anymore," Julia said.

"All right," Booker said wearily. "Do something else. Nobody said you had to model. I just thought that's why you've been so mopey lately, because you hate the offers you're getting."

"That's just it," Julia said. "I don't know how to do anything else. I quit college after one semester, remember?"

"And now's your chance to go back to school, if that's what you want," Booker jumped in. "Or not. I don't give a damn. I just want you with me. I want us to get married, have a kid—if I've still got any swimmers—and get old together. Is that so awful?"

"No," Julia said. "Not awful. Sweet. You're sweet, and I'm a mixed-up bitch." Now, she thought. Now was the time to tell him the truth. Maybe she couldn't even have a baby. Telling the girls was such a relief. How had she walked around with this secret for so many years? What had she been afraid of?

She walked over to the bedroom window and looked idly out at the beach. There was a full moon, and now she could see a couple standing at the end of the boardwalk, on the little deck there. It was a man and a woman, and they were standing close, and now they were embracing. The girl pasted herself to the man's chest, and the moment was so sensual, Julia almost turned away. Almost. A second later, the girl pulled away and began running back towards the house.

"Good Lord," she breathed. "Ellis!"

"What?" Booker demanded. "What's wrong?"

"Nothing," Julia chuckled. "I just saw our Ellis, outside in the moonlight, making out with a strange man."

"I thought you said this was a chick thing. No guys allowed."

"I did. They weren't," she said.

"Julia," Booker's voice was plaintive. "Have you heard a single word I've just said?"

She was staring down at Ellis, who was walking towards the house at a fast clip. She was in her pajamas, for God's sake. And even from where Julia stood, with the moonlight making things absurdly bright, she could see the bemused smile on Ellis's face. Well good for Ellis. But who on earth was the man? He stood for a long while on the deck, staring at the house. Julia hadn't turned the light on in her room, so she was sure he couldn't see her, but just in case, she took a few steps away from the window.

"I hear you, Booker," she said sofly. "But I can't talk about this any more. Love you. G'night."

He was still sputtering when she disconnected. Julia heard the downstairs screen door open and close, and then the sound of the front door closing. Ellis's bare feet trod lightly on the stairs.

Julia stayed at the window, peering out. Finally, the man walked slowly up the boardwalk towards the house. Julia held her breath. Delicious! Was he going to follow Ellis into the house, sneak into her bedroom for a secret tryst? Wait. He was heading towards the garage. What? When he stood for a moment under the garage light she saw his face clearly. It was the garage guy, Ty Bazemore. Ellis and Ty! What a lovely, unexpected development, Julia thought.

Maryn awoke with a start, and sat straight up in bed. For a moment, she struggled to remember where she was. The air in the room was hot and stagnant. Her sweat-soaked nightgown clung to her body. Then she heard the crunch of tires on the crushed shell driveway outside, and with a jolt, she knew exactly where she was.

She glanced at the cheap clock radio on the nightstand. It was 2 A.M. A car was rolling slowly down the driveway. Bile rose in her throat, and for a moment, she felt paralyzed. Then she got up, knelt down, clawing at the thin mattress, until her fingers closed over the pistol she'd hidden there. She ran to the window opposite her bed and peeked out between the faded cotton curtains. She exhaled slowly. It was the red Bronco, the one driven by the man who rented the garage apartment.

Maryn watched as he pulled into the garage. A moment later he walked out of the garage, illuminated by the motion-activated light at the edge of the porch. He was dressed in faded jeans and a white T-shirt, and wore a green baseball cap with the bill pointed backwards. His name was Ty, Dorie had said, and he was a day trader. He looked tired as he slowly climbed the wooden staircase on the exterior of the garage.

She stayed at the window, watching, until she saw the lights switch on in the garage apartment. She could see him through the uncurtained windows, walking around. He went to a table near the window and looked out. She backed away from her own window, not wanting to be seen. She looked down at the .32 still clenched in her right hand.

It was Don's pistol. He'd given it to her not long after they first started dating and she was living in that rat-hole apartment on Pinelawn. Her car had been broken into and her cell phone stolen, and he was insistent that the neighborhood wasn't safe. Which it wasn't.

The next night when he came over, he had a brown paper bag which he carefully set down on her kitchen table.

She gasped when he pulled the gun from the bag. She'd never been around guns. Her father never owned one.

"Don't be afraid, baby," Don had said gently. He showed her how to load it and unload it. Then they'd driven out to the country. He set a row of beer cans on a tree stump, and he showed her how to aim and fire.

"Don't I need a permit for this?" she asked, after he was satisfied that she knew how to use the thing.

"Nah," he'd said. "I've got a permit, and anyway, if you ever have to use the damned thing, you'll shoot first and ask questions later."

She'd thought it was sweet, that he wanted to protect her.

When he insisted that she move out of the apartment and into the condo in a complex he owned closer to town, it was so she'd be living someplace nicer. The rent was twice what she could afford on her salary at the insurance company, but since Don owned the condo and had no intention of letting her pay rent, that wasn't a problem. It hadn't dawned on her that it was more convenient for Don, her living there. He came by most nights, bringing takeout Chinese or a steak that they'd grill on the little enclosed patio off her living room.

They'd met at the office. Don had grown up with the Prescotts, and now he was the firm's accountant. She never would have met him at all, except that one day, two years ago, Marie, Robby Prescott's administrative assistant, had jury duty, and Maryn was drafted to answer the boss's phone. As luck would have it, that was the day Don Shackleford showed up to take Robby Prescott to lunch.

It was a chilly fall morning, and he wore an expensive-looking cashmere coat over his suit. She was on the phone when he entered the office, and he stood impatiently at her desk, tapping his fingers on the papers in Marie's in-box, glancing at his watch, which had annoyed her. Was he tapping to let her know what a big, important man he was? Too important to be kept waiting? So she let him wait, pretending to be listening long after her call had actually ended, just so he knew she was busy too.

"Yes?" she'd said coolly, looking up as though she were seeing him for the first time.

"I'm here for Robby," he said impatiently. "Where's the other girl?"

"Marie? She has jury duty."

"And you work here too? What's your name?"

"Maryn," she said. "I work in claims processing." She said it with the faintest hint of a smile. "I'll let Mr. Prescott know you're here." She got up from her desk, stuck her head in the boss's office, and quietly let him know he had a visitor. Prescott was on the phone, but mouthed he'd be out when he was done.

When she got back to her desk, Don had seated himself on a leather wing chair opposite her desk. "He's on a call, but he'll be out as soon as he can," she told the visitor. She went back to her computer, to the file she'd been working on, but she felt his eyes on her. He was checking her out, which was fine, because she was checking him out too.

And she liked what she saw. Don Shackleford was in his early forties, with thick white-blond hair, a deep tan, ice blue eyes above pronounced cheekbones, and a wide mouth and perfect teeth. He wasn't particularly tall, maybe five-eight, and he had a thick neck and athletic build. She noticed right off that he didn't wear a wedding ring.

Maryn wasn't surprised when Don was back the next week. This time, he hunted her down at her own desk, on some pretext that they both knew was absurd. He asked her to lunch, and she refused, saying she had plans. What about next week, he'd persisted.

"Next week when?" Maryn had asked, not caring.

"Any day next week," he'd said. "Or the week after that. Come on. You know you're going to go to lunch with me. Why not make it sooner than later?"

"Next Friday," Maryn told him. "But I only get an hour. Come by for me at one."

That next Friday, she'd worn her best outfit, a Marc Jacobs pantsuit she'd bought—the tags still on it—at an upscale consignment shop in Philly. The red jacket fit her like a glove, and she'd worn high-heeled black boots that made her only two inches shorter than him.

"You look good," Don said, holding the door of his silver Carrera. They'd gone to the Valley Brook Country Club for lunch, and they'd dined in the men's grill, where all the men sitting around in golf clothes greeted Don like they'd known him for years. He saw their questioning glances at Maryn, but he didn't bother to introduce her. "Horny old bastards," he said with a laugh.

He'd taken her to lunch again the next Friday, but the Friday after that, he'd driven directly to the condo, with no explanation. "Whose place is this?" she'd asked, once they were inside, and he was unzipping her skirt.

"Mine," he'd said, his mouth on hers. There were no more questions. He knew she only had an hour for lunch.

It hadn't taken Maryn by surprise, really. She was surprised he'd waited this long. Don Shackleford was a man who was used to taking what he wanted, and she'd known, the first time she met him, that he wanted her.

If she were honest with herself, Maryn would admit she'd been attracted to Don because of his single-minded pursuit of her. It was absurdly flattering to be so desired, so adored. Nobody had ever wanted to take care of her the way Don did. It didn't occur to her until many months later that he didn't want to just take care of her. He wanted to possess her.

Two months after their first date, she was living in Don's condo. Adam, not surprisingly, made it clear that he didn't approve of Don.

"He's using you," Adam would say when she'd come back after lunch, her hair still damp from her hurried shower.

"How do you know I'm not using him right back?" Maryn had asked. She didn't care who knew she was sleeping with Don. She was doing her job, wasn't she? So it was nobody's business.

Adam was Maryn's age. He'd gone to work at R.G. Prescott Insurers two years earlier, right out of the local community college. There were five other women in their office, but with the exception of that bitch Tara Powers, they were older, married, and clearly none of them, especially Tara, liked or approved of Maryn—or Adam, for that matter.

So it was Adam and Maryn, just hanging out as friends, although Adam clearly wanted more from her than that. She always insisted on paying her own way when she was with Adam. She saw lots of guys, but there was nobody special. Not until Don came along.

"He's way too old for you," Adam said. "I mean, come on, Maryn, what is he, forty?"

"He's forty-two," Maryn said. "Anyway, my mother always said I'm an old soul. I've always dated older guys. You're just jealous of Don, that's all."

"You're only sleeping with him because he's rich," Adam said accusingly.

"And he's amazing in bed," Maryn said, taunting him. When Adam's face flushed, she regretted what she'd said, knowing she'd hurt his feelings.

"I don't like him," Adam had said finally.

And Don didn't like Adam, either. He made that very clear when Maryn had suggested, once or twice, that Adam join them for drinks after work. "That loser?" he'd sneered. Eventually, she'd quit asking.

She got a twinge in her stomach thinking of Adam. She needed to talk to him so badly.

# 19

Raindrops tapped at the tin roof of the old house, and the thin cotton curtains billowed at the windows of Ellis's bedroom. She stretched and yawned and sank blissfully back into the pillows. She couldn't remember the last time she'd slept so soundly. The breeze and the rain had a narcotic effect, she decided.

But then she thought again about last night. The kiss. Her lips curved dreamily at the memory of it. When had she last been kissed like that? Wait. Had she *ever* been kissed the way Ty Bazemore kissed her on the beach the night before?

Definitely not.

She wondered what it could mean. Ty had chosen her. From his vantage point on that deck, he surveyed a vast buffet of beautiful women sunning themselves on the beach below. And he had the kind of looks that could make even a sane woman yowl at the moon. Julia and Dorie for sure had proclaimed him their instant summer crushes. He could probably have any woman he liked. But he liked her. He'd told her so himself, last night.

So what? the practical Ellis taunted. She'd been standing right there in the moonlight, only half dressed in those skimpy pjs. Easy pickings. And it didn't mean a thing. Not to him anyway.

She sat up and swung her legs out of bed. The rain sluiced down the windows, and now it was pooling on the scarred wooden floor. She went to the window and looked out at the sky. Heavy gray clouds covered the horizon. There would be no beach today. And no chance encounter with Ty Bazemore either. Reluctantly, she closed the window and headed for the shower.

Maryn slept badly. Unable to shake the sense of dread settling into her psyche, she'd tossed and turned the rest of the night, and not even the gentle rain beating on the roof just above her head could lull her back to sleep.

Finally, at six, she got up and fetched a paperback romance novel she'd bought on one of her bike rides around the island. But the plot—all dizzy, frothy nonsense about true love and undying devotion—bored her to tears.

Her thoughts kept turning to that terrifying scene back home, of Don, white-faced with fury, gripping her arm, his fingers digging into her flesh, his eyes burning into hers.

After the meeting with Adam, Maryn had to know the truth. Was she married to a thief? Where did all Don's wealth come from? She'd waited until the end of the week, a morning when she knew he had a standing golf date with a client who always wanted to play thirty-six holes. Taking his spare office keys from a tray he kept on his dresser, she drove to his office in a bland strip mall and let herself in.

It took most of the day, fumbling around in his computer files, before she'd finally blundered into a file with rows and rows of damning figures. She wasn't a CPA, but she'd taken enough accounting classes to get their meaning. As she read, she grew nauseous.

Everything Adam had said was true. Don had helped himself to, from what she could tell, at least two million dollars, writing checks to bogus companies controlled by him on five different Prescott accounts. Sick with fear, she'd locked up the office and left, so upset she never noticed Don's Escalade trailing her all the way home.

He'd stormed into the house moments later.

"What the hell are you up to?" he'd demanded, grabbing her by the shoulders and slamming her against the wall. "I saw you pulling out of the parking lot at my office."

"Nnnnothing," she stammered. "I went shopping and thought I'd stop by to see if you were back from golf."

"I saw you coming out of the office," he said quietly. "Watched you lock up and leave. What were you doing in my office, Maryn?"

She'd never seen him so angry before. Should she tell him what she knew? Confront him with the truth?

"Tell me," he said, grabbing her by the forearm, squeezing until she thought she could feel her bones crumble to dust.

"Don, for God's sake, stop. You're hurting me." For a moment, she wasn't even sure he knew what he was doing. But he knew. He always knew exactly what he was doing.

"I asked you a question, Maryn." He tightened his grip, and she thought she would pass out from the pain.

"I know," she said, nearly screaming. "I know you've been stealing from Prescott. Adam knows too. He told me."

Don let go of her arm, and she slumped to the floor, crying softly.

"Adam knows what?" he said, looking down at her. He prodded her with the toe of his golf shoe. "I asked you a question, Maryn."

"He knows there's something funny about the way you've handled Prescott's finances. The company has hired outside auditors! They know you've been stealing from them."

"Adam doesn't know dick," Don said calmly. "The auditors don't know dick." He jerked her up by the arm to a standing position. "And you don't know anything either. Do you hear me?"

"Don," Maryn said, her eyes riveted to his. Maybe there was a mistake. Maybe she'd misunderstood. "I saw the files in your office. It doesn't look right."

"Shut up," Don said. "And listen carefully. You didn't see anything in my files. You don't know anything."

"I hear," she mumbled.

"Understand me, Maryn," Don said, a strange light coming into his pale-blue eyes. "If you say anything to anybody, I will bury you. Someplace where you'll never be found. Nobody will even know you're missing until it's too late. Not Adam, not your mother, nobody will know what happened, where Maryn has gone." He'd smiled at the thought of that. A moment later, he'd released her, but not before bending his head to her forearm and tenderly kissing the angry red welts he'd left there.

He glanced at his watch. "I'm meeting Robby and a couple of the guys at the club for drinks, and I'm already late. The other wives are meeting us for drinks and an early dinner, and Robby made a point of letting me know he expects you to join us."

Maryn had stared at him wordlessly. Five minutes ago, he'd threatened to kill her. Now he was casually inviting her to dinner—with his client, who was also her former boss at R.G. Prescott Insurers, Robby Prescott, from whom, she was certain, he'd embezzled a couple of million dollars.

"I . . . I'll try," she'd stammered. "My mother called, and she's been begging me to come for a visit. . . ."

"No," Don said, shaking his head curtly. "Tell your mother you're busy. If Robby wants you to have dinner with us, that's what you're going to do. And you'll be just as relaxed and charming as you always used to be. Understood?"

"Well . . ." Maryn started, her mouth dry.

"Then I'll see you at six," Don said, heading for the front door, content that he'd given her the day's marching orders. His golf cleats clicked across the marble foyer. "And for Chrissake," he added, his look taking in her disheveled hair and tearstained face, "get yourself put together before you show up at the club tonight." He'd reached in his pocket, pulled out his money clip, and flung a wad of fifties at her.

After Don was gone, Biggie stood by the bedroom door, his liquid brown eyes bewildered. He knew a suitcase meant a trip, and every other time, if they went to the Jersey shore, or just away for the weekend, Biggie went too. Maryn knelt down beside him and cradled his graying muzzle in her hands. "Not this time, buddy," she said, stroking his soft fur.

There was no time for more. She'd been dressed for shopping, her cover story in case Don got home early, in a cream sleeveless silk-wrap blouse, black slacks, her favorite black patent leather slingbacks. She changed into a top that would hide the angry red welts on her arm and she threw clothes into a duffle bag she found on the closet floor, not wanting to take the time to drag her big suitcase out of the guest-room closet. She tossed in some toiletries, her makeup bag, a jumble of shoes, unsure of what she'd need or want since she had no destination in mind. Just away. Far away. She grabbed the cash hidden in her boots and her Rolex Oyster watch and threw them into her cream Prada bag. At the last minute, she remembered her laptop. She slung the strap of the black-leather carrying case over her shoulder and ran for the front door.

And there was Biggie, sitting by the door, ears pricked up, the red-leather leash in his mouth. "Oh, Big," she'd said, mourning the dog already. She stepped outside and closed the door quickly, but she could hear him scratching at it.

Maryn ran to the Volvo SUV and threw the duffle bag and laptop case on the passenger seat. She drove without purpose, intending only to put miles between her and the stranger she'd married.

And now, nearly a week had passed. This house was quiet. Too quiet. She had to know what was going on at home. Had the auditors discovered the extent of Don's embezzlement? And what about Don? He'd been leaving messages on her phone. She'd been too terrified to listen to any of them, deleting them as soon as they arrived.

She had to know something. She picked up her cell phone, intending to call Adam, or at least see if she had any other missed calls. Damn. The phone was dead. In her haste to flee the town house, she'd left the wall charger behind, and she'd been keeping the phone charged with her car charger. Which was, of course, out in the car. In the garage.

But there was still the laptop. She hadn't even bothered to look at it since she'd moved into Ebbtide, unsure of whether or not the house had wireless Internet.

Only one way to find out. She picked up the black-leather case and lifted it onto the bed. For the first time, she was struck by how heavy it was. Don was a nut for new gizmos, and he'd bought both of them the latest ultra-slim Mac-Books back in the springtime. She mostly used hers to play online games or to shop. Frowning, she unzipped the case and reached in to grab the computer. Instead, her hand closed over a thick rubber-band-bound bundle of paper.

Not just paper, though. Currency. She was holding an inch-thick stack of bills. With trembling hands, she rifled the stack. All hundred-dollar bills. Now she picked up the case and dumped the contents out onto the bed. The MacBook slid out, and so did nine more identical bundles of bills.

Maryn stared down at the money and the MacBook. Her laptop was hot pink. This one was white. In her frenzy, she'd grabbed Don's briefcase. And his computer. And his money.

So much money. Thousands. Hundreds of thousands, probably. Her hands shook as she picked up one of the bundles of bills. Where had this much money come from? Too much for Vegas winnings. What was Don doing with all this cash? And what would he do when he discovered it—and Maryn—were missing?

Suddenly, there was a soft tap at the bedroom door. Maryn's heart felt as though it would leap right out of her chest.

"Madison?" It was Dorie, the strawberry blonde who'd befriended her in the luncheonette.

"Yes?" she managed to croak.

"I hate to bother you, but since it's Sunday, and it's raining cats and dogs out, we decided to fix a big ol' brunch. Julia's making waffles and bacon, and I've got fruit salad, and we're having mimosas. Why don't you join us, Madison? We've hardly gotten to see you at all since you moved in."

The smell of bacon and coffee wafted all the way up to the third floor. Her stomach growled. She hadn't eaten since lunch yesterday. Maryn looked down at the pile of money on the bed, and then back at the door. All week, she'd managed to avoid the women except for a couple of brief, awkward encounters while she was coming and going from the house on her bike. Now, it was raining out, so she couldn't very well take off on her bike. Her stomach growled again. She'd been a hermit long enough. Maybe one meal wouldn't hurt. Hurriedly, she began scooping the money back into the briefcase. She would figure out what to do about it later.

"Brunch sounds nice," she called finally. "Just let me get myself presentable, and I'll be right down."

"She's coming down," Dorie reported to the others. "See, I told you we should ask her."

"Oh goodie," Julia said sarcastically, bowing and grandly waving her spatula like a scepter. "We finally get a real audience with the queen." She dipped a quick curtsy. "Hello, your majesty."

"Shh, she'll hear you," Dorie said. "You wait. She's not stuck-up. She's just . . . an introvert, I think."

Julia drummed her fingertips on the wooden tabletop. "I don't buy that bit about her being in 'transition' after a breakup with some man. What's she really doing here? Money obviously isn't a problem, so why hang out in a dinky little beach town like this? Why isn't she someplace glamorous? Why doesn't she have any friends or family? She keeps her bedroom door locked every second she's gone. I know, because I've checked. And she hasn't moved that car of hers since she parked it in the garage. I'm telling you, she's hiding from somebody or something, and I intend to figure it out."

"She's a mystery, all right," Ellis agreed. She popped the cork on the bottle of champagne and started filling the plastic flutes they'd picked up at the dollar store earlier in the week. Dorie put her hand across the top of her own flute. "No champagne for me, remember?"

"Of course," Ellis said. "But orange juice is good for you. No coffee, though, right?"

"Nope," Dorie said, shaking her head. "Caffeine's not good for the baby, sad to say. I'm missing that a lot more than the alcohol. And I'm already getting tired of drinking all that milk."

Julia glanced over her shoulder at Dorie. "Have you even gained any weight yet?"

"Actually, I've lost seven pounds," Dorie reported. "But that's just because I had hideous morning sickness the first two months. The nurse-midwife at my obstetrician's office says I'm doing just fine. She says some women don't really start gaining until they're in the middle of their second trimester."

Julia shook her head. "Only you, Dorie Dunaway, could get pregnant and actually lose weight."

"Is somebody pregnant?" Madison stood in the doorway, looking elegant even in white capris and an oversized pink-and-white striped shirt. Her blond hair was in a ponytail, and she wore pink Ferragamo ballet flats.

Dorie blushed and Julia looked chagrined.

"Well . . ." Ellis began.

"I am," Dorie said, smiling brightly. She sat down at the kitchen table and held up one of the champagne flutes. "Come sit and hear my tale of woe."

Madison sipped the mimosa cautiously as Dorie calmly repeated the story she'd told her friends just the night before.

"Wow," Madison said, when Dorie had finished. "So . . . your husband doesn't know yet?"

"No," Dorie said, nibbling on a piece of bacon she'd snagged from the platter in the middle of the table. "I'm such a coward, I just really haven't been able to face talking to him yet—let alone tell him about the baby."

"Well," Madison said, "I admire your courage. I don't know how I'd feel about being a single mother. My folks split up when I was thirteen. It was rough. I mean, raising a baby alone, that's a lot."

Julia slid a waffle onto Madison's plate. "So," she said, trying to sound casual. "What about you, Madison? Kids? Husband?"

"Neither," Madison said without looking up. "I guess I've been too busy concentrating on work to settle down and start a family."

Julia's eyes flickered meaningfully at Maryn's ring finger—the one with Don's diamond solitaire. "Oh, this?" Maryn said, fluttering the finger in question. "This is an old family piece."

"Some family," Julia said.

"Julia and I have already appointed ourselves Dorie's baby's godmothers," Ellis was saying.

"Fairy godmothers," Julia added. "Of course, she'll be the most beautiful child in the world. With Dorie's hair and eyes."

Madison glanced at Dorie. "Oh, you already know you're having a girl?"

"No," Dorie said. "I don't want to know the baby's sex ahead of time."

"Julia thinks she's a witch," Ellis explained. "She thinks she can just *will* Dorie to have a little girl so we can spoil her rotten."

"Naturally," Julia agreed. "An angelic little girl. With red-gold curls and green eyes. Her Aunt Julia will teach her how to dress and accessorize— skills her mommy, unfortunately, never learned."

"Hey!" Dorie said good-naturedly, smoothing the wrinkles in her faded Our Lady of Angels soccer tournament T-shirt. "I think I resent that."

"Her Auntie Ellis will teach her math, and how to swim, and of course, we'll read lots of books together. I'll take her to the zoo, and the beach. . . ."

"I'll take her to New York and Bergdorf's," Julia said.

"And if it's a boy?" Dorie asked, spreading the palms of her hands across her belly.

"We'll put him on a raft and gently shove him out to sea," Julia declared.

"Julia!" Ellis and Dorie exclaimed.

"Kidding," Julia assured them. "Mostly."

# 20

It was nearly three by the time Maryn managed to pry herself away from the other women. Brunch had been a leisurely affair, and truthfully, she'd been surprised to find how much she enjoyed their company. They hadn't made her feel like an outsider at all. It felt good to laugh, relax, let her guard down. And with women her own age. That was the big surprise. But she'd only allowed herself to relax a little. Ellis and Dorie seemed genuinely warm and friendly. But Julia was a different story. Julia listened intently to every little shred of information Maryn had reluctantly imparted about herself.

Lying about her marital status had been a mistake. When had she become such an accomplished liar, Maryn wondered. She should have just admitted that she'd left her husband. They would have been sympathetic. Instead, Julia was now even more suspicious. She wasn't overtly hostile, but Maryn could tell from long practice when another woman was sizing her up. Just as Maryn was accustomed to sizing up every woman she met, right from the start. Well, that was fine. Julia was watching her. And she was watching Julia.

Maryn knelt beside the bed and reached for the briefcase. She laid the stacks of bills out on the bed and counted the money, her heart pounding as the amount grew. Ten thousand dollars in each stack, a hundred thousand dollars in all. The stacks were bound with green rubber bands, not the neat paper bands a bank would use. And the bills weren't new; their numbers were nonsequential.

Her mouth felt dry. What was Don doing with this much cash? She looked warily at the laptop. Were the answers locked somewhere inside Don's computer?

She grabbed the power cord and plugged in the MacBook. It booted up right away. But she didn't have Don's password. For twenty minutes, she played around with different combinations of letters, words, and numbers. His birthday, her birthday. Their anniversary. That was a laugh!

She'd managed to lie to herself just as convincingly as Don had lied to her, right from the very start of their relationship. As it turned out, he already had a family. Of course, she hadn't known about his wife and teenaged children until they'd been practically living together for three months.

Adam had broken the news to her. Reluctantly, he claimed. It had been a terrible blow to Maryn. She'd never claimed to be an angel. She'd slept with her share of men, broken her share of hearts. But she had a rule. No married men. Ever. She'd never do to some other woman what another woman had done to Maryn's mother. She was a lot of things, but she wasn't a home wrecker. Or so she thought.

Another lie. There had been so many, she'd forgotten what was truth and what was not.

She'd confronted Don about his lies, and he'd laughed them off. "We've been living apart for years," he told her. "Abby doesn't care what I do or who I sleep with, as long as the money keeps flowing. She thinks I'm her personal ATM. So why do you care?"

"What about your kids?" she'd demanded. "Don't you care about them?"

"I see the kids," he'd said carelessly. "It's not like they're in first grade. Ashley's what, fourteen? Cash is sixteen. They have their own lives, their own interests. They're not interested in taking a trip to Disney World with Daddy, Maryn."

He'd left a copy of the divorce papers on the dresser, where she'd see them.

And three months later, on a Friday in early February, he'd come home and proposed. If she were brutally honest with herself, she had to admit that the diamond solitaire, twinkling from its white satin cushioned box, had blinded her. To everything. She'd wanted a real wedding, with at least her mother and Aunt Patsy—and Adam—present, but Don had flatly refused. In the end, they'd gotten married before a justice of the peace Don knew, and flown to Aruba for a five-day honeymoon.

Those five days had been the happiest of her life. Don was relaxed, he was tender, attentive, everything she'd dreamed a husband would be. He'd talked about their future together. He'd already bought a lot where they'd build their dream home: ten thousand square feet, five bedrooms, five baths, a three-car garage. And it was on a lake. Maryn would have a bathroom with a fireplace and a whirlpool tub, all marble. And a kitchen that would rival any in the best restaurants in town.

"And kids," Maryn said dreamily. "I know you've done that already, but I want kids of our own, Don. I'm thirty-two. My clock is ticking."

"Whatever," he'd said, brushing aside any specifics.

She tapped away now at the laptop keyboard, trying different passwords. His company name, his kids' names—Ash and Cash, he called them—the nickname his golfing buddies used for him, Shack. None of them worked.

Madison fetched her duffle bag from the armoire. She stacked the money in the bottom of it, and put a dirty T-shirt on top before placing the duffle under her bed. Her thoughts drifted back to Adam. She had to talk to him, let him know where she'd gone.

Rain pelted her as she stepped out onto the rusted iron spiral staircase. She locked the door behind her and, clutching the rail with both hands, picked her way down the steps, feeling the staircase sway with every step. When she got to the bottom, she ran to the garage and unlocked the car. She turned the key in the ignition, plugged in her phone, and sat waiting as the battery re-charged.

When the phone's display window lit up, she saw that she had eleven missed calls. All from Don. He'd left voice-mail messages too. Now she forced herself to listen.

Don's voice was low. "Maryn. Where the hell are you? We need to talk. Look, I admit I lost my temper. But you know I never intended to hurt you. I love you, baby. Call me, okay? And let me know you're all right. You're starting to worry me."

She snorted. Oh yeah, he was worried all right. Maybe a little about her. What she'd seen, who she might tell. But mostly, she was sure, he was worried about that briefcase full of money. And his laptop computer and whatever secrets it might hold. She went down the phone log and tapped each of his messages, deleting without listening. She was done listening to Don Shackleford.

She called Adam's cell phone, and it went directly to voice mail.

"Adam, it's me," she said breathlessly. "I've . . . I've left Don. I'm down south. Look, a lot has happened. You were right. About everything. I really need to talk to you, okay? Call me as soon as you get this, no matter what time it is."

Madison considered calling her mother, but rejected the idea immediately. They hadn't talked in months, why call her now? She didn't think Don would have contacted her mother. He had no interest in her family, and she was fairly sure he didn't even have her mother's phone number.

Idly, she tapped the phone. A wallpaper screen came up, a photo she'd taken right after they'd returned from Aruba. Don, sitting on the porch of the town house, relaxed, smiling, his arm draped companionably across the shoulder of his one true friend. Biggie.

Biggie! Why hadn't she thought of that? Maryn jumped out of the car and ran, splashing through the rain, for the house. And Don's laptop.

# 21

Ellis found herself drawn to the window in her bedroom. She told herself it was the scenery, the dark blue-green waves crashing on the sand, the rain and wind blowing and bending the tufts of sea oats lining the dunes below. She pulled a wooden chair up to the window, and rested her forehead against the moisture-beaded glass. And if she leaned in just the right way, she could see the weather-beaten boards of the garage, and the apartment above, and the dull glow of one lit lamp within.

He was home. She could see his Bronco parked to the side of the driveway. What was he doing on this rainy Sunday afternoon? Probably working, planning his next trade. She decided he was definitely not doing what she was doing. No way he was reliving that moment on the beach last night. No way he was analyzing that kiss, that amazing, lingering kiss, or the feeling of dizzying heat when they'd embraced. No way Ty Bazemore was telling himself to get over himself. Which was what Ellis was doing.

She tried reading. She had a stack of book club books, the ones she'd been too busy to read over the past year, back when she had a career. They were all highly recommended books, literary masterpieces, food for the mind. Stacked on her nightstand, they gently reproved her. But right now what she craved was mind candy, the idle, delicious retelling of a love story—featuring a heroine who looked uncannily like Ellis Sullivan and a hero with sun-streaked hair who could only be Ty Bazemore.

At five o'clock, she watched as Ty came splashing down the wooden stairs from his apartment. He wore khaki cargo shorts, top-siders, and a black T-shirt with CADILLAC JACK'S in hot pink script across the back. He jumped in the Bronco and headed down the driveway. Ellis watched him go, and a plan took root.

At seven, Ellis wandered into the kitchen, where she found Julia, dressed in cut-offs and a faded black tank top, and Dorie, still dressed in cotton pajama pants and an oversized Braves T-shirt. They were studying a handful of takeout menus.

"Pizza or Chinese?" Julia asked, looking up.

"Neither," Ellis said. "We've been stuck inside all day and I've got a bad case of cabin fever. I say we get dressed up and head out and do the town. We could do girls' night out, like the old days."

"What town?" Julia asked. "Are you telling me there's a club scene in Nags Head?"

"Not really a club scene," Ellis said hesitantly. "But I've heard about a place—Cadillac Jack's. They've supposedly got a halfway decent menu, and a bar, and music. Sunday nights it's supposed to be the place to see and be seen."

Julia raised one eyebrow. "By who?"

"By whom, you mean," Dorie said, yawning. "You guys go on without me. Since I can't drink, I might as well stay home and eat leftovers. Anyway, I'm gonna turn in early tonight."

"That leaves us," Ellis told Julia. "Unless we want to include Madison?"

Dorie turned from the refrigerator with a bowl of leftover chicken salad. "She's not here. I saw her drive off about thirty minutes ago."

"Really?" Julia narrowed her eyes. "Wonder where she was headed?"

"Who cares?" Ellis said impatiently. "What do you say, are you in?"

"Why not?" Julia headed for the hallway. "Just give me fifteen minutes to get changed."

Twenty minutes later, Julia sat in the living room, thumbing through a magazine. She was dressed in faded denim capris and a tight black T-shirt that barely covered her tanned midriff. She wore brown leather gladiator-style sandals, and she'd done her hair in a loose braid that hung over one shoulder. Large gold hoops gleamed from her ears.

"Ellis!" she hollered, staring up at the ceiling. "Hurry up and get down here before I change my mind and decide to stay home with Dorie."

"Keep your shirt on," Ellis said, carefully taking one stair at a time.

Julia swung around to see her friend.

"Hey!" she said suspiciously. "You didn't say this place was dressy."

"This isn't dressy," Ellis said, walking into the living room.

"That's a dress you're wearing," Julia said, stating the obvious.

It was, in fact, a dress Ellis had never even worn before—a short, cotton Lilly Pulitzer sundress with a pattern of stylized hot-pink-and-yellow daisies. The dress's spaghetti straps were of a contrasting lime green, and the tight-fitting bodice showed a healthy stretch of Ellis's freckled cleavage. She wore lime green ballet skimmers, and a pair of dangly pink-pearl earrings nearly brushed her shoulder tops. Ellis had swept her hair into a French twist updo, with feathery bangs.

"No fair," Julia said, coming closer to examine her friend. "You look like the queen of the Junior League summer country club dance!"

"And you look like a gorgeous high-fashion model who happens to be slumming it in Nags Head," Ellis said. "I've gotta bring out the big guns if I'm going anywhere with you."

Julia studied Ellis carefully. "You're even wearing makeup."

"First time since we got here," Ellis agreed. "Are you going to stand there giving me the fish-eye, or can we go?"

"Waitin' on you," Julia said.

Cadillac Jack's was actually in Kitty Hawk, eight miles up the road. It was housed in a former Piggly Wiggly supermarket. The old neon sign with the jaunty winking pig still stood by the roadside, but the 1940s-era stucco building had been painted charcoal gray, and the large plate glass windows were shaded by scalloped pink-and-black striped canvas awnings. Ellis joined the line of cars streaming into the parking lot, where a burly off-duty cop in jeans and a navy T-shirt with SECURITY stenciled on the back waved them into one of the few remaining spots, at the rear of the lot.

"This joint is jumping," Julia said as they walked towards the entrance. "How'd you hear about it?"

"I think I read something in a magazine," Ellis said vaguely.

"This is kinda cool," Julia said when her eyes had adjusted to the semi-darkness. The club's walls were still plastered with age-darkened signs advertising specials like CREAM OF WHEAT and COLLARDS and HAM HOCKS with Eisenhower-era prices, but now black leather-upholstered booths filled one wall of the cavernous room and round tables were scattered around the center, with a postcard-sized, slightly elevated wooden dance floor. Music thumped from speakers mounted around the ceiling. Ellis thought she recognized Lady Gaga's latest hit, but nobody was dancing. The crowd was an eclectic mix, with groups of couples and singles Ellis's age, but also lots of college kids, the girls in clingy tops and short skirts, guys in preppy polo shirts.

A bar took up the back wall of the room, with the grocery's retro neon MEAT MARKET sign flashing off and on, the light reflecting in the rows of bottles and glasses on the back bar.

"Are we the oldest ones in here?" Ellis asked anxiously, staring at the bobbing heads of girls who looked a generation younger than herself. She suddenly felt horribly, terrifyingly out of place in her childish pink-and-green getup.

"Who gives a shit?" Julia said, tugging at Ellis's hand. "Come on, let's get a drink and snag a table."

"Wait," Ellis said urgently. "It's so crowded. I didn't think there'd be so many people. Maybe we should just find a quiet restaurant. . . ."

"Too late," Julia declared, plunging into the crowd, dragging Ellis by the hand towards the back of the room, and the bar.

People were stacked three deep at the bar, but Julia expertly managed to wedge herself into a spot at the corner, between a pair of middle-aged men who were nursing beers and eyeing the crowd.

"Get you somethin', darlin'?" The taller of the two men had horn-rimmed glasses and wore a pale blue ball cap with UNC embroidered on the bill. He grinned at Julia, and even seemed to include Ellis in his admiring glance.

"No thanks," Julia said, flashing him a smile that managed to turn him down without shutting him down. It was a uniquely Julia art, one Ellis had always coveted.

Now Julia was leaning over and across the bar, her long, tanned arm waving in the air. "Excuse me," she called loudly. The bartender, whose back had been to her, turned, and on seeing who was calling, put down the glass he'd been polishing.

"Hey there," Ty Bazemore said, walking towards them. "Ellis. Julia. This is a nice surprise." His easy grin took in both the women, but Ellis thought, just maybe, the warmth was directed at her.

"Wow, yeah," Julia said, half turning and shoving Ellis forward. "It sure is a surprise. I didn't know you worked here. Did you, Ellis?"

Ellis felt her face turn as pink as her dress. "Oh, well, yeah, I think maybe I did know that."

"Hmm," Julia said, enjoying her friend's discomfort for a moment.

"Can I get you something?" Ty asked.

"What have you got?" Julia asked.

"Well drinks are two for one for the next ten minutes," Ty said. "But you don't want any of that rotgut. I've got a decent pinot and a cab, or I could fix you something else. . . ."

"Tanqueray and tonic for me," Julia said decisively.

"Uh, well . . ." Ellis floundered.

"Give her a cosmo," Julia said. "You don't happen to have any food, do you? We actually didn't eat dinner."

He frowned. "The kitchen closes early on Sunday, but I'll see what I can do." He turned away, fixed their drinks, and was back a minute later. "I hope you like quesadillas. Go ahead and get a table, and I'll get somebody to bring them over."

"Thanks," Julia said, pushing a twenty-dollar bill across the bar. "I think you just saved our lives."

"Well," Julia said when they'd settled into a booth on the far side of the bar with a pair of two-for-one drinks for each of them, and a heaping plate of chicken quesadillas. "That was quite a coincidence, wasn't it? Running into garage boy at Cadillac Jack's of all places?"

"Umm-hmm," Ellis said, sipping her drink.

"I think he is totally hot," Julia said, looking past Ellis at Ty moving up and down the bar, slinging drinks and making small talk with fluid efficiency. "Don't you?"

Ellis shrugged nonchalantly. "I guess he could grow on you. It was nice of him to get us some food after the kitchen was closed."

"I think he likes you," Julia said, her tone lightly teasing. "I checked my watch. Happy hour ended half an hour ago, and he still gave us the special."

"Oh, no," Ellis said, busying herself by slathering the quesadilla with sour cream. "He was just being polite. But what makes you think he likes me?"

"I'm a witch, remember?" Julia said, resisting the impulse to admit that she'd seen Ellis and Ty in a moonlit clinch the night before. "I can read the future. And I definitely see a man in your future, Miss Ellis Sullivan."

"Hope so," Ellis said fervently.

"Since when are you looking for a man?" Julia challenged.

"You think I'm not interested in men?"

Julia shrugged. "Are you?"

"Well . . . why not? Look, I know we promised each other that this would be a chick trip. But to be honest with you, I haven't really dated in a while."

"How long a while?"

Ellis knew exactly how long it had been. Five years, give or take a month or two. She'd made a brief, disastrous stab at online dating. Nine dates with four different guys. She actually felt queasy thinking about it.

She toyed with a piece of lettuce on her plate. "Please don't make me talk about this," she said quietly.

"How bad could it be?" Julia asked.

"Awful," Ellis said, taking a large swallow of her cosmo. "Soul-searing."

"Which is exactly why you *should* talk about it," Julia coaxed. "Dorie and

I are your oldest, bestest friends. There's nothing you could say that would shock *me*, of all people, for God's sake."

It was true. If the game were truth or dare, Julia's confession of the night before had raised the stakes for all of them.

"If I tell you about it, will you swear never to tell another living soul?"

Julia leaned in until her forehead nearly grazed Ellis's. "Of course. But, you don't even want me to tell Dorie?"

"No. Dorie wouldn't understand. She's so gorgeous, she's never had to worry about meeting men. Not that you've ever had that problem either."

Julia cocked her head. "Hey, don't you remember what I looked like in junior high? That bad perm my mom gave me, the braces, the flat chest? And my God, my acne! I was the original pizza face. Not to mention I weighed, like, eighty-seven pounds and looked like a damned stork."

Ellis sighed. "Yeah, but by the time we were seventeen, the braces were off, the acne cleared up, and you grew boobs. It was like revenge of the ugly duckling."

"Turns out my mother was right," Julia agreed. "I really *was* a late bloomer."

"Not as late as me," Ellis said, her voice low. "I'm thirty-four, Julia. And I haven't really been with a man since . . ." She paused, and then forced herself to say it. "Since Ben."

Julia's eyes widened. "For real?"

Ellis took another sip of her drink and forced a smile. "Yeah. I'm a freak, right? Eleven years without sex. Not quite the forty-year-old virgin, but close."

"You are not a freak, Ellis Sullivan!" Julia said fiercely. She gestured at the couples on the dance floor, and in particular at a woman about their age who was grinding her hips into her dance partner, her arms locked around his neck, eyes closed, lips apart. "The freaks are these chicks who'll give a lap dance or a blow job to some asshole they just met at a bar while on vacation."

"You're just saying that," Ellis said. "Although I appreciate the sentiment."

"Okay, fine," Julia said. "I'm not going to make you tell me." She raised an eyebrow, as though daring Ellis.

Ellis slurped up the last of her cosmo and took the bait. "Oh well. I guess it won't hurt. I mean, lots of people do it. . . ."

"I knew it," Julia said triumphantly. "You were online dating, weren't you? Come on. Out with it. eHarmony or Match.com?"

Ellis buried her face in her hands. "Match.com. It was the year I turned thirty. I made this stupid New Year's resolution that I was going to really be out there, you know, in the marketplace. Never again. I'd rather die alone, the crazy lady living in a double-wide down by the river, with forty-seven cats and a houseful of hoarded tin cans and toilet paper, than try that again."

Julia rubbed her hands in delight. "Tell me everything. Don't leave out a single, grotesque detail."

"I only did it for three months," Ellis said. "Two different women I worked with met their husbands that way, and they were totally normal, average to above-average nice guys. But I think those women got the last two normal guys on the planet. Either that, or I'm just a major creep magnet."

"Details," Julia interrupted. "Gimme."

"Gawwwwd," Ellis moaned. "I've spent years trying to forget all this stuff. And now you want me to dredge up all the dirt again. Isn't it enough that I admit I made a major mistake?"

"No," Julia said. "Quit stalling."

"Okay," Ellis said, wincing at the memory. "The first guy—his name actually was Guy—seemed nice, at first. We e-mailed back and forth for a couple weeks, until I convinced myself he wasn't some kind of psycho axe murderer. We met at a coffee shop on a Saturday morning. He was wearing jeans, a polo shirt, well-groomed, nothing scary at all about him. Until he ordered."

"What? What did he order?"

"It wasn't what he ordered, it was *how* he did it. I mean, he made the waitress repeat our order back twice to him, and then when she brought the coffee and his danish, he made this big stink about how she'd screwed it up, and insisted he'd asked for decaf. And I heard him. He did not ask for decaf! And then he said the danish was stale, and it tasted fine. He harangued this poor girl for five minutes, until she was in tears, and when we finished, he left a penny for a tip."

Julia rolled her eyes. "I can't stand a waitress baiter. Or a stingy bastard. I'm guessing you never saw Guy again."

"Never," Ellis agreed. "But the next guy was worse." She shuddered. "I've blocked out his name."

"No you haven't."

"Okay. It was Bart. Or Barf, as I came to think of him afterwards."

"What was wrong with Bart?"

"He was maybe the best-looking guy I've ever gone out with. I mean, gorgeous. Tan, muscular, elegant manners. He took me to dinner at this really nice Italian restaurant. And of course, he ordered in Italian, which was a little bit of a turnoff. I mean, who gives an entire order in Italian?"

"You can't hate the guy just because he spoke Italian."

"He did kind of remind me of Kevin Kline in *A Fish Called Wanda,* but it wasn't the Italian that was the turnoff. It was the fact that he took me on a date—commando!"

Julia guffawed. "Seriously? How do you know? Maybe he was just wearing, like, you know, low riders."

Ellis blushed beet red and giggled. "I know, okay? He was totally commando."

"I don't believe it," Julia said, taking a long sip of her drink.

"No, Julia," Ellis said, leaning forward again. "The way his pants were cut, sort of loose, you know, I could tell he was, you know . . ." she whispered, "free balling. That's what Baylor used to call it. But Baylor only did it at the beach, when he was a teenager. Not on a first date at a nice Italian restaurant!"

Julia's face contorted, and she pressed a paper napkin to her face. "No fair! You made me snort gin out my nose. What did you do when you realized he wasn't wearing any underwear?"

"What could I do?" Ellis said. "I didn't realize it until he got up to go to the men's room, and he was walking back across the restaurant, and you know, his goods were kinda jiggling around as he walked."

"Oh no," Julia laughed. "Eeeeww. Poor Ellis."

"It wasn't that funny at the time," Ellis said, laughing now. "I just had to get out of there, but I'd already ordered dinner. So I scarfed down my entrée, then I faked a migraine, told him I was so nauseous I'd better leave immediately. I literally ran out of the restaurant, hailed a cab, and hightailed it home. And that was it for me and online dating."

"Oh my God," Julia giggled. "I've been with Booker so long, I had no idea things were that awful out there in the dating world."

"You don't know the half of it," Ellis agreed.

"So what changed your mind about dating again?" Julia asked.

"Nothing," Ellis said. "And everything. Losing my job—it's corny, but I think it's time to take stock. And I've decided it's now or never. If I meet a nice guy, who knows? Anyway, Ty's not really a bartender. He's a day trader. He's just moonlighting here because the stock market is so crappy right now."

"I'm no snob," Julia said. "I wouldn't care if he really was just a bartender. He seems like a nice guy. I think you should go for it, Ellis. Come on, a little summer fling would do you a world of good."

Ellis toyed with her second drink. "You think?"

The waitress was back with another round of drinks, and this time she didn't look happy. "Ty asked me to tell you ladies that he gets off in thirty minutes," she said. "He was wondering if you're going to stick around that long."

"Oh," Ellis said. "Well, sure. I mean, does that sound all right to you, Julia?"

Julia finished off her drink. "You stay, Ellis," she said casually. "If you don't mind, I'll take the car and go on back to the house. I think I feel a migraine coming on. Maybe Ty will give you a ride home."

"No!" Ellis said, feeling panicky. "You can't go already, Julia."

"You can stay," Julia said, reaching over and patting her friend's hand. "You're a big girl. You can do this."

The waitress cleared her throat to let them know she was waiting.

Ellis gulped. Her heart was racing. She looked up at the waitress. "Tell him I'll be here."

Julia stood up and put a twenty-dollar bill on the tabletop. "There's the tip," she said, nodding at the money. She dropped a kiss on the top of Ellis's head. "Have a good time," she whispered. "And don't worry. I've been watching Ty all night. He does a lot of bending and stretching, getting beers out of that cooler on the back bar. I'm a hundred percent sure he's wearing underpants."

# 22

"Strawberry Shortcake is staying, but her friend is outta here," the waitress told Ty.

"Nella!" Ty said reprovingly. "Don't be mean. It doesn't suit you."

"Can't help it," Nella Maxwell said, dumping her tray full of dirty glasses into the bar sink. "It's my nature. Who is she, anyway?"

"Her name is Ellis," Ty said, filling a shaker with ice and vodka. "She's a friend."

"Doesn't look like your usual variety of 'friend,'" Nella pointed out. "The hottie who left is more your type."

"Julia?" Ty frowned. "Not really. Anyway, I like Ellis. She's . . . different." He gazed over at Ellis, sitting alone at her table, chin propped up on her fists, watching the swirl of people around her. She was wearing a girlish pink-and-green sundress, and with her hair swept off her neck, he could see a sprinkling of freckles on her sunburnt shoulders and chest, and a surprising amount of cleavage, especially from a woman whose bathing suit looked like something you'd wear to a swim meet. Nella was right about one thing, Ty thought. Ellis looked just like a sweet, pink confection. Totally out of place in a bar like Cadillac Jack's, with its writhing mass of on-the-make college kids and black-clad hipsters. He wanted to sweep her up and out of there, maybe back to the beach, someplace quiet, someplace without the throb of music and din of shrill voices.

He'd been unaccountably thrilled to look up an hour ago and see Julia towing Ellis along in her wake, steaming towards the bar. He'd never expected Ellis would actually take him up on his invitation to drop by the club. She didn't seem like the type to go club hopping, but maybe it had been all Julia's idea. Not that he really cared. He was happy Ellis had come and even happier that Julia had bowed out.

Ty looked down at his watch and frowned. "It's after nine, and I'm supposed to be off. Angie told me Patricia was coming in to work the rest of the shift. You seen her?"

"Nope," Nella said. "But I need two frozen 'ritas and a Natty Lite for one of my tables five minutes ago."

"Patricia better get her butt in here," Ty said darkly, dumping ice and margarita mix into the blender jar. "I'm tired of covering for her. Do you have her cell number?"

"Patricia's?" Nella hooted. "Get serious. Even if I had her number, she wouldn't answer. She and Jason had a big fight last night, and he threw her out of the apartment. And you know that piece-of-crap car of hers quit running a week ago, so with Jason out of the picture she's either gotta ride her bike or thumb a ride to get here."

"Swell," Ty muttered, looking around the bar. It was a typical summer Sunday night at Cadillac Jack's. The place was jammed and people were still coming in. Patricia Altizer was a sweet kid, in her midtwenties, but she had terrible taste in men, and worse luck when it came to managing her own life. When she made it in on time for her shift, she was a hard worker, but Ty had already had to fill in for her the past couple of times she was supposed to work, and he had the sinking feeling that tonight would be another of those nights.

Sure enough, at 9:30, Angie, the club owner, slipped behind the bar, a look of chagrin on her face. "Patricia's a no-show, as I'm sure you already figured," she started. "Ty, honey, I hate to ask, but can you stay 'til closing?"

"You can't get anybody else?" he asked. "I've kinda got something to do tonight. And you swore you weren't going to keep asking me to close."

Angie turned and looked in the direction of the table she'd seen Ty gazing at as she approached the bar. Ellis had finished her drink and was fiddling with her cell phone. Ty had been so busy, he hadn't even had time to send over another drink—or an apology for keeping her waiting.

"Yeah, Nella told me you've got a new friend," Angie said, a note of sarcasm in her voice.

"Nella needs to mind her own business," Ty said.

"Look, Ty," Angie went on. "I'm desperate, okay? Patricia's definitely not coming in, and I've called all over, trying to round up somebody else to work, but you're it. If you'll stay 'til closing, I'll owe you big time. You name it, you got it. Just don't walk out of here and leave me without a bartender."

Ty thought about it. Angie really was in a jam. If he left now, with only Nella and one other girl waiting tables, there'd likely be a riot. Anyway, he was in a jam of his own, wasn't he? It was mid-August, and September was closing in. He needed to make some money, and he needed to make it fast. He looked over at Ellis, who returned his gaze. She smiled, raised her eyebrows, and gave a little wave.

He sighed. "You're gonna have to spell me for half an hour. Then I'll be back, and I'll stay and close. But this is the last time. And it's gonna cost you."

"Anything," she said fervently. "Name it."

"You're paying me twenty bucks an hour tonight," Ty said. "Plus tip out. And no skimming. Nella and I can tell what tips oughta be tonight, and if you try and short us, it'll be the last time I set foot in this place. Understand?"

"That's extortion."

"Yep," Ty said. "And you could always refuse to pay, and I could take a walk."

"Hey," Ty said, sliding into the booth across from Ellis.

"Hey yourself," Ellis said. "Pretty busy tonight, huh?"

"Yeah, and I've got bad news," Ty said. "The chick who was supposed to be coming in at nine isn't coming. Which means I've got to stay and close up—and I won't get out of here 'til at least 1 A.M."

"Oh," Ellis said, trying to hide her disappointment. "That's too bad."

"It's a pain in the ass," Ty said. "But they can't get anybody else this late, so it's all me. Look, I've got, like, a fifteen-minute break. I'll run you home, and if you'll give me a rain check, maybe we could hang out another night."

"Sure," Ellis said, trying to sound noncommittal. "But don't worry about me. I can get a cab or something. . . ."

"No way." He held out his hand. "C'mon. The quicker we get out of here, the more time I can spend with you."

"All fifteen minutes," Ellis said.

Ten minutes later they pulled into the driveway at Ebbtide. The porch light was on, and Madison's room on the top floor of the house was lit up, but the rest of the house was dark.

Ty left the Bronco's motor running. "This really sucks," he said fervently.

"It's all right," Ellis said. "It's not like we had a date or anything."

"We didn't really have a date, but that's not all right with me," Ty said. "What about another night this week? Most of the best restaurants are closed Mondays. Maybe Tuesday night?"

"Uh," Ellis said. Her brain was frozen. He was asking her out. For a real date. Suddenly, she was fifteen again, tongue-tied and paralyzed with shyness.

"Wednesday night, then?" Ty asked.

"No, I mean, yes, Tuesday night would be fine," Ellis finally managed.

"Great," Ty said, relieved.

Grateful that the awkward moment had ended, Ellis fumbled around, looking for the door handle. But before she could find it, Ty leapt out of the car, jogged around, and opened it for her.

He took her hand and helped her out of the car, pulling her to him in one fluid movement, just as naturally as if he had done it a million other star-filled summer nights. And to her amazement, her arms went around his neck, just as though she'd been doing this all her life too. He found a tendril of dark hair trailing on her shoulder blade, and tucked it behind her ear, kissing first her shoulder blade and then her ear. Finally, his lips found hers. He teased her lips open with his tongue. And then the front pocket of his jeans began to vibrate, and then ring.

"Damn it," he said, reluctantly letting her go. "That's Angie, screaming that I gotta get back. Which I do."

He kissed the tip of Ellis's nose. "To be continued, right?"

"Right," Ellis agreed. "Absolutely."

She made a concerted effort to march briskly up the steps to Ebbtide, turning at the door to watch Ty's car backing down the driveway. She hummed lightly as she swept through the ground floor of the house, checking the locks, corking a bottle of wine somebody had left on the kitchen counter, turning off the lights.

Ellis was halfway up the stairs when she recognized the tune she'd been humming. "Dancing in the Dark." In her bedroom, she hung up the pink sundress, slipped into her cupcake pjs, and climbed under the covers. She stretched and yawned contentedly, and clicked off the lamp on her bedside table. A summer fling! Ellis Sullivan was having herself a summer fling. As Julia had said, "It's about damned time."

# 23

Tuesday morning, Dorie rolled down the elastic waistband of her pajama bottoms so that they barely rested on her pubic bone. She lay flat on the worn chenille bedspread, lifted her chin, and stared down at the soft, pale roundness of her belly. Sometime in the past ten days, when she'd been preoccupied with the future, the present caught up with her.

She closed her eyes and rested the palms of her hands lightly on the bump. Her belly. Her baby. This was really happening. She'd dog-eared her second-hand copy of *What to Expect When You're Expecting*. And at fourteen weeks, she—and the baby—were right on track. Her boobs had grown at least a cup size, spilling out of all her bras and the last bathing suit that still fit. The nausea was gone, she was starting to regain her energy, and just the night before, she was sure—positive, really—that the flutter she'd felt was the baby stirring. Now, if only the rest of her life would get on track.

It was 10 A.M. She'd been watching the clock since waking shortly after seven. At every hour mark, she thought about Stephen. He'd always been an early riser. Should she call him at daybreak? Dorie couldn't bear to think about her husband waking up in Matt's bed. Or would he be alone? At eight, she forced herself to rehearse what she would say when she did call.

"Stephen? There's something I need to tell you. I'm sorry to do this on the phone, but I just couldn't see you before. And I didn't know how to tell you. But now I do. And the thing is . . . I'm pregnant."

She'd imagined a dozen different responses from him. Shock. Disbelief. Anger. Confusion. Happiness? Could this possibly be news he'd welcome? Could he possibly feel what she'd come to feel—deep, unalloyed joy?

The joy was something else that had taken her by surprise. Not that she wasn't still worried about the future—she was! But thinking about this baby gave her a feeling of peace, of such completeness, such absolute rightness, she was almost afraid to allow herself to dip her toe in such a fountain of happiness. The baby books said it was hormonal, but she didn't care. Whatever else happened next, nothing could change the fact of this baby.

At nine, Dorie told herself she should wait. Just a little longer. Let Stephen settle into the day. He would be at school now, she thought, putting together lesson plans for the coming year. Or maybe he'd be in meetings with the rest of the coaches, plotting the soccer team's upcoming season.

Thinking about school, about their colleagues there, made Dorie queasy, and not for the first time. Our Lady of Angels Academy was a small community. Six hundred girls, thirty teachers. It was a Catholic school with conservative values, ruled by the sixty-six-year-old Sister Mary Thomasine, who'd been running OLA with an iron will and a velvet voice since way before Dorie's own school days there. What would Sister Thomasine make of Dorie and Stephen's situation—of Stephen leaving his wife, and for another man? And what would she say about Dorie—and her pregnancy?

Stephen was such an introvert; he had friends on the faculty, but Dorie couldn't think of anybody he might have confided in about the demise of their marriage.

At ten o'clock, she could stand it no longer. She tapped the icon on her phone for Stephen's number, holding her breath, half afraid he would answer, half afraid he wouldn't.

On the third ring, he picked up.

"Dorie?" he was out of breath.

"Hey, Stephen," she said softly.

"Hi," he said. He took a deep breath. She did the same. "It's good to hear your voice."

"Yours too," she said, frowning. He could have called her. He hadn't even tried.

"So," he said finally. "You're still in Nags Head? With the girls?"

"Yes," she said. Stupid question. He knew perfectly well where she was.

"How's it going?" he asked. "Is it as hot there as it is here?"

"Maybe a little cooler," she said. "We had a big rain Sunday, and that cooled things off. How is it down there?"

This was ridiculous, Dorie thought. If she wanted a weather report, she could just look it up on the Internet. She had to quit stalling.

"You know," Stephen said wearily. "It's Savannah in August. Hot. Muggy. Buggy. Pretty much unbearable."

"How's your dad?" Dorie asked. "Any better?"

"Oh." His voice dropped. "Oh, God, Dorie. I . . . you didn't know?"

"Know what?"

"Dorie, I left you a message. On the house phone. I thought you knew. Dad . . . Oh Jesus. Dorie, we lost Dad. It's been, what? A week? I thought you knew."

"What?" she cried. "How would I know? I never check the house phone for messages, Stephen, you know that. Why didn't you call my cell?"

"It all happened so fast," Stephen said, his voice sounding defensive. "They put him in hospice care on a Thursday, and Mom thought, well, we'd still have some time. And the next morning, as soon as she got to his room, he just . . . his heart just stopped."

"Stephen!" She was weeping now. "I am so, so sorry." Sorry for the sweet man Henry had been. For Stephen's mother, a quiet, reserved Midwesterner whom Dorie had never quite felt comfortable calling "Mom." And yes, she was crying for Stephen, and for herself, and for this baby she was carrying, who would never know its grandfather Henry.

"Is your mom okay?"

"You know," he said. "She's sad, she misses him, but my mom isn't one to talk a lot about that kind of stuff. Stoic, I guess that's the word for her."

"Have they already had the funeral?" she asked, sitting up, dabbing at her eyes with the corner of her bedsheet.

"Well, yeah," Stephen said. "It was last week."

"And you didn't think to try to call me? To make sure I knew?" Dorie's face grew hot as her voice rose. "How could you?"

"I just . . . I don't know," he said, his voice drifting away. "I'm sorry, Dorie. After what's happened with us, I didn't know if you would, you know, care."

"So that's it?" she cried. "You sleep with somebody else, move out, and you think that's it, you just click your heels together and we're done? All our history, what we had together, all that's over because you've decided you don't love me anymore?"

"Dorie!" Stephen's voice cracked. "Don't. You know it's not like that."

"No, Stephen," she said. "I don't know that it's not like that. How would I? We haven't talked all summer."

"I tried to call you. I came by the house. You saw me. I know you did. I'm sorry I didn't let you know about Dad. Truly. He loved you, Dorie."

"And I loved him," Dorie said. "Which is why it hurts that you didn't let me know." She was being unbelievably bitchy, unfeeling, cruel even. She sounded just like her mother had, screaming at her father, back in the bad old days. And she just couldn't stop herself. "Let me ask you something, Stephen."

"What?"

"Did you tell *Matt* about your dad's death?"

"Stop it, Dorie," he said.

"Just tell me. Did you?"

"Of course. He was standing right there when I got the call."

"And did *Matt* go to your dad's funeral?"

"God. No. Just stop it, Dorie. I mean, what's the point of all this?"

"Did he go to Omaha with you? Did he?"

"I'm not discussing this with you."

"He did, didn't he?"

"Cut it out."

"No. I won't cut it out. I think I have a right to know who's taking my place. So, I think we've established that Matt went to Omaha. How did you introduce him to your mother? 'Hey Mom, Dorie's out of the picture, meet the little mister?' So now the next question is this: did the two of you sleep in your old room? The one with the *Star Wars* bedspreads and all your soccer trophies? In the same bed *we* slept in?"

"Fuck you, Dorie," he said. "I'm hanging up now."

She had never heard him use that kind of language before. But then, she'd never talked to him this way before either. "Don't you dare hang up," she said shakily. "Wait just a minute. There's a reason I called you today. And I'm so glad I did, since we seem to be sharing secrets."

"What? I've gotta go, Dorie. I don't have time for your crap."

She hesitated, feeling the bile rise in her throat. This was not how she wanted to share this news. Not this way. She did not want to float the baby news on this regrettable torrent of anger. But the toothpaste was out of the tube now, as her grandmother would say. And there was no going back.

"Congratulations, Stephen," she said finally. "You're going to be a father. I'm pregnant."

"What? What did you just say?"

Not the reaction she'd been expecting from him, this sudden deafness.

Dorie took a deep breath, enunciating each syllable with care. She didn't intend to repeat herself again. "I said . . . I'm pregnant."

There was a long silence. She could hear his breathing, rapid and ragged. Maybe he'd just gotten back from a run. Or maybe her news was giving him a heart attack.

"Stephen?"

"I'm here," he said. "Oh, God, Dorie. A baby? When?"

"February. I'm almost four months pregnant."

"Wow. Just . . . I don't know what to say, Dorie. I mean, you call me up and yell at me because I didn't tell you about my dad, and now you just casually blurt out the news about this baby?"

Dorie tried to laugh, but it wasn't funny. "Not so casual. I've been trying to figure out how to tell you for weeks and weeks. I even rehearsed what I'd say.

Somehow, it didn't go as well as I'd planned. I'm sorry I yelled at you. And I'm really so sorry about Henry. The sweetest, dearest man . . . I wish he could have known about the baby."

"A baby," Stephen repeated. "And you're four months already? You couldn't have told me sooner?"

"No," she said simply. "I found out right around the same time we found out about your dad's cancer. I felt guilty, giving you something else to worry about. So I kept waiting for the right time, when you weren't so upset about your dad. And then you were acting so weird and withdrawn, and then, well, Fourth of July happened."

"I see."

Her palms were sweaty. She switched the phone to her right hand, which was trembling. "Well, what do you think?"

"About the baby? I don't know. It hasn't sunk in yet. What do *you* think? I mean, it's not something we'd talked about. And now . . ."

"I'm happy," Dorie said simply. "Despite everything that's happened, I am so happy and excited about this baby. I've got a lot to figure out, but for right now, I am going to concentrate on this child I am carrying. And I am going to be a good mother. I swear, I won't be anything like Phyllis."

"You're nothing like your mother. But do I get any say in any of this?" Stephen asked.

"If you want," she said carefully. "But I think we both know the marriage is over."

"Is it?"

She shook her head. Was he really this dense?

"Yeah. It really is over," she said. "Stick a fork in us. We're done."

His breath slowed, and now she wondered if he was having a stroke instead of a heart attack. "I still love you, you know."

She put her right hand over her belly, and wondered if the baby could hear what he'd just told her. "Do you really?"

"Yeah," he said sadly. "It kinda sucks, doesn't it?"

"And what about Matt?"

He sighed. "What can I tell you? You want me to lie and say there's nothing there? That it was all a big mistake? I can't tell you that, Dorie. No more lies. When my dad got sick, when I flew out there to see him that last time, I knew I probably wouldn't see him again. And I realized it was time. Time to quit lying to myself about who I was and what I wanted."

"It would have been good if you could have told *me* who you were and what you wanted," she said quietly.

"I didn't know how," Stephen said. "I was scared. And ashamed. God help me."

"Oh, Stephen," Dorie said, reaching for the sheet to wipe her eyes again. By the time they were done talking, she'd have to change the bed. "What are we gonna do now?"

"I guess we better start figuring that out," he said. "What about school? Have you told Sister? About us? Or the baby?"

"No," she said. "I haven't told anybody else, besides you and the girls. But I've got a contract, and I intend to work just as long as I can. How about you? Have you told anybody . . . that we've split up?"

"No," Stephen said. "I thought we should talk first. Figure out the next step."

She rolled her eyes. This was how it was going to be. Stephen was never going to be the person to take the first step. He was going to avoid the reality just as long as possible.

"Ellis's brother Baylor has a friend who's a divorce lawyer," Dorie said briskly. "I'm going to talk to him about getting the paperwork started as soon as possible. We'll have to sell the house, I think."

"Why?" Stephen said. "You love that house."

"But I can't afford to live there on just my paycheck. And neither can you." She pointedly did not ask him where he intended to live.

"Dad left me a little money," he started.

"Enough to pay off the mortgage?"

"No, nothing like that," he said hurriedly.

"I rest my case," Dorie said. "Look. I'm going to talk to Baylor's friend. I think you'd better find a lawyer too. And a real estate agent, so we can get the house listed. I'll call you when I find out how we file the papers and everything."

"I don't want a lawyer," he said dully. "You can have everything, Dorie. I want our baby to have a home. And this is all my fault. I did this to you. I hate fighting with you. And I hate the idea of a divorce."

"I hate it too. But you don't want to be married to me anymore. It looks like you want to be with Matt," she reminded him. "You can't have it both ways, Stephen. I don't want to fight with you either, and I have no intention of taking you to the cleaners. I just want half the proceeds from the house. And I'll need child support, of course."

"Dorie?" Stephen sounded urgent. "About the baby. When do you think it happened? I mean, I thought you were taking precautions."

"May," she said, closing her eyes, trying to shut out the memory of that night. "The night before graduation. The end-of-the-year faculty party at Kristin and Bruce's house. We'd both had too much to drink, remember? So instead of driving home, we stayed in their guest room. And . . . you'd been so distant, but that night, you were so being so sweet and silly. It was like when we first met. So . . . we ended up making a baby."

"Yeah," he said softly. "I guess we did. And . . . I guess, despite the rotten timing, I'm glad too. Are you feeling okay? Taking care of yourself?"

"It was a little rocky at first, but the nausea's finally subsided and I'm feeling great now," Dorie said, smiling for the first time. "The girls are totally pampering me."

"Good," Stephen said. "Look, I really have to go now. Will you call me as soon as you get back to town? I really need to see you."

"I will," she promised. "But I'm warning you, I'll be a blimp. See you then."

# 24

It was the first hot, sunny day in nearly a week. Right after breakfast Julia had set up their camp—the quilt, the chairs, the cooler—on their favorite stretch of beach. Then she'd gone for a jog. Julia hated running, but with all the eating and drinking she'd indulged in since arriving in Nags Head, her inner disciplinarian had finally kicked in. Despite what she'd told Booker, eventually, when this month was over, she'd have to find work again. And nobody was going to hire her for a modeling assignment if she showed up looking like the Pillsbury Doughboy. She'd even reverted to her old regime: black coffee and a hard-boiled egg—without the yolk—for breakfast.

And now she was pounding down Virginia Dare Trail when she spotted a familiar figure on a silver beach cruiser pedaling along in front of her. Julia sped up until she came up beside the bicyclist.

"Madison, hi," she called.

Madison looked over, startled. The bike swerved off the pavement and onto the shoulder of the road, and the cool blonde tumbled headfirst over the handlebars.

"Oof." She was sprawled out on her back, in a patch of sandspurs.

"Oh my God," Julia cried. She ran over and squatted down beside the fallen woman. "Are you all right?"

Sand clung to Madison's arms and bare legs and the right side of her face. Blood oozed from a scrape on her elbow.

"Fine," she said, glaring at Julia. "You startled me."

"Sorry," Julia said, offering her a hand up and looking away from the blood, the sight of which was already making her feel light-headed.

Reluctantly, Madison took the hand and hauled herself to a standing position. She looked down at the bike, which had landed hard on the pavement. The front wheel rim was bent. "Damn it," she muttered.

She picked the bike up and grabbed the rim, grimacing as she tried, ineffectively, to straighten it out. Then she set the bike upright and tried to wheel it away, but it wobbled crazily.

"Well, that's all screwed up," Madison said, slamming the bike back onto the pavement.

"I really am sorry," Julia said, taken aback by Madison's burst of anger. "Look, I'll go get Dorie's van. We can load it in there and take it to the bicycle repair shop. There's one just up the road, I noticed it on my run."

"Whatever," Madison said, stony-faced.

Julia touched the other woman's elbow gingerly and looked away quickly. "You're bleeding. Come on, we're just a block from home. Ellis has a first aid kit. We'll get you cleaned up and then come back for the bike. Nobody's going to steal it while it looks like that."

Madison looked back at the bike and sighed. "All right."

Julia was soaked in sweat, her orange nylon running shorts and white tank top clung to her tanned body, and her hair was held back with a white visor. She looked over at Madison, dressed in cheap black capris, a pale blue T-shirt, and no-name sneakers, limping along beside her.

"Did you do something to your ankle?" she asked sympathetically.

"I think maybe I twisted it," Madison grimaced.

"I really am sorry," Julia repeated. "I'll pay to have the bike fixed."

"Don't worry about it," Madison snapped. "It's a piece of junk. Not a big deal." Despite her injured ankle, she sped up.

Julia sped up too, until she was alongside the other woman again. "Have I done something else to offend you?" she asked. "Have the rest of us—Dorie and Ellis—done something to piss you off?"

"No," Madison said. "What makes you think that?"

Julia shrugged. "Every time we see you, every time we ask you to come down and eat with us, or join us on the beach, you act like we want to poison you or something. Dorie says you're just shy, but I think there's something else. Maybe you just plain don't like us?"

Madison kept walking. "I don't have anything against any of you. You all seem like perfectly nice girls. It's just . . . I'm not one of you. Okay? And that's fine with me. I don't want to pledge your little sorority or be your BFF. I just want to pay for my room, and eat my meals, and ride my bike in peace."

"O-kaaaay," Julia said, stung by the outburst. "Fair enough. I'll let the others know. We'll keep our distance, if that's what you want."

They walked on in silence. When they reached Ebbtide, Ellis was on the porch, sweeping off the night's sand deposit.

"What happened?" Ellis asked when she saw Madison, limp and bleeding.

"I fell," Madison said.

"Come on inside, and I'll get the first aid kit," Ellis said.

Dorie was sitting at the table finishing her breakfast when the two women walked in. "Good Lord," she said.

"I fell off my bike," Madison repeated. "It's no big thing."

Ellis got Madison to sit at the table while she gently washed the sand off her scraped elbow, dabbed the abrasion with antiseptic cream, and bandaged it. "What about your ankle?" she asked, lightly touching Madison's ankle, which was already swollen and discolored. "Do you think maybe it's sprained?"

Madison flinched. "It's just a twist," she said, determined to avoid further contact. "It'll be fine."

Dorie jumped up, went to the freezer, and scooped up a handful of ice cubes. "I'll put these in a ziploc bag and we'll fix you up an ice pack to get the swelling down." She looked over at Ellis. "Do you have some aspirin or ibuprofen in that kit?"

Ellis shook a couple of tablets from a bottle and handed them to Madison, who rolled her eyes but swallowed them without water.

Julia came into the kitchen then. "I'm going to take the van and go get your bike and take it to the repair shop," she announced, brushing aside Madison's protests. "You probably don't need to be walking on that ankle."

"She doesn't," Ellis agreed.

"I'm fine," Madison repeated. "I'm just going to go up to my room and wash off all this sand."

"You shouldn't be going up stairs on that ankle," Ellis said, but Madison grabbed the ice pack, pretended not to hear, and kept walking out of the room and up the stairs.

"Geez," Ellis said, watching her go. "What the hell did you do to her, Julia?"

"Nothing! I was jogging back towards the house, and she was in front of me on her bike, so I ran along beside her and said 'Hi!' and she just freaked out and fell off," Julia insisted. "I apologized, I offered to pay for the bike, I totally groveled, but she acts like I did it on purpose."

"She's so prickly," Ellis said, shaking her head. "I totally don't get her."

"I even asked her if we'd done something to offend her."

"What did she say?" Dorie asked.

"She basically told me she doesn't want to play in our sandbox," Julia said, laughing uneasily. "I'm telling you, Ellis, there's something going on with that woman. And I intend to find out what it is."

"Julia," Ellis said, a note of warning in her voice, "leave her alone. You are not Nancy Drew."

"That's what you think," Julia said. "Dorie, I'm gonna take the van and pick up her precious bike and take it to get it fixed. Be back in a few."

Julia pulled the minivan onto the shoulder of the road, directly beside Madison's mangled bike. It was nearly noon and the sun blazed white hot overhead. Her running shoes sank into the soft sand as she stood over the bike, and a bead of perspiration trickled down her cheek. Impatiently, she yanked her top over her head and tossed it inside the car. Dressed in her bright orange running shorts and hot pink sports bra, she bent over and grasped the bike's handlebars with one hand and the rear wheel with the other. As she was transferring the bike into the back of the van she heard a soft clunk. A cell phone had fallen from a purple-and-black foam cup holder bolted to the bike's handlebars.

She knew at a glance whose cell phone it was. The few times Madison had deigned to join the other girls, she had that cell phone clutched tightly in her hand, and Julia had never seen her without it.

She picked it up, and just as she did so, a car's horn blared, and there was a chorus of loud wolf whistles. A battered black Land Cruiser full of shirtless, sunburnt college boys pulled up alongside her. "Hey baby," the driver called. "You need a hand?"

She flashed them what Booker always called her "money smile," the one she'd perfected in her early days of modeling, after studying Farrah Fawcett's iconic red-bathing suit poster. Julia raised her chin, tilted her head slightly to the side, and shook her long hair back over her shoulders. "Fuck off," she said sweetly. She shoved the phone into the pocket of her running shorts, slammed down the van's hatch, and got back in the driver's seat.

The Land Cruiser's driver treated her to another blast of his horn, and then peeled away, leaving a trail of oily black exhaust. "Assholes," Julia muttered. But she was secretly pleased that at thirty-five she still had the looks—and the power—to stop a carload of randy college boys and drive them just a little bit nuts.

Bikes on the Beach occupied the end slot in a small strip mall on Croatan Highway. Every slot in the parking lot was full, so she double-parked and ran into the shop. A middle-aged woman with waist-length dyed black hair sat on a stool at a counter, leafing through a catalog of bicycle parts. "Help you?" the woman asked, looking up.

"I've got a bike in my van with a bent wheel," Julia said. "Is that something you can fix?"

"Sure thing," the woman said. She eased herself off the stool and followed Julia out to the van. The woman easily hefted the bike out of the van. Inside the shop, she gave Julia an index card to fill out, with her name, address, and cell phone number. "My husband does the estimating and repairs, and he just left to deliver some beach chairs down the road. I'll have him call you as soon as he gets a chance to look at it," the woman said.

"How long before it's fixed?" Julia asked, remembering Madison's annoyance at the prospect of being without her bike.

The woman shrugged. "If we've got a replacement wheel, it could be done this afternoon. But if he's got to get one sent over from a supplier, it could be a few days."

"Great," Julia said.

"We got plenty of rentals," the woman said, gesturing at the front of the shop, where a couple dozen bikes of all description were parked.

"I'll let her know," Julia said.

She was getting back into the van when she heard an unfamiliar noise. It sounded like a dog's urgent bark—but it was coming from her hip. Julia reached for her pocket and brought out the cell phone. Madison's phone. The display screen was lit up. UNKNOWN CALLER.

Julia hesitated, but then curiosity got the better of her. "Hello," she said. "Madison's phone."

"Maryn?" It was a man's voice and he didn't sound happy. "Come off it. I know it's you."

Julia frowned. "Who is this?"

"Who the hell is this?" the man demanded.

"This is Julia Capelli," Julia shot back.

"Put Maryn on."

Swiftly, Julia disconnected. "Maryn?" she said softly. "Who the hell is Maryn?"

The phone rang again, almost immediately, and again, the display screen said UNKNOWN CALLER. This time, Julia let it ring. A moment later, the phone dinged, and she saw that the caller had left a voice mail.

She glanced around to see if anyone was watching. The shopping center was nearly a mile from Ebbtide. There was no way Madison could have walked all this way with a sprained ankle, especially not in this heat. But Julia decided not to take any chances.

She pulled the van around to the back of the shopping center and parked behind a dumpster. She touched the icon for voice mail, and the screen showed eight voice mails. Four of them were from someone named Don. She touched the icon and listened to the call that had just come in.

"Maryn, damn it, call me back." It was the same man she'd hung up on. "Don't do this to me. I'm going crazy here. I know you're pissed about what happened, but I can explain. Call me back, okay? Just let me know where you are, and that you're all right. I'm sorry, you know? I didn't mean to hurt you. I would never deliberately hurt you."

It was easily ninety degrees inside the van, but Julia shivered despite the heat. She touched the icon for the next voice mail, and the next, each from someone named Don. In each message, Don addressed his caller as Maryn, and each time, implored her to call him, the urgency in his voice increasing with each message. It was clear to Julia, from the first time she heard Don, that he was also the unknown caller.

"Who the hell is Maryn?" Julia wondered aloud. One caller might have misdialed Madison's phone by accident. But this caller, this Don, had repeatedly called somebody he knew as Maryn.

With her index fingertip, Julia touched the icon that would play back the phone's voice mail message. "This is Maryn," she heard a familiar woman's voice say pleasantly. "Leave me a message and I'll get back to you as soon as I feel like it." The voice was indisputably Madison's.

"I knew it," Julia said. "I knew that chick was a phony."

She looked down at the phone with renewed interest. In just a few moments, she could check call history, she could check Madison's e-mail on that phone too. Just as she was about to do so, the phone began barking again, startling Julia so much that she dropped the phone to the floor of the car. Julia looked warily at the screen. To her amazement, it was Dorie calling.

"Hello?" she said hesitantly.

"Julia, is that you?" Madison's voice was brittle with anxiety. "So you found my phone? Thank God! Was it with my bike?"

"Uh, yeah," Julia said, guiltily. "It fell out of the cup holder. I was just bringing it back there to you."

"Great," Madison said. "See you in a few."

Julia held the phone in her right hand and considered what she'd been about to do. Madison, or Maryn, or whoever she really was, was back at Ebbtide, and she knew Julia had her cell phone. Julia was not somebody who was easily intimidated. But Madison, with her icy stare and aloof demeanor, was potentially a very scary person. As was this unknown man, Don, whoever he was, who had hurt her, and was now begging her to come back.

Gingerly, Julia set the phone down on the passenger seat and started the van's engine. The air conditioner came on, full blast, and Julia shivered again. This time, she didn't know if it was from the frigid air, or the realization of just exactly what she'd gotten herself into.

As soon as she pulled into the driveway at Ebbtide, Madison was out the front door, hobbling towards the van, her hand outstretched for the phone.

"Here ya go," Julia said, handing it over. "Uh, the lady at the bike shop said she'd call me and let me know when it's going to be ready."

"Thanks," Madison said. She looked at the phone, and then at Julia, who found herself going crimson with embarrassment.

"You had a couple of missed calls," Julia offered.

"Uh huh," Madison said. She turned without another word, and went back into the house.

Julia went inside too, and followed the sound of voices coming from the kitchen, where Ellis and Dorie were constructing bacon, lettuce, and tomato sandwiches.

"Want one?" Dorie asked, pointing to the platter of crisp bacon and tomato slices.

"Okay," Julia said. "Well, maybe just the bacon, lettuce, and tomato. No bread." She went out into the hallway and looked up the stairwell, and then came back in the kitchen.

"Did she go back to her room?" Julia asked, her voice soft.

"Who, Madison?" Dorie asked. "Yeah. She said she wasn't hungry. I swear, I don't know why she's so shy."

"Her name's not Madison," Julia said softly. "And she's not just shy. She's a phony."

"What?" Dorie said, putting down her butter knife with a frown. "What are you talking about?"

"Why are we whispering?" Ellis asked.

"I don't want her to hear me," Julia said urgently. "You guys! Her name is really Maryn. Or something like that."

"And how do you know that?" Dorie asked.

"Because while I was retrieving her bike down the road, her cell phone rang, and I just answered it. You know, sort of without thinking."

"Nuh-uh," Ellis said. "You did it on purpose. Don't even try to pretend otherwise. This is us you're talking to, Julia Capelli."

"Okay, fine. I answered it because I wanted to know who was calling her," Julia said readily. "It was a man, and when I answered, I said something like 'Madison's phone', and the guy said, 'Maryn, quit screwing around.' Then, when he realized it really wasn't Madison—or whatever the hell her real name is—he wanted to know who I was. So without thinking, I told him my name. And then I got scared and hung up."

"*You* got scared?" Dorie said, looking incredulous. "Since when does a man scare *you?*"

"This guy was really pissed," Julia said. "So I started messing around with the phone, and I saw she had a bunch of missed calls, and I listened, and they were all from the same guy. Don somebody. Each time, he called her 'Maryn'. He was begging her to call, to come home, telling her he didn't hurt her on purpose. You guys, it was really creepy."

"Maybe he had a wrong number," Ellis offered.

"Nope," Julia said. "I thought of that too. I listened to the message on her voice mail. It's Madison's voice, but she calls herself Maryn."

"Maybe she's in trouble," Dorie said, her brow wrinkled. "She did tell us she'd broken up with her guy. If he physically hurt her, and he's looking for her, maybe that's why she acts so skittish."

"Or maybe she's some kind of criminal on the lam," Julia suggested.

"Oh, Julia," Ellis said, "I'm sure there's a good explanation. Don't be such a drama queen."

"I'm not," Julia protested. And then she had an idea.

"Dorie," she said, holding out her hand. "Give me your cell phone."

"What do you want with it?" Dorie asked, handing it over.

Julia opened a kitchen drawer and found a pencil and pad of paper. She flipped Dorie's cell phone open and scrolled down the call history until she found the number she was looking for.

"What on earth do you think you are you doing?" Ellis asked.

"Just a little detecting," Julia said smugly, snapping the phone closed. She held up the piece of paper. "This is our friend's cell phone number."

"So?" Ellis said.

"So now that I've got it, I'm going to see what I can do to find out who that phone of hers is registered to."

"For Pete's sake," Dorie said. "Don't you have anything better to do with yourself?"

"Not really," Julia admitted, tucking the phone number in her pocket. "Anyway, let's hit the beach while the sun is still shining. I can look this up later."

# 25

An hour later, Julia, Ellis, and Dorie were stretched out on the beach.

"Dorie," Ellis said, tapping her friend's ankle. "Turn over. Your back is getting blistered already."

"I know," Dorie said, propping herself up on an elbow. "I think it must be all the hormones." She stood up and adjusted the beach umbrella, tilting it forward until the upper half of her body was now in its shade. She sat back down and fixed her chair's headrest so that she was propped up at a forty-five-degree angle. Finally, she slathered more sunscreen on her legs, and uncapped a bottle of water from the cooler.

"That's better," she said, after emptying half the bottle in one prolonged gulp. She settled back onto her chair and picked up her magazine again.

"Dorie?" Ellis began. "I'm not trying to be nosy, but did I hear you talking on your phone this morning?"

"Yep," Dorie said. "You guys will be proud of me. I called Stephen and I told him about the baby."

"You did?" Ellis squealed.

"What?" Julia asked, removing her iPod ear buds. "What's she saying?"

"She called Stephen and told him about the baby!" Ellis said excitedly.

"For real?" Julia asked. "Good for you. What'd he say?"

"He was . . . taken aback," Dorie said. "And even more so when I told him we're getting a divorce."

"This came as a shock to him?" Julia asked. "What planet is he living on?"

"The planet denial," Dorie said simply. "He claims he still loves me. But he's totally not ready to give up Matt."

"He told you that?" Ellis asked.

"In so many words," Dorie said. "God. He is just so screwed up, he doesn't know which way to turn."

"Not your problem anymore," Julia said. "You've got yourself and the baby to think about. He's just going to have to get over himself and act like a grown-up."

"You don't know him like I do," Dorie said. "I know I shouldn't but I feel so sorry for him. You guys, his father died. Like, a week ago! And he didn't even call. I yelled at him, and he just said he didn't think I would care. Can you believe that? Henry was my father-in-law! So then I really screamed at him, and I made him admit that he took Matt out to Omaha for the funeral. I was such a bitch! So he told me to fuck off. I don't think I have ever heard him use that kind of language before. God. You should have heard me. I totally sounded just like my mother. It was depressing."

"It was the hormones!" Julia said loyally. "Anyway, whatever you said to him, he totally had it coming."

"You said it yourself," Ellis said. "He's all screwed up. So what next?"

"Well, I'm going to have to do all the heavy lifting when it comes to the divorce," Dorie said. "He doesn't want anything. He says it's all his fault, and he says I can have everything, including the house."

"So take it," Julia advised. "He's the one who screwed around on you. You deserve it."

"No," Dorie said, shaking her head. "We bought the house together. I told him we'll sell the house and split the proceeds. Neither of us can afford to keep it on our own. Although Stephen doesn't know that. I always took care of all the finances. He doesn't have a clue about that kind of stuff."

"If you sell the house, where will you live?" Ellis asked.

"I've been thinking about that," Dorie said slowly. "I guess I could move in with my mom. . . ."

"Phyllis?" Julia said, "Are you nuts? Why would you subject yourself to that kind of torture?"

"She is my mother," Dorie said. "And her house is only five minutes away from school. It's in a much nicer neighborhood than I could afford on my own. I'm pretty sure she'd let me have Nash's old garage apartment, since he's basically living at Granny's house on East Forty-eighth. It's got a little studio kitchen and a bathroom. It's nothing fancy, but that way we wouldn't actually be under the same roof with Phyllis. She retired from teaching last year, so maybe, at first anyway, she'd be willing to help with the baby, just until I get day care figured out."

"Oh, Dorie," Ellis said sympathetically. "Is that really what you want to do?"

"No," Dorie admitted. "But I think it's what I have to do. At least for the short run. I know Phyllis can be pretty difficult sometimes, and I'm dreading telling her about . . . everything . . . but she really does love me. She'd never turn her back on me. Or her grandchild. She's devoted to Willa's kids."

"There has to be a better way," Julia said, flopping back down onto her chair.

"I'd be open to any suggestions," Dorie said. "But in the meantime, it is what it is."

"It sucks," Julia said.

"It really does," Ellis agreed. "But we'll think of something. In the meantime, take my advice and start buying lottery tickets. That's what I've been doing ever since I got downsized."

She took a deep breath. All morning she'd been trying to figure out how to tell Dorie and Julia about her date with Ty without making it seem like it was a big deal. Although it was a big deal for her. A huge deal.

"You guys," she said slowly. "I know we made a girls-only pact when we got down here. But I've got a confession to make."

"You, a confession?" Dorie said lazily. "What did you do? Steal from the grocery kitty?"

"I already know. Ellis has a boyfriend, Ellis has a boyfriend," Julia sing-songed.

Pink tinged Ellis's tanned face.

"Really?" Dorie lifted her sun visor. "Somebody you met here?"

"Right here," Julia said smugly. "On this very beach."

"You met a guy on the beach? Where was I?" Dorie said.

Julia could stand the suspense no longer. "It's garage boy," she said. "Ty Bazemore. Tell the truth, Ellis, you've got a date with Ty, right?"

"Reaallly?" Dorie sighed happily. "That's great, Ellie-Belly."

"Please don't call me that," Ellis said. "Especially within earshot of Ty."

"I wouldn't," Dorie assured her. "Although there's no telling what Julia might do."

"I would never do anything to screw up a romance for Ellis," Julia said loyally. "Just as long as she shares all the smutty bits with us."

Ellis rolled her eyes again. "It's just dinner. I swear, we are not planning to elope. He's . . . nicer than I knew. Really a sweet guy."

Dorie raised her right hand and made the gesture of a benediction. "Then you have our blessing. Anyway, the 'no boys' rule wasn't my idea in the first place. It was Julia's."

"I give," Julia said readily. "Now let's go get our little girl ready for her big night out. Did anybody bring any condoms?"

Dorie giggled. "Don't look at me. Apparently I flunked that lesson."

"Ditto," Julia said, rolling her eyes.

# 26

Ellis had just gotten out of the shower and was peering into the tiny, clouded mirror over her dresser when Julia burst into her room.

"What are you wearing for your big night tonight?" Julia asked, flouncing down onto the bed.

Ellis pointed at the yellow floral sundress hanging on the outside of her closet door. "That."

"Really?" Julia got up and walked over to the closet. She fingered the cotton fabric, rubbing it between her fingers. She glanced at the label sewn into the inside of the dress. "Meh."

"What's wrong?" Ellis asked anxiously. "Too low-cut? Too slutty?"

"Slutty?" Julia asked with a hoot. "My first communion dress showed more skin than this rag. Don't you have anything more . . . tantalizing?"

Ellis's bedroom door opened again and Dorie wandered in, dressed in her pajamas and eating a Popsicle. "What are we doing?" she asked, seating herself on the bed.

"Trying to find something for Ellis to wear out to dinner with Ty that won't make her look like June Cleaver," Julia said. She brandished the yellow sundress. "This is what she had in mind."

"Meh," Dorie said. And then, quickly, "Although Ellis does look nice in yellow."

"Nice is not how you want to look on a date with somebody like Ty Bazemore," Julia said.

"Well, no," Dorie said.

Ellis rolled her eyes. "How should I look, if not nice?"

"Hot," Julia said, without hesitation. "Mind-blowingly hot. Smoking hot. Right, Eudora?"

"Oh yeah," Dorie nodded vigorously. "What you said. Pardon the expression, sex on a stick."

"Easy for you two to say," Ellis retorted. "You wake up in the morning looking hot, and just get better through the day. I wake up looking like . . . me. And Ty's picking me up in an hour, and since we don't have time for a whole-body makeover, I'll settle for nice, if you don't mind. Now you two run along and find something else to do."

"Fine," Julia said, giving the sundress a dismissive flick with her index finger. "Suit yourself. Have a *nice* time tonight. Maybe you two kids can share a banana split after the putt-putt."

Dorie got up too. "Have a good time, sweetie," she said, blowing Ellis an air kiss.

The two friends were at the door when Ellis caved.

"Okay," she said. "I know I'm probably going to regret this, but what did you have in mind?"

Julia and Dorie exchanged high fives. Julia opened Ellis's door with an exaggerated flourish. "Follow me," she said.

Dorie uncapped a frosted jar of moisturizer and applied it to Ellis's face with feathery, practiced strokes.

"Mmm," Ellis said, her eyes closed. "What is this stuff?"

"Fluide d'Agneau," Julia said, tossing an armful of clothes onto the bed.

"It's supposed to be made out of the amniotic fluid of sheep raised by monks on shaded slopes of the Swiss Alps. Two hundred dollars an ounce. You believe that?"

Ellis's eyes flew open. "Good God!"

"Relax," Julia said. "The beauty editor at *Self* loaded me up with goodies from the sample closet the last time I was over there for a shoot." She held up a short zebra-print skirt. "This?"

"No animal prints," Ellis said firmly.

Julia nodded and tossed the skirt aside. She picked up a low-cut orange spandex tank dress that resembled a rubber band with shoulder straps. "Too short?"

"Ellis is five inches shorter than you," Dorie pointed out. "Tight is the issue here. That dress will only work if she wants him to jump her as soon as they get in the car."

Julia picked up and quickly discarded half a dozen more garments. Finally, she held up a flirty short skirt in black flower-sprigged chiffon. The hem of the skirt ended in a bias-cut ruffle. "Too girly?" she asked, holding the skirt at arm's length.

Ellis held her breath. She actually liked that skirt. A lot. But she knew if she made a fuss over it, Dorie and Julia would automatically nix it.

"Not bad," Dorie said. She took the skirt and held it up to Ellis. "It's normal length on her. Don't take this the wrong way, Julia, but you must look like a hoochie mama when you wear this thing."

"My legs are my best asset," Julia said. "And Booker loves me in short skirts."

"Hmm," Dorie said, peering at the skirt's waistband. "I don't see a label. Is this another magazine sample or something?"

"Nope," Julia said. "It's mine."

"You mean you actually bought it with your own money?" Ellis asked.

"No, I actually designed it and made it with my own hands," Julia said.

"No way!" Dorie said. "Really? I didn't know you could sew."

"I fool around with it a little bit," Julia said lightly. "Don't you remember, in eighth grade, when you guys took French II, I took home ec instead? Sister Marguerite made me rip out my zipper, like, two hundred times while you guys were conjugating verbs."

"We took French, but I can just barely order bouillabaisse," Ellis said. "And in the meantime, you're making your own clothes?"

"Not all the time," Julia said. "When I get bored, or I get an idea, if I have the time, I'll make something. I actually like the drawing part better than the sewing, because I can do that on planes or in a hotel room."

"Amazing," Ellis said, turning to Dorie. "Did you know she could sew?"

"She's pretty good at secrets," Dorie said. "It's part of that whole witch thing. What kind of a top?" she asked, turning back to the skirt.

"I have a cute white blouse," Ellis started to say, knowing immediately that this was a misstep.

Dorie wrinkled her nose. "No white. What do you wear that with, Julia?"

Julia's eyes lit up. "Wait. This will be genius." She went to the battered wooden dresser and pulled out what looked like a scrap of black lace. "Ta-da!"

"Okay," Ellis said, eyeing the lace warily. "What do I wear over the bra?"

"This is not a bra," Julia said. "It's a corset top. Just the hottest look this season. It's a knockoff of a Gaultier. I wore it for a shoot in the Bahamas this past winter." She held the top up against the skirt.

"Yum!" Dorie said enthusiastically.

"Nuh-uh," Ellis said, defiantly crossing her arms over her terry cloth–clad breasts. "I am not going out on a first date wearing a bra for a blouse. No how, no way."

"You're not listening, Ellis," Julia said, trying to stay patient. "This is not the bra."

She went back to the dresser and brought out a pink lace push-up bra. "*This* is your bra." She held it up in front of her own black tank top, and then placed the corset over it. "See? Two sets of straps. Very alluring."

"Oh yeah," Dorie chimed in. "Adorable. You gotta wear it, Ellis."

"I don't know," Ellis said. "I'm already jumpy as hell. You guys wouldn't understand. I haven't dated, uh, in a really long time. I need to wear something that's in my comfort zone. Maybe if this thing with Ty works out, I could wear this next time."

"Nuh-uh," Julia said, holding her ground. "We've seen your comfort zone. Granny panties and cotton schmatas. Come on, Ellis, just try it on, okay?"

"Yeah, Ellis," Dorie said. "If you really, really hate it, you don't have to wear it. Just try it on for me. Pretty please?"

"Oh, all right," Ellis said. She threw her robe onto the bed and grabbed for the bra. She glanced at the shell-pink satin label. "34C?" She looked over at Julia. "Since when are you a C cup?"

Julia gave them a sheepish grin. She cupped her hands under her breasts. "Since last year," she said. "Implants. The girls were starting to get a little droopy, so I had them hiked up and upsized."

"Really?" Dorie's eyes were big as saucers. "I hadn't even noticed. What was that like?"

"No big thing. I couldn't work for a couple weeks, 'til the swelling went down and they removed the drains."

"Drains?" Ellis made a face. "That doesn't sound like fun."

"It's not supposed to be fun," Julia said. "It's business, that's all. But the boob job wasn't nearly as bad as when I had my nose done. Now that was a major pain. You should have seen the bruising. I looked like I'd been worked over with a baseball bat."

"Julia!" Ellis said. "I had no idea you'd had your nose done. And I've known you all your life." She got up and stood inches away from Julia's face, gingerly touching her nose. "You can't even tell."

"That's because I had the best plastic surgeon money could buy," Julia said.

"What was wrong with your old nose?" Dorie asked. "I mean, it couldn't have been all that bad. You've been modeling since you were nineteen."

"Too ethnic," Julia said. "I had the Capelli schnoz. And I gotta tell you, the first time my daddy saw me after the surgery, and figured out what I'd done, he was brokenhearted. It really hurt his feelings. But I told him it's just business. When you're in this business, your body and your face are your equipment. And you gotta take care of your equipment."

Dorie sat back down on the bed and leaned against a stack of pillows. "Julia, you keep talking about how you're too old and your career is over. But I don't get it. You're more beautiful than ever. Your skin is great, your body is to die for. Who wouldn't hire you?"

Julia flashed Dorie a grateful smile. "You're sweet, Eudora. But you don't understand my world. I'm thirty-five. The girl on the cover of *Elle* this month is seventeen. She wears a size zero. If that. And don't talk to me about Heidi Klum, because she is not the norm. Anyway, I was never Heidi Klum. I was Julia Capelli, who had a couple of lucky breaks and knocked around Europe and did some editorial and runway work. And now, well, that's all winding down. I look good to you guys because you love me, and you don't know any better. But it's okay. Don't worry about me. I'll get it figured out. I always do, right?"

Ellis had been concentrating on lacing up the black satin ribbons criss-crossing the corset top. She sucked in her breath and tied the ribbon in a double knot.

"There is so much more to you than just your looks, Julia," Ellis said. "You're smart. Really smart. And don't give me that crap about never going to college. I'm not talking about degrees. You know real stuff. You've traveled everywhere, you know art and books and music. You've met people! Look at me, I've got a degree in finance, but I spent nearly fifteen years locked up in a bank vault—and what did it get me? Fifteen years of hanging out with pencil pushers and bean counters. And now I don't even have a job."

"And what about me?" Dorie put in. "I'm ten credit hours away from having a master's degree in secondary education. I spend my days trying to pound sentence structure into teenage girls who could give a crap. Don't get me wrong, I love my job, and I love the girls, but a sanitation worker in Savannah makes more money than I do."

"But you have careers," Julia said. "And you both have a piece of paper that s*ays* you're smart. And I don't. I'll tell you the truth: If it weren't for the money, which is very, very nice, I wouldn't care if I never got another modeling job. I even told Booker that the other night. I am so over all of that. But modeling is all I know."

"No, it's not," Ellis said. "You know a lot about lots of stuff." She picked up the black chiffon skirt and slipped it over her head, then turned with her back to Julia so that she'd zip it up. "What about this?" she said, turning and shaking her hips so that the flounce softly flared. "This skirt is amazing. I'd totally buy something like this, wouldn't you, Dorie?"

"If they made it in a maternity size," Dorie said. "What about it, Julia, have you ever thought about designing clothes instead of modeling them?"

Julia shrugged and waved her hand dismissively. "This is just something I like to mess with. Anyway, you don't know how the industry works. You don't just buy a bunch of sewing machines and call yourself a fashion designer."

"But you do know how it works," Ellis pointed out. "You've been around the business since you were a kid. Come on, Julia. Tell the truth, if you could do anything at all with your life, what would it be?"

"You mean when I grow up?" Julia snorted.

"Yes," Dorie said quietly. "Next week. Next year. What would you be?"

"Hold that thought," Ellis said, peering into the mirror on the back of Julia's closet door. She held her arms out. "I can't wear this, y'all. I'm sorry. But I feel naked in this rig."

"Here," Julia said, thrusting a filmy black jacket in her direction. "Put this on. And quit being such a baby."

Ellis slid her arms into the jacket. It was a nearly sheer, cobwebby fabric, with tight-fitting sleeves that flared gently at the wrists. At least it covered her shoulders. She did a little pirouette. "You think?"

"Absolutely," Dorie said, applauding. "Perfection. You look amazing." She turned to Julia. "And you, my friend, are a genius. So how are we going to put all that talent to work?"

Julia took a deep breath. "Well . . . actually, the job I want isn't in front of a camera. It's behind it."

"You want to be a photographer?" Ellis asked. "I've never even seen you with a camera."

"Not a photographer, a stylist," Julia said. "A photo stylist."

"Really?" Dorie asked, starting to apply makeup to Ellis. "What all does that entail?"

"The stylist is the one who's responsible for the look of a shoot," Julia said. "She shops for all the props and accessories, fluffs everything and makes it pretty—whether it's a modeling shoot, or a food or interiors piece. I've always loved to mess around with that kind of stuff."

Ellis lifted her face to allow Dorie to brush mascara onto her lashes. "So do it, already."

"I'd love to," Julia said. "But it's nearly impossible to break into. It's really competitive. And unfortunately, with print magazines going out of business right and left, the job market sucks right now."

"Could Booker help you get a job as a photo stylist?" Dorie asked. She was lightly fluffing powder over Ellis's cheeks.

"Probably."

Julia leaned in to assess Dorie's handiwork. She picked up a flat black compact and a long-handled brush and handed it to her. "Excellent. Now put some of this blusher across her cheekbones and contour it just along the edge of her jawline."

Dorie nodded and went to work. "Have you told Booker you want to be a photo stylist?"

"Noooo," Julia said, picking up a comb and going to work on Ellis's hair. "It's just something I've been thinking about. I'd probably have to get a job as a stylist's assistant first."

"What does a stylist's assistant do?" Ellis asked.

"Grunt work," Julia said. "You make the cappuccino runs, help load and unload the props and equipment, catalog and return the props to the stores where you bought or borrowed them. Nothing glamorous about it. And the pay is shit."

"And you told me Booker wants you to move back to the States and marry him," Ellis added. "So tell me something, Julia Capelli. What's your problem?"

"I don't know," Julia admitted. "I wish I did."

Julia gathered Ellis's thick straight hair in one hand and picked up a pair of scissors in the other. "Good Lord, Ellis," she complained. "You've been wearing your hair—parted straight down the middle, down to your shoulders—like this since sixth grade. Talk about a rut."

Ellis looked up in alarm. "You are not going to make me change my hair. I can't. I just can't."

Dorie and Julia exchanged a look.

"Ellie-Belly," Dorie said plaintively. "Don't you trust us?"

"No," Ellis said firmly, taking the scissors away from Julia. "I'll wear the corset-thingy. I'll wear the skirt. I'll even wear this damned pink push-up bra that is poking me in the ribs. But I am not letting her cut my hair. Not. Happening."

"All right," Julia said, her expression clearly saying it was not all right. "I'll do what I can. But at least let me try something new. Okay?"

"No cutting," Ellis said between her clenched teeth.

"Wimp," Julia muttered.

"Bitch," Ellis answered back. But she was grinning. And as Julia gathered her hair at the nape of her neck, twisted, and then expertly pinned it up, she blinked. Between the hair and the makeup, she looked like someone completely different. Like herself, but prettier.

There was a polite tap at Julia's bedroom door. The three of them turned to see Madison leaning into the room. Her face was pale beneath the bandage on her cheek, and ugly bruises had already blossomed on her elbow.

"Wow," Madison breathed. "Ellis, you look amazing."

"See?" Julia and Dorie cried in unison.

"Hey, Dorie," Maryn said. "I hate to bother you, but I'm wondering if I could borrow some more ibuprofen. My ankle's kinda starting to throb."

"You poor thing," Dorie said, getting up from the bed. "It's in my room. I'll get it and come right back." As she passed her in the doorway, Dorie bent down to get a better look at Madison's ankle. "It's really swollen now," she reported. "I've got an Ace bandage in my first aid kit. I'll bring that too." She gestured towards Julia's bed. "Sit over there," she ordered.

"Oh no," Madison demurred.

"Sit!" Ellis repeated.

Madison clearly looked uncomfortable perched on the edge of Julia's bed. She looked around the room, and then back at Ellis. "Special occasion?" she asked.

Ellis blushed. "Just a dinner date. But Julia and Dorie decided I needed an extreme makeover."

Madison nodded hesitantly at Julia. "Great job."

"Thank you," Julia said, reluctant to accept the compliment.

Ellis glanced at the clock on Julia's bedside table. "Okay, are we done here? Because he's picking me up in, like, ten minutes."

"What about shoes?" Julia asked. "I shudder to think what kind of shoes you'd planned to wear tonight."

"I didn't bring that many shoes," Ellis said. "Mostly just flip-flops and tennis shoes. The only thing I have that would go with this rig is my black ballet flats."

"God no," Julia said swiftly. She went back to the open closet, but stopped and frowned. "No good. My feet are like gunboats. I wear a ten, and you're like, what, a size six?"

"Six or seven," Ellis said. "The ballet flats will be fine."

"Ballet flats?" Dorie said, arriving with pill bottle and first aid kit in hand. "No, no, no. You need some strappy little sandals with heels with that skirt. I've got just the thing. Can you squeeze into my fives?"

"Not if I want to walk," Ellis said dryly. "Guys, it's fine. It's just a pair of shoes."

"It's never *just* a pair of shoes."

All three heads swiveled in Madison's direction. She stood, wincing. "Don't move. I'll be right back."

"Where are you going?" Dorie cried. "You really shouldn't walk until I get you taped up. . . ."

But Madison was already limping down the hall, towards the stairway.

Five minutes later, she was back, dangling a pair of wicked-looking sandals. They had a tangle of black grosgrain ribbon straps, three-inch spike heels, and the soles were an audacious red.

"Perfect!" Dorie said, clapping her hands in delight.

"Christian Louboutin?" Julia said, raising one eyebrow. "You bring Christian Louboutins to the beach?"

Madison handed the sandals to Ellis and sank down onto the bed. "So kill me. I have a thing for nice shoes. Anyway, I got them on end-of-the-season clearance last summer." She nodded at Ellis. "I'm a seven and a half, but Louboutins run small. Go ahead. Try 'em on."

Ellis examined the shoes carefully. "But these have hardly been worn," she said, tapping the bright crimson, unmarred shoe sole. "I can't wear your brand-new shoes."

"Sure you can," Madison said easily. "Look, in my old life, I had several pairs like this. But all that's gone. I don't even know why I packed 'em. Please, Ellis. I would love it if you'd wear them tonight."

"I don't know," Ellis said, but she slid her feet into the sandals and fastened the straps. She stood, wobbily, and did a slow pirouette.

Dorie and Ellis applauded and whistled. Even Madison gave a quick golf clap.

"Wait one minute," Julia said. She scrabbled around in a quilted satin box on her dresser before triumphantly holding up a pair of dangly chandelier earrings made from crystals and jet beads.

Ellis screwed the earring backs to the posts. "Done," she said. She blew kisses to her friends and tottered towards the door. "Gotta go. Thanks, guys. I mean it. You're the best."

"Run along," Dorie said. "Have fun. Okay? You do remember how to have fun, right?"

"And don't do anything I wouldn't do," Julia advised.

"I can't think of anything you wouldn't do," Ellis said.

Julia nodded approvingly. "That's my point."

# 27

The girl who answered the door at Ebbtide looked only vaguely like the Ellis Sullivan Ty had seen on the beach and on Sunday night at Cadillac Jack's.

Ty was no fashion expert, but it looked to him as though Ellis had been transformed. She was wearing some kind of lacy, low-cut black lingerie-looking top with a cobwebby jacket sort of thing over it. The hem of her skirt barely brushed the tops of her knees, and she was wearing some ridiculously high heels. Her hair was in some kind of sophisticated updo, with earrings that nearly brushed the tops of her nearly bare shoulders.

She opened the screen door and stepped onto the porch, giving him a shy smile. "Hey," she said.

He knew he was staring, but he couldn't help himself. "You're beautiful," he blurted. Mental headslap. Of course she was beautiful. Ellis Sullivan was beautiful in those goofy cupcake boxers, with her hair in a lopsided ponytail. But tonight, she was different. He'd have said she looked spectacular, if he were the kind of guy who ever used the word "spectacular."

Ellis blushed. "Julia and Dorie double-teamed me," she said. "I feel sorta like Cinderella. This is all borrowed finery. The only thing I'm wearing that's my own is my panties." She gasped and blushed even harder. "Sorry. TMI again. You seem to have that effect on me."

"Whatever you're wearing, it's working," Ty said. He gestured down at the khaki slacks he'd so laboriously pressed and the starched white button-down shirt, which he'd found still in the dry-cleaner's bag at the back of his closet, along with his navy blazer, which he hadn't worn since the time when, in one last desperate attempt to rein him into the family fold, Kendra had dragged him to a cocktail party at her father's country club. He'd even polished his best loafers until they shone like they hadn't since the day he bought them. No socks, though. He had to draw the line somewhere.

"Sorry, but this is all my own stuff," he joked. "Good thing Julia and Dorie aren't here to see me."

He took her hand and led her down the porch steps to the Bronco, which he'd washed and vacuumed earlier in the day. He'd even thrown away all the beer bottles and fast-food wrappers.

"Oh, they can see you, all right," Ellis said, nodding her chin just slightly north. "They're watching us from the window in Julia's room."

Ty glanced up, but all he saw was the slightest twitch of a curtain. "Let's give 'em something worth watching," he said, taking Ellis's hand and kissing the back of it before he opened the car door and helped her in. Then he turned and waved, and the curtain twitched again. As he pulled the Bronco out of the driveway, he saw Ellis, glancing nervously in the rearview mirror.

He'd chosen a seafood restaurant in Duck, twenty minutes north of Nags Head. It was a tiny place at the end of a gravel road, at a marina overlooking the sound. It had weathered cedar-plank walls, a rusted tin roof, and a buzzing neon sign out front that said FISH FOOD.

"Don't let the decor scare you," Ty said, parking the car. "This is the best food on the Outer Banks."

"This looks very nice," Ellis said with a look of surprise after they'd been shown to their table at a window overlooking a long row of docks. "You know, before we came down, I sent away for the chamber of commerce information packet, and I even bought the Mobil Outer Banks travel guide, and not one of them mentioned this place."

"You sent away for stuff?" Ty laughed. "Who does that?"

"I do," Ellis said. "I don't like surprises. And anyway, they usually have good coupons. You know, for, like, a free appetizer or dessert."

"I thought all women loved surprises," Ty said. "Anyway, you won't find Fish Food in a restaurant guide. And I'm pretty sure they don't give coupons. This is kind of a local place. Eddie, the chef, used to wait tables at a restaurant I worked at in high school. He's got kind of a squirrely sense of humor, but he knows his way around the kitchen."

The waitress came, and Ty asked Ellis if she wanted a drink. "I'll have a Blue Dawg—you've got that on draft, right? And she'll have . . ." He looked over at Ellis, trying to remember what she'd ordered Sunday night, at Cadillac Jack's. "A cosmo, right?"

They chatted aimlessly until the waitress was back with their drinks and the menus.

"What's good here?" Ellis asked, looking down at the grease-spattered photocopied sheet of paper.

She was sitting up very straight in her chair and was fiddling with the ribbon that seemed to tie her top together in the front. When she wasn't trying to hike the top up to keep her breasts from further spilling out, she was tugging at the hem of her short skirt, which was a lost cause anyway. The skirt barely brushed the tops of her thighs, which were lightly dusted with freckles, as was her nose, or what he could see of her nose underneath the layer of sparkly powder covering it. Ty's fingers itched to reach across the table and yank at both ends of the ribbons, just to see what would happen. Was that pink lace bra thing attached to the girdle-looking top she was wearing? He decided that would need further study.

"Ty? Oh my God, is that really you?"

He looked up. Kendra and Ryan were standing, waiting to be seated at the next table over. He felt the blood drain from his face. And now Kendra was actually coming over to their table, with Ryan, that fuckhead, trailing right behind.

Kill me now, Ty thought. Right here.

"It is you," Kendra said shrilly. "All dressed up in your Sunday best."

Ty Bazemore had been "raised right," at his mother's and grandmother's insistence. Two years of cotillion, relentless etiquette drilled into him. You addressed your elders as "sir" and "ma'am." You stood when a lady entered the room, and you greeted a gentleman by looking him in the eye, smilingly, with a firm handshake. Reluctantly, Ty stood. "Hi, Kendra," he said, his face expressionless. He nodded in Fuckface's direction. "Ryan." He would not shake Ryan's hand. If his mother had been alive, even she would have understood. If his grandmother had been alive, she would have applauded, or maybe smacked Fuckface across the face with her ever-present flyswatter.

"Hey, dude!" Ryan, clueless, held out his hand, but when Kendra shot him a withering glance, he dropped it back to his side.

"How are you?" Kendra gave him a hug, standing on her tiptoes, even in heels, to do it. He was enveloped in a toxic cloud of her signature scent, which, to him, smelled like overripe pineapples.

"Just fine," Ty said, extending only a wooden, one-handed half hug. When she finally released him, he took a step backwards, just in case Fuckface got any ideas. He would throw away this blazer and shirt when he got home. *If* he got out of here alive.

"Really?" Kendra said, frowning. "You're sure? I've been thinking about you a lot lately. Ever since we moved back. Did you know? Daddy finally talked me into joining the firm. Of course, I think he only did it because he knew he'd get Ryan as part of the package. A twofer, he calls it."

"Great," Ty said. "Congratulations." If there was a bigger, more pompous asshole than Boomer Wilcox on the Outer Banks, Ty had never met him. Ryan and Boomer deserved each other.

"We heard you're day trading," Kendra said, her voice oozing concern. "I know that's got to be tough in this economy, right?"

"It's all right," Ty said, managing to unclench his teeth. "You win some, you lose some." He looked desperately around the room, hoping that some-thing, somehow, would make this horror show grind to a halt. A lightning bolt, maybe. But he'd settle for a minor grease fire.

And now he saw Ellis, still seated, looking up at him, smiling expec-tantly. In his mind's eye, he could see his grandmother's flyswatter hovering at the back of his neck, just waiting to deliver a smack, should he forget his upbringing.

"Kendra, Ryan, this is Ellis, my, uh, friend."

"Oh, hi," Kendra said, her voice going up a decibel. "Alice?"

"Actually, it's Ellis," Ellis said. "With an E."

"Hiya, Ellis," Ryan said, automatically extending his hand. Ellis, who had apparently also undergone some rigorous training—and who, after all, had no history with Kendra or Fuckface—stood, smiled radiantly, and shook both their hands.

"Ellis is such an unusual name," Kendra was saying. "I don't believe I've ever met a woman named Ellis before. Are you from around here?"

"No," Ellis said, "I'm originally from Savannah. My friends and I are visit-ing here for the whole month."

"How did you happen to pick the Outer Banks for vacation?" Kendra asked. "I mean, of course, we adore it, but then, I grew up here."

"It was sort of a compromise," Ellis explained.

"Wonderful!" Kendra trilled. "Where are you staying? Here at Duck?"

"We're staying down at Nags Head," Ellis said.

Ty felt his scalp prickle at the mention of Nags Head. A slow dread started to work its way south. He knew what was coming, and he was powerless to stop it.

"Oh!" Kendra said. "Nags Head. That's my old stomping grounds, you know. Mama and Daddy have Cedar Haven. Do you know it? It's that huge, rambling, old pile of junk on the Beach Road."

Ryan wrapped a proprietary arm around Kendra's waist. "She calls it a pile of junk," he said with a chuckle. "What she doesn't tell you is that Cedar Haven is one of the original houses on Nags Head. There's only about a dozen of 'em. The 'unpainted aristocracy,' they call them. It's a showplace. Five thousand square feet, and it sits on an ocean-side double lot. Her grandfather built the first swimming pool on Nags Head there."

"I think I know that house," Ellis said excitedly. "It's about a mile from where we're staying. On Virginia Dare, right?"

Don't say it, Ty pleaded silently. Do not go there.

"Where are you staying?" Kendra asked.

"The house we're renting is kind of a dump," Ellis confided. "I mean, it could be wonderful, but it hasn't really been maintained in a while."

Ty looked frantically around the dining room. The waitress was approaching with a basket of bread and a cruet of olive oil. Deliverance. He wanted to kiss her on the lips.

"Hey, listen," he said. "Here comes our bread. We don't want it to get cold. They have awesome yeast rolls here. Eddie makes them himself." He pulled Ellis's chair away from the table and practically shoved her into it. "Good to see you guys," he said, giving Kendra and Ryan a dismissive nod.

Kendra gave him an odd look, but she allowed herself to be herded back to her table.

"They seem nice," Ellis said, helping herself to one of the yeast rolls.

If you only knew, Ty thought.

Dinner was agony. He ordered for both of them, and he tried to act normal. But every time he looked at Ellis, he saw the table just behind her. Kendra and Fuckface, laughing, talking, their golden heads bowed together. Every once in a while, Kendra would see him looking, and she'd lean in closer, her hand hiding her mouth, whispering something in her husband's ear. They were talking about him, he knew. Mocking him in his yellowing dress shirt and frayed college graduation blazer with the sleeves just a quarter inch too short. His stomach burned.

Their entrées took a lifetime to arrive. He couldn't have said what he ordered. It was hot, and it was vaguely seafoodish looking. Somehow, he managed to choke it down. Ellis picked at her broiled swordfish, nibbling delicately at the steamed broccoli and the couscous on her plate.

At one point, the waitress appeared with a bottle of chilled wine. It was Moët & Chandon Nectar Imperial Rose; Ty knew the label well. Sixty bucks a bottle, and that was if you bought it at Harris Teeter. "We didn't order this," he said, pushing the wine bucket away.

"The lady and gentleman at that table there sent it over. With their compliments," the waitress said.

He looked up, and Kendra gave him a little finger wave. The Imperial Rose was her favorite, and it had triggered many a fight when they were practically penniless first-year law students at Carolina. Their friends were all in the same boat, living on ramen noodles and Hot Pockets. When they had parties, they were glad to swill whatever rotgut was on sale. But Kendra, who said life was too short to drink bad wine, would appear with a bottle of her Moët & Chandon, paid for with the money Boomer had transferred into their checking account every month.

"How nice," Ellis murmured. Ty couldn't send the bottle back, not without making a scene. So he allowed the waitress to pour Ellis a glass, but he'd be damned if he'd touch the stuff himself. Instead he asked for another draft Blue Dawg.

He emptied the glass in a couple of long swigs. Ellis sipped hers slowly.

A dead, awkward silence fell over the table. He thought he'd averted disaster, but he'd been wrong.

The waitress came back to their table. She was a local, with purple-streaked blond hair and too much black eyeliner and a tattoo of an octopus whose swirling tentacles slithered all the way across her chest and probably cost more than the girl made in a week working for Eddie. She looked down at their half-eaten meals and shrugged, although she didn't bother to pick them up. "Dessert?" she asked, putting a large black slate on a stand on the table. "Eddie's got fresh peach cobbler with homemade lemon-basil gelato, and the cheesecake tonight is turtle track, which means it's done with toasted pecans and butterscotch topping..."

Ty gave Ellis a questioning glance. "I don't know," she started to say.

"Just the check, please," Ty said brusquely.

And of course it took her forever to come back with the check. Ellis sipped her wine and Ty drummed the tabletop with his fingers, determined not to look over at Kendra's table.

Finally, the waitress brought the check. He was tucking the cash in the leather-bound check holder, his escape imminent, when out of the corner of his eye, he saw Ryan get up from his table and start to approach.

Ty tried to calm himself. Even Fuckface had a right to go to the men's room, and he couldn't get there without passing the table where Ty and Ellis had been seated.

But no, Ryan stopped right beside their table. Ty stood and pulled Ellis's chair out, his back to Ryan, determined to make his escape unscathed, even if it meant ignoring Fuckface.

"Hey Ty, buddy," Ryan said, putting his hand on Ty's sleeve, leaning in, talking low, confidentially. Like they were old pals. "Look, Kendra and I were just talking. We saw the notice about Ebbtide in the legal ads. Kendra was saying Ebbtide's been in your family as long as Cedar Haven's been in hers. Helluva note, losing it after all these years. Thing is, we're in the market for a place of our own. So maybe we could help each other out."

Ty froze. Could this really be happening?

Ryan reached into the inner pocket of his sport coat and came out with a sterling silver monogrammed card case. Somewhere, in the boxes he'd never unpacked after moving back to Nags Head, Ty had an identical card case, although with his own initials monogrammed on it. His had been a wedding gift from Kendra's mother, who was never noted for her originality.

Now Ryan was holding out a business card, casually, between his thumb and forefinger. "Gimme a call, will ya? No need to let the bank take Ebbtide."

Ty dropped the card onto Ellis's plate of half-eaten swordfish. He took Ellis's hand and pulled her not so gently away from the table. Away from a restaurant called Fish Food. And Kendra and her fuckface new husband and their sixty-dollar bottle of pink wine.

# 28

Ellis allowed herself to be rushed out of the restaurant and practically slung into Ty's Bronco. She managed to keep her temper tamped down for maybe five minutes. Then she exploded.

"*You* own Ebbtide?"

He winced, then nodded. "I do. For now, anyway."

"And Mr. Culpepper? Our crusty-but-kindly landlord?"

Ty sighed. "You're looking at him."

"This whole time? I've been e-mailing *you*? Asking Mr. Culpepper about *you*? Complaining about *you*?"

"Afraid so," Ty admitted.

"Cute," Ellis said, biting off the word. "I bet you think you're really cute, pulling one over on me like that. I bet you've been laughing your ass off at me, over there in that garage of yours."

"Look, it wasn't just about you," Ty said. "I never tell my tenants about Mr. Culpepper. If they knew the landlord lived just over the garage, I'd never get any peace. They'd be hammering on my door at midnight, bitching about the hot water heater, or the bugs, or any damned thing. Or they lose their key. And I'm supposed to drop what I'm doing because they can't keep track of something as simple as a key? You wouldn't believe what a pain in the ass people can be. This way, I'm just some anonymous slacker dude next door. If they want something from Culpepper, they have to e-mail him. And he takes care of it. Eventually."

"And I'm the biggest pain in the ass of all, right?" Ellis said. "Bitching night and day."

"Well, yeah, at first," Ty said truthfully. "I mean, I thought you were a pain in the ass at first, but then, when I met you, well, it was different. Hey, I got you a new stove, didn't I? And those dishes with the pink flowers? Those were my grandmother's dishes, you know. And I wanted to tell you about Mr. Culpepper, I really did."

"But you didn't," Ellis said, crossing her arms over her chest. Julia's underwire bra was cutting into her rib cage, and the corset thing was tied so tightly she couldn't breathe, but she didn't dare touch the ribbons lacing it together, for fear she'd explode out of the stinking thing. Why the hell had she let the girls talk her into this outfit? What was she doing with this loser, this liar?

"I was going to," Ty said. "Like, tonight. I was going to tell you. But I didn't get the chance."

"Unbelievable," Ellis said. She turned and stared out the window.

Eventually, they pulled into the crushed-shell driveway at Ebbtide. He parked the Bronco beside the garage, and before he could get out and come around to open her door, she opened it herself and was out of the car like a shot.

"Ellis," he started.

"Thanks for dinner . . . Mr. Culpepper," she said. It was all she could do to keep from running into the house. Anyway, she couldn't have run in those damned high-heeled sandals Madison had loaned her. She walked, head up, back straight, just as fast as she could, without as much as a backward glance at Ty Bazemore, aka Mr. Culpepper. And when she got to the screen door at the house, its slam echoed in the still, hot, summer air.

. . .

Dorie and Julia heard the screen door slam from the kitchen, where they'd been playing a desultory game of Hearts.

"What the hell?" Julia said, glancing at the kitchen clock. It was barely nine o'clock.

They heard the furious tapping of the stiletto heels on the worn wooden hall floors, then heard them ascending the stairs, and then the second slam, of a bedroom door.

"Uh-oh," Dorie said. "That can't be good."

"Damn," Julia nodded in agreement. "And I had such high hopes." She raised an eyebrow. "Do you think we should go up there and talk to her?"

"Ix-nay," Dorie said, yawning. "If she wanted to talk about it, she'd come looking for us. You know how Ellis is."

"I do," Julia agreed. She sighed loudly. "I really thought this guy might be it, you know? He's totally hot, and he's hot for her, and I thought she was kinda hot for him."

"You know something I don't?" Dorie asked suspiciously.

"I kinda saw them making out the other night," Julia said sheepishly.

"What?" Dorie slapped her cards down on the table. "And you held out on me? In my condition?"

"It was totally by accident," Julia said. "Not like I was spying on them or anything. It was late, and Booker called, and I was kinda pacing around the room talking to him. I just happened to look out my window, and I saw this couple—just, wrapped up in each other, out on that boardwalk over the dunes. And it was just so sweet, you know? Summer love, that whole thing. It wasn't until they pulled apart—reluctantly, I might add—and the girl was walking back towards the house, that I realized it was our Ellie-Belly. With garage guy."

"I'd never say this to Ellis, but Ty doesn't really seem like her type," Dorie mused. "I mean, don't get me wrong, I think he's adorable, but nothing like the guys she used to be attracted to."

"She is, though," Julia said. "Sunday night, when we were at Cadillac Jack's? That whole 'I've got cabin fever, let's us girls go out on the town?' All a ploy. She knew he was working there that night. She only dragged me along so it wouldn't look like she was stalking him. You should have seen Ty's face when he caught sight of her, Dorie. There were all these hoochie mamas and pretty young things hanging around the bar, hoping he'd give them a glance, but when he saw Ellis, it was like he'd just been handed the biggest lollipop in the store." She sighed. "So, so, sweet. And of course, Ellis was all nervous and tingly. Dorie, did you know she hasn't, like, been with anybody since whatsisname?"

"Doesn't surprise me," Dorie said. "After whatsisname, I didn't think she'd ever allow herself to fall for another man."

"She tried, though," Julia said. "She was doing online dating! Do you believe that?"

"I know a lot of girls who've met their husbands online," Dorie said. "But I am a little surprised that our Ellis got up the nerve to try it. And that she admitted it to you."

"I swore not to tell," Julia said. "But she had to know I'd tell you."

Dorie patted Julia's hand. "That's all right. You're great at keeping your own secrets, but everybody else's? Not so much." She yawned again. "God, I feel like I can never get enough sleep. I'm going to bed. Maybe by tomorrow, things won't look so bad to Ellis. Maybe this was just a little tiff. Or something. I want this for Ellis."

Julia cocked her head and studied Dorie. Her strawberry blond hair was gathered into pigtails, and her face was pink from the sun and just a little fuller than usual. It was hard to believe her old friend, who looked barely out of her teens, would be a mother in a few months.

"What do you want for Ellis?" Julia asked. "A good lay? God knows, she's due. It's been twelve years or something. Who knows, she might have forgotten how."

Dorie rolled her eyes. "No, not just a good lay. Stop being such a cynic. Ellis deserves everything. True love, a husband, children, all of it. I don't care what you say, Julia Capelli, I think that's what all of us really want. You just think it's not cool to admit it."

"I do?"

"Absolutely. You had a great career, and I know you say that's all over, but it still looks pretty fabulous from where I'm sitting. And you've got this great guy, Booker, who loves you and wants to marry you and give you whatever you want. And you're just too stinkin' cool to say yes."

Julia pushed her chair away from the table. "Thanks for the cut-rate analysis, Eudora. Now, let me ask you something. Are you telling me that after all you've been through with Stephen, who has essentially left you for another man—while you are carrying his child—that you still believe in that happy-ever-after fairy tale stuff? Can you tell me that, straight-faced, with your own screwed-up family history, you buy that crap?"

Dorie leaned forward, her green eyes glittering with intensity.

"Look at me, Julia. I am telling you, yes. Yes, with absolute sincerity, despite Stephen, despite my parents' shitty marital history, despite all evidence to the contrary, that yes, I do still buy what you call 'that crap'. I have to believe Stephen really did love me, and that I loved him, and that we will love this baby I'm carrying. I'm furious and sad about what happened with us, but that doesn't make me believe that what we had wasn't real. And it doesn't make me believe that I won't find something that real again. I may be looking at being a single mother, at having to move in with my mom again, at working my ass off teaching school for peanuts, but you're the one I feel sorry for, Julia. Because you do have it all, but you don't believe it, and you don't appreciate it. And that's the saddest thing of all."

Ellis kicked off the high-heeled sandals and peeled herself out of Julia's clothes. She climbed into her cupcake pajamas and went into the bathroom, where she brushed her teeth until they bled, and scrubbed off every trace of the face Dorie had so carefully painted on her only a few hours earlier.

"Idiot," she said, scowling into the mirror at the real Ellis Sullivan.

Back in her bedroom, she got out her cell phone, and erased each and every duplicitous e-mail she'd sent or received from Mr.Culpepper@Ebbtide .com.

When she was done, she padded back and forth in her bedroom, stopping every so often to glare out the window in the direction of the garage apartment. The lights were all on, but she couldn't see Ty. Wait. As she watched, he came down the stairs from the apartment and went over to the Bronco. A moment later, the headlights flashed on, and he was backing out and down the driveway. Well, it was only 9:30, after all. Maybe he had another date. Maybe he was heading over to Cadillac Jack's, to hook up with one of the willing women who'd flocked around him at the bar there. She didn't care, Ellis told herself.

Screw him.

But the thing was, she did care. She'd let down her guard, let herself believe somebody like Ty Bazemore could care about her, let herself believe that she could ever be with somebody like him. Which was a joke, right? And she was the punch line.

Eventually, she heard footsteps on the stairs, light ones that must have been Dorie, barefoot, going to bed early. Maybe half an hour later, she heard the soft flapping of leather-soled sandals—those would be Julia's. She heard their bedroom doors close, thankful that neither of her best friends had knocked on her own door to enquire about her "big date."

What a laugh.

She tried to read her paperback, but gave up after realizing she'd reread the same chapter three times. Ellis settled back into the pillows on her bed, staring up at the ceiling fan whirring overhead. She studied all the cracks in the plaster ceiling, the watermarks on the faded flowery wallpaper. The air conditioner wedged into the window by the bed wheezed and rattled the window glass in a futile attempt to cool temperatures that were probably in the eighties. The place really was a dump. She'd been so happy to finally be here with her friends, so full of anticipation of the month, she'd glossed over the truly deplorable condition of Ebbtide.

It had been a grand old house at one time, she could tell. Large, square, high-ceilinged rooms, generous windows with amazing views of the ocean and dunes. Ryan, that guy at the restaurant, had mentioned that the house had belonged to Ty's family. And that the house was about to be foreclosed on.

Served him right, Ellis tried to tell herself.

But it didn't wash. Ty had told her he was a day trader, trying to recoup his losses in the stock market. The reality was that he was trying desperately to keep from losing his family home. Which explained why he rented out the big house and lived in the garage apartment. But it still didn't explain why he couldn't have just told her, after their first encounter on the beach, that *he* was Mr. Culpepper.

Not that it mattered. He didn't owe her anything. She was just another pain-in-the-ass summer renter.

With only two weeks left at the beach.

Screw it, Ellis thought.

She jumped out of bed and padded barefoot down the stairs, and out through the kitchen. She wasn't worried about encountering Ty Bazemore again, as she had last time. He was out tomcatting around Nags Head.

Ellis found the deck of cards the girls had abandoned on the kitchen table. She dealt herself a hand of solitaire, but gave up on it after fifteen minutes. She couldn't even beat herself at cards, she thought, slapping the cards down in disgust. It was hot in the kitchen too—suffocating, really. She wet a paper towel and dabbed her forehead and wrists to cool herself down.

A walk on the beach, she decided, might be the only thing to calm herself down. Upstairs, she pulled on a pair of shorts and a T-shirt. She picked up the sandals Madison had loaned her only a few hours earlier, and tiptoed upstairs. She paused outside Madison's door. The light was on, but she heard no movement from inside. She was probably reading. Ellis thought about knocking, about blurting out the truth of her whole, awful evening to a pair of neutral ears, but decided against it. Madison wasn't the kind of girl who wanted to hear about somebody else's drama. Instead, Ellis set the shoes carefully on the floor and left.

She let herself out the kitchen door and sped over the boardwalk and down to the beach. A slight breeze ruffled the sea oats, but otherwise, it was quiet. She left her flip-flops on the soft sand at the base of the steps and hurried out to the water's edge, not stopping until her toes were licked by the cool wavelets. The moon was still near full, shining brightly on the gleaming silvery beach.

Better. She took a deep breath and started walking on the hard-packed wet sand. She wove her way up the beach, side stepping the incoming tide, although occasionally a wave caught her, slapping water up as high as her thigh. She kept walking. The farther south she went, the closer together houses were packed. Lights were on in some of the houses, and occasionally she heard a drift of music, or laughter, but the beach was otherwise deserted.

Ellis stopped occasionally, bent over and picked up a seashell, but dropped the ones that were crushed or broken. At one point, she found a perfect, white, palm-sized sand dollar at the water's edge. With her fingertip, she traced the indentations in the brittle surface of the shell, trying to remember what Sister Marguerite, her biology teacher back at Our Lady of Angels, had told her the indentations meant. Something about the cross, and the trials of Jesus. Carefully, Ellis tucked the sand dollar into the pocket of her shorts and kept walking.

At some point, the wind picked up, and the waves began crashing harder into the sand, the tide creeping up. Ellis stopped, turned around, and stared up at the cluster of unfamiliar buildings at the edge of the dunes. She shivered and crossed her arms over her chest. Just how far had she come?

Time to turn back. The encroaching tide had driven her closer to the dunes. She tried walking faster, struggling as her feet sank into the powdery soft sand. Each time she came to a set of stairs leading up and over the dunes, she looked up, trying to decide if it was her stairway, leading back to Ebbtide.

But now, in the dark, all the dunes and stairways looked alike. She felt her heart racing, and told herself this was silly. She wasn't lost. Couldn't be. After two weeks, she knew her own stretch of beach perfectly. There was a faded, pale yellow catamaran pushed into the beach rosemary and sea oats below Ebbtide. The battered red metal trash barrel bolted to a piling near their house was crisscrossed with painted-on graffiti: "TIGERS RULE, COCKS SUCK" and "RENE LOVES BUSTER."

And her shoes! Her lime green flip-flops. She'd left them right at the base of the steps. All she had to do was find those flip-flops. She powered onwards, squinting in the dark, looking for the catamaran and the red trash barrel. After another thirty minutes, her calf muscles burned, and she was nearly out of breath. The tide kept inching closer, until it was lapping right at the base of the dunes, and still there were no familiar signs.

Finally, exhausted, she stopped and sat on a worn wooden step. The water swirled around her ankles, and she realized it would have swept her flip-flops away. What should she do? She stepped into the water and craned her neck to look up. These steps led up to a boardwalk similar to the one at Ebbtide, and a house that looked nothing like Ebbtide. Should she climb up, cross the boardwalk, and find her way to the road?

And then what? Walk barefoot on the asphalt for who knows how far, with cars whizzing past and God-knows-who looking at her in her soggy shorts and windblown hair, not to mention the fact that she was braless?

No. She'd stick to the beach. She stood and started trudging. Ten minutes later, she heaved a sigh of relief when she spotted the yellow catamaran. Thank God! She almost felt like kissing the paint-spattered red trash barrel. Almost. Instead, she grabbed the handrail of the staircase and heaved herself up the steep first step.

It wasn't until she'd reached the top step that she smelled it. Cigar smoke. In the darkness, she saw the glowing red tip first, and then the outline of the beach chair. And Ty Bazemore, beer in hand.

# 29

He'd been sitting on the deck for at least an hour, smoking a cigar, nursing a Heineken. After the disastrous aborted date, he'd gone up to the garage, shed the jacket and khakis, and tried to forget about it and just get some work done. He'd been reading about a small agribiz company in Kentucky that had recently patented a new kind of grass seed with promising drought-tolerant qualities. But he was glassy-eyed from reading all the technical reports, not to mention the company's P&L statements.

Ty's heart wasn't in it, anyhow. He'd tried to shake off the depression that was settling over him like a thick woolen blanket, but didn't have much luck. And anyway, he was seriously starving. So he'd jumped in the Bronco and hit the drive-through at the burger joint up the road.

Sometimes, a good greasy cheeseburger and fries were the only antidote to misery. He'd eaten the burger and half the fries, and lit up the last of his good cigars, but he wasn't feeling that much better about life. He was, however, developing a bad case of heartburn.

The wind had picked up, and the surf was pounding away at the beach below. And suddenly, he looked up, and there she was, climbing up the last stair.

Cinderella was gone, and in her place the old Ellis Sullivan seemed to have washed ashore. The carefully arranged hairdo had been blown all to hell. She was barefoot, her baggy pink shorts were soggy, and her damp T-shirt clung to her body. It was apparent, even from where he sat in the darkness, that she'd been crying.

"Oh," she said when she spotted him. "It's you."

"I live here," Ty said. He stubbed out the last of his cigar on the top of the beer can. "Are you all right?"

She looked down at her sandy legs, wiped her nose with the sleeve of her T-shirt, and nodded. "I think the tide took my shoes. Other than that, I'm just peachy. I thought you were gone."

"I was," he said, gesturing to the paper sack with the remnants of cheese-burger and French fries. "I ran out for a little midnight snack. But now I'm back. What were you doing down there? Going for a midnight swim? Not to scare you or anything, but there are sharks out there."

"I went for a walk," Ellis said, leaning against the deck railing. "What time is it?"

He consulted his watch. "Nearly midnight. Must have been a hell of a stroll. I've been out here for over an hour."

She slumped down onto the deck, her legs suddenly rubbery with fatigue. "I guess I lost track of where I was going. God, I must have walked a couple of miles along the beach. And then the tide started coming in, and I sort of freaked out. At night, in the dark like this, all these stairways look alike."

"I'll give you a tip," Ty drawled. "Tomorrow, when you go out on the beach, look up at the stairways. Most of 'em have metal address numbers attached to 'em. Ours even says EBBTIDE, although you have to really get pretty close up to see it."

Ellis leaned her head back against the railing and stretched her legs out on the deck planks, which still retained some of the heat from the sun. She wanted to jump up and run down the walkway, back to her room, away from Ty Bazemore. But she was exhausted. Physically and mentally.

Ty sat back in his chair and looked at her expectantly. Waiting for her to blast him again.

"Maybe," she said, after a couple minutes of awkward silence, "maybe we could just pretend tonight never happened. You could go back to your garage and computer, and I could go back to . . . whatever."

He got up from his chair and sank down onto the deck beside her, sitting so close that they were brushing shoulders.

"Why would we want to do that?" he asked. "I mean, was there any part of tonight that you enjoyed?"

"Seriously?" she asked, shaking her head in disbelief. "Are you telling me you had a good time tonight?"

"You didn't?"

"I asked first," she pointed out.

"But I paid."

"Okay," she relented. "Are you sure you want me to go off on you again?"

"Why not? Everybody else does."

"As far as first dates go?" she said, brushing at the sand on her shorts and her legs. "This was pretty awful. Catastrophic, you might say."

He tilted his head and looked at her. "If you had to pinpoint it, where would you say it all started to go wrong? The jacket? I guess it has gotten a little short in the sleeves."

"The jacket was fine," Ellis said. "Except for the dry-cleaner's tag attached to your right sleeve."

"You coulda said something."

"You could have told me you own Ebbtide," Ellis said. "So we're even. Anyway, it was a first date. You don't tell that kind of stuff on a first date."

"Oh."

Ty went back over the evening in his mind again. "I did notice you didn't eat very much. So, you didn't like the restaurant? I considered a steak house, or Italian, but then I thought, seafood. Who doesn't like seafood at the beach?"

"I loved the restaurant," Ellis said, hesitating.

"But?"

She wrinkled her nose. "Swordfish. Ugh. Hate, hate, hate swordfish."

"Again, you could have said something."

"I was trying to be polite," Ellis said.

"Next time, just tell me what you want to eat," Ty said, exasperated.

"Next time maybe you could ask me what I want to eat. Wait," she said. "There's going to be a next time?"

"I only ordered the swordfish because it was the most expensive thing on the menu," he went on. "I was trying to impress you, in case you didn't notice."

"Really?" She tilted her head and considered him. "That's sweet."

"Okay. Aside from the swordfish, and the dry-cleaner tag, and the finding out about Mr. Culpepper thing, what else was bad?" Ty asked. "You know, so I can improve on my technique."

Ellis rolled her eyes. "It's not your fault, I suppose. But it's still pretty awkward running into your old girlfriend and her husband when we're on a date."

Ty made a choking sound. "That wasn't an old girlfriend."

"No? You could have fooled me. I definitely sensed some history there. Also hostility. Not so deeply repressed hostility, I might add."

"Oh, Kendra and I have history, all right," Ty said ruefully. "If you consider two years of marriage to be history."

"Marriage? You were married? To her? For two years?"

"It seemed a lot longer at the time," Ty said.

"Wow. Just . . . wow." Ellis said. "How long have you been divorced? If you don't mind my asking."

"It was a long time ago."

Ellis hugged her knees to her chest, to warm up a little. "She's beautiful."

"She certainly thinks so," Ty agreed. "And I guess most people would agree."

"You must have thought she was pretty at some point," Ellis said. "You did marry her."

"We dated in high school, got married after college," Ty said. "Everybody always said we were perfect for each other."

"And then?"

"Kendra is the kind of girl who always has a plan," Ty said. "I guess she gets that from her old man. Boomer used to be in politics, was in the state house, like that. Now he concentrates on running his law firm. And his daughter's life. And that's fine with Kendra, fits right in with her plans."

"But it didn't fit with yours?"

"It did at first," Ty admitted. "Law school seemed like a great idea. I made decent grades in high school and as an undergrad. We got out of college, worked for a couple years, mainly so I could save money to go back to grad school, but then Kendra got the bright idea we should go to law school together. I thought, why not? We both applied to law schools. Kendra got accepted a bunch of places. Me? Looking back on it, I think Boomer probably pulled some strings to get me in at Carolina. He was on the board of visitors."

"And then what? If you don't mind my asking?"

"Ancient history now," Ty said with a shrug. "It just wasn't a good fit for me. Kendra and I were doing okay. We lived in a ratty little apartment off Franklin Street, and we were starving law students, just like all our friends. Or at least, I was. Kendra had a separate bank account, and her daddy kept it filled up all the time. So we fought about that. And a lot of other stuff. And by the time I was halfway through my second year, I knew, absolutely, that law school was not the place for me. But I stuck it out, finished the year. Then, when I told Kendra I was dropping out, she announced that she was dropping me."

"Ow," Ellis said. "Ryan?"

"I prefer to think of him as Fuckface," Ty said. "They were on the law review together. According to Kendra, things just . . . happened."

"Where have I heard that before?" Ellis sympathized.

"She claimed they were 'just friends,'" Ty said. "Of course, when she moved out of the rat hole, she moved in with him. Just a coincidence, I'm sure."

"Again, ow. What did you do then?"

"I got a job working as a glorified office boy at a stock brokerage firm in Chapel Hill. Kept my eyes and ears open, started doing some trades, and figured out I kind of liked it. Turns out, I'm an information junkie. The guy I worked for taught me a lot, and I hit some lucky breaks. I stayed with his firm for a couple more years, then moved to Charlotte to work for another couple years. But I always missed being on the coast. I lived lean, saved my money, and eventually moved back here to Nags Head."

"To Ebbtide," Ellis said.

"Nah. I moved in with my dad," Ty said. "Ebbtide belonged to my mom's family. When my grandmother died, she left it to my mom's brother, my uncle Ralph. He lives out west and didn't really have much interest in the place. He was gonna sell it last year. By that time, real estate prices here were in the tank, and I'd managed to squirrel some money away, so I got the bright idea to buy it and keep it in the family."

"I think that's nice," Ellis said. "Has your family always owned it?"

"Always," Ty said. "And until I bought the place, virtually nothing had been done to it in all those years. Turns out, the joint is a money pit. It needs a new roof, new plumbing, new electrical. And you see the shape the kitchen and the bathrooms are in. I moved in right after I bought it and started working on it, but then the stock market did a nosedive, and I ran out of money."

"The economy sucks," Ellis said sympathetically. "I know, that's what happened to me at the bank I worked for in Philly. We got swallowed up by another bank, and everybody in my department got pink slips."

"Have you got another job lined up?"

"Not yet," Ellis admitted. "I've got résumés out, but . . ."

"Yeah," Ty said. "I feel your pain. When I first moved back here, I tried finding a job, but let's face it, Nags Head ain't Charlotte. It's all about tourism here. Anyway, I'm tired of working for other people. I'd rather figure it out on my own, even if I have to live on next to nothing while I do that. That's why I moved into the garage apartment and started renting out the big house. But it was too little, too late.' "

Ellis shivered and hugged her knees tighter.

"You're cold," Ty said. He slipped an arm around her shoulder and pulled her to him. "We could go inside," he offered.

"I'm all right," Ellis said. She looked up at him. "What Ryan said tonight, about Ebbtide? Is it really in foreclosure?"

"Prick," Ty muttered. "Yeah, that's right. I got in over my head, pure and simple. I don't want to sound too melodramatic, but if I don't figure out a way to raise some money, fast, by September fifteenth, I'll lose Ebbtide. That's why I've been moonlighting at Caddie's."

"It would be so sad to lose your family home," Ellis said. "Isn't there anything you can do? Have you talked to anybody at the bank? I mean, I was never in the mortgage side of things, but it seems to me the last thing a bank wants right now is to have to manage another foreclosed property. Maybe you could work something out with them?"

"I'm trying," Ty said, "but they're not local. The bank I got my mortgage from got taken over by another bank, in Virginia. I've called and written letters, but I can't ever seem to get in contact with a real human being. And in the meantime, the clock is ticking. The legal ads have started to run. And the vultures have started to circle."

"Like Ryan and Kendra," Ellis said.

Ty's face darkened. "I'll burn it to the ground before I let them get their hands on my house."

Ellis's eyes widened at the ferocity of his response.

"Not literally," Ty said. "I'll think of something. Anyway, could we change the subject?"

"What did you have in mind?" she asked.

Ty pulled Ellis closer. He nuzzled her hair and her neck. "I was hoping maybe we could discuss your giving me a do-over on this evening."

Ellis reached for the paper bag he'd left sitting beside his chair. "Only if you agree to share whatever's in this bag. I didn't have much dinner, remember?"

"Later," Ty said. He turned her face to his and found her lips in the dark.

# 30

There was a knock at Julia's bedroom door. When she opened it, Madison stood there, holding her cell phone in her hand. "We need to talk," Madison said, her dark-ringed eyes still and serious. Her unwashed hair hung from a center part, and her cheap brown T-shirt was wrinkled and shrunken from the wash. She limped into the room without being invited, and sat down on the edge of a rickety orange-painted wooden chair.

The chair was one Julia had found at a charity thrift shop on Croatan Highway over the weekend, and in a fit of boredom, painted a shade called Valencia.

"Hey," Julia started to say, but Madison held her hand up, palm outwards, stopping her before she could get started with any fake outrage.

Julia sank down onto her bed, which she'd just made up with a cheap cotton spread with bright pink, orange, and turquoise stripes, picked up at the Target store on her way back from the paint store.

"What's up, Madison?" Julia asked, smoothing out a nonexistent wrinkle in the spread.

"What did you say to him?" Madison asked.

"Who?"

"Him!" Madison said, thrusting the phone at Julia. "Look, I know you think you're smart, messing with my phone, checking my messages. But you have no idea who you are messing with here. So just cut the act and tell me exactly what he said. And what you told him." She crossed her legs and added, "Please."

Julia sighed. "Is Maryn your real name?"

"That's none of your business."

Julia leaned forward. "Oh, but it is my business. You're living under the same roof as me. I've got a right to know who you are and what you're doing here."

"Okay, fine. You got me. I lied. Now tell me what you told him."

"You mean Don? I didn't tell him anything. Who is he, anyway?"

Madison's face was taut. "He told you his name?"

Julia thought about that. "No. He asked for Maryn, I told him you weren't there. He asked who I was, and then he hung up."

"You're sure that's all that was said? Julia, this is really important. What did you say when he asked you who were?"

She shrugged. "I said I'm Julia Capelli. Who the hell are you? When the phone rang, the caller ID just said 'unknown caller.' After he hung up, I listened to some other messages on your phone from 'Don.' It was the same voice."

Madison crossed and uncrossed her legs. She nibbled on a ragged bit of cuticle. Julia noticed that she wasn't wearing the big diamond engagement ring. "You actually told him your name?"

"Why wouldn't I tell him my name?" Julia asked. "Madison, why don't you just tell me what's going on here and stop with the twenty questions? Who is this Don guy? And why are you running away from him? What's got you so scared?"

Madison shook her head violently. "You wouldn't understand. Anyway, it's not your problem."

"The hell it isn't! I told him my name!"

Madison looked down at the phone. "His name is Don Shackleford. He's my husband. I found out he's into some bad stuff. So I left. End of story."

"Nuh-uh," Julia said. "You didn't just leave. You ran. And you're traveling under an assumed name. I think you owe us an explanation."

"The only thing I owe you guys is the rent on that crappy room upstairs," Madison said. "Which I already paid. And if you hadn't been so damned nosy, messing with my phone and snooping in my private life, none of this would be an issue."

"What kind of bad stuff is he into?" Julia asked, her eyes glittering with excitement. "Drugs? Gun running?"

"You watch too much television," Madison said. "It's nothing that exciting. He's . . . dishonest, that's all. I should have known better. I did know better, once."

She stood up abruptly. "Look, my rent's paid up. I'll leave as soon as I figure out my next step. Probably by the weekend. In the meantime, could you please keep this to yourself? The less people who know my real name, the better. Don doesn't have any reason to think I'd come someplace like Nags Head. I didn't know I was coming here myself until I saw the sign on the interstate for the turnoff."

Julia followed her to the door. "I already told the girls I know Madison isn't your real name."

Madison rolled her eyes. "Another big surprise."

"You don't have to go, you know," Julia said. "Maybe we could help. You know, help get you out of whatever kind of jam you're in."

"No!" Madison said quickly. "I don't want any help. I'll be out of here by the weekend. Just do as I ask—don't be running off at the mouth about me, and stay out of my business."

She left the room as quickly as she'd come, leaving Julia with more questions than answers.

# 31

Maryn slammed her bedroom door and locked it. There was no getting around facts: she had to leave Ebbtide and Nags Head. What if Julia was lying about her conversation with Don? God knows what she might have told him.

Her mouth went dry at the prospect. But no, she sternly told herself. Julia might be a nosy little sneak, but she was well-meaning. And besides, she had no reason to lie once she'd been confronted. Not that it mattered now. No matter how innocuous Julia's comments to Don seemed, she couldn't risk staying.

She took the duffle bag out from beneath the bed, propped it on the wooden chair by the door, and started to pack. She was surprised and irritated at how sad the idea of leaving this place made her. This cruddy little room in this big, crumbling old house had become her refuge, a home in a way that the gaudy, nouveau riche town house where Don had installed her would never be a home. And these women—Ellis, Dorie, and even Julia— they weren't friends, not really. But they were decent, generous women who might have become her friends if she'd dared to let down her guard. But she couldn't. And now it was too late.

She had no idea where she would go next, but go she would. Maybe she'd head west? Mexico was too obvious—and anyway, she didn't speak a word of Spanish. And what about all that money? The stacks of cash terrified her. She was no Pollyanna, but she was sure Don hadn't earned that money legally. So far, except for her rent, she'd mostly resisted spending it. She'd need money to get as far away as possible.

The ring. Her engagement ring. She dug the black velvet box out of her dresser drawer and flipped the top open. The huge solitaire seemed to wink impishly at her. Don was a phony. Their marriage was phony. She only hoped that the diamond was real, because it was looking like her ticket away from both Don and the marriage.

Maryn was making a mental list of all she needed to do before leaving— gas up the car, find a decent road map, look up a jeweler who might buy, or at least appraise, the ring—when she realized that her cell phone, which she'd tossed onto the bed, was buzzing.

For a moment, she felt paralyzed. But then she grabbed the phone, and when she saw the caller ID on the readout, she could have cried with relief.

"Adam!" she said, fighting back tears. "Where are you? All you all right?"

"I'm fine," he said. "I'm in Philly. But where the hell are you? I've been worried sick about you."

"Don . . . he didn't hurt you?"

"No. Why would he?"

"He caught me, after I left his office. Oh God, you were right about him. I took his key and I went over there, and I found some of the Prescott files. He's been robbing them blind." The words tumbling out of Maryn in a torrent. "Don flew into a rage. He . . . hurt me. And I couldn't help it, I told him what you'd told me, about the auditors and everything. Of course, he denied everything. He even wanted me to go to dinner with him and Robby Prescott that night. As though nothing had happened. But he told me if I didn't do exactly as he said, he'd kill me, and hide my body where nobody would ever find me."

"So you ran?" Adam said. "Why didn't you call me?"

"I tried to call you," Maryn said accusingly. "I left messages, didn't you get any of them? I was frantic with worry, afraid he'd come after you next. Where were you?"

"Oh, Maryn," Adam said. "I am so sorry. I was on vacation. Don't you remember? I told you I was going hiking with my brother and some friends. I just got back and saw all the missed calls."

She had no such memory. Adam, hiking? But it didn't matter now.

"Listen," she said. "Has Don called, looking for me?"

"Yeah," he said, his voice dripping disdain. "I think he must think I'm hiding you or something. Prick."

"He's more than just a prick," Maryn said. "He's a lunatic. A dangerous lunatic. And what's worse is, I married him."

"So . . . what are you gonna do?" Adam asked. "Get a lawyer and divorce his ass?"

"Eventually," Maryn said. "But right now, I've got to get as far away from him as I can."

"Aren't you being a little overly dramatic?" Adam asked.

"You didn't see the look in his eyes when he was threatening me," Maryn said. "I did."

"Okay," Adam said quickly. "I get your point. What can I do to help? Where are you, anyway? You still haven't told me."

Maryn hesitated. But Adam was her best friend. He'd tried to warn her about Don, but she'd refused to listen. And look what had happened.

"I'm on the Outer Banks," she said. "Nags Head."

"That's in North Carolina?" Adam asked. "What made you go all the way down there?"

"Nothing in particular," she said. "After I ran, I'd been driving all night, and I was exhausted, and I saw a billboard, so I just headed east and ended up here."

"Here, where?" Adam wanted to know. "Are you in a hotel or something?"

She looked around the barren little room and laughed ruefully. "Not hardly. I'm renting a room in an old house, right on the beach. I'm sharing it with three other women. It's too long a story to go into right now. Doesn't matter, anyway, because I'm leaving here just as soon as I can."

"Why's that?"

"It's not safe," Maryn said. "One of the women happened to pick up my cell phone, and Don called, and she answered it. She swears she didn't tell him anything, but I just can't risk staying here."

"Just what is it that makes you so terrified of him?" Adam asked. "I'm not saying you shouldn't be afraid, but you just sound . . . so . . . unhinged. Why not just come back home, get yourself a good lawyer, and proceed to take him for every last dime?"

"You don't get it," Maryn said, her voice growing shrill. "Don is a criminal. And no, I am not overreacting. Adam, when I left the house, I was terrified. I threw some clothes into a suitcase, grabbed my laptop case, and got the hell out. When I got down here, I went to unpack my laptop, and that's when I discovered it—I'd grabbed Don's computer instead of mine."

"Did you find any secret documents or smoking guns?" Adam asked.

"Not really," Maryn said. "Don's too cagey for anything like that. I didn't find anything on the computer—it's what I found in the computer case that's got me nervous."

"Like what?"

"Like a hundred thousand dollars," Maryn said. "Neat little bundles of hundred-dollar bills."

"Holy shit," Adam breathed.

"Now do you get why I can't come back there?" Maryn asked. "That money is dirty. It has to be. And Don knows I have it. And his computer."

"So . . . give the money back," Adam said. "Tell him you don't want it, and you don't want him, either."

"You make it sound so easy, so rational," Maryn said. "But Don's not rational. And I don't think he'll just let me walk away—not from any of it. I don't know where I'm going next, but the one thing I do know is that I'm not coming back there, or anywhere near where Don can find me."

"Where will you go? And what'll you do?" Adam asked.

"I don't know," Maryn repeated. "I haven't thought that far ahead. Somewhere. I'll get a job again. Earn my own keep. I did it before I met Don Shackleford, and I'll do it again."

Adam laughed. "You're telling me you're going to go back to driving a ten-year-old Honda and wearing markdowns from Loehmann's? Living in some cruddy studio apartment like that dump you were in when you met him? All just to prove you don't need a sugar daddy?"

Maryn's eyes rested on her Louboutin sandals, which she'd found outside her bedroom door when she'd gotten up to use the bathroom in the middle of the night. They'd cost eight hundred dollars, and she'd bought them without a second thought after Don gave her the American Express Black Card. She wished now that she'd told Ellis to keep them.

"I damn well don't need somebody like Don!" Maryn cried. "I don't understand why you're talking to me like this, Adam. You're the one who always accused me of only dating Don because of his money. I thought you were my friend."

"I *am* your friend," Adam assured her. "But I just want you to stop and think things all the way through before you do anything else drastic. Why spend your life on the run if you don't have to?"

"I don't see any other way," Maryn said, rubbing her eyes. She was suddenly exhausted, physically and emotionally. And now, damn it, she was crying. And she'd never, ever been a crybaby.

"Look," Adam was saying, "I've still got a few days of vacation left. I'm not due back at work 'til Monday. Why don't I come down there? We'll have a couple of drinks, take a walk on the beach, and talk. We can figure it out together. Okay? What do you say?"

"I don't know," Maryn said, feeling her resolve weakening. "What if Don figures out where I am? He talked to Julia. She swears she didn't tell him anything, but now she knows my real name. It just doesn't feel safe anymore."

"You're giving Don too much credit," Adam said soothingly. "He's just not that smart, Maryn. You say you're not staying at a hotel, so you're not registered anywhere, right? How's he gonna find you?"

"He is that smart," Maryn retorted. "You don't know him like I do."

"Whatever," Adam said. "Will you do that for me? Just hang for another day or so. I can drive down there tomorrow. We can hang out, talk. And if you still feel like you've got to take off, fine. I can help you figure that out. I know you, Maryn. You put on that tough girl front all the time, but at some point, you've got to quit being a loner. You've got to trust somebody. Right?"

"I guess," Maryn said, relenting. Maybe Adam was right. Maybe it was time to lean on somebody else. At least for a little while.

"Okay," she said, sniffling. "I'll wait here. You'll leave tomorrow?"

"First thing," he assured her. "But you've got to tell me the address there."

"You know, I don't even know the address," Maryn said. "Just the name of the street. South Virginia Dare. Oh yeah, and the house name. All the beach houses down here have names. It's Ebbtide."

"Ebbtide," Adam repeated. "I'll leave here first thing in the morning, and I'll call you when I'm about an hour away. Get some sleep, okay?"

"I'll try," Maryn promised. "See you tomorrow."

# 32

When she got back from her morning run shortly after nine, Julia walked, breathless and sweat-drenched, into the kitchen, where she found Dorie and Ellis already dressed for the beach, loading ice and cold drinks into their cooler.

Julia helped herself to a bottle of water, gulping it down so fast it splashed onto her tank top. She sank down on a kitchen chair and rolled the icy bottle across her forehead and neck. "Cute suit," she said, eyeing Ellis's midriff-baring coral tankini. "Is that new?"

"Kinda," Ellis said, as she smeared sunscreen on her chest and arms. "I bought it in Rehoboth Beach last summer, but I never wore it because I wasn't sure I really liked it."

"You mean you were too shy to wear it out in public," Julia said bluntly. "Ellis, this is the perfect suit for you. The top's not too low cut, but it shows off your nice flat tummy and that cute little booty of yours. Now, promise me you'll throw out that hideous black one-piece you've been wearing. I mean, my nona had a suit just like that one."

"It is not an old-lady suit!" Ellis protested. "Is it, Dorie?"

Dorie wrinkled her nose and helped herself to the bottle of sunscreen, squiggling lines of lotion up and down her arms and legs.

"Really?" Ellis sighed. "Dorie, I thought you were on my side."

"I'm not on either side," she said. "I'm neutral. Like Switzerland. I will say, however, that I like this bathing suit a whole lot better than the other one."

"Yeah," Julia said. "That black suit looks like something out of the 1968 Miss USSR pageant."

"Fine," Ellis said, slipping a cover-up over the pink suit. "Go ahead, gang up on me. I'm a big girl, I can take it."

She picked up her beach towel and tote bag, and grabbed the handle of the rolling cooler, heading for the back door. "Are you coming down to the beach with us, Julia?"

"After I shower," Julia said. "Have you guys seen Madison this morning?"

"Nope," Dorie said. "And I've been up since seven. I went out to the store at eight, to pick up more cereal and orange juice, but her bike was already gone."

"Her car's still parked in the garage," Julia said. "So that's good." She walked to the front of the house and peered out the living room window, then came quickly back to the kitchen.

"Listen," she said, lowering her voice. "I'm going up to Madison's room to check things out. One of you go out front and watch for her. If you see her coming, give me a signal, okay?"

"Julia, no," Dorie said, her voice sharp. "You've got no right. . . ."

"Madison admitted to me last night that she's been lying to us," Julia said. "Her real name is Maryn. That guy who called her cell phone? Don? He's her husband. She's terrified of him, you guys. She told me last night that she found out he's into something bad, and she ran away. That's how she ended up here, on Nags Head."

"What?" Ellis said. "She just suddenly opened up and confessed? When did all this happen?"

"Last night, while you were out on your hot date with garage guy," Julia said smugly. "And don't think we don't expect a full report about last night, either, Ellis Sullivan. We want to know why you came home so early. And why you left again and were out past midnight."

"What are you, Harriet the Spy?" Ellis asked, blushing nonetheless. "It was a date, that's all. Nothing to tell."

"Hmmph," Julia said. "We'll get back to you later. So, yes, Madison, or rather, Maryn, did open up to me. She came into my room not long after you left, ready to bitch me out because she'd figured out I'd been snooping around her cell phone."

"She had a right to be pissed at you," Dorie pointed out. "We're your best friends, so we expect a certain amount of nosiness, but it's different for her."

"She was pissed," Julia admitted. "But she wanted to know what I'd told her husband, Don, when he called. Then she really grilled me, so I grilled her right back, or tried to. But she wouldn't tell me much. So now, I'm just going to take matters into my own hands. Watch the front door, okay?"

Julia pulled her cell phone from the plastic case clipped to the waist of her running shorts. "If you see Madison coming, give me a call, and then try to keep her occupied until I can get out of there."

"Absolutely not," Dorie said. "You can't just go rifling through her things. You've got no right."

"Don't sweat it, Dorie," Ellis said. "Julia can't get in there, anyway. Madison locks her bedroom door every time she leaves the room."

Julia gave a conspiratorial smile. "True that. But I don't necessarily need a key. Madison sleeps with the windows open. I noticed it when I was out on the beach the other day. There's an access door onto that widow's walk on the third floor from the attic. I'm just gonna go out the door, climb onto the widow's walk, and then crawl in her bedroom window. It's a teeny-tiny room, it won't take but a few minutes to check it out."

Dorie crossed her arms over her chest. "I can't stop you, but I'm not gonna help you, that's for damned sure. If Madison's in trouble, we need to help her, not turn on her."

"I *offered* to help," Julia said. "She just told me to mind my own business. She says she's leaving by the weekend, if not sooner. So it's now or never."

Julia turned to Ellis. "What about you? Are you in, or are you out?"

Ellis sighed. "Oh hell. I don't like it, but I don't like the idea of her lying to us, either. How do we know she's not the one who ran away because she's into something illegal?"

"My point exactly," Julia said triumphantly. "Okay. Cover me, Ellie-Belly. I'm going in."

Dorie snorted. "You two are crazy as bat-shit. And when Madison comes home, and figures out you've been messing with her stuff, I do not want to be around to pick up the pieces."

But Julia didn't bother to respond. She took the stairs to the second and third floor at a trot. When she got to the third floor, she twisted the doorknob of Madison's room, just to make sure. As Ellis had predicted, the door was locked.

Julia went down to the end of the hall and tugged at the door to the attic. But the summer's heat and humidity had caused the old wooden door to swell. She tugged harder, then braced one leg on the door frame, and yanked with all her might. The door swung open suddenly, throwing Julia backwards, landing on her butt on the splintery wooden floor.

"Damn," she muttered, picking herself up. She gasped as a wall of heat engulfed her when she stepped into the low-ceilinged attic. She pulled the door nearly shut, to ensure she could make a quick getaway once she'd finished searching Madison's room.

A single window high in the roof peak illuminated the room. Julia picked her way past piles of cardboard boxes and dust-shrouded furniture, sneezing as she headed for the door onto the widow's walk. It had to be close to a hundred degrees in the attic, she thought, as sweat poured down her face, back, and arms.

The access door had an old-fashioned slide lock as well as a dead bolt. Julia's hands, slick with sweat, couldn't budge the lock mechanism. In frustration, she yanked off her top and used it to grasp the lock and jerk it open. She took a step backwards and kicked the door as hard as she could with her running shoe. The brittle old wood splintered, and the door flew open.

Gasping for air, Julia stepped out onto the widow's walk, dressed only in her shorts and sports bra, the tank top tucked into the waistband of her shorts. The temperature outside was already in the mid-eighties, but the air was refreshingly cool compared to the blast-furnace atmosphere in the attic. And the view was spectacular. The beach spread out below, and Julia believed she could see all the way to Currituck, to the south, and Corolla, to the north. But there was no time for sightseeing. She had a job to do.

The wooden widow's walk was narrower than it looked from the beach, only four feet wide, with a wooden railing that stood not quite hip high. The railing was rotted in places, as was the decking of the walkway. She glanced down and gulped. If she fell, it was at least a fifty-foot drop.

But she wouldn't fall. She edged down the walk until she came to the window outside Madison's room. It was propped halfway open. Julia grasped the window sill and pushed upwards. Stuck. She gritted her teeth and pushed harder, and slowly, the stubborn window inched higher. When she'd raised it a full eighteen inches, Julia managed to wriggle into the room, feet first.

"Gaawwwd," she groaned, falling in a heap onto the floor.

She was struck, instantly, by the clinical neatness of Madison's room. In contrast to Julia's own room, with its unmade bed, discarded magazines, empty soda cans, and clothes strewn haphazardly over every surface, Madison's room reminded her of a nun's cell. Or an army barracks.

The worn cotton sheets were pulled taut on the narrow iron bed, two pillows were stacked atop each other, the faded chenille bedspread was folded in a crisp rectangle at the foot of the bed. The nightstand held a lamp and a dog-eared paperback romance novel. The top of the wooden dresser was bare, except for a black vinyl zippered cosmetic case.

But a wooden chair beside the door held an open duffle bag, filled with a stack of neatly folded clothing. Madison hadn't been lying about that, Julia thought. She really did intend to leave. And soon.

Julia opened the armoire door. A couple of inexpensive cotton sundresses and some blouses still hung there. Lined up on the floor were a pair of black canvas espadrilles, a pair of pink flip-flops, and the Louboutins. On the shelf sat a black leather laptop case. Julia tugged it down. She unzipped the case and lifted the computer out.

Julia stared down at the laptop. In the movies, the heroine always managed to power up the computer, figure out the passwords, and instantly uncover all the data locked within in a matter of seconds. But Julia's knowledge of computers was mostly limited to reading her e-mails and playing games of Freecell when she was bored. She had neither the time nor the necessary expertise to unlock Madison's secrets. Reluctantly, she slipped the computer back into the case and hefted it back onto the shelf. She tried sliding it all the way to the back of the shelf, but something was back there.

She grabbed the wooden chair and dragged it over to the armoire, climbing up to peer inside. She reached up to move aside whatever was at the back of the shelf. Her fingers closed on a stack of paper.

When she saw what she'd grabbed, Julia nearly fell off the chair. It was a stack of money. Hundred-dollar bills, bound by a paper bank wrapper. She took the laptop and set it down on the floor, and reaching in with both hands, grabbed an armload of similar money bundles. Thousands of dollars.

"Whoa," Julia breathed. "What the hell are you into, Madison?" Her fingers itched to take all the bundles down, to count it and examine it, but there was no time for that. Hurriedly, she shoved the money to the back of the shelf, then set the laptop in front of it.

She closed the armoire door and moved quickly to the dresser. The drawers were half empty, the clothing within neatly folded and stacked. As Julia rifled through the clothing she reflected that for a person with all that money stashed in her closet, Madison's clothes were appallingly cheap, most of them apparently purchased either at thrift or discount stores. So how did that jibe with the Prada pocketbook, the Louboutin sandals, and the honking big diamond ring?

Mildly disappointed that the dresser didn't hold any more money, Julia searched the nightstand's single drawer for more clues to the Madison puzzle, but all she found was a plastic bottle of aspirin.

Julia glanced around the room. There was nothing much else to search. She flopped down onto her belly and peered under the bed, halfway expecting to find another suitcase full of cash. But the only thing she found was a single white sock.

She scooted onto her knees, and as a last thought, did what they always do in the movies. She lifted the thin, worn mattress and ran her hand under the space between it and the box spring. When her fingertips closed on the cool, smooth, metal object there, her mouth went dry.

She pulled the object out and stared down at it. A gun! Julia knew a little bit about guns. Her father and brothers were hunters, stalking deer in the piney woods of Georgia and quail at a friend's South Carolina plantation. This was a revolver, a Smith & Wesson. Her hands trembled badly as she fumbled with the barrel.

*Briiing! Briinng!* Startled, she dropped the revolver onto the bed. Her cell phone vibrated in its plastic holder at her waist.

She fumbled again, trying to get it out of the holder. The screen told her Ellis was calling.

Julia flipped it open.

"She's coming!" Ellis whispered. "Madison just rode up on her bike. I made Dorie go out and stall her, but you know Madison isn't chummy. Get the hell out of there!"

"Shit!" Julia said. "Do something. Anything. Keep her downstairs. Ellis— Madison's got a gun under her mattress. And a shitload of money hidden in the back of her closet."

"Oh my God," Ellis breathed. "Oh shit. Shit. Shit. Shit. She's coming in the house. I think I'm gonna have a heart attack. Or pee my pants."

"Don't you dare!" Julia clicked the phone closed. She started to shove the revolver under the mattress, but then, thinking better of it, shoved it in the waistband of her shorts. She smoothed the rumpled bedcovers, then ran across the room, hoisted herself out the window, and closed the window back to its original position.

This time around, she didn't linger long enough to consider the view, or the possibility of falling to her death. She scurried back inside the attic door, pulled it shut, and a moment later was taking the stairs, two at a time, back to her own bedroom on the second floor.

# 33

It was Dorie who saved the day. It was Wednesday, trash-pickup day, and even though they'd theoretically discarded Ellis's chore chart, it was Dorie's turn to take out the trash. She was just wheeling the overflowing plastic bin down to the curb, muttering to herself about *certain people* who couldn't be bothered to separate recyclables from the real trash, when Madison came pedaling down the street towards the house.

And then, despite all her protestations to the contrary, she found herself an unindicted co-conspirator.

"Madison," Dorie called, her mouth going dry with fear. "Hey! You're up early today. How was the bike ride?"

Madison coasted up to where Dorie was standing and braked. "It was fine," she said briefly. "I like to get out before all the tourists wake up and start clogging the roads with traffic."

"How's the ankle?" Dorie asked, glancing at Madison's leg. It was neatly taped with the Ace bandage.

"It's fine," Madison said, wiping a bead of sweat from her brow. "Thanks to you and your ice and ibuprofen."

She started to wheel away.

Dorie swallowed, trying to think of something to say, a way to stall Madison and keep her from going up to the house where Julia was, right now, rifling through Madison's belongings.

"Do you like that bike?" Dorie asked. Dumb question. Really dumb question, but it was all she could think of. Could pregnancy really do this to a person? Could the baby growing inside her really be siphoning off all her normal intelligence? She remembered a couple of the teachers at school joking about the dumb stuff they'd done while they were pregnant. Mommy minds, they called it, and Dorie always thought they were exaggerating, but now she knew different. She was dumb, and she was pregnant, and yes, pregnant by her gay husband, which made her just too stupid to live.

"The bike's all right," Madison said. "It's cheap, but it rides pretty good."

"I've been thinking about buying myself a bike," Dorie babbled. "It's supposed to be such good exercise, everybody says. But God, I don't think I've ridden a bike since I got out of college. I bet I wouldn't even remember how."

"Sure you would," Madison said. "That's why they always say what they say about riding a bike."

"What do they say?" Dorie asked. She was blanking, she really was. This baby better be a friggin' rocket scientist, she told herself, because it had already sucked out every brain cell Dorie had ever possessed.

Madison shifted impatiently from one foot to the other. "People always say something easy is like riding a bike, because you supposedly never forget how to ride a bike." She leaned closer and peered into Dorie's eyes with something like concern.

"Dorie, are you all right? You seem kind of, uh, spacey this morning."

"The teachers at school say it's something to do with your elevated hormone levels," Dorie explained. "Sharon? She's teaches freshman English? She was pregnant last fall, and not once, not twice, but three different times she got me to give her a ride home from school, and then remembered that she'd actually driven to school that day. I had to turn right around and take her back to school to get her own car."

"Yeah, that's crazy," Madison said. "Well, anyway, it's just a temporary condition, right?"

"I certainly hope so," Dorie said fervently. Madison was starting to walk her bike down the crushed-shell driveway. Dorie caught up with her. "So, we were just getting ready to go down to the beach. Supposed to be a beautiful day today. Not too humid. Anyway, not as humid as it gets in Savannah, which is, like, a million percent humidity. Maybe you could come hang with us at the beach today."

"Maybe later," Madison said. She stopped and turned towards Dorie. "Look, I know Julia told you guys about me. I'm sorry I lied to you. But I had my reasons. Anyway, not that it matters, because I'm leaving tomorrow, but I just wanted to tell you, you know, thanks. For letting me stay here. And everything."

Impulsively, Dorie gave Madison a hug. "Thank you," she said. "That morning we met, at that restaurant, I was really feeling pretty desperate. My sister flaked out on us, and I was so depressed and worried about money. I guess you thought I was some kind of nut, a perfect stranger, trying to rent you a room."

"You were nice," Madison said shyly. "And I'm sure Ellis and Julia—especially Julia—gave you some crap about renting to me without consulting them."

"They were fine with it, once they got over the initial shock," Dorie insisted. "They're really not so bad, once you get to know them. I think they'd like you as much as I do if you'd let them, Madison. Or should I call you Maryn?"

"Doesn't matter now, but I've kind of gotten to like being Madison."

"What made you pick that name?" Dorie asked, again, trying desperately to stall.

"Remember that movie, *Splash*? Where Daryl Hannah plays the mermaid, and she rescues Tom Hanks from drowning and falls in love with him? And she names herself Madison, because she sees the street sign for Madison Avenue? That was my favorite movie as a kid," Maryn said. "I named all my dolls Madison. I even named my kitten Madison." She smiled wryly. "I guess I wasn't a very imaginative kid."

"I named my kitten Kitty," Dorie said. "So, what does that tell you about me?"

"Tells me I hope you do better with this baby you're having," Maryn said, and they both laughed.

But now Maryn was walking towards the house again, picking up the pace, and Julia—oh God, she only hoped Julia had chickened out. Unlikely, knowing Julia.

"I wish you wouldn't go," Dorie said, meaning it more than the other woman could know. "I wish you'd stay here, and let us help you with whatever kind of trouble you're having."

"You can't," Maryn called over her shoulder.

"Get out, Julia," Dorie thought. "Get the hell out. Now!" She turned around, walked back to the curb, and fetched the unwieldy trash bin, trundling it halfway back to the house when it struck her: "Mommy mind, my ass," she grumbled, run-walking the still-full bin back towards the street because she had to pee. Again.

Ellis made an elaborate show of setting herself up on the beach, tilting her beach chair at what she thought would be her most flattering angle, slipping out of the filmy cover-up, and reclining facing the water. She did not allow herself to glance in the direction of the garage apartment. That would be just too obvious. Instead, she busied herself with her book and the cooler of cold drinks.

Dorie flopped down into her own chair and took the bottle of water Ellis offered. "Is everything okay?" she asked. "Is Julia coming down?"

"In a minute," Ellis said. "And when she gets down here, I am going to read her the riot act. You were right, Dorie. She had absolutely no business breaking into Madison's room. I swear to God, when I saw her walking that bike down the driveway, I nearly had a myocardial infarction. I haven't been that scared since your mom came home early from work that time we were seniors in high school and almost caught you and Kevin Boylan doing it on your dad's Barcalounger."

Dorie took a sip of water. "That wasn't Kevin Boylan. It was Kieran, his older brother. And we weren't technically doing it. Just messing around, as Kieran liked to say."

"Yeah, well, I wasn't about to explain the technicalities to Phyllis," Ellis said. "It was bad enough that we'd cut school and I'd drunk half a bottle of Jägermeister and puked in the backseat of Willa's Camry. And then here comes Phyllis, and I'm trying to act sober and tell her you had cramps so Miss Deal gave me permission to drive you home from school early. And the whole time I'm praying to the Baby Jesus that Kevin will get his pants on and get the hell out of your den before Phyllis asks where you are."

"It was Kieran, not Kevin, wasn't it?"

Ellis and Dorie looked up as Julia unfolded a quilt and spread it out on the sand beside them.

"I was just explaining that to Ellis," Dorie said. "Kevin Boylan had terminal dandruff. I would never have let Kevin Boylan get to third base. I did have certain standards, you know."

"Oh, please," Julia said, dropping down onto the quilt. "Don't talk to us about standards. We were there, remember? You only let Kieran get into your pants because he drove a cool car and you thought he'd invite you to all his fraternity parties at Georgia."

"And you guys agreed to go along with our little party because you assumed I'd get you dates with his KA brothers," Dorie said serenely. "And, if I recall correctly, Julia Capelli, you were the one who shoplifted that Jägermeister from Johnnie Ganem's Liquor Store."

"The beginning of a life of crime," Ellis said somberly. She flicked her towel at Julia. "And you, you idiot, are never to pull a stunt like that again. Ever." Ellis fanned herself. "My nerves can't take the strain."

"Your nerves," Julia drawled. "What about mine? When I found all that loot stashed in the back of Madison's closet? Not to mention the gun under her mattress."

"What?" Dorie sat straight up on her lounge chair. "You are making that up." She turned to Ellis. "Phyllis was right about one thing, though. Julia Capelli was, and still is, a bad influence."

Julia did a cursory sign of the cross. "On my daddy's grave. I'm telling you the truth. Madison must have, I don't know, like, twenty thousand dollars in cash. Shoved to the back of the shelf in her armoire. But that's not the scariest thing." She plunged her hand into her beach bag and withdrew a menacing-looking black handgun.

"This," she said triumphantly, "is what she had under her mattress. Now tell me again about poor, unfortunate, innocent Madison-slash-Maryn."

Ellis and Dorie stared goggle-eyed at the gun, until Julia shoved it back into the bag.

"Is it real?" Dorie asked.

"Is it loaded?" Ellis demanded.

"Not anymore," Julia said.

"You actually stole her gun?" Dorie groaned and shook her head.

"I did it for you guys," Julia said. "Who knows what she planned to do with that gun?" She held out one hand. "Diet Coke, please. All this sleuthing has left me absolutely parched."

"Oh my God," Dorie said, still eyeing Julia's bag. "Madison must be in awful trouble. Y'all, we have got to try to help her."

When Julia had finished her Diet Coke, and they'd made her recount the search and seizure of the contents of Madison's room not once, but twice, the three women agreed that it was time to do something.

"She told me this morning, she's leaving tomorrow," Dorie pointed out. "So it'd be a waste of time to kick her out. Anyway, I don't want to kick her out. I want to figure out how to help her."

"Dorie," Ellis said, sounding calmer than she felt. "You don't help a woman who has a closet full of cash and a loaded weapon. You just keep out of her way."

"Not happening," Julia said, her voice low, as she nodded in the direction of the stairway from the dunes.

Madison, or Maryn, was steaming down the stairs, blood in her eyes.

She kicked her shoes off at the base of the steps and kept coming, until she was standing at the very edge of their little beach camp, a damp tank top clutched in her right hand.

"Hi, Madison," Dorie attempted.

"You bitches!" Madison spat the words. "I knew moving in here was a mistake. Knew you'd never trust me and that I could never trust any of you."

Madison stood, hands clenched on her hips, staring down at Julia. "You've got some goddamn nerve, breaking into my room," she said. "Did you think I wouldn't find out?"

Julia's complexion paled a little under her tan. She propped herself up on her elbows. "What are you talking about? Me? Why would I be interested in your room?"

"I don't know why," Madison snapped. "Maybe because you're a pathetic loser, with no life of your own, so you have to go snooping around in mine?"

"I resent that," Julia said.

"Fuck you," Madison said. She glanced over at Dorie and gave her an even more withering look. "And you. With all that phony bullshit compassion, telling me you want me to stay. All the while you're really just stalling me so I won't catch *that* one in the act of burglarizing my room."

"It wasn't phony!" Dorie blurted out. "I mean, yes, I was stalling you, because I didn't want you to catch Julia. But I meant what I said. And I mean it even more now. Julia told us about the money."

"So now what? You've concluded that I'm a bank robber? An embezzler? Or maybe just a madam for a high-class call girl outfit? I'm surprised there's not a patrol car parked up at the house. You did call the cops, right?"

"It was a lot of cash," Julia pointed out.

"I don't have to explain myself to you people," Madison said, shaking her head in disbelief.

"Let me ask you something," Julia piped up. "How did you figure out I'd been in your room? I mean, I was so careful. Did you set up some kind of booby trap or something, just in case somebody did go snooping around?"

"Some cat burglar," Madison sneered. She held up the garment in her hand, which turned out to be a still-damp, white nylon running shirt, and flung it in Julia's face. "You left this."

# 34

The three women watched as Madison/Maryn gave her best effort towards stomping off in the damp khaki-colored sand. When she'd abandoned the beach, they returned their attention to Julia, who'd slumped back onto her beach towel, her hands thrown across her eyes, blocking the sun and their inquisitive stares.

"Your top?" Ellis said finally, flicking the sweaty garment with a dismissive fingertip. "Really, Julia? You didn't notice you'd left your top behind?"

"I'm sorry," Julia cried, her voice so shrill that a nearby seagull squawked in answer, and a small child walking by scampered quickly away, towards the water and an incoming wave. "Don't look at me like that. Jesus! You saw how I was dressed. I'd just come back from my run. And that attic—the temperature must have been about two hundred degrees. I couldn't get the door latch to open—sweat was pouring off of me, my hands were slippery, so I took off my top—for God's sake—I was wearing a sports bra! And I used it to get the latch open. And then I climbed in the window, and I was rummaging around in her room. She didn't even have the air conditioner on up there.

Why am I explaining all of this to you? She's the one with the stash of cash and the gun under her mattress."

"This was just a really, really bad idea," Ellis said, her voice low. "Unforgivable. I should never have gone along with this. I knew it wasn't right, but I did it anyway. I feel awful."

"Me too," Dorie said. "And I'm just as bad as you guys. I could have stopped Julia, if I'd really tried."

But Julia was unrepenetant. "Okay, so maybe I shouldn't have ransacked her room. I'm sorry. Okay? It was all my idea, and you guys are off the hook. But can we just get back to the matter at hand—which, after all, is what do we do about Madison and her gun and her giant stack o' cash?"

Dorie looked uneasily at Ellis. "I think you should go talk to her."

"Me?" Ellis was indignant. "Why me? I'm not the one who invited her to live here. And I'm not the one who is chasing her off because I went prying into her private business."

"Who else?" Dorie asked. "She hates Julia. And she doesn't trust me anymore, that's for sure. You're the calm one. The smart one. You can talk to her. You can talk to anybody. Weren't you the one who persuaded Phyllis all those years ago that the moaning coming from our den was me, writhing with cramps, instead of Kieran Boylan, crying like a little girly man because he cut his knee crawling out the back window?"

"Just ask her where the money came from," Julia advised. "But don't say anything about the gun, okay? I mean, we don't want to piss her off, just in case she's got another one hidden in her car or something."

"No!" Ellis said, flinging the sweaty top at Julia. "I am putting my foot down." Despite her protests, Ellis knew it was no use arguing or stalling. They were all in their thirties now, but she, Ellis Sullivan, was still designated driver for life.

She took a deep breath and knocked lightly on Madison's door.

"Go away," came the muffled response.

"Madison," Ellis called. "Please let me in. I want to talk to you. I want to apologize . . . for all of us."

"Fine. Whatever," Madison called. "I'm leaving in the morning, so just let it be. Let me be."

"I can't," Ellis said plaintively. "You know Julia. She's not going to let up on any of us until I talk to you. Face-to-face."

The door opened abruptly. "Make it fast," Madison said, gesturing her inside. "But this is a complete waste of time."

Ellis crossed the threshold and looked around the room. The thin, white, cotton curtains ruffled listlessly in the faint breeze.

"May I sit down?" Ellis asked.

"It's your house," Madison said bitterly. "I'm just a boarder here. With no property rights."

"About that," Ellis said, clearing her throat and perching on the edge of the narrow bed. "We owe you an apology. All of us. Except maybe Dorie. She was totally against what Julia did, but we pressured her to act as lookout, and in the end, she caved."

"Nice to know," Madison said. She was emptying the drawers of the wooden dresser, folding clothes and placing them in a duffle bag.

"We really would like to help you," Ellis said. "If you'd let us."

Madison wheeled around, fire in her eyes. "Why should I let any of you near me? Why should I trust any of you?"

"I don't know," Ellis said truthfully. "Maybe you should trust us because we've trusted you. We rented you a room, based solely on what you told us, which turned out to be a lie. We know you're mixed up in something . . . complicated. And that you're afraid of your . . . is he your ex-husband?"

"Not yet," Madison said grimly.

"What did he do?" Ellis asked. "To make you run the way you did? You don't strike me as a scaredy-cat."

"If I tell you, will you just let me alone?" Madison asked. "Not try to meddle in my affairs?"

"I'll try," Ellis said. "I can't speak for Julia—nobody speaks for her. And nobody controls her."

"My husband . . ." Madison started. "He's an accountant, back in Jersey. He handled the books for the insurance company where I used to work.

That's where we met. He asked me to lunch, I went, and pretty soon, we were living together."

"And?" Ellis said gently.

"Don was married when I met him," Madison blurted. "Of course, I didn't know that, he didn't bother to tell me he still had a wife and two teenagers. They were separated, and he did get divorced, but he was definitely still married when we started dating."

"Would you have dated him if you knew he was married?" Ellis asked, raising one eyebrow.

"Hell, no!" Madison said. "But I should have figured it out. There was a lot about Don Shackleford I should have figured out before we moved in together."

"You told Julia he was into something really bad," Ellis prompted. "What did you mean by that?"

Madison bit her lip. "He's a thief and a con man. He's been stealing from his clients, at least two million just from the insurance company, that I know about. There's probably more, though."

"How do you know?" Ellis asked. "I mean, you didn't have anything to do with it, right?"

"Oh, because of the money, right?" Madison said bitterly. "You just assume I'm a thief too?"

"I don't know what to think about you," Ellis said, exasperated. "You keep everything such a freakin' secret, what am I supposed to think?"

"I may be a lot of things, but I'm not a thief," Madison said. "Swear to God. The money was Don's. Or whoever he was stealing it from."

"So how do you know your husband was stealing?"

"Adam—he's a friend from work—told me that a team of auditors had been in the office, looking at all the files. They were investigating Don. I didn't want to believe Adam. He's always been jealous of Don, he had kind of a crush on me. So I snuck into Don's office and checked, and Adam was right. Don had all these bogus companies set up, being paid from Prescott accounts."

"What did you do?" Ellis asked. "Did you confront your husband? Did he bother to deny it?"

Madison's laugh was mirthless. "You don't *confront* Don Shackleford. It was the other way around. He drove up to the office as I was leaving and followed me home. He knew I'd been up to something, and he . . . made me tell him what I found out."

"He hurt you?"

"Not in a way that would be visible to anybody else. He grabbed me, threw me up against the wall, and calmly informed me that if I told anybody about my suspicions that he'd kill me and hide the body where nobody would ever think to look."

Ellis studied Madison's face. "You think he's capable of something like that? Murder?"

"I do now," Madison said soberly. "He's capable of that and worse."

"So you ran?"

"I didn't know what else to do," Madison said. "I was terrified. I'd begun to understand a little bit about Don—about his coldness, his dishonesty, but I truly didn't know he was capable of something like that. Not until I saw it with my own eyes. As soon as he drove off, I knew I had to get out."

"You couldn't call somebody? A relative?"

Maryn's voice was colorless. "You wouldn't understand. I don't have a lot of family, just my mom and my aunt, and we're not close. Emotionally or geographically."

"What about a girlfriend? Somebody from your office?"

"Don made me quit my job right after we got married. And anyway, I wasn't exactly chummy with the women in my office. Adam was my only friend there. He's coming here tomorrow. Him I can trust."

"Like you can't trust us?"

Maryn shrugged. "Breaking into my room, that was a really shitty thing to do. Friends wouldn't do something like that."

"You made it very clear that you didn't need any friends," Ellis reminded her. "But you're right, it really was shitty. At some point, when she starts to really think about it, Julia will realize that too."

"Doesn't matter now," Madison said.

"You still haven't told me about the money," Ellis reminded her. "You've got to admit, it's kind of shady, having all that money hidden in your closet."

"It's a long story," Madison said. "Just go, okay? Tell the others they don't have to worry about me any more."

"I'd still like to hear it, if you don't mind," Ellis said.

"Whatever," Madison said. She'd stopped folding clothes and was leaning against the wall opposite the bed where Ellis sat.

"After he threatened me, Don just left," Madison said. "It never would have occurred to him that I might disobey him. Or leave.

"But as soon as he was gone, I knew I was outta there. I threw some clothes and stuff into that," she said, gesturing towards the duffle bag. "I didn't have a plan. I mean, I had some money squirreled away." She laughed again. "My mother used to call that 'get outta town money', and how right she was. It came to a little over six thousand dollars. I grabbed that, and on the way out the door, I remembered my computer. My laptop. Don bought us new computers a few months ago. They came with matching cases, too. So I grabbed my laptop and threw it in the back of the car. And I left."

"And drove until you got to Nags Head," Ellis said. "What made you come here?"

A ghost of a smile flitted across Madison's lips. "I told myself it was a co-incidence. I was driving south, saw a billboard for Nags Head, and headed in this direction. But on all those long bike rides I've been taking, I've done some soul-searching. Nags Head was no accident."

"You'd been here before?"

"As a kid, with my parents. It was the only vacation they ever took me on. We stayed in a little motel, swam in the pool, went on the bumper cars, ate ice cream—all the stuff normal happy families do. I'd saved my allowance, and I bought a little shell-covered jewelry box with NAGS HEAD, NC, written on the lid; the first thing I ever bought with my own money."

"I think I had a jewelry box just like that," Ellis volunteered. "Except mine said TYBEE ISLAND, GA. I still have it, come to think of it."

"Mine's long gone," Madison said dully. "My parents split up when I was thirteen. We'd been living in Fayetteville, North Carolina. As soon as school was out that year, my mom loaded me in the car and we moved to New Jersey to live with my Aunt Patsy. We just drove off, with our clothes in some cardboard boxes from the liquor store. Left everything else in the house."

"Oh Lord," Ellis said. "What about your dad?"

"He got remarried," Madison said. "To a woman who'd been my mom's best friend."

Ellis looked down at her right hand, at the narrow gold band lined with tiny diamond chips that her father had given her for her thirtieth birthday. It was the last of a long line of gifts her father had given her over the years.

"Did you ever see him again?"

"Who? Oh, my dad? Not much. They moved to Daytona."

"I'm sorry," Ellis said.

"It is what it is," Madison said, practiced at not caring.

Ellis wanted to change the subject. "Your ring. The one you said was an old family piece. I noticed you stopped wearing it."

"My engagement ring. Don bought it for me, right before we got married. I'm thinking of pawning it. Wanna make me an offer?"

Ellis glanced at Madison's now-bare hands. "Why do you need to pawn it? With all that money?"

"I'm not touching that money," Madison said. "I didn't even know it was there, not until I went to unpack my laptop and realized I'd actually grabbed Don's by mistake."

"And the money was in his laptop case? Do you mind if I ask how much?"

Madison shrugged. "Close to a hundred thousand dollars."

"For real?" Ellis's eyes widened.

"I've got Don's money. And I know he's stolen millions more. He probably thinks I meant to take the cash. Now do you see why I was in such a panic when I found out Julia talked to him? What if he finds me?"

"You think he'd hurt you? To get at the money?"

"A few months ago I'd have said no. Now, for sure. With Don, it's not just about the money. It's about control. Ownership."

Ellis looked down at her hands, then out the window, thinking about her own brief marriage, and its sudden, emotionless ending. It had been so painful at the time, but maybe, in comparison to what Madison was going through, Ben's way was preferable.

"So . . . you and Don were already having problems before this?" Ellis asked.

"Yeah," Madison said sourly. "If by problems you mean he was sleeping with somebody else and I'd moved into the guest bedroom."

"Oh," Ellis said weakly.

"Don't know why I was surprised," Madison said, tossing her head, as though she didn't really care. "He cheated on his ex-wife with me, why wouldn't he cheat on me with somebody else?"

"Any idea who she is?"

Madison reached in an open dresser drawer, balled up some shirts, and tossed them at the duffle bag. "I've got a very good idea who."

Now that she'd starting talking to Ellis, it was as though she'd turned on a spigot and was powerless to turn it off. The words just kept spewing.

"Tara Powers! We worked together at the insurance company. We weren't friends or anything—but she knew Don was married to me."

Ellis kept thinking about all that money. "A hundred thousand dollars. Do you think he meant to give it to his girlfriend?"

"No way," Madison said quickly. "Not his style. Don keeps his women on a tight leash."

"So, what was he doing with all that money?" Ellis persisted.

"I don't care anymore," Madison said. "After tomorrow, I'm out of here. I'm only sticking around today because Adam begged me to. He thinks there's something he can do to get me out of this."

"Adam? That's your friend you used to work with?" Ellis asked, her curiosity aroused. "He's coming here? To Nags Head?"

"He should be about halfway here," Madison said. "He's kind of a nerd, but in a really sweet way."

"You two worked together?"

"Yep. And he's still there. He's taking a vacation day to come down here."

"You told him everything that happened?" Ellis asked, surprised.

"Most of it," Madison said. "He was on vacation when I took off. I kept trying to text him, but he never got back to me until last night. You won't believe this—he actually thinks I should go back to Jersey and calmly start divorce proceedings against Don. As if!"

"Let me ask you this," Ellis said. "You say you're not going back. What about the insurance company, the one you used to work for, that he ripped off? Don't you care about any of them?"

"I care!" Madison said. "But I don't have any proof. Those files I saw at his office? All gone now, I guarantee."

"What about his laptop? You've got that, right? Maybe there are incriminating files on that."

"I don't have the password."

"And you have no idea if the auditors found anything about the embezzlement to tie it to Don, or whether or not the insurance company has brought charges against your husband?"

"No," Madison said. "I rode my bike over to the library, thinking I could get online on their computers, see if there's been anything in the news up there," Madison admitted. "But they won't let you use the Internet unless you've got a library card. And I wasn't about to apply for one and start giving out personal information."

"Hmm," Ellis said, looking out the window. She could just see the edge of the deck of Ty's garage apartment. She could access the Internet with her iPhone, but she had an ulterior motive—seeing Ty.

"I know somebody who's got Internet access," Ellis said. "And I think maybe he'd be willing to let us use his computer, too. That is, if you want our help."

Madison hesitated. "No, never mind."

"Suit yourself," Ellis said, shaking her head. "I did my best, but you really just don't let anybody get close, do you?"

She got off the bed and went to the door. "I'll tell the girls . . . what? You're leaving tomorrow, or the day after, when your friend gets here? Dorie will be sad. She really thought she could reach out to you."

Madison let her get down the hallway before she called after her.

"Ellis?"

She turned and walked back, poking her head inside Madison's bedroom.

"What the hell," Madison said. "I've been wondering what that garage apartment looked like inside."

"Me too," Ellis said.

# 35

Ellis came flying down the stairway, with Madison trailing reluctantly behind. Julia and Dorie sat at the table in the dining room, pretending to play cards.

"We're going over to Ty's, to look up some stuff on the Internet," Ellis started.

"We know," Julia interrupted.

"What?" Madison said, stopping short, her eyes narrowed. "You bugged my room while you were ransacking it?"

"Sorry," Dorie said meekly. "We really didn't mean to eavesdrop. We were up in my room, and as it turns out, the airshaft from Madison's room runs right through my closet. We kinda heard everything you guys were saying."

Ty answered the door before they could knock. His hair was still wet from the shower, and he was dressed in khaki cargo shorts and the black Cadillac Jack's T-shirt.

"Hey!" he said, his face lighting up when he saw Ellis. He leaned forward and kissed her cheek lightly, as though they'd been doing this forever.

"You're Madison, right?" he said, holding out his hand. "The new girl. Nice to meet you."

"And you," she said stiffly.

Still swooning from the scent of Ty's soap and shampoo, Ellis blushed happily. "Are you on your way out?"

"Yeah," Ty said. "They're short a bartender again, and God knows I can use the money, so I agreed to come in and cover lunch, then hang around 'til closing. Hey, maybe you and the girls could all come over later. They're having a special drink promotion for some new citrus vodka. It probably tastes like crap, but the drinks are cheap."

"Maybe," Ellis said. "But we were wondering if we could use your computer. For research."

"Sure," Ty said, looking puzzled. "Come on in."

The apartment was even smaller than it looked from the outside. The walls were knotty pine, the varnish blackened with age, and worn green-and-white checkerboard linoleum covered the floor of what was essentially an all-in-one living room, dining room, and kitchen. The kitchen consisted of an old white-painted Hoosier cupboard stocked with a mismatched assortment of plastic dishes; a two-burner stove; and a small, rust-spotted refrigerator.

"Welcome to my office," Ty said, gesturing towards a stout oak kitchen table. A PC was set up on the table, and a metal, rolling office chair with cracked leatherette upholstery was pulled up to the makeshift desk. Nearby a rickety blue-painted bookshelf held an assortment of business books, magazines, and stacks of folders.

He leaned over, pressed a button on the computer's monitor, and the screen lit up. "The printer's right there," he said, pointing to a small table doing double duty as end table and printer stand beside the lumpy two-seater sofa. "Anything else you need, just help yourself."

"Thank you," Madison said, pulling out the desk chair and seating herself. Ellis walked out onto the deck with Ty.

"Wait," he said, ducking back inside. When he came back, he held out a single key.

"Just lock up when you leave," he said. "And keep it, if you want."

Ellis raised an eyebrow.

"I already have a key to your place," he said, with that slow grin. "Not that I'd use it without your permission, though." He glanced back towards the apartment. "What's going on with you guys? I thought you said Madison was pretty standoffish."

"She was," Ellis said. "But Madison is in real trouble. Her husband, back in Jersey, is some kind of criminal, and . . . well it's too complicated to go into right now. But she's trying to figure some stuff out, and I want to try to help her."

"That's nice," Ty said absentmindedly. "So . . . listen. When can I see you again? Tonight? Any chance you might wait up for me after I get off work?"

"There's a chance," Ellis said lightly. "Text me when you're leaving. And maybe I'll see you at Caddie's, depending on what we figure out about Madison's situation."

"We're good now, right?" he asked, catching her hand in his.

"Very good," she said. "Talk to you later."

Madison was staring quizzically at the computer screen when Ellis rejoined her. "I figured out how to open his Internet browser, but now what?" she asked.

She saw Ellis's look of surprise.

"I'm not really a computer person. I mean, I used one at work, but they had all kind of rules about using the computers for personal use. And as for my laptop at home? All I really use it for is to play online blackjack."

"Okay, well, let's go to the website for the *Philadelphia Inquirer*," Ellis suggested. She leaned over Madison's shoulder and started typing into the browser bar.

Madison quickly got up and yielded the chair to Ellis. She leaned eagerly over Ellis's shoulder and watched as she navigated around the *Inquirer's* website. "How do you spell your husband's last name?"

"S-H-I-T," Madison said, snickering, and then quickly supplying the correct spelling. Ellis typed the name into the site's search bar, and waited for a moment.

"Here it is," she said, tapping the screen.

"CHERRY HILL BUSINESSMAN WANTED FOR QUESTIONING IN EMBEZZLEMENT SCHEME," the headline read.

"Oh my God," Madison whispered as she read.

The story was over a week old.

Sources close to an investigation by local police have revealed that prominent Cherry Hill financial wiz Donald Shackleford has been implicated in an embezzlement scheme that may have drained millions of dollars from several of his client companies, including R.G. Prescott Insurers, also of Cherry Hill.

"So, you were right. The insurance company wasn't the only client he ripped off," Ellis said.

Attempts to contact Shackleford for comment have been unsuccessful, although neighbors in the upscale town house development where Shackleford lived with his second wife, Maryn, say neither he nor his wife has been seen in recent days. According to Shackleford's company website, D. Shackleford & Assoc. provides accounting and investment services to a range of firms throughout the state. Investigators have begun contacting other companies that were clients of Shackleford in an effort to determine how widespread the alleged fraud may have been.

The rest of the newspaper story detailed Don Shackleford's ties in the community and ended with a statement from his attorney saying he was confident any investigation would prove that the complaints against his client were baseless and not worthy of further comment.

Madison ran her hands through her hair and stared at the computer screen. "Can you find out if there have been any more recent stories?"

Ellis began typing into the search bar on the newspaper's website, and a moment later, links to two stories appeared.

She clicked and started reading. "Here's a piece that ran last Sunday," she said.

"EMBEZZLEMENT SUSPECT HAD TIES TO VICTIMIZED INSURANCE COMPANY," the headline read.

> As forensic accountants try to piece together what local investigators charac-
> terize as an ever-widening probe into embezzlement claims against Cherry Hill
> financial wiz Donald Shackleford, investigators say they have also begun look-
> ing into the possibility that Shackleford's wife, Maryn Vance Shackleford, 32,
> and her close associate, Adam Kuykendall, 33, of Camden, may also be involved
> in Shackleford's alleged scheme to embezzle and defraud local firm R.G.
> Prescott Insurers of millions of dollars. Maryn Shackleford and Kuykendall
> were employed in "sensitive positions" at Prescott for the past two years,
> and investigators believe they may have aided Don Shackleford's criminal
> activities.

"What?" Madison shrieked. "They think I had something to do with this shit? Sensitive position? I was a claims processor, for God's sake. Adam worked in accounting, but there's no way he had anything to do with this mess. 'Close associate'? Are these people freakin' nuts? We're not the thieves, Don is."

"Calm down," Ellis said, glancing at Madison. "It's just a newspaper story. And you'll notice none of the information has any kind of real attribution. 'Sources said'? I'm sure these reporters are just fishing for a real story without knowing any of the facts."

"Look at this!" Madison cried, flicking the computer screen. "Can you believe this?"

> At least one R.G. Prescott employee, Tara Powers, 28, an account executive at
> the firm, characterized her former coworkers Maryn Shackleford and Adam
> Kuykendall as "shadowy types" who rarely mixed with others at the insurance
> company. Powers pointed out that Maryn Shackleford met her future husband
> while acting as personal assistant to the company's president, R.G. "Robby"
> Prescott III, a position that gave her unlimited access to the company's financial
> records.

"That bitch," Madison screeched. "Shadowy types? Personal assistant? I filled in for Robby's secretary one freakin' day! That's all. One freakin' day. It happened to be the day I met Don, but what's that got to do with anything? I had access to nothing—except Robby's phone and an old copy of *People* magazine his real assistant left on top of her desk. And as for Tara being an account executive? Don't make me laugh. She works in the file room. If I ever get my hands on the little slut . . ."

"What about this?" Ellis asked, pointing to the next paragraph in the story.

Sources say Maryn Shackleford left the company several months ago, and that Kuykendall abruptly resigned from his position yesterday. Investigators questioned Kuykendall the day he resigned from R.G. Prescott, but they have been unable to contact Maryn Shackleford, who they say abruptly disappeared from the area within the past ten days. The insurance company is offering a $10,000 reward for information leading to the whereabouts of Maryn Shackleford.

Madison pounded the desktop. "God! They've put out an APB on me. And a ten-thousand-dollar reward. For what? I didn't do anything. I don't know anything."

"But this is your friend Adam, right? The one who tipped you off that auditors were looking at Don's records?" Ellis asked.

"Yeahhh," she said, looking perplexed. "But when we talked yesterday, he didn't tell me he'd quit his job. In fact, he told me he's been on vacation."

"Why would the cops question Adam about Don's embezzlement scheme?" Ellis asked.

"Maybe because he worked in the accounting department?" Madison said, looking perplexed. "I guess I'll ask him that when he gets here tomorrow."

Ellis's stomach lurched. "Madison, um, did you tell him about the money you found in Don's briefcase?"

"Yeah," she said quietly. "Sure? Why wouldn't I tell him?"

"You don't think he had anything to do with any of this, do you?"

"No!" she said. "Adam is, like, my best friend. He was my *only* friend in that office. All those backstabbing bitches I worked with treated me like a pariah. You know, they didn't even have a going-away lunch for me when I quit? Adam was different. I trusted him. My last day of work, he took me out to lunch, and we got hammered on tequila shooters. I never even went back to the office after lunch. I mean, what was the point?"

"Did you tell him where you're staying?" Ellis inquired.

"He knows I'm in Nags Head. I didn't give him the exact address, because to tell you the truth, I don't even know it."

"That might be just as well," Ellis said. "I mean, I'm not saying anything against him, but maybe, just to be cautious . . . I mean, for one thing, there's that ten-thousand-dollar reward. Adam knows what kind of car you drive, right?"

"Of course," Madison said, getting impatient. "He also kinda knows where I've been staying. I told him it's on South Virginia Dare. I told him the name of the house. Ebbtide. But I'm telling you, I know him. Adam wouldn't hurt a fly." She held up her cell phone. "I'll call him right now, get this straightened out."

Madison scrolled through her phone's recent call log, punched in a number and waited.

"Adam? It's me. Look, we need to talk. Call me right back, okay? This is really important."

She closed the phone and looked at Ellis. "I know this guy, okay? He's not like Don. He wants to help me."

Ellis wasn't totally convinced. But she didn't want to make Madison any more anxious than she already was. "Okay," she said finally. "We'll just wait and see what happens, right?"

# 36

"What did you find out?" Julia demanded as soon as Ellis and Madison got back to Ebbtide. "Is there an APB out for Maryn?"

"Madison," Dorie gently corrected her. "Remember, she likes Madison better."

"Whatever," Julia said, slapping the dining room tabletop with the palm of her hand. "Come on. Give."

Ellis glanced at Madison, and she nodded.

"So . . ." Ellis began. "We may have a problem."

She filled Dorie and Julia in on what they'd discovered from the newspaper stories.

"They're offering a ten-thousand-dollar reward for me!" Madison blurted out. "Like I'm the criminal! Like I had anything to do with stealing that money."

Ellis took a deep breath. "And there's some question about her friend Adam. He told Maryn he's on vacation, but the paper said he quit his job."

Madison shook her head and frowned. "Adam can't afford to quit. He just bought a brand-new Camaro, back in the spring. And I know for a fact his credit cards are always maxed out. Bill collectors were always calling the office looking for him."

Dorie looked horrified. "You think he'd turn you in for that ten-thousand-dollar reward?"

"No!" Madison exclaimed. "He's my friend. He wouldn't do that to me. There's gotta be an explanation for all this. Look, probably the newspaper got it wrong about him quitting his job. There's a woman at the office, Tara, I'm pretty sure she's sleeping with Don. She's the one telling the paper all these lies about me and Adam."

Dorie and Julia exchanged a look.

"I think," Ellis said, "maybe we should call the police. Just in case."

"And tell them what?" Madison said heatedly. "Here's the woman they're looking for up in Jersey? The one who maybe helped her husband steal a couple million dollars?"

"If I was a cop, I'd lock your ass up in a heartbeat," Julia said matter-of-factly. "And that's before I knew you had a hundred grand hidden on the top shelf of your armoire."

"Maybe we don't call the police right away," Dorie murmured.

"Okay," Ellis said. "What do we do—to keep Madison safe until she can go home and clear her name?"

"Look," Madison said, sounding braver than she looked. "Adam Kuyken-dall isn't exactly Al Capone. He's not even six feet tall, weighs maybe 160 pounds, soaking wet. He wears Coke-bottle glasses, and I happen to know he flunked out of community college. Twice. He's not that scary and he's really not that smart."

"But from what you say, he's in debt up to his eyeballs, and he's definitely motivated," Ellis reminded her. "That sounds like a scary combination to me. Plus, he knows where you're staying."

"I could leave," Madison replied heatedly. "I will leave. As soon as I let Adam know what's going on, I'm outta here."

"That's not necessary," Dorie said. "If you say your friend can be trusted, we believe you. We want you to stay. Right?" she said, glaring first at Julia, and then at Ellis.

"Right," Ellis mumbled.

"I never said she should go in the first place," Julia muttered.

# 37

Dinnertime. Julia stared into the refrigerator, studying its contents with a mixture of disdain and outright disgust. "Leftovers. A jar of marinara sauce. A package of chicken thighs. Since it's my night to cook, I move that we go out for dinner tonight. My treat. All in favor?"

Madison's hand shot up in the air. Dorie glanced apologetically at Ellis, and then raised her hand too.

"Oh, all right," Ellis grumbled. "I'm sick of chicken too. What did you have in mind? Do we have any coupons?"

"Pizza!" Dorie crowed. "I have been craving pizza all day. Thick, gooey, triple-cheese pizza."

"Pizza? Here?" Madison said. "What do southerners know about pizza? Have you people ever tasted real pizza? There's a place at home. Carmine's. The owner is right off the boat from Italy. The crust is so thin, it's like paper. The cheese is real fresh-shaven parmigiano-reggiano, not that crap from the green can, and they make the tomato sauce themselves, smoke and cure their own pepperoni, and they bake it in a real wood-fired pizza oven."

"Oh, God," Julia moaned. "Not a pizza snob. Spare me, please. I really don't care where we go, I just need to get out of this house tonight. I'm getting cabin fever."

"I know," Ellis said meaningfully. "It's been a long day."

"I've got a better idea than pizza anyway," Julia announced. "What about that place up the road, Tortuga something? The menu is in that notebook of yours, Ellis, and it looks pretty good. But more to the point, did you know they've got a beach-volleyball court in the back of that place?"

"Since when do you play beach volleyball?" Ellis asked.

"I don't, but guys do," Julia replied, waggling her eyebrows. "Hot, sweaty, tanned, ripped, buff guys. And did I mention shirtless? Yes, shirtless. Mmmm. How does that sound?"

"I'm in," Dorie said breathlessly.

"Dorie!" Ellis exclaimed.

"What? Look, I'm pregnant, not dead. This all-girl stuff is fine as far as it goes, but my hormones are friggin' raging out of control right now. I just want to engage in a little harmless spectator leering. Is that so wrong?"

"I wouldn't mind staring at some man-candy myself," Madison admitted. "Take my mind off my worries."

Ellis was leafing through her notebook. "Here it is," she cried triumphantly. "Tortugas' Lie! Two-for-one weeknight appetizers. But we've got to get there before seven."

"It's twenty 'til," Julia announced, getting up from the table. "Let's roll!"

They ordered steamed shrimp and crab, conch fritters, and Baja fish tacos, and ate all of it from paper plates, sitting on the wooden bleachers overlooking the restaurant's sand volleyball court, where a dozen shirtless men, as promised, jumped and spiked and dove and joked and hollered.

"Ah," Julia said, sniffing the air appreciatively. "The sweet smell of testosterone." She took a long swig from her lime-spiked Corona and tilted up the brim of the straw cowboy hat she'd grabbed on her way out the door.

"Y'all, I have a confession to make."

"This'll be good," Ellis told Madison under her breath.

"I folded. I called Booker this morning and invited him down for the weekend."

"Yay!" Dorie clapped her hands. "When's he coming?"

"He's driving down after work tomorrow. I hope nobody minds."

"Not me," Ellis said. "Does this mean you're considering his offer?"

"Offer?" Madison said.

"Booker has been begging Julia to marry him for the past year. He's taken a job as art director for a magazine in DC," Dorie explained. "He wants to buy a house and get married."

"And knock me up," Julia said dryly. "And no, this does not mean you guys should start shopping for bridesmaids' dresses. It just means that we haven't seen each other in over a month. A girl has needs, you know."

"When the trailer is a-rockin', don't come a-knockin'," Dorie quipped happily.

"Actually," Julia added, "I think he's just as interested in seeing the house as he is me."

"Which house?" Madison asked.

"Our house. The one we're staying in. Ebbtide. I've been e-mailing him the pictures I've been taking of all of us with my cell phone, and for some reason, he's fascinated with the place. I'd suggested maybe we'd want to get a hotel room, just for the weekend, you know, but Booker says he's dying to see the house. If you guys don't mind him staying with us."

"I think we might all feel a little safer with a guy around," Dorie said, and Madison nodded her agreement.

"He'd better get a good look at the house while he's here," Ellis said glumly. "Ebbtide is in foreclosure. If Ty doesn't find a way to catch up on his payments by September fifteenth, the bank will auction it off on the courthouse steps."

"What's Ty got to do with Ebbtide?" Julia asked.

Ellis smiled enigmatically. "Turns out Ty Bazemore is actually Mr. Culpepper. He owns the place! His mother's family built the house in the thirties, and Ty bought it last year from his uncle, who'd inherited it. He's been living in the garage apartment, renting out the big house, trying to raise enough money to fix it up and keep it. But then the economy went to hell, and now, if he doesn't figure something out, he'll lose it."

"Garage boy is actually Mr. Culpepper?" Dorie repeated. "Why didn't he just tell you that from the beginning?"

Ellis shrugged. "He says he never tells the tenants that he lives on the property, because then they'd be pestering him night and day. He does all the rentals, all the communication by e-mail, like he did with me. That way, he can concentrate on doing his stock research and trading."

"Hey," Julia said. "You never did tell us how your date went last night. Come on, give. And don't you dare leave out the sexy bits."

Eventually, the sun went down, and the volleyball players, sweaty and covered in sand, retreated into the bar to be joined by hordes of girlfriends and thirsty college kids.

"Where to now?" Julia asked, shouting to be heard over the din.

Ellis hesitated. "Ty mentioned that they're having some kind of special promotion at Cadillac Jack's tonight, for a new citrus-flavored vodka. Cheap drinks and karaoke. You, know, if anybody's interested."

"Karaoke? Hmm," Julia said. "So corny."

"So fun!" Dorie insisted. "Come on, you guys. Let's go. I'm finally starting to get some energy again. And I love karaoke. You guys can party and not worry. I'll be the designated driver."

Twenty minutes later, they were pulling into the parking lot at Caddie's. A huge hot-pink canvas banner fluttered from the front of the building. PUCKER-UPPER NITE, it proclaimed. PUCKERADE COCKTAILS, $2.

"I can't wait to see what goes into a Puckerade cocktail," Julia said as they elbowed their way into the crowded bar.

"There's Ty," Dorie said, pointing towards the bar. "Come on, let's get a table." She gave Ellis a gentle push in that direction. "Let him know we're here, and order us some drinks, okay? See if they can make me something without any booze, will you?"

"Well, hello," Ty said, when Ellis finally managed to slither through the three-deep row of women pressed up against the bar. "How about a Pucker-Upper? Tastes like shit, if you ask me, but these women seem to be lapping them up."

And it was true, it seemed that each woman in the crowd was clutching, or sucking from, a yellow, vaguely lemon-shaped plastic orb with a straw sticking out of the top.

"Okay," Ellis said. "Three Pucker-Uppers, and something nonalcoholic for Dorie."

Ty handed her one of the lemon cups, and Ellis, feeling suddenly overcome with shyness, took a long drink. And then another.

"Not so bad," she pronounced.

"The others came too?" Ty asked, obviously pleased. "Even Madison?"

"Even Madison," Ellis nodded. "Hey, thanks for letting us use your computer. It looks like Madison may be in more trouble than we knew. According to the Philly paper, it looks like the police back in Jersey want to talk to her about the money her husband embezzled from the insurance company where she worked. There's sort of a reward out for her."

"You really think somebody might come looking for her? Is it safe?"

"I'm not sure," Ellis admitted. "Madison's friend from work, a guy named Adam, is somehow mixed up in all this stuff, and he's supposedly on his way here to see her. I'm a little worried because he knows she's staying at Ebbtide. Not the address, exactly, but he does know the street name and the name of the house. So yeah, I don't want to sound too paranoid, but I'm actually a little worried."

Ty frowned. "I've got a friend who's a sheriff's deputy, Connor Terry. In fact, he's working the door tonight. I could ask him to roll past the house in his county cruiser, keep an eye out."

"Could you?" Ellis said gratefully. "That would make me feel a lot better."

"Sure, no problem," Ty said. "Where you sitting? I'll send Nella over with the drinks as soon as she comes back."

Ellis reached for her pocketbook to pay, but Ty shook his head. "On the house," he said.

Julia took a cautious sip of her drink. "Not bad," she admitted.

Madison sipped, but made a face, pushing the souvenir cup away. "Kinda tastes like lemon Pledge, if you ask me."

"It's okay," Ellis said, working on her second drink of the night. "Anyway, the price is right."

"Ooh, free drinks," Julia drawled. "Aren't you clever, shagging the bartender?"

"I am not..." Ellis started, and then dissolved into a fit of Pucker-Upper fueled giggles.

"Yet," Dorie said, hopefully.

"Yet," voted Madison, suddenly realizing how much she enjoyed the company of these women, how much fun it was to tease Ellis, and yes, even to bait Julia.

An hour later, their tabletop was littered with yellow plastic Pucker-Upper cups. Karaoke had started, and three sunburnt chicks wearing UNC-Greensboro T-shirts stood on the postage-stamp-sized stage, arms locked around each other's shoulders, swaying as they shrieked a drunken, tuneless version of "Lady Marmalade."

"Sounds like a cat got skinned," Madison complained. "Voulez vous shut the fuck up?"

"Think you can do better?" Julia retorted.

"Not a chance," Madison said. "I'm a wanted woman, remember?"

"Ellis!" Dorie cried. "You have to. Please?"

"Who, me?" Ellis laughed. "You know me better than that. As far as I'm concerned, karaoke is strictly a spectator sport."

"Don't look at me," Julia warned. "This was your idea, not mine."

"Spoilsports," Dorie said, pretending to pout. "Y'all are no fun anymore."

So they stayed, and drank, and danced as a pack, even persuading Madison, once, to join them in the Electric Slide, and Ty kept sending drinks over, and Ellis kept glancing over her shoulder to watch him in action behind the bar. He was so fine, she thought. So fine. And mine.

In the end, it was Dorie's bladder, not exhaustion, that did them in. "Y'all," she complained, hopping from one foot to another. "The line to the ladies room is like twenty people long."

"Oh, just go in the men's room," Julia grumbled. "There aren't hardly any men here tonight. No *straight* men, that is."

"There's twice as many girls in the men's room line," Dorie said. "Come on, y'all, if I don't get out of here right this minute, I'm gonna pop."

"Might as well," Ellis said, getting somewhat unsteadily to her feet. "They close at two. C'mon, Julia, let's get little mama home."

She tried to catch Ty's eye as they were leaving the club, but there was still a crowd standing at the bar, and Dorie was tugging at her, urging her to hurry.

When they got back to Ebbtide, Dorie pulled the red van almost to the edge of the porch, put the car in park, and jumped out and raced for the front door, fumbling for her keys as she went.

Madison hesitated, getting out of the backseat of the van. She looked up at the silent house, and the dull, yellow glow of the porch light they'd left burning, and then back again at the end of the driveway, bathed in a pool of pale white from the street lamp. No cars drove past. It was eerily quiet, except for the thrum of cicadas.

For the tenth time, she pulled her cell phone from her purse to check for missed calls. Nothing. She frowned.

Ellis climbed out of the van in time to see Madison tuck her phone away.

"Maybe Adam changed his mind," she offered.

"He should have been here by now," Madison fretted. "Something's wrong. I just know it. It's not safe. If Don figures out I'm here . . ."

"He won't," Ellis assured her. "Anyway, Ty is friends with a sheriff's deputy here. He was actually working the door at Caddie's tonight. Ty promised he'd get the guy to drive past the house tonight and tomorrow in his sheriff's cruiser. You know, just in case."

"A sheriff's deputy?" Madison shrugged. "I guess it couldn't hurt."

"Anybody hungry?" Dorie asked hopefully, standing in the kitchen doorway.

"After all that stuff we ate tonight?" Madison shook her head. "I guess you really are eating for two now."

"She's always been like that," Julia said. "Ever since she was a kid. Eats like a little piggy and never gains an ounce."

"What did you have in mind?" Ellis asked. "Have we got any dessert?"

"Fudgsicles and some store-bought pound cake and some strawberries," Dorie reported.

"Okay, you talked me into it," Julia relented. "All that dancing we did tonight has to have burned off a boatload of calories. And I'll run off the rest in the morning."

"I'm in," Ellis said. "Madison?"

"Not me," Madison said. "I'm turning in." She turned and headed for the stairway, but then stopped, and came back into the kitchen.

"Hey, ladies," she said shyly. "Thanks. I had a good time tonight. So thanks . . . for everything. Really. In case I forget to tell you tomorrow."

Julia managed a crooked smile. "And Madison? I really am sorry about the, you know, uh . . ."

"Break-in?" Madison shrugged. "What break-in?"

Julia groaned and pushed away the half-eaten bowl of strawberries and cake. "Gawwd. Why did I let y'all talk me into eating this mess? I'm going to bed. Booker will be here tomorrow, and I've got to get my beauty sleep."

"I'm coming too," Dorie said, stacking the bowls in the sink. "You, Ellis?"

"I'll be along," Ellis said casually. "I think I'll just tidy up in here a little bit." It was after two, and she'd promised Ty she'd wait up for him. She had her cell phone on the counter, and kept eyeing it, waiting for his text.

"You don't fool me, Ellis Sullivan," Julia said, yawning again. "You're waiting for a call from garage guy."

"Actually," Ellis admitted, "he said he'd text me when he was leaving the club."

Julia gave Dorie an elaborate wink. "She's gonna have to pay for all those free drinks one way or another."

"You're such a romantic, Julia," Dorie said. She grabbed Julia's hand and tugged. "C'mon. I'll race you for the bathroom."

# 38

Alone in the kitchen, Ellis washed, dried, and put away the dishes. She smiled as she traced the faded pattern of green leaves and pink rosebuds on the delicate gold-edged china. Such a sweet gesture on Ty's part, giving them his grandmother's dishes.

It was nearly 2:30 in the morning. To kill time, she got a bottle of spray cleaner and spritzed all the counters. Then she swept the floor, and finally, took the damp dish towel out to the back porch to dry on the makeshift clothesline the girls had rigged up between the weathered gray porch posts.

It was still unbelievably hot and humid outside. She glanced at the rusted Sunbeam Bread thermometer tacked to the wall beside the kitchen door. Eighty-six degrees! Still, she thought, glancing up at the deep, velvet sky, the stars were so plentiful and bright this time of night. Maybe she'd take a walk on the beach while she waited for Ty. She'd read a magazine article about how summertime was the season when sea turtles lumbered ashore all along the East Coast to lay eggs, and had even seen signs on the beach warning people not to disturb the turtle nests. Wouldn't it be amazing if she came across a nest of sea turtle eggs? She ducked back into the house, grabbed her cell phone, and strolled down the boardwalk over the dunes.

Leaving her shoes at the bottom of the beach staircase, Ellis let her feet sink into the cool, damp sand. The tide was out. She walked to the water's edge, letting the incoming waves tickle her ankles. She inhaled deeply, taking in the scent of salt and sun-baked sand, and started walking north, confident that she would not get lost or panicked this time.

She walked for fifteen minutes, zigzagging between the waterline and the dunes, before she saw it: two wavy, parallel lines in the sand, which crossed in a X shape, leading up to a sort of crater shape in the soft sand at the edge of a dune.

Ellis tiptoed over to the crater. The sand here had clearly been disturbed. Had she found a turtle nest? She looked back towards the water, wondering about the odd X-shaped lines, until it occurred to her that if she had indeed discovered a nest, maybe one track was from the turtle, making its way up to the dune line, and the other was the turtle's return track to the ocean.

She knelt in the soft sand and peered down at the impression in the sand, holding her breath, as though even the softest sound might disturb what was under the sand. Should she touch it if it was a nest? And if it was a nest, and she did touch it, would that deter the mother sea turtle from returning to tend to its eggs? She frowned, wishing she knew more. She really wanted to feather the sand aside, to see if, by some miracle, there could be eggs there. She straightened and looked around, but the beach was deserted. As she looked up, she felt a drop of water on the back of her neck.

It had started to rain. Reluctantly, she stood up, brushing sand from her knees. She looked around for something to mark the nest, so that she could find it again in the morning. Finding a piece of a windbreak, she managed to wrench off a weathered wooden stake, and poked it into the sand a few inches from the nest.

"Okay, turtle babies," she whispered, as the rain began to fall harder. "I'll check back with you little guys later, okay?"

As she trotted back through the rain, she heard her cell phone ping, and looked down at the text message there.

I'M HERE. WHERE ARE U?

Ellis smiled, tucked the phone back into her pocket to keep it dry, and picked up her pace.

She was soaking wet and out of breath as she climbed the last step to the garage apartment deck. The light was on inside, and she tapped on the door. Ty opened it and laughed when he saw her bedraggled condition.

"Get lost again?" he asked, pulling her inside and out of the rain.

"No," she said excitedly. "I was walking on the beach, and I saw these tracks in the sand. Ty, I think maybe I found a sea turtle nest!"

"Really? Cool. This is definitely nesting season. Were there any eggs in it?" He disappeared into another room and came back with a dry towel.

"Thanks." She started toweling off her arms and her hair. "I was afraid to disturb it. I mean, I know sea turtles are endangered, and I didn't know if it was against the law to tamper with a nest, so I just found a piece of wood and stuck it down in the sand to mark it. If it really is a nest, maybe I can find it in the morning and check it out."

"You did the right thing," Ty said approvingly. "Did you notice what mile marker the nest was near?"

"It was at number seventeen," she said proudly.

"I'm sure it'll be fine," Ty said. "I'll call the Sea Turtle Patrol hotline and let them know you found it, and they'll cordon it off and monitor it. Sometimes, if they find a nest in a high-traffic area, they'll even move it to a safer place, where it won't get disturbed."

Ellis's face glowed with excitement. "We could go back now, couldn't we? And just shift the sand a little, to see if there are any eggs?"

He gestured towards the deck. "In this rain?"

She looked out the window and saw that the rain was coming down in sheets now.

"Oh," she said, sounding deflated. "I guess maybe not."

She looked down at the floor, where a small puddle of rainwater had formed beneath her feet, and shivered.

"You're cold," he said, and he ducked into the next room. When he came back, he was holding a faded, navy blue terry cloth bathrobe.

"Here," he said, handing it to her. "You're soaked. Get out of those clothes, and I'll put the kettle on. And," he said, sternly, "don't give me that look. I'm not gonna jump you, for God's sake. I'm not that kinda guy."

Ellis laughed despite herself. "How do you know I'm not that kind of girl?"

"Some things you just know," Ty said.

She went into the adjoining room, his bedroom, and closed the door. She looked around with interest. The walls here were the same bleached-out cedar as the exterior of the apartment. The wooden floors were painted battleship gray, covered with a faded red-and-white-striped rag rug. The bed was a double with a lumpy mattress, but it was tidily made up with a quilt of blue-and red patchwork stars. A standing fan in the corner stirred the air in a desultory way.

Ellis stripped off her wet clothes. She went into the adjoining bathroom, found another towel, and finished drying herself off before folding herself into the oversized bathrobe, inhaling its perfume of aftershave. The bathroom was tiny, with a scarred linoleum floor, a miniscule wall-hung sink, and a commode. She gazed into the cloudy mirror and fluffed her damp hair, finger combing it away from her face. She squeezed a dollop of Ty's toothpaste onto her index finger, and scrubbed her teeth as best she could.

Tonight, she thought, shivering in anticipation. She placed her wet clothes on the towel rack, belted the robe snugly, and padded barefoot out into the living room.

"Here," Ty said, handing her a heavy china mug. "I don't have any milk or anything. How about some honey?"

"Honey would be good," Ellis said. She watched as he pulled a plastic bear-shaped bottle from the shelf of the Hoosier cupboard and drizzled honey into the cup. And before she could stop him, he added a healthy slug of Jack Daniel's from a bottle he had standing on the counter.

"Hot toddy," he said, handing the cup back. He picked up his own mug, and steered her towards the sofa.

She sat down and took a sip of the steaming tea, enjoying the sweet burn of the whiskey. Ty sat beside her. She propped her bare feet up on a coffee table made from a battered ship's hatch, and snuggled into his arms. The robe slipped open at the hem, but Ellis decided she didn't care. Tonight.

"Long night," Ty said, as he yawned.

"Long day. All that drama with Julia burglarizing Madison's room. I really thought she was gonna tear Julia limb from limb," Ellis said. "I think maybe we're okay now, though."

"Good," Ty said, yawning elaborately again. "I saw you guys dancing together. It looked like you were having fun with the Electric Slide."

Ellis blushed. "It was all those Pucker-Uppers you kept sending over."

"Just trying to keep the ladies happy," Ty said nonchalantly.

She turned and looked at him. "You did." After a moment she said, "Ty?"

"Hmm?" He kissed the top of her head, and they yawned in unison.

"This is kinda nice," Ellis said, after a long, companionable silence. His hand found its way inside the neckline of the robe, and he was stroking her bare collarbone. She closed her eyes, savoring the warmth of his skin on hers. This, this was what she'd been missing all these years. She felt warm and safe and . . . cared for.

"Mmm-hmmm," Ty said. "Ellis?"

"Mm-hmm?"

"Do you think this could be our do-over date?"

"Kind of a weird date, don't you think?"

"Yeah, but it's nicer than our first one."

"That's true." She put her head on his shoulder and yawned sleepily.

"So, that would make this, like, our third date, if you count the first do-over."

"Whatever."

Her eyelids drooped, and he gently removed the mug from her hand.

A lifetime later, she stirred, and turned her head because the sun was shining in her eyes. She stretched luxuriously, and then, startled, sat up. She was stretched out on the sofa, with the blue-and-red patchwork quilt tucked around her, and sunlight was streaming in through the slats of the wooden blinds.

She walked to the bathroom, washed her face, and squeezed another line of toothpaste onto her finger and applied it to her teeth. The clothes she'd peeled out of the night before were laid out on a wooden bench at the foot of the empty bed, still damp. She shrugged. So much for her big plans for last night. What a dud she was. Tightening the belt of the bathrobe, she went back to the living room. The computer was on, and there was a stack of papers and books beside it.

Ellis opened the screen door to the deck. Ty was looking out at the ocean, his back to her, with the wind blowing his sun-streaked blond hair. His baggy white boxers rode low on his lean, tanned hips, and his bare shoulders gleamed in the sunlight, muscles rippling just beneath the skin as he lazily raised his arms and did a full stretch. Oh God, he was so gorgeous. She could see the outline of his butt through the thin white cotton of his boxers, and she was so aroused, and so surprised by how aroused she was, it took her breath away. And then he turned, caught her watching him, and his lips did that slow, secret-smile thing. Just for her.

"Mr. Culpepper?" Ellis said.

"That's me," Ty said, opening his arms. "What can I do for you?"

"I'm sorry about last night," she said, snuggling up to his bare chest. "Please don't take it personally. It was all that booze. I can't believe I just passed out on you like that."

"Entirely my fault," Ty told her. "But I think I know how you can make it up to me."

He took her hand and led her into the bedroom. "I'm gonna need that robe back," he said, stretching out on the bed.

"Right now?"

He nodded solemnly. "Afraid so."

Her fingers fumbled as she tried to unknot the belt. Damn it! She could do this. She'd been ready to do it last night. Why was she so nervous now—in the daylight? She had done it before, hadn't she? Ty tugged at the belt and pulled her down till she was sitting on the edge of the bed beside him. "Allow me," he said. "I have some experience with this type of thing."

"I bet you do."

He had the grace to blush. "I meant, it's my robe. That's all. It was a high school graduation present."

"From Kendra?" She regretted it the minute the words were out of her mouth.

But Ty seemed unfazed. "No, from my nana. Mrs. Culpepper."

"Ohhh," Ellis said.

Ty unknotted the robe and slipped it from her shoulders, running his hands down her shoulders, to her bare hips, pulling her closer. He cupped her breast in one hand, lowered his head and kissed it delicately. Ellis shivered, and he gathered the other breast and did the same. Was this really happening, at last?

He looked down at her and smiled. "You're beautiful, you know that, Ellis Sullivan?"

She shivered again, and felt suddenly shy. "You're just saying that."

"No," he shook his head. "I've thought it since the first time I spotted you the day you moved in here. You're gorgeous. Especially now. Especially naked. Naked, you're a goddess."

She laughed, and then his face grew serious. He pulled her down beside him, and his lips found hers. But then his hand inched lower, touching her between her legs with feather-soft stokes, and she grew dizzy as her body remembered long-forgotten pleasures. He touched her, and she arched up to meet him, and her body throbbed in a way she was sure it had never done before.

Ty flicked his tongue across her nipple, and she heard herself gasp. She trailed her fingers down his chest, lightly, lightly, until they rested just below the waistband of his boxers. She felt him shudder, and she slid her hands down his hips and effortlessly rolled the boxers down to his ankles. He kicked them free of the bed, rolled to one side, and fumbled for something in the nightstand beside the bed.

He held the foil-wrapped package so she could see it. "Ellis Sullivan, are you usually the kind of girl who does this on a fourth date?" he asked, his gray-blue eyes twinkling.

"Not usually," she told him truthfully, taking the condom from him and ripping the foil. "But in your case, I'm willing to make an exception."

# 39

Ellis was relieved to see that the red van was gone. She unlocked the front door and tiptoed into the house. She'd almost made it to her bedroom when Julia's bedroom door opened and she popped her head out.

Julia's glance took in Ellis's disheveled appearance, the borrowed bathrobe, and the armful of Ellis's own, damp clothing. "So," she grinned approvingly. "It finally happens. Ellis Sullivan does the walk of shame. Wish Dorie were here to enjoy it with me."

"Shut up," Ellis said happily. "Where is Dorie?"

"You won't believe it," Julia said. "Remember that bouncer at Caddie's last night? Ty's friend Connor?"

"Ty mentioned him, but I didn't get to meet him," Ellis said.

"No, but Dorie apparently did get to meet him at some point last night, and make a favorable impression," Julia said. "He 'dropped by' a little while ago, allegedly to check on our security, but actually to check out Dorie. You should see this dude! Six-four, and bald as a billiard ball."

"Allegedly?"

Julia's lips pressed together with barely suppressed mirth. "I realize that you've been a little, ahem, *preoccupied* today, but yes, if you'd seen the way he looked at her, you'd know he's definitely interested in Dorie."

"Oh, come on, Julia," Ellis said, leaning on the bathroom doorjamb. "Does everything always have to be about men with you?"

"Me!" Julia said with a wicked cackle. "I'm not the one who snuck out after midnight and came strolling home at noon wearing nothing but a smile and her boyfriend's bathrobe."

"Ty's not my . . ." Ellis stopped in midsentence. If Ty wasn't her boyfriend, what was he, and what did that make her, since she had just spent the whole delicious morning in his bed?

"You still haven't told me where Dorie is," she said, changing tack.

Julia rolled her eyes. "You haven't been listening. She's gone off with Connor Terry. He was driving his county unit, and even though he's off duty, there's some kind of rule against civilians riding in a cop car. Unless they're under arrest. So she was following him in the van. Of course, they left here three hours ago, so God knows where they've gone now. Or what they're up to," she added hopefully.

"You have a one-track mind, Julia Capelli," Ellis said primly. "A smutty one-track mind. And I, for one, am headed for the shower."

"What?" Julia said mockingly. "You and Ty didn't shower off together?"

Ty had, in fact, strongly suggested a communal shower. But since the garage apartment's shower consisted of a tiny wooden stall on the deck overlooking the beach, with only a slatted wooden door separating a bather from the beach, and said beach was already teaming with summer sun-seekers, Ellis had firmly assured him that she would just as soon shower at Ebbtide, thank you very much.

"Next time," Ty had said, reluctantly, his hand just barely brushing her breast as he handed her the robe. "It's got hot water and everything."

Ellis shivered with delight at the thought of the next time. And the next. How had she gone this long without sex? And how could she have mistaken what she had with Ben for what she had with Ty? And when could she have it again?

.   .   .

Ellis was slipping a clean T-shirt over her head when her cell phone rang.

"Hey," she said, feeling unaccountably shy.

"Hey," Ty said. "Listen, I completely forgot we were supposed to go check on that sea turtle nest you found last night."

"Oh, my gosh, you're right," Ellis said. "I guess, uh, with everything else . . ." Looking in the mirror over her dresser she saw that her face was in flames.

"Yeah, I guess you could say something came up," Ty laughed. "And now, damn it, I've got to go in to Caddie's. I can't afford to turn down a shift right now. So, if I give you the Turtle Patrol number, can you call them and tell 'em where to find it?"

"Absolutely," Ellis said, scrabbling around in the drawer of her nightstand for a pencil and paper.

"Great," Ty said. "I'll call you later, okay?"

"Okay," Ellis said.

"You doing anything tonight?" he asked.

"Only if you want to," Ellis said.

"I want."

Julia and Ellis were sitting on the porch when Madison came pedaling down the driveway towards Ebbtide.

"We're gonna go grab some lunch," Julia said casually. "Wanna come?"

"No thanks," Madison said, mostly out of habit. And then, "Oh, hell. Who am I kidding? I'm starved. Where did you have in mind?"

"Let's just cruise down the main drag and see what looks good," Ellis suggested.

"That place," Madison said, when they'd driven a couple miles north on Croatan Highway. She was pointing at a roadside diner. BOB'S GRILL, the sign said in large letters, and in even larger letters, EAT AND GET THE HELL OUT.

"I've been riding my bike past that joint for two weeks, laughing my ass off every time," Madison said. "Breakfast all day. Let's check it out."

They ordered Diet Cokes and perused the menus. Ellis decided on the

Southwestern omelet, with sour cream, extra salsa, and bacon, Madison ordered a club sandwich, and Julia, reluctantly, asked for scrambled eggs, one slice of dry whole wheat toast, and a bowl of melon. "I got an e-mail from my agent, and he's booked me for a JCPenney catalog shoot the first week of September," she said gloomily. "Holiday and midpriced resort wear. Week after next."

Ellis felt a pang of panic. Only one more week of August. One more week of Ebbtide. One more week with Ty.

"You don't sound too excited," Madison observed.

Julia shrugged and sipped her Diet Coke. "It's work. I've got to make a living. It's as simple as that."

"Not really," Ellis said. "You hate modeling. You told us yourself. Booker wants to marry you. He makes a good living, and he'd support you no matter what you decide to do next."

Julia looked over at Madison, who was busy shredding her paper napkin. "Would you tell her, please? Tell her what happens when you get married to somebody just to keep a roof over your head? What happens when you sell yourself?"

"Julia!" Ellis said sharply, her face burning with embarrassment for Madison.

But Madison didn't look angry or embarrassed. "Is that what you think I did?" she asked, rubbing her bare arms absentmindedly.

"Didn't you? That was the impression you gave us when you talked about Don Shackleford," Julia said.

"My mistake wasn't in marrying Don," Madison said. "It was in falling in love with him. My mistake was lying to myself about what he was, and then, when it became painfully clear what he was, in telling myself that I could change him. My timing really sucked," she said, laughing ruefully. "I didn't decide to leave him until the minute he decided he would never let me leave."

Julia sat back in the diner booth and looked blankly at the woman opposite her. The woman who'd been living in their third-floor bedroom for the past three weeks, an enigma personified, was suddenly baring her soul as casually as she'd just ordered lunch.

"Deep down, I knew Don for what he was," Madison went on. "And if I'm being brutally honest, I probably suspected he was married when we met. Even though I always talked the talk about not dating a married man. The signs were there. I just chose to ignore them."

"That doesn't make you a bad person," Ellis said, feeling suddenly loyal.

"Nope, just an incredibly stupid one," Madison agreed. "I think Amy Shackleford was probably ecstatic I took Don off her hands. She got the money, and she didn't have to live with him. Smart lady."

Madison stopped fiddling with her paper napkin. She leaned across the table and stared directly at Julia. "You're a smart lady too, Julia. If you love this guy, if you want to be with him, and make a life with him, do that. Stop worrying about your mother's marriage, or mine, or anybody else's. Life is too damned short. . . ."

"I'm only thirty-five," Julia protested. "I've got plenty of time."

Madison raised one eyebrow. "And how old is Booker?"

The waitress arrived with a tray full of food. She set their meals down. Julia took one look at the scrambled eggs and dry toast and handed it back to the waitress.

"Sorry, but I changed my mind," she said. "I'll have the breakfast burrito with cream cheese and crabmeat, a side order of country sausage. And a biscuit. A big ol' biscuit. With butter and jelly."

She looked at Ellis and Madison.

"I decided you two might be right," she said simply. "Life's too short to eat dry toast. I'm still working on the rest."

Ellis waited as long as she could, and then took a bite of her omelet. "I'm sorry," she said. "It's terrible, with all that's happened. But I can't help it. I am truly about to faint from hunger."

"Go ahead," Madison said, waving airily. "I'm hungry myself." She lifted the edge of the top layer of toast, and delicately salted the deep red tomato.

"Not as hungry as Ellis," Julia said mischeviously. "I think she probably skipped breakfast, but I'm not certain, since she never came back home last night."

Madison picked up a piece of bacon and nibbled. "Why, Ellis!" she said. "Congratulations."

# 40

W ell, hello," Ellis said, propping herself on her elbows and shading her eyes from the low-lying sun. "Where on earth have you been all day?"

Dorie giggled as she spread out a blanket on the sand beside her friend. "I've been . . . everywhere." She unloaded a *People* magazine, a tube of sunscreen, and a bottle of water from her tote bag.

"Alone?"

"Nope," Dorie said, "I've been with Connor. All day."

Ellis lowered her sunglasses and peered over them at Dorie. Her hair was windblown and her nose and cheeks were sunburnt. Over her bathing suit she wore an oversized T-shirt with the Dare County Sheriff's Department logo emblazoned on the front, and she had a black DCSD baseball cap jammed on her head.

"Is that so?"

"Yes, it is," Dorie said. She rolled up a beach towel, propped it under her head, opened her magazine, and began humming.

"Is that . . ." Ellis strained to catch the melody.

"Don't bother," Dorie said airily. "I guarantee you don't know it."

"Hum some more," Ellis ordered. It was an old game she and Baylor played as children on long family car rides. Their own version of *Name That Tune*, even though they were decades too young to have ever seen the old television show.

Dorie hummed another bar. "Give up?"

"Oh, all right," Ellis said. "What's the song?"

"'Crazy Ex-Girlfriend.' Miranda Lambert."

"Country music?" Ellis said in mock horror. "Since when?"

"Since today," Dorie said. "Connor loves country music. We went for a ride in his boat after lunch, and we listened to a country radio station. But not that old twangy 'my dawg died and my mama's in prison' crap. We listened to Miranda Lambert and Lady Antebellum and Big & Rich. . . ."

"Hmm," Ellis said.

Dorie looked up from her magazine. "What's that supposed to mean?"

"Nothing. Just hmmm. I mean, you just met this guy when he came roaring up in his police cruiser this morning, then you spend the entire day with him, and suddenly you're a country music expert. The next thing we know, you'll be picking out china patterns."

"Not funny," Dorie said, snapping the pages of her magazine. "He's a nice guy, that's all. And for your information, I'd met him earlier."

"How much earlier?"

"At the club," Dorie said, sniffing. "Ty introduced us when I was coming back from my ninth or tenth trip to the bathroom. He said he loved my Electric Slide, and he wanted to know if he could buy me a drink."

"And you said . . . ?"

"I said, 'Hi, my name's Dorie. I'm not currently drinking alcohol because I'm four months pregnant, but I'm getting divorced. Are you a Virgo?'"

"Hmm."

"Kidding!" Dorie said. "I didn't even give him my phone number. Anyway, you're the one who asked Ty to have his bouncer-slash-cop friend drive by the house, so this is really all your doing."

"Not my business," Ellis said.

"Look," Dorie said, slapping the magazine down on the blanket. "I'm not like you or Julia. Okay? I like guys. Always have. I like talking to them, hanging out with 'em. And I like sex. Always have. That doesn't exactly make me a dirty girl, you know."

"I know," Ellis said hastily. "I'm really not judging you...."

"Good," Dorie said. "Connor is a decent guy. He makes me laugh. He's so different from Stephen. He's... uncomplicated. He says what he thinks. He loves country music, and riding around in his boat. He's got a Harley too. He likes his job. Loves his job, actually. I told him I'm gonna be living alone when I get back home, and he's offered to take me to the firing range and show me how to fire a gun. And I'm going to do it, damn it."

"You're sure this is not about being on the rebound from Stephen?" Ellis asked.

"Maybe, but I don't think so. Look, this sounds conceited, but you've known me my whole life. Guys come on to me. All the time. They just do. And you know I'm not doing anything to encourage them. Just since I've been up here, I've been hit on by the seafood manager at Food Lion, the pimply gross guy at the pizza place, even the pharmacist at Walgreens, for God's sake, when I was picking up my prenatal vitamins!"

Ellis sighed. "It's a fact. You're a man magnet."

"And I have totally blown off each and every one of those guys," Dorie said. "Just not interested. Until Connor. He really is different from those other guys. I'm not saying I want to marry him. But I would like to spend time with him, and see what comes of it."

"Did you tell him... ?"

"Yes," Dorie said, sounding exasperated. She pulled up the tank top and pooched out her tummy. "I really can't hide it in this bathing suit. And I didn't want to. I told him the short version. That I'm pregnant, and I'll be getting a divorce as soon as I get home."

"What was his reaction?"

"He was so sweet," Dorie exclaimed. "He's got a sister who's exactly the same number of weeks pregnant as me. It didn't seem to faze him a bit, Ellis. He's a little bit younger than us, but I swear, he's way more mature than Stephen could ever hope to be. So that's where we stand."

"Are you gonna see him again?"

"As a matter of fact, we're supposed to have dinner tomorrow night," Dorie said. "I know it all seems like this is happening pretty fast, but I'm only here for another week. I want to see how this plays out. And so does he. And there's just one more thing I've been thinking about."

"What's that?" Ellis asked warily.

"Well," Dorie said, giving her an exaggerated wink, "I can pretty much do whatever I want right now. You know, romance-wise."

"How's that?" Ellis asked.

"'Cuz I'm already knocked up!"

"Incorrigible," Ellis laughed. "Eudora the incorrigible. Anyway, I really, really hope this thing with Connor will work out."

"Because?" Dorie gave her a fishy look.

"Because I would just love to see the look on Phyllis's face the day you introduce her to your gun-totin', Harley-riding, country-music-loving, bald-headed cop boyfriend. I bet she'd blow a gasket."

"Definitely," Dorie agreed. "Plus I forgot to mention he only went to college for two years. And," she crowed. "Get this: Connor is Baptist."

"Oh yeah," Ellis said. "That'd put her in the grave for sure."

At some point, Ellis dozed off. When she awoke, it was nearly six, and Dorie was also, apparently, rousing herself from a catnap. The tide was coming in, and the languorous waves were lapping perilously close to their base camp.

Ellis stood and began to gather her belongings.

"Where you headed?" Dorie asked.

"Up to the house," Ellis said. "I've had enough beach for one day."

Dorie reached for her cell phone and checked the time. "Might want to give it another thirty minutes or so."

"Why's that?" Ellis asked, stowing her book and towel in her bag.

"I was up at the house for a potty break, around four o'clock, and Booker had just gotten in," Dorie said. "I think Julia was hoping for some 'quiet time.' "

"Gotcha," Ellis said. "I haven't seen Booker in ages. How is he?"

"He's okay. Still not what I expected for Julia. But nice. Kinda quiet. I guess I knew he was older, but maybe I forgot. His hair is totally gray, which I personally think is sexy as hell. Julia, for all her blasé attitude, was really, really excited that he was coming. After you guys got back from lunch she even went to that day spa down the street and got a pedicure and a Brazilian wax."

"Ow," Ellis said.

"Ditto," Dorie said. "Makes me glad I'm a natural redhead." She swung her head around and studied Ellis. "You ever get one of those?"

"Hell, no," Ellis said emphatically. "I don't even like to get my eyebrows waxed. I am definitely not letting some strange Vietnamese chick pour boiling wax on my girlie parts. Anyway," she added, "I really haven't needed to worry about landscaping that area of the territory until recently, if you get my drift."

Dorie grinned. "Until very recently, from what I understand."

"No comment," Ellis said. "I suppose Julia already spilled the beans?"

"Absolutely. What did you expect? Anyway," Dorie said primly, "I don't judge."

"Ha!"

But when Ellis and Dorie came trudging up the boardwalk towards the house, they were met by the sight of Booker, laying flat on his stomach on the deck, with a long-lensed camera, snapping photographs of the house, with Julia standing beside him, another camera lens in hand.

"Hey, Booker," Ellis said.

"Hey there," Booker said, looking up from the camera and giving her a brief smile before turning back to his camera.

"He's trying to shoot the back of the house before he loses the light," Julia explained.

"Okay," Ellis said. "We're going to head for the house, will we be in the way?"

"Not at all," Booker said. "In fact, it'd be good to have somebody in a few of the shots. When you get up to the porch, stand at the rail and look back towards me, if you would, please. But not at me, right?"

Dorie and Ellis got up to the porch and stood self-consciously for a moment, looking out at the dunes and the deepening twilight. A slight breeze bent the sea oats, and large dragonflies skimmed just over the waving fronds.

"It's so beautiful this time of day," Dorie said, pushing a strand of hair from her face. "I'm really gonna miss this place."

"Yeah, me too," Ellis said, feeling the now-familiar pang in her chest.

"I'm gonna miss you guys even more, when I get home," Dorie said. "I'd forgotten how much fun we always have. I've got friends at home, but it's different with you guys."

"Same here," Ellis said. "I really hate to see this month end."

"You could move back to Savannah," Dorie said impulsively. "We've got tons of banks in Savannah. And Willa's husband knows everybody in town."

Ellis smiled, and glanced over at the garage apartment. Ty's Bronco was gone, but he'd sent her a text telling her he was working at Caddie's again tonight.

"I think I'm done with banks, Dorie."

"Really? What are you gonna do for a job, then?"

"Haven't a clue," Ellis said. And for the first time in a long time, she realized that it had been many days since she'd clenched her teeth in panic about her future.

The smell of charcoal wafted from the back of the house. Ellis, her hair still wet from the shower, found Booker and Julia in the kitchen. Julia was shucking ears of corn from the farm stand down the beach road, and Booker was shooting pictures of Julia in the unlikely role of domestic goddess.

Ellis helped herself to a slice of tomato from a platter at Julia's elbow. "Are we shooting some kind of documentary?"

"Better," Julia said, her eyes shining with excitement. "Booker, the brilliant, brilliant love of my life, has a brilliant, brilliant scheme."

Booker chuckled. "You heard that, didn't you? I'm the love of her life? Not to mention brilliant?"

"I'm your witness," Ellis agreed, sitting at the kitchen table. "So what's the scheme?"

"What scheme?" Dorie said, wandering into the kitchen. She was dressed in a jade green tank top and matching loose-fitting drawstring pants, and her damp hair fell in a braid down her back. With her sun-speckled breasts spilling from the low-cut top, she looked like a modern mermaid.

Julia finished up the corn and wiped her hand on a dish towel. "You tell 'em, Booker."

"It's not really all that brilliant," he said modestly. "You know that Julia's been snapping photos of everything, the house, the three of you at the beach, everything she sees, really, since you got here. And she's been e-mailing them to me. Right?"

"Riiight," Ellis said.

"She's really a pretty talented amateur photographer," Booker said. "Of course, it makes sense, since she learned from the master. I know she's always had a fabulous eye, but those photos she sent were especially evocative."

"And I was only shooting with my cell phone," Julia interjected. "You know, just messing around, trying to show Booker where we were staying."

"Anyway, I forwarded some of her photos to a friend of mine, who works out in California."

"He's a location scout for the movies!" Julia said. "And Booker never told me a thing about him."

"I hadn't seen the guy in a couple of years," Booker said mildly. "We used to do some work together, when I was doing fashion shoots. Anyway, he was intrigued with Julia's photos."

"Especially the ones of Ebbtide," Julia said. "You guys, he thinks this house would be perfect for this movie he's working on. It's a chick flick, and I'm not allowed to say who all is in it, but let's just say *Legally Blonde, Pretty Woman, Miss Congeniality!*"

"Julia," Booker lowered his camera and gave her a reproving look. "They haven't actually all signed on yet, remember."

"I didn't mention any names," Julia said coyly.

"Anyway, Simon, my friend the location scout, has actually hired me to take scouting shots of the house, and the beach, and some of the nearby houses and businesses and things," Booker said. "I've already e-mailed the shots I did this afternoon, because he's meeting with the producers tomorrow. They're on a very tight production schedule because all these, um, unnamed actresses only have a brief window of availability. They were going to shoot at a beach house on the West Coast, but the art director hated all the houses they showed him. Too contemporary, too glitzy."

"But he loves how shabby and worn-out Ebbtide looks," Julia interrupted. "Of course, he hasn't seen the bathrooms."

"The movie is supposed to be set on Cape Cod, in the summer," Booker explained. "But all the houses they scouted there looked too elegant and old-money. Which brings us to Nags Head, and Ebbtide. If the producer likes what he sees, Simon will want to talk to your friend, Ellis, about the possibility of renting it for three or four months."

"For real?" Ellis asked. "When would they want it?"

"Right away, I imagine. Production is supposed to start September fifteenth. They want to wait until after Labor Day, when tourist season is over and crowd control won't be such an issue."

"Isn't that awesome?" Julia asked. "Won't Ty just flip over the idea?"

"Awesome," Ellis repeated. "If he can hang on to the house until then."

# 41

The dinner dishes had been cleared away, the last of the wine drunk. Booker had graciously accepted all the women's compliments for the dinner he'd masterminded: tuna steaks on the grill; chipotle-pepper-roasted corn on the cob; and risotto with green peas, asparagus, shallots, and basil. Dorie and Ellis spilled a five-hundred-piece jigsaw puzzle depicting the Cape Hatteras lighthouse onto the dining room table and declared their intentions of finishing it by midnight. Madison, who'd finally given in to their pleas, joined them for dinner, but declared herself hopeless at puzzles. For the first time since she'd been living in the house, she seemed at ease with the group.

"Come on, Book," Julia said, flipping him lightly with her dish towel. "I can't stand all this excitement. Let's take a walk on the beach."

She led him down the beach stairs and onto the sand. They left their shoes in the pillowy sand at the base of the steps and walked hand-in-hand out to the water's edge.

"Which way?" Booker asked.

"Hmm, north, I think," Julia said. "Cottage Row is just up ahead."

"What's that?"

"What's left of the original old houses built in Nags Head at the turn of the century," Julia said. "There were originally, like, a dozen or so houses. All of 'em wooden, like Ebbtide. They call them the 'unpainted aristocracy.' Ebbtide's not one of them. Ty told us his family had the house built in the 1930s."

They walked slowly, stopping to gaze at the stars, or just stand in the moonlight, looking up at the rows of houses, lit up with summertime occupants. Voices and the sound of a radio playing drifted down from the houses beyond the dunes.

"These are the oldest houses," Julia said, when they'd walked a little further. The houses were further apart here, sprawling wooden structures with outward-canted porches, their wooden walls gleaming a dull brownish-silver in the moonlight.

"Not very fancy," Booker said approvingly.

"Nope," Julia agreed. "From what Ty tells us, the old-time Nags Headers consider it crude to flaunt your money by fixing up your house or adding on a wing. Nothing at all had been done at Ebbtide in decades, until Ty bought it from an uncle and started trying to fix it up."

"You like it here," Booker said, sounding surprised.

"It has a certain charm that grows on you," Julia admitted. "At first, I was pretty grossed out by the place. I mean, I didn't want to hurt Ellis's feelings, since she did all the research and work of tracking down the house and getting it lined up and everything, but it was seriously skanky when we moved in."

"Not exactly the kind of beach house you're used to." Booker laughed, nudging her gently.

"We had a little bit of a rocky start," Julia said. "Ellis was being so . . . bossy. She even made up a chore chart for the kitchen, if you can believe it."

"And we all know how Julia Capelli deals with authority, now, don't we?" Booker said.

"We worked things out," Julia said. "Pretty much. It's been an interesting month, that's for sure."

"And what about you?" Booker asked. "What's been going on with you? Aside from the pictures and a couple phone calls, you've been surprisingly quiet for the past month, Julia."

"I know," she said, squeezing his hand. "You've given me a lot to think about."

"Come to any conclusions?"

"Some."

"Such as?"

Julia brushed her long hair back from her face. "I'm done modeling."

Booker nodded. "Have you told the agency?"

"Not yet. They've booked me for a JCPenney catalog shoot when I leave here. I guess I'll have to go ahead and do it, because I don't want to leave Jessica in the lurch. But that's it. No more."

"Sounds reasonable," Booker said.

"The girls think . . ." she started. "No, I think I'd like to try doing photo styling."

"You'd be a natural," Booker said. "You've been doing it on your own for years, anyway. I've always said you have the best eye in the business, Julia."

"I'd need your help," Julia said, giving him a sidelong glance. "You know everybody. The magazine people, the photographers, art directors."

"Not everybody," Booker said. "But I do have some resources."

"I know I'd have to start off as an assistant," Julia went on. "Doing the grunt work. Cataloging props, making coffee runs, ironing shirts and pillowcases."

"Not very glamorous," Booker said.

"I was thinking of asking Annette Joseph if she'd take me on," Julia said.

"Do I know her?"

"I met her at a catalog shoot in Miami last year," Julia said. "She works out of Atlanta, but she does a lot of work for shelter magazines, so she gets assignments all over the East Coast."

"Atlanta," Booker said, his face impassive.

"It makes sense because of the airport," Julia said.

"We have two airports in DC, you know."

"Hear me out," Julia said, taking a deep breath. "We could sell the flat in London."

Booker stopped walking. "You'd consider it?"

Julia swallowed hard. "If I'm not working in Europe, it doesn't make sense to keep it. I know the real estate market is crap right now, but Mayfair is so trendy, even in a down market we should be able to make a killing when we sell it."

"Or lease it, long-term," Booker said. "In case you change your mind."

"I won't," Julia promised. "I've been in a holding pattern for too long, avoiding the inevitable. London was wonderful, my work was exciting, but it isn't anymore. Hasn't been in a long time. You're here in the States. I want to be with you. It's that simple. I *have* missed you, Booker."

"Have you?" He put his arms around her waist and pulled her to him.

She wound her arms around his neck and kissed him fiercely. "I do love you, you know," she said, resting her forehead on his chest. "This month, at the beach, with everything the girls have been through, sort of forced me to stop and take stock of things. Dorie basically told me off the other day."

"Dorie? Sweet little Dorie?"

"Not so sweet if you really get to know her," Julia said ruefully. "And then, Madison, who barely knows me at all, said something at lunch today that kind of tipped the scale for me."

"And what was that?" Booker inquired, running his hands up the back of the thin cotton peasant top Julia was wearing, and kissing her neck.

"She kind of called me out," Julia said. "She said I couldn't keep making chickenshit assumptions about marriage based on other people's mistakes."

"Smart girl," Booker said, holding her closer.

"I guess . . ." Julia stopped and pulled away, but Booker had no intention of letting her go.

"You guess what?"

She turned, so that her back was to him. "I guess I don't think I deserve somebody like you. Somebody as good as you. Maybe that's why I keep trying to push you away."

"What?" He put his hands on her shoulder and wheeled her around. "What kind of crap is that?"

Julia shrugged and swallowed hard. She took a deep breath. "There are things about me . . . things you don't know."

He chortled. "We've lived together for nearly ten years. Tell me one thing about you that I don't know. Come on. I dare you."

She bit her lip. "The thing is . . . I got pregnant when I was eighteen. It was an ectopic pregnancy, Book. I only have one good fallopian tube. I don't know if I can have children." A tear rolled down her cheek. "I'm sorry. I should have told you years ago."

He traced the tear with the tip of his thumb. "And you think this is some kind of deal breaker for me? Julia, love. Is this the thing that's been eating at you all this time?"

She nodded sadly, the tears flowing nonstop now. "People think I'm this perfect model *thing*. But I'm not! It's all plastic! I've had my nose fixed, and my boobs done, and for all I know, I'm infertile, too."

"Stop that," Booker said sternly. "And listen to me. The only person who thinks you're plastic is you. You are the warmest, realest woman I have ever met. I don't give a damn about your nose or your fallopian tube, or your hammertoes or whatever. I fell in love with you, Julia Capelli. The whole package. And as far as I'm concerned, you are perfect. Hell, look at me. I'm pushing fifty. Maybe I'm infertile too. Yeah, I want kids. But only if you do too. So maybe we do this the modern way. Test tubes, petri dishes, adoption, I don't care. I just want you. Have you got that?"

Julia sniffed and nodded, slowly. She rested her cheek on Booker's shoulder, and surreptitiously rubbed her runny nose on his shirt. He rubbed her back reassuringly.

"Madison said I should just quit worrying about other people's lives, and get on with ours."

"I think I like that girl," Booker said, slowly working his thumbs under the edge of Julia's bra.

"And she reminded me that life is short, and nothing is guaranteed. Carpe diem, baby, you know?"

"Latin?" Booker said, with an exaggerated groan. "You know how turned on I get when you talk foreign."

"Grow up," Julia said. But she'd slipped her hands into the waistband of his shorts and was fully aware of how turned on Booker had gotten.

"I think," Booker said solemnly, "we had better turn back to Ebbtide so you can take advantage of me. I mean, how will we ever know if we can make babies unless we actually try?"

"Mmm," Julia said. "You're probably right. The house would be much more civilized than the beach. Wouldn't want to scare the seagulls."

They made it all the way back to the stairway at Ebbtide and sat on the bottom step to brush the sand off their feet.

"I hate to break this golden moment," Booker said finally. "But I can't help wonder how you're going to be with me in DC, and at the same time work in Atlanta."

Julia kissed his nose. "With the money we'll make from selling the London flat, I can rent something tiny and convenient in Atlanta. A pied-à-terre, if you will. I'll live full time in this amazing house you've found us in Alexandria, and travel to shoots wherever I'm needed. Of course, this is all predicated on a couple of things. First off, I'll have to persuade Annette to give me a shot at learning the business."

"Not a problem. You're a very persuasive girl, in my experience."

"And then," Julia said, dusting the sand off her shorts and climbing onto Booker's lap, "I'll have to figure out how to plan a wedding before Dorie gets as big as an elephant and Ellis takes a new job God knows where. And since you've just started a new job, when will you be able to take some vacation time?"

"A wedding?" Booker mused. "Is somebody having a wedding?"

"We are, if you'll have me," Julia whispered. "Just name the date."

"Oh, I'll have you, my love," Booker said. "You'll just have to let me consult my calendar. It's upstairs. In your room."

# 42

Saturday morning, Ellis raced over to the garage apartment, bursting with the news about Booker's friend Simon, the movie location scout. But the Bronco was already gone.

She considered calling his cell, but decided against it. He could be anyplace, and she wanted to tell him the news in person. She fished the key Ty had given her out of the pocket of her shorts, and climbed the stairs to the apartment.

He'd obviously come in late the night before. A Styrofoam takeout tray sat on the table Ty used as a desk, along with an empty Corona bottle and a crumpled newspaper. A cereal bowl with a film of milk sat in the sink, along with a spoon and an empty juice glass. The counter was cluttered with a cereal box, empty orange juice carton, and a sugar bowl with a spoon stuck in it. A single fly buzzed lazily around, batting against the wire window screen.

Ellis walked into the bedroom. The quilt and bedcovers lay in a rumpled heap at the foot of the bed, and Ty's T-shirt and shorts were thrown on the floor, along with a still-damp towel.

She sighed happily and started to put the tiny apartment to rights. She washed and rinsed the dishes, putting them away in the Hoosier cupboard, and wiped off the gummy kitchen counter. She opened the door to the deck and swept what seemed like a pound of sand out the door and through the cracks in the deck boards, just as she remembered her mother sweeping out the houses they rented at the beach at Tybee during her childhood summers.

Ellis smiled contentedly as she stripped Ty's bed, gathering the sheets and discarded clothing into a bundle. She would wash them in the laundry room at Ebbtide, she decided, and surprise Ty when he got back from his errands.

As she was stepping out of the apartment onto the deck, a car came bumping down the Ebbtide driveway. It was a sleek dark gray Mercedes convertible, with a man at the wheel and a woman with long blond hair sitting beside him, her eyes shaded by a pale blue sun visor. The driver pulled the car directly up to the garage, as though he knew exactly where he was going.

Were these prospective renters for Ebbtide? Ellis wondered. Ty hadn't said anything about showing the house while she and the others were still in residence, but she assumed he'd want to rent the house out again as soon as they vacated the place next Saturday.

There was that stabbing feeling in her chest again. Vacate. Saturday was only a week away.

The woman got out of the convertible and looked up at Ellis in curiosity.

The blonde was Kendra. Ty's ex-wife. And the driver was Ryan, or as Ty referred to him, Fuckface.

"Hey there," the blonde called, waving. "Is Ty around?"

"Nope," Ellis said. "Haven't seen him this morning." She turned and went back inside the apartment. What should she do? Call Ty?

Before she had a chance to decide, she heard footsteps pounding up the wooden staircase, and a brisk knock at the door.

She opened it, and Kendra gave her a breezy smile. "Oh! It's you." She knit her brow, searching for the name. "Hi there, Ellen, right?"

"It's Ellis."

"Oh, right. So, I'm Kendra, and I guess you remember we met at Fish Food the other night. Kinda awkward, right, bumping into the ex like that?"

Ellis shrugged. "Ty's not here," she repeated. "I'm not sure when he'll be back."

Kendra's full red lips pouted. "I've been calling and calling, leaving messages. He never returns any of them. That's why we finally decided to run over here this morning, to see if we can talk to him about Ebbtide. You know, before next month."

"I don't know what to tell you," Ellis said. "He stays pretty busy. But I can let him know you dropped by." She gathered up the bundle of laundry and stepped outside onto the deck, locking the door behind her.

Ellis hurried down the stairs. Ryan had gotten out of the Mercedes and was walking around the outside of the garage, leaning down, poking at the boards, walking around inside the garage itself, staring up at the old rafters with the assortment of junk hanging from the beams: rusted lawn chairs, rotting hanks of rope, what looked like an old sail.

"Can I help you?" she called sharply. Fuckface had some nerve wandering around the place like he already owned it.

"Nope," Ryan said, immune to her tone. "Say, you have any idea how many square feet are in that apartment up there?"

"No," Ellis said woodenly.

"But it's got a kitchen, right, like an efficiency? And a bathroom? Is it a full or half bath? We're trying to figure out if the apartment would work out as income property. It's hell to get new bathrooms approved, is why I ask, so if there's an existing full bath up there, that would be awesome."

"Honey, I think I remember that it's got a sink and a toilet, with the shower out on the deck," Kendra called down.

Ellis whirled around. Kendra was not only still on the deck, she was actually peering in the glass insert in the door, her hands cupped to shut out the glare of the sunlight. "The kitchen's small, but it's got everything you'd need. We'd want to replace the appliances, and the linoleum would have to go right away too. New cupboards and countertops, of course. It might be worth a trip to IKEA for that stuff."

"Hey!" Ellis called. "I don't think Ty would appreciate having you poking around his apartment while he's gone."

"Okay," Kendra said. She came bopping down the stairs and joined her husband, who'd finished inspecting the garage. Ellis noticed that Kendra's sun visor was the exact same shade of Carolina blue as her sleek sleeveless top and running shorts. And, of course, her Carolina blue running shoes matched everything else she wore, including the scrunchy that held her long blond hair in a ponytail.

"Say, Alice . . ." Kendra started.

"It's Ellis. E-L-L-I-S."

"Right, sorry. Listen, you don't happen to know who's renting Ebbtide right now, do you?"

"No," Ellis lied.

"Hmm," Kendra said, turning to stare up at the house. A trio of damp bathing suits clipped to the clothesline stretched between the porch posts flapped in the breeze. As she watched, Booker emerged from the house with a camera slung around his neck.

"I really, really need to get a look inside the house, hon," Kendra told her husband. "Ty's nana was sweet, but she was really *not* much of a house-keeper, and God knows, Ty never cared about that kind of stuff. As long as the fish were biting or the surf was up, he didn't care what the house looked like."

She pursed her lips, still looking up at the house, thoughtfully. "Window air conditioners. And I'm sure there's no insulation, or even a furnace. Guess I'm not surprised. I don't think the Culpeppers ever did winterize the house." She gave Ellis a sad smile. "Ty's grandparents were the salt of the earth, but there was never much money there."

"Roof looks pretty bad too, sweetness," Ryan added. "We'd have to gut the place."

Ellis's stomach twinged at the word "gut." She wanted to grab the broom she'd recently abandoned and chase these two opportunists down the drive-way and off the Ebbtide property. Even though it wasn't her place, she felt strongly that Ty would approve of such a course of action.

Before she could suggest that Kendra and Fuckface vacate the premises, she was saved by the cheery chirping of Kendra's cell phone.

"Hi-i-i," Kendra said, her face brightening. "No, nope. He's not here. His *friend* says she doesn't know where he's gone, or when he'll be back. What's new about that, right? Probably off surfing with some of those lowlife buddies of his."

Kendra's caller talked for a while, and she listened intently. "No, we won't give up. I'll leave him another message, and if that doesn't work, we'll just check back later. I promise you, Daddy, when we hand him a check, he'll be happy to take it and walk away. Okay? See you at lunch, then."

She clicked disconnect and pocketed the phone. "So," she said brightly. "You'll be sure and tell Ty we came by?"

"As soon as I see him," Ellis promised.

Kendra turned to her husband. "Daddy wants us to meet them at the club for lunch. That leaves us a couple hours to kill. We could run up to Duck in the meantime. Bailey and Ferris have been pestering me to drop by and see what they've done to their place, and then we'd have an excuse to leave."

Ryan nodded enthusiastically, and without another word to Ellis, they jumped in the Mercedes and sped off.

Ellis watched them go, her fists clenched in rage. She marched herself back to Ebbtide, dumped her load of laundry into the washing machine, spun the dial, and punched the start button.

Late afternoon, and the house was eerily quiet. Booker had insisted on treating all of them, including Madison, who'd tried without success to beg off, to a late lunch at the Beach Grill.

When they were seated at a table overlooking the dunes, Booker gave Julia an ill-concealed wink. She produced a bottle of champagne from her big straw beach tote, and Booker stood up and tapped his water glass with a spoon.

The other diners in the restaurant turned, gave them a look of mild interest, and then turned back to the Braves baseball game they were watching on the big-screen television mounted over the bar.

Booker pulled Julia to her feet, and for the first time any of the girls could remember, Julia was actually blushing.

"I have an announcement to make," Booker said, wrapping an arm around Julia's waist and struggling to look serious.

"Yessss!" Ellis squealed.

"Oh, hell yeah!" Dorie squealed in unison.

"Quiet!" Julia demanded. "Have you no sense of decorum?"

The waitress returned to their table, bearing a tray of cloudy, water-spotted champagne glasses and a basket of individually wrapped saltine crackers. "Thank you," Booker said, dismissing her with a nod.

"Now, as I was saying," Booker continued. "As you may know, I have been pursuing this flower of southern womanhood, Julia Elizabeth Capelli, for well over a decade. And as you also know, your friend Julia has, thus far, refused—nay, scorned—my entreaties to allow me to make of her an honest woman."

"Boo!" Dorie booed.

"Hiss," Ellis hissed. "Get to the good part, would you?"

Julia rolled her eyes. "Now you know what I've been dealing with for all these years."

"Be that as it may," Booker went on, gesturing grandly. "Last night, under the influence of a full moon, not to mention nearly two bottles of very good French pinot gris, your friend, and my beloved, did me the great honor of agreeing to, at a date to be announced, make me the happiest man on earth. May I introduce to you all my fiancée, the future Mrs. Julia Capelli-hyphen-Calloway."

With that, Booker grabbed the champagne bottle and popped the cork, and with the champagne spewing over his hands, he clasped Julia and planted a huge, noisy kiss directly on her laughing lips, while Dorie, Ellis, and Madison cheered wildly.

The lunch that followed was the happiest, craziest, loudest meal Ellis could remember attending in recent memory.

Julia had finally, after much baiting and begging, agreed that the wedding would take place sometime in the fall. "Before you get too fat," she told Dorie, "and he," she said, turning fondly to Booker, "has time to change his mind and find another girl."

But Booker had more than one surprise up his sleeve, they soon discov-

ered. When their appetizers arrived, Julia stared down at her plate of cala-
mari, and finally, with a fork, picked up a vinaigrette-drenched ring—platinum,
with a band of small diamond chips surrounding an enormous, glittering
cushion-cut diamond.

"Booker!" Julia sputtered. "What the hell?"

Booker lifted the ring from the tines of Julia's fork and slid it, dressing and
all, onto her left hand. He kissed the ring, and then Julia's palm, and finally,
her lips.

When she'd recovered from the shock, Julia held her hand up and twisted
it back and forth, admiring the glint of sunlight on the diamond. "It's perfect," she declared. "If I'd designed it myself, it could not have been more perfect. It looks so much like my grandmother's engagement ring. How did you
know? And where on earth . . . ?"

Instead of answering her, Booker stood, picked up the camera he'd slung
over the back of his chair, aimed, and started shooting photos of the group
around the table.

"It *is* your grandmother's," he told her.

"But . . ." Julia sputtered. "Mama left it to my brother Joe."

"And your sister-in-law decided it was hideously old-fashioned," Booker
said, planting yet another kiss on Julia's cheek. "I'd e-mailed to ask if there
was a piece of family jewelry he might be willing to part with, in the remote
event that you would ever agree to get married, and he was only too happy to
let me take this off his hands."

"You!" Julia squealed. She got up, backed him into a chair and then planted
herself on his lap, kissing him passionately.

"Get a room," Dorie called.

After lunch, as the group was filing out of the restaurant, Booker pulled
Ellis aside.

"Great news," he said. "Simon texted me just as we were getting in the car
to drive over here. The producers loved the scouting shots. He's flying in with
them first thing Monday to work on lining up the rest of the locations. Have
you told Ty about any of this?"

"That's so great," Ellis said, trying to refrain from squealing. "I haven't talked to Ty, he's been gone all day. But I'll call him right away and let him know you need to talk to him."

"Good, because Simon says the whole production schedule's been sped up. It's supposed to be top secret, but one of the leading ladies just disclosed that she's pregnant."

"I wonder which one," Ellis said, watching Dorie climb into the driver's seat of the red van. "Um, Booker, do you have any idea how much the movie people will pay to use the house?"

"Nope," Booker said. "That's something Ty will need to negotiate."

It was close to six when Ellis saw the Bronco pull into the garage. A few minutes later, her phone dinged, announcing the arrival of a text message.

COCKTAILS ON MY VERANDA? MR. CULPEPPER.

She grinned and texted back:

B RITE OVER.

Ellis pulled on a pair of white shorts and a scoop-necked lime green top that made her tan look golden. After slicking on some lip gloss and spritzing on some perfume, she strolled over to the garage apartment.

Ty was just emerging from the shower, a beach towel wrapped around his waist, when she got to the top of the deck stairs.

"Oh," she said, blushing. "Uh, guess I'm early."

He laughed at her modesty and pulled her to him. He was still damp from the shower, but she didn't mind at all that her top and spotless white shorts were getting equally damp.

"There's some beer and a bottle of white wine in the fridge," he told her. "And I think I've got some chips and salsa, if you're hungry. I'll get dressed and be out in a minute."

Ellis set out the chips and salsa, poured herself a glass of wine, and took it out to the deck. She stood at the rail, looking out at the beach, which was mostly deserted now, with the exception of two adolescent boys riding skim-boards at the water's edge.

She'd noticed the boys earlier in the morning and realized they'd spent the whole day lounging on the beach, playing Frisbee, and now skimboarding. It was probably their last free weekend before school started, Ellis realized, feel-ing that prickle of sadness again. She couldn't remember when she'd been so sad to see the end of summer.

Ty was behind her now, his arms around her waist, kissing her neck. "You smell good," he said, breathing in her scent. "Is that for me?"

"All for you," she said, turning to return his kiss.

They sat companionably in the teak Adirondack chairs, sipping their drinks and catching up.

"I know you hate swordfish, but how do you feel about grouper?" Ty asked. "A buddy of mine called me early this morning and asked if I wanted to crew on his charter. That's where I've been all day. We caught the hell out of the grouper and snapper."

"I love grouper," Ellis said. "Are we having dinner?"

"Thought I'd try to impress you with my culinary skills," he said. "You're not one of those girly girls who won't eat fried fish, are you?"

"Not me," Ellis said.

He nodded approvingly. "Okay. Fried grouper sandwiches and coleslaw for dinner. You're in charge of the coleslaw."

"I can do that," Ellis said, following him into the kitchen. "But first, I've got a proposition for you."

# 43

*Summer Fling* could be the thing that saves Ebbtide," Ellis said, outlining what Booker had told her about his friend Simon. "A big Hollywood movie. If they use your house for filming, they'd probably pay enough in rent to get you out of the hole."

Ty gazed out the kitchen window at the big house. "But Ebbtide's a wreck. You said so yourself. Who would want to shoot a movie here?"

"Apparently they like what they've seen," Ellis insisted. "Starting with the crummy pictures Julia took with her cell phone, and including the professional-quality photos Booker's been taking for the past couple of days. Maybe the movie's about an old house. They make movies like that all the time, and they can't all be filmed from specially built sets."

"I guess," Ty said, placing the flour-coated grouper into a cast-iron skillet full of bubbling oil. "I never go see movies anymore. Probably the last one I saw was *Die Hard 2*."

Ellis buttered the hamburger buns and put them in the tiny oven to brown. "Well, I see lots and lots of chick-type movies, and I can tell you that my favorite ones are the ones where the houses are as much a character in the plot as the actors. And," she added, "with the actresses that have supposedly already been signed for *Summer Fling*, it sounds like a really big-budget flick."

With a long-handled fork, Ty flipped over each of the fish fillets. "You like tartar sauce, or do you wanna try my super-secret sauce?"

"What's your super-secret sauce?"

"If I tell you that, it won't be a super secret, now will it?"

"What if I swear not to tell?" Ellis asked. "Pinky swear?"

"I've got a better idea," Ty said, wrapping his arms around her waist and kissing her.

"And the secret?" Ellis asked, stepping away from his reach.

"Bottled chili sauce, lemon juice, horseradish, and Duke's mayo," Ty said.

He laid out the grouper on a brown paper grocery store sack to drain, deftly mixed up his sauce, and five minutes later, they'd pushed aside the papers on the tiny dining table/desk to eat.

"Mmm," Ellis said, biting into her sandwich. "I am officially impressed. This might be the best grouper sandwich I've ever had. And growing up in Savannah, I've had a lot."

Ty lifted a forkful of coleslaw. "This slaw's not too shabby either. How'd you make the dressing? It's not mayonnaisey, which I like."

"It's my mama's recipe, and my daddy taught her how to make it," Ellis confided. "You just sprinkle sugar and salt on the shredded cabbage, and you crunch it together with your hands 'til the cabbage kinda 'weeps.' Then you heat up some apple cider vinegar on the stove, and put in some more sugar and some celery seed. You just pour that over the cabbage while it's still warm, mash it around with a wooden spoon, and put it in the fridge. It's even better if you let it sit a day or so."

"We make a decent team," Ty said, resting his elbows on the table. He looked around the room. "Apparently, somebody broke in here today and cleaned the joint up. They even did my laundry. You ever hear of a burglar doing that?"

"It was me," Ellis admitted. "Don't know what came over me. I was so excited about this movie thing, I ran over here this morning to tell you about it.

I let myself in, and I kinda got carried away." She flashed him an apologetic grin. "Sorry. It won't happen again."

"Why not? I mean, who am I to tamper with your domestic urges?"

"Oh my gosh," Ellis said, setting her fork down. "I completely forgot! You had a visitor while I was here cleaning up. So much has happened today—what with Julia and Booker getting engaged, and the movie stuff—it totally slipped my mind."

"Who came by?" Ty said, his mouth twisted sardonically. "Another bill collector?"

"Your ex," Ellis said. "And her husband."

"I hope you ran 'em off with a pitchfork," Ty said. "What the hell did they want?"

"To get a better look at this apartment, and the house, of course," Ellis said. "They actually wanted me to let them inside so they could figure out if this apartment would make a good income property."

"That's Kendra," Ty said bitterly. "Never lets any dust settle under her feet once she's on a mission."

"She said she's been calling you and leaving messages that you never return."

"Hmm," Ty said. "Guess I must have forgotten."

"I couldn't believe how nervy they were," Ellis said. "She was up here peering in the windows, trying to scope out the kitchen, while he was down in the garage with a measuring tape! And then, she had the gall to ask me if I thought your tenants in Ebbtide would let them in to look around."

"Amazing," Ty said, shaking his head in disbelief. "What did you tell her?"

"That I had no idea who the tenants were," Ellis said, pleased with her subterfuge.

"Good," Ty said sharply. He got up from the table and began to clear their plates. "Now, can we think of something else to talk about? Anything else?"

The mood in the room had subtly shifted. Before, they were just messing around, flirting, having fun, getting comfortable together. But now, Ellis sensed, Ty was moody, withdrawn. She was sorry she'd mentioned Kendra. She wouldn't make that mistake again.

She helped him wash the dishes, and while he was drying and putting them away, she picked up the broom from the corner and started to sweep the kitchen floor, needing a way to work out her nervous energy.

"You don't have to do that," Ty said, taking the broom from her hands. He looked around the room for a diversion. "Can't watch television."

"Maybe you should call the cable company," Ellis suggested.

"And lie and tell them I promise to pay them next month?"

"Oh." She'd put her foot in it again, reminding Ty of his financial situation.

"I'm sorry," Ty said, catching her hand in his. "None of this is your fault. It's just . . . One minute I think I'm digging myself out of the hole I've gotten myself into, and the next minute, Kendra and Fuckface are knocking at my door, looking to buy my house out from under me."

"I understand," Ellis said softly. And she truly did. "Look," she said. "It's been a nice evening. Dinner was great. But I think maybe you could use your space tonight."

"No," he protested. "Stay. It's early yet. I thought we'd take a walk on the beach. . . ."

"Another night," Ellis promised. "I want to go back to the house and make sure we've got everything tidy. Remember, the movie people are flying in to-morrow."

"There's no way they'll want Ebbtide," Ty said. "It's just an ugly, falling-down old dump. Look around. These days, places like Ebbtide are a dime a dozen."

"They'll love it!" Ellis insisted. "Please don't talk like that, Ty. I know it's discouraging, but I honestly believe this could work out and be the break you've been waiting for."

"Break?" Ty looked dubious. "People like me don't get breaks. I'll just have to figure something else out. My dad offered to loan me the money, but I can't let him touch his retirement." He gestured towards his computer, which Ellis had jokingly covered with a dish towel during dinner. "There's a stock I'm watching. I've been reading the reports on this company, and I think it's radi-cally undervalued. They're working on a new software application, and if they get it patented before anybody else, *that* actually could be the break I need."

"Okay," Ellis said, feeling herself being dismissed, literally and emotionally. "Thanks for dinner, Ty. I'm going to give your cell phone number to Booker so he can give it to Simon, and you can talk to him directly, instead of having me be the go-between."

"What? Now you're mad at me? Did we just have a fight?"

"Nope," she said, trying to make her voice sound lighter than she felt. "I just don't happen to agree with you. No fight. We'll talk tomorrow."

She was climbing the first step to Ebbtide's porch when she heard her cell phone ding in her pocket. She took it out and saw that she had a text. And it was from Ty.

I'M AN ASS. I'M AN ASS. I'M AN ASS.

"You certainly are," she muttered to herself. She put the phone back in her pocket and went into the now-dark house.

She found Madison stretched out on the sofa in the living room, reading a moldy-looking paperback detective novel.

"Where is everybody?" Ellis asked.

"Dorie had a dinner date with her new cop friend, and I think Julia and Booker decided to go catch a movie," Madison said.

Ellis flung herself into an armchair opposite the sofa, kicking her legs over the arms. "What's that you're reading?" she asked, squinting to get a look at the lurid cover illustration.

"John D. MacDonald, *The Turquoise Lament,*" Madison said. "There's a whole shelf full of them here. My grandfather always used to read John D. MacDonald, and he used to talk about Travis McGee as though he were a real person."

"Never heard of him," Ellis said. She got up and roamed idly around the room, leafing through books and putting them down, picking up magazines only to discard them.

Her cell phone dinged and she looked at the screen.

PLEASE COME BACK.

Ellis snorted and with the press of a button, cleared the screen of its latest text. "Men are idiots, you know that?"

Madison looked up from her book. "Who me? You're talking to me?"

"Of course," Ellis said.

Madison put the book facedown on her chest and sighed. "Having man problems, are we?"

"It's Ty," Ellis blurted. "He doesn't even want to help himself. I told him about Booker's friend, the movie scout, and no matter what I say, he just seems to think this is some big fantasy of mine. And now he's got his panties in a wad because I told him his ex-wife and her new husband came around the house while he was gone today, sizing it up to buy it out of foreclosure. Like any of this is my fault."

"You said it yourself," Madison said. "Men are idiots. And take it from me, on that I *am* an authority. The problem is, there really aren't a lot of good alternatives. So you just have to decide if you want to deal with a whole gender of people who are intrinsically flawed."

"I have been doing without men for years. A decade, actually," Ellis said gloomily, slumping down in her chair. "I finally thought I'd found a guy who was different, who was smart and funny. . . ."

"And sexy as hell," Madison said meaningfully. "Ty Bazemore is all that."

"And he's got a chip on his shoulder the size of Texas," Ellis added. "I don't need that."

"Of course not," Madison said. "You can just go right back to Philly and your old life there, and leave his stupid foreclosed self right here in Nags Head. Let him figure out how to save his house on his own."

"I will," Ellis said. "That's just what I'm going to do."

"Good for you," Madison said. She picked the book up again.

"Have you heard anything from Adam?" Ellis asked, determined to forget her own problems.

"Not a word," Madison said. "He still hasn't returned any of my calls. I'm definitely getting bad vibes now."

Ellis's cell dinged again. Madison raised one eyebrow, but otherwise remained motionless.

Ellis got up and walked into the kitchen. She could see the yellow light burning in the window at the apartment above the garage. *I miss you,* Ty's text said. She looked up and could see him now, standing in the window, looking directly at her; she was perfectly silhouetted in the dim kitchen light. The phone dinged again.

DEAR ELLIS SULLIVAN. I CAN'T DO WITHOUT YOU. PLEASE GIVE ME ANOTHER CHANCE. PLEASE? MR. CULPEPPER.

"Madison," she called, heading for the kitchen door. "I'm going out for a while."

"Tell Ty I said not to mess it up this time," Madison called back.

At dawn, they sat in the Adirondack chairs, drinking coffee made in Ty's grandmother's battered aluminum percolator, watching the sunrise. A lone pair of fishermen stood ankle deep in the water, surf casting, but the beach was otherwise deserted.

"Nice morning," Ellis said with a yawn, feeling completely at peace.

"Nicer night," Ty said, putting down his coffee cup.

"Mmm, hmm," Ellis said.

"Know what would be really, really nice?" Ty asked, pulling her to her feet.

"Again?" Ellis clutched the blue terry cloth bathrobe a little tighter.

"Oh. Well, maybe later. For now, I was thinking that I really, really need a shower," Ty said. "And if I just had somebody to help wash my back..." He had the bathrobe belt nearly unknotted. He was a very fast worker, Ellis thought.

"I don't know," Ellis said uneasily. "Those guys out there..." She nodded towards the fishermen.

"They've pulled in two bluefish, just while we've been sitting out here," Ty pointed out. "Those guys are in the zone. They're oblivious to us."

He was tugging her towards the wooden shower enclosure, pulling his own T-shirt over his head. He turned on the faucet, opened the door, and stepped out of his boxers. "Come on," he grinned, pulling at her belt. "You'll love it." The bathrobe fell open, and she was just as naked as Ty.

"Oh well," Ellis said. She let the robe fall to the deck and stepped into the shower.

"One minute," Ty said, picking up the fallen robe. He put his hand in the pocket and brought out a foil-wrapped condom, holding it up for Ellis's approval. "Be prepared," he said solemnly.

Warm water sluiced down on her head. Ty had a bottle of baby shampoo. He squirted some into his hands and rubbed it into her hair, massaging her scalp expertly with long, tapered fingers. She took the bottle from him and returned the favor, running her fingers through his thick, soapy, sun-bleached hair.

They stood under the water, blinking and giggling. Ty took the shampoo bottle and traced a line of amber liquid from her shoulder to her right breast, and then her left. He put the bottle back on the little wooden shelf, and turned his attentions to Ellis. He worked the shampoo into a fine white foam, caressing her breasts, soaping her belly, slowly tracing a line in the soap lower, and lower, finally sliding into her.

They moved together, and Ellis forgot to be self-conscious, forgot to be inhibited, forgot all the rules. "Splinters," she whispered at one point, as her soapy butt rubbed up against the rough-hewn cedar planks, but that too was quickly forgotten.

They were on their second lather, and the water was just beginning to get noticeably cooler, when Ellis heard footsteps on the wooden stairs.

"Ty!" she whispered.

"Hmm?" He was behind her, soaping her back.

"Somebody's here."

"Hmm?" He turned her around and nuzzled her neck.

"Hellooo!"

Ellis froze. She knew that voice.

"Shiiiit," he whispered. He knew it too. All too well.

"Oh my God," Ellis breathed. "Hide me."

"Why?" he whispered back. "What do you care?"

"Ty?" her voice came closer. They could tell Kendra was almost at the top step.

"Do something," Ellis pleaded. "I'll die of embarrassment if she sees me like this."

"Stay here," Ty whispered. "I'll get rid of her and be right back."

Ellis looked down and realized that if Kendra got any closer she'd surely notice two sets of legs inside the wooden shower stall. She sat on the narrow wooden bench and drew her legs up to her knees.

Ty shut off the water, snatched up his boxers, and pulled them on. The next minute, he was wrapping the bathrobe around himself and stepping out, firmly pushing the shower door shut.

"Kendra," Ellis heard him say. "What the hell do you want?"

Ellis looked down at the water streaming off her body. She shivered and saw the fine goose bumps prickling her bare skin. *Hurry,* she thought. *Hurry!*

# 44

Tyyyy," Kendra's voice was shrill, teasing. "Did I catch you at a bad time?"

"You always manage to catch me at a bad time, Kendra," Ty snapped. "It's barely 7 A.M. What the hell do you want?"

"If you'd return my phone calls, you'd know what I want," Kendra said, totally unfazed by Ty's rudeness. "Ryan and I want to talk to you about buying Ebbtide."

"Talk to the bank, not me," Ty said. "It's out of my hands, as you well know."

"We could help each other," Kendra said sweetly. "You need to get out of debt, and Ryan and I are looking for a beach house. A beach house with age and character, just like Ebbtide. But we'd like to just take a look around the place before we make an offer. I'm thinking it's gonna need an awful lot of work, and we'd like to ballpark it before we get to auction."

"Nothing doing," Ty said flatly. "Go away."

"You don't have to give me attitude," Kendra said. "I'm not the bad guy, you know."

Ellis hugged her knees tightly to her chest. The sun hadn't fully risen yet, and the morning air was still chilly. As chilly as Ty's voice.

"Sure you are," Ty said. "You and your asshole husband are a couple of vultures, circling around my house, looking to swoop in and snatch it away from me. And if you think I'm gonna actually help you do that, you're dumber than I thought."

"I'm dumb? I'm not the one who dropped out of law school and threw away a brilliant career as a lawyer. I'm not the one who walked away from a marriage the first time it hit a bump in the road, because my fragile little ego couldn't take a dose of reality. And I'm certainly not the one who's fixing to lose his house, and everything else, because I refused to face facts and cut a deal with somebody who could save my bacon."

"You've got an interesting take on history, Kendra," Ty drawled. "I wonder if ol' Fuckface knows you regard him as 'a bump in the road.' "

"Stop calling him that," Kendra snapped.

"Stop showing up at my house, uninvited and unannounced. Stop calling me, and stop leaving me messages," Ty said. "And now, get the hell off my property, before I call the cops."

"I'll go," Kendra said, and Ellis heard her feet moving across the deck. She breathed a sigh of relief.

"But throwing me out doesn't change anything, Ty," she taunted. "*Ryan* and I will still be on the Dare County Courthouse steps on the fifteenth, and we'll have our checkbook out. And there's not a damned thing you can do to stop us. We're gonna buy Ebbtide, Ty. And when we do, the first thing we'll do is kick your white trash ass right to the curb."

"Beat it," Ty said. "Now."

The footsteps were rapidly retreating. Evidently, Ty looked as menacing as he sounded. Ellis heard an engine roar to life, heard the accelerator being floored, and then, the eminently rewarding sound of Kendra's tires, spinning ineffectively in the crushed shell driveway.

Ty chuckled. He walked over to the shower stall and poked his head inside.

Ellis was curled in a ball on the bench, her knees pressed to her chest. She managed to smile up at him through lips turned blue. "Y-y-you d-d-da m-m-man. Now, could I please have a t-t-towel?"

# 45

Ellis heard the thrum of the vacuum cleaner as soon as she opened the front door. Dorie was running it across the worn rug in the living room. She waved at Dorie, and walked into the kitchen to find Madison waxing the floors. Upstairs, Ellis found Julia flitting about among the bedrooms, her arms full of new linens, pillows, quilts, and throw rugs.

"What's going on?" she asked, catching Julia coming out of her own room. "What's all that stuff?"

Julia pushed a strand of hair behind her ear. "Getting the house styled up for its big moment. And this," she said, pointing with her chin at the stack of linens in her arms, "is lots of stuff to girly up the bedrooms. Booker and I did a little shopping at HomeGoods last night. A lot of shopping, actually."

"But, who's gonna pay for all of it?" Ellis asked. "Ty's broke."

"Don't worry," Julia assured her. "The price tags are all intact. As soon as these guys leave, I'll take it all back for a refund."

"Can you do that? Is it legal?"

"It's not like anybody actually slept on the stuff, Ellis," Julia said, rolling her eyes.

"Where's Booker?" Ellis asked.

"If you were coming from Ty's, you probably walked right past him," Julia said, ducking into the hall bathroom. She began folding and arranging a stack of fluffy, white bath towels. "He's out in the garage, trying to get the lawn mower started. Which I can't wait to see—Booker using a lawn mower."

"And all of this is for the movie people?" Ellis asked. "I was gonna just make sure all the beds were made, but Julia, this is above and beyond the call."

"It's nothing," Julia said. She opened a shopping bag and lifted out a clear-glass apothecary jar, which she began filling with sun-bleached seashells from another shopping bag. She placed the jar on the back of the toilet tank, then stepped back to critique her handiwork.

"What do you think?" she asked. "Too fussy?"

"Very pretty," Ellis said. "But is all of this necessary?"

Julia shrugged. "It couldn't hurt, right? And anyway, we're kind of having fun. It's like getting ready for a big, important party. Besides, this is not all self-less. If Simon's people use the house for the movie, Booker gets a nice finder's fee. And if they make a movie here, maybe I can snag a job working for the set dressers. Wouldn't that be awesome?"

"If, if, if," Ellis said worriedly. "So much riding on this."

"The house is going to look fabulous," Julia assured her, steering her towards her own room. When Ellis opened the door, she almost didn't recognize the space that had been hers for nearly a month. The yellowing sheers at the windows had been replaced with simple, white-cotton curtains with ball fringe, caught back on the sides with lengths of rope. The threadbare bedspread was gone too, and in its place was a quilt in soft sea-glass shades of blue, green, and aqua. Three fat pillows were plumped at the head of the bed. The cheesy art in the room, blurry prints of lighthouses and ducks, had been replaced with large, atmospheric, black-and-white photographs of Ebbtide, the dunes, and the beach right outside their back door.

"Booker?" Ellis asked, touching one of the frames.

"Yup. We had some of his shots printed at Kinko's, and then we stuck 'em in frames from Kmart," Julia said. "He does nice work, doesn't he?"

"They're gorgeous," Ellis agreed. "Do you think he'd sell me copies of some of these? They'd be a great souvenir to remind me of Nags Head and Ebbtide."

Julia gave her a curious look. "Do you need a souvenir?"

"Too soon to tell," Ellis said. "Now, give me a job."

"Easy. Booker says the thing that will sell the producers on the house is the amazing light, and the location, of course. So we need to wash all the windows, which it doesn't look like has happened since the Reagan administration."

"I'll hit the inside windows, but I'll have to get Ty for anything requiring ladders," Ellis said.

She went down to the kitchen and filled a bucket with ammonia and water, and found a stack of old newspapers to wipe the windows. While she was texting Ty, Dorie walked into the kitchen and sat down at the table, her cell phone in hand, a stunned look on her face.

"Anything wrong?" Ellis asked, her heart racing. "The baby's okay, right?"

"Huh? Oh, yeah. The baby's fine. I'm just . . . shell-shocked, I guess. Stephen just called."

Ellis sat down in the chair opposite Dorie's. "What did he want?"

Dorie had both hands resting lightly on her tummy. "He said he was just checking in, he wanted to see how I'm doing. He asked about the baby, you know—if I'm showing yet, if it's kicking yet, et cetera."

"That's kinda sweet," Ellis said, waiting for the other shoe to drop.

"He's hired a divorce lawyer and started proceedings," Dorie said, her lower lip trembling. "And . . . he wants to buy out my share of the house."

"Really? That's good, right? Isn't that what you wanted?"

Dorie's eyes filled with tears. "I guess. It's just sort of sudden, you know? I thought I was going to have to be the one to get the ball rolling, because Stephen is such a procrastinator, but all of a sudden, he's in a big hurry to get all these papers signed and get shed of me."

"You were the one who was insisting on the divorce, Dorie," Ellis reminded her. "And you just told me yesterday that it's time for you to get on with your life. You're even dating. Sorta."

"Connor and I aren't really dating," Dorie protested. "I didn't even let him buy me dinner last night. I paid for my own."

"Have you kissed him?"

Dorie blushed.

"Maybe Stephen wants to get on with his life too," Ellis said.

"Oh sure, he gets to have his life all neat and perfect," Dorie said. She looked up at Ellis. "He's leaving Our Lady of Angels. He's been offered a job at Savannah College of Art and Design, in the development office. He says it's a big pay raise, and something he's always been interested in. I guess that's how he can afford to buy me out."

"That and the fact that he has a rich boyfriend," Ellis reminded her. "Anyway, a raise means he won't be making the same crappy salary you make. If he's working at SCAD, it'll mean he can afford to pay a decent amount of child support."

"It doesn't seem fair," Dorie said bitterly. "He's the one who screwed up our lives. He got me pregnant, and he cheated, and he walked out. Now, he gets the house, he gets a great new job . . . and what do I get?"

"You get to be a mom," Ellis said softly. "That's more important than a house, or a job, or money. Right? You get what you've always wanted: a child. None of that other stuff matters. You will be a fabulous mother, and Stephen will always have to know that he walked away from sharing a life with you and his child."

"You make it sound like a Hallmark card," Dorie said, sniffing. "What if I screw this up? I know I made a lot of noise about wanting this baby, but Ellis, I'm terrified. I don't know if I can do this all by myself."

"You won't screw up," Ellis said. "And you won't be by yourself. For better or worse, you have to let Stephen be a father to this baby. And you've got Willa, and Nash, and the rest of your crazy, screwed-up family. And Connor, it sounds like. And us. You've got us, Dorie. You know that, right? We've got your back. Always have. Always will."

"Willa!" Dorie said. "I almost forgot. Willa knows about the baby. Stephen ran into her this morning, and he just assumed I'd told her, and so he said something about her being an aunt. He said she nearly dropped dead of a heart attack."

"If only," Ellis said. "Oops."

"So now I've got to call her and tell her the whole sordid story," Dorie said, slumping in her chair. "And then she'll tell Phyllis, and there'll be this big shitstorm."

"You could just do an end run and call your mother yourself," Ellis suggested. "Sort of a preemptive strike."

"Nuh-uh," Dorie said glumly. "I'll face Phyllis when I get home. And not until."

Dorie propped her elbows on the table and rested her chin on her fists. "I am *not* looking forward to having this conversation with my sister."

"I'm surprised she hasn't called you," Ellis said.

"Oh, she has," Dorie said. "Repeatedly. I just haven't chosen to call her back."

"Coward," Ellis said.

"Yup, that's me."

"He's here," Julia announced at six that evening, walking into the kitchen where the girls were congregated. Dorie was making guacamole and Ellis was squeezing limes for margaritas. Madison was coating the rims of newly purchased glasses with a mixture of lime juice and salt. "Booker just pulled into the driveway. He and Simon are walking around outside, talking."

"Look," Ellis said, dropping a halved lime onto the countertop. "My hands are shaking. I can't believe how nervous I am."

"Relax," Julia said, tossing her hair. "He'll love the place. Hell, I love it, now that we've got it all pimped out like this."

"You did a great job, Julia," Dorie told her, tossing the diced avocados with some of the juice from Ellis's limes. "I never thought this house could look so good."

"I'd make a movie here," Madison added. "Hell, I'd live here, now that you've fixed it up like this."

"It's no biggie," Julia said lightly. "Any idiot could do what I did. Clean windows, waxed floors, some potted geraniums and ferns on the porch. . . ."

"All the furniture rearranged, new curtains in all the windows, new rugs, new art, flowers in every room, the deck pressure washed, the whole yard landscaped, porch rails repaired," Ellis said, ticking off the day's accomplishments on her hands. "I'm exhausted just talking about it. And I think Ty's totally overwhelmed by the change. I think he's actually starting to think this movie thing just might happen."

"It will happen," Julia vowed. "You wait and see. Booker says Simon is not easily impressed. So if he's here, the deal is almost certainly going to happen. Where is Ty, by the way?"

"Showering," Ellis said. "Or more likely, asleep standing up in the shower, after all the work you had him doing today."

"It's all going to pay off," Julia said. "I guarantee."

"I believe you," Ellis said. "The trick now is to make Ty believe."

The dining room table was littered with glasses, empty Corona bottles, shards of chips, and globs of salsa and guacamole—not to mention Dorie's empty caffeine-free Diet Coke cans. It was ten o'clock. The women, worn out from trying to make a good impression, had all scattered to their rooms. Simon had been wined and dined, plied with shrimp and grits and fried green tomatoes, all served up by Julia, Ellis, Madison, and Dorie, turned out in low-cut sundresses that showed their gleaming summer tans and welcoming Southern smiles.

Simon was in his late forties, balding, the remainder of his white-blond hair gathered into a tight little braid at the back of his head. He wore a snug-fitting black T-shirt with the word FAÇADE in white letters across the front; black linen shorts, which Julia cuttingly referred to as "manpris" behind his back; and high-top black sneakers worn unlaced.

He'd toured the house for two hours, looking in every nook and cranny, not saying much. Following that, he'd been driven up and down Croatan Highway by Ty and Booker. He'd stood on the bay side, watching the sunset with a practiced eye, and taken a cursory look at two other old houses Ty had found that might work for other locations for the movie. Now he leaned back in his chair and looked across the table at Ty, who was still sipping his first and only beer of the night.

"It'll work," he said succinctly. "Not perfect, but we can make it work. When can you be out?"

"Out?" Ty said blankly.

"Move out," Simon said. "We'll need access immediately. Didn't Booker tell you?"

Ty rubbed his eyes and yawned. "He said you wanted to start shooting in September?"

"Shooting, yes," Simon said impatiently. "But we've got to get our crews in here right away. This place, if you don't mind my saying so, needs a lot of work."

"I thought you wanted an old house," Ty protested. "Booker said . . ."

"We need to make it look even older than it is," Simon said. "The art director wants the house to be weathered blue shingles. Like on Cape Cod."

"But this house doesn't have shingles," Ty said.

"It will when we're done," Simon said. "Also, Joe wants awnings. Striped awnings, for Chrissakes. We need a gazebo on that deck of yours, overlooking the water, and that piece-of-crap garage? That's going to be a barn. A faded-red barn."

"It's a garage," Ty pointed out. "It doesn't look anything like a barn."

"It will," Simon said. "When we're done, you'll wonder where the cows went."

"Oo-kay," Ty said slowly.

"So you can move immediately?"

Ty blinked. "Why can't I stay in the garage apartment?"

"Because it's going to be a barn," Simon said, speaking slowly, as though he were dealing with someone with a marked learning disability. "We're going to make a movie in it, remember?"

"Let's back up," Ty suggested. "First off, my tenants, you remember my tenants? Julia, Ellis, Dorie, Madison? They have this place rented for another week yet. I can't just kick them out."

"Fifty thousand dollars," Simon said pleasantly. "For three months. We'll throw in a housing allowance for you, as long as you don't try to gouge us. How does that sound?"

Ty swallowed and tried to look uninterested, although his pulse was racing, his throat was dry, and his heart was hammering so hard he was afraid to look down at his shirtfront. He took another sip of the warm beer as a stalling tactic.

"The girls stay 'til the end of next week, as planned," he said finally. "They have a rental agreement, and I won't break it. Your people can work around them, can't they?"

Simon shook his head. "They'll stay out of the way?"

"Of course," Ty said. "Who'll be doing the work on the house, the construction and painting and all that?"

"A crew," Simon said. "Maybe you can help us line up some decent locals? Union, of course."

"Maybe I can be the general contractor," Ty said easily. "I've done all the work on the house up to now, but I've got buddies who are carpenters, painters, electricians.

"About the money," Ty said. "I'm gonna need a big deposit."

"How big?"

Ty felt a vein in his neck bulge, but chose to ignore it. "Half up front."

Simon shook his head vehemently. "Not happening."

"Okay," Ty said, taking another swig of beer. "No hard feelings. Maybe you can find another house on the water with somebody willing to turn a garage into a barn in, like, a week."

Simon eyed him. "Are you dicking around with me?"

"Yeah," Ty said. "But I need twenty-five thousand dollars up front, along with a signed agreement, and all the usual stuff I'm sure you people do with insurance and bonds and all. Or it's no deal."

Simon pushed his chair back from the table and stood up. "I'll get back to you in the morning. You wanna give me a ride to my motel, or are you gonna charge me extra for that too?"

"No charge," Ty said smoothly. "It's my pleasure."

"One more thing," Simon said. "What do you know about that lot next door? The one with the burnt-out house? That might work for us too."

"I'll get back to you on that," Ty said.

# 46

The trucks came rumbling down Ebbtide's driveway around two o'clock on Tuesday. Ellis had just come up from the beach, and now she stood on the front porch, with a red Solo Cup of iced tea, watching the parade approach. The first one was a lumber company tractor-trailer, piled high with pallets of wooden shingles, plywood, rolls of roofing, and lumber of every description. Right behind it came a big box van with RELIANCE AIR stenciled on the doors. It was followed by two beat-up cargo vans, which were followed by a red pickup truck, which was followed by Ty, in his weatherbeaten Bronco, minus the surfboard.

Ty parked the Bronco close to the street and jogged down to the house, directing the drivers where to park. Finally, he walked up to the porch, greeting Ellis with a brief kiss.

"What's all this?" she asked. "It looks like invasion of the house snatchers."

"Close," Ty said. "They're just going to do a little 'fixing up,' as Simon puts it. But I made 'em promise you girls won't be bothered too much. They're going to start on the garage first."

"You mean the barn?"

"Right."

Ellis pointed to the Reliance Air truck. "And that would be?"

Ty grinned. "Just a brand-spanking-new heat pump and two two-and-a-half-ton central air units. Hollywood likes the illusion of old, but talent as expensive as they've hired can't shoot a movie without air."

"Really? Do you get to keep it after the movie's done?"

"Absolutely. All the 'improvements' stay with the house afterwards, including the new cedar shake roof, the gazebo, and the barn. Although I still can't believe they can make that garage look like a New England barn."

"Yippee!" Ellis said, clapping her hands. "Air! How long will it take them to hook it up? I mean, I hate to complain, but the unit in Dorie's room is dead, and the one in my room is close to it. Madison gave up on hers as soon as she moved in."

Ty frowned. "Maybe you guys should consider moving over to a hotel. I told Simon I wouldn't let him run you off, but if the air's not working, that's not good. I'll make them pay for your rooms. I really didn't think they were gonna get everything going this fast. It's crazy, isn't it?"

"It makes my head spin," Ellis admitted. "You never told me if you were able to work things out with the bank. Did it go okay?"

"It did," Ty said. "I finally got a face-to-face with an actual human being. I showed him my contract with the movie people and wrote them a check for twenty thousand dollars, with the understanding that there'd be another payment as soon as shooting is completed and I get the rest of my money. For now, the foreclosure sale has been canceled."

"That's great," Ellis said. "You only gave them twenty thousand dollars? But you said Simon gave you twenty-five thousand."

"Right," Ty said. "I used the other five thousand to put an option on some land."

"I don't understand," Ellis said. "I'm not trying to second-guess you, but Ty, don't you need to put every penny back into saving Ebbtide?"

"Not every penny," Ty said. "The land I optioned is right over there." He pointed to the sandy lot next to Ebbtide, the one with the burnt-out foundation.

Ellis still looked puzzled. "You want to build a house right next to the house you already own?"

"Nope," Ty said. "Not right now, anyway. I'm going to rent it out to Simon and his buddies for the movie. They need an old-timey country store because one of the characters in the movie runs one. They've been looking all over the Outer Banks, but everything here is too shiny and new. So Joe and his people are going to build a store." He gestured with his chin. "Right over there."

"How did you know?"

"Simon asked me Sunday night, when we were negotiating, in a casual kind of way, about that lot. I figured they wanted it, and I told him I'd look into it."

"You knew who owned the lot?"

"Of course. Ruthann Sargent owns it. Her mother was my grandmother's best friend. Ruthann hasn't been to Nags Head since before Miss Penny passed away, four or five years ago. Not long after Miss Penny died, the house was struck by lightning and burned to the ground."

"How awful," Ellis said.

"Not so very awful," Ty said cheerfully. "The house was falling to pieces before the fire. Ruthann was more than happy to sell me a six-month option on it. If the movie people rent it, I'll give her half of what they give me. She's a nice gal, took care of my grandmother after her heart attack."

"I'm impressed," Ellis said. "You really are more than just a pretty face."

"You're just saying that because you want to get into my pants," Ty countered. "Now, what about the motel? Do you think you wanna move over there?"

"It's only for five more days," Ellis said, trying to sound lighthearted. "Four really, because our rental agreement clearly states that checkout time for Ebbtide is 10 A.M. Saturday."

"Yeah, well, I happen to know the landlord," Ty said. "Culpepper's a crusty old sumbitch, but I think we can probably get him to cut you some slack on that. But are you sure you want to stay with all this going on?"

"I don't know about the girls, but I don't mind. It's actually pretty exciting. I've never seen a movie being made."

"Don't know about the exciting part," Ty said. "It's going to get noisy and crowded, I guarantee, once all the subs start piling in here."

"Maybe we'd be in your way," Ellis said.

"Never," Ty said. He touched her chin with the tip of his finger. "Seriously, Ellis, I know it's selfish, but I want you here. Look, I need to talk to you about that. I mean, I don't want you to leave. Not just Ebbtide. I don't want you to leave Nags Head. I don't want you to leave. . . ."

A gleaming black Land Cruiser came bouncing down the drive, sand and crushed shells spinning from beneath its wheels, its horn honking madly. A man's arm was waving from the driver's side window.

"Oh shit," Ty said, distracted. "That's gonna be Joe, the art director. He's called me, like, twenty times already today. I better go deal with him. Can we talk about this later? Tonight?"

"Sure," Ellis said. "I'm not going anywhere. Yet."

As promised, carpenters and electricians and movie-type people started crawling all over Ebbtide. When Joe, the art director, set up an office on the kitchen table, the girls decided it was time to have dinner at Barnacle Betty's.

Their appetizers had just arrived at the table. "I think," Julia announced, spearing a fried shrimp with a fork, "I may have snagged myself a job with the movie folks."

"Really?" Dorie crowed. "That's fantastic. What would you do? When would you start?"

"I'll be a gofer," Julia said, dipping the shrimp in a plastic cup of cocktail sauce. "And I won't start for another week or two, which'll give me time to go up to DC and take a look at this house Booker is so hot to buy."

"Is there any chance they'll let you do something more artistic than just running errands?" Madison asked.

"Maybe," Julia said. "They're not making me any promises, but I figure, I'll hang around, schmooze, and worm my way into their hearts. It's kind of my specialty."

"It really is," Dorie told Madison. "Julia, when she's not being a bitchy diva, can really be totally charming."

"Hard to believe," Madison cracked, and they all burst out laughing.

"I've got news too," Madison said, choosing her words carefully. "I'm going to take off in the morning."

"Madison, no!" Dorie said. "Why? We've got the house 'til Saturday, and things are just starting to get interesting. I'm hoping maybe Cameron or Reese will show up later in the week. Don't you want to be able to say you met them?"

"Not really," Madison said. "It's just . . . time to go. You guys have been great, and I truly appreciate all you've done, but . . . I don't have a good feeling about Adam. I still haven't heard from him. And Don has stopped calling too. It's . . . eerie."

"Where'll you go?" Ellis asked.

Madison grimaced. "Believe it or not, I've decided to go back to New Jersey. I'll hire a lawyer, contact the authorities, and tell them what I know about Don's embezzlement. I've got the cash, or most of it, and that should make them sit up and listen. I hope."

"Ballsy move," Julia nodded approvingly.

"I'm tired of running," Madison said. "It's time for me to figure out what I'm going to do with the rest of my life. So, tomorrow's just as good a day as any to get started."

"No it's not," Julia said. "You've got to stay 'til Friday night. Please?"

"What's so important about Friday night?" Madison asked warily.

"My birthday," Julia said.

Dorie clapped her hand over her mouth. "Oh my gosh, Julia, I'd forgotten."

"Me too," Ellis said guiltily. "And you guys know I never forget a birthday."

"I'll be thirty-six," Julia said. "I never thought I'd get that old. But this year, thirty-six doesn't seem so ancient."

"We're having a party?" Ellis asked. "You went and planned your own party?"

"Karaoke," Julia said. "At Cadillac Jack's. Friday night. Our last night. Who's in?"

"Me," Dorie said.

"Me too," Ellis added.

They all looked expectantly at Madison.

"Oh, all right," she said, caving. "A couple more days won't make that much difference. I guess I can just as easily leave Saturday as tomorrow. One more thing," she said, glaring at all of them in turn. "I *do not* karaoke."

"Karaoke is not a verb, Madison," Dorie said sweetly. "Anyway, we'll see about that."

Ellis was climbing into Dorie's van for the ride back to Ebbtide when she heard her cell phone ding. She dug through the contents of her purse, eager to see if the text was from Ty.

"Oh Lord, y'all," Julia announced. "Ellis has gone boy crazy on us. She and Ty are texting each other day and night. He's probably wanting to know when she's due back at the love nest."

"Shut up, Julia," Ellis said, laughing. "We're not that bad."

"Yeah, you are," Dorie said, turning around from the driver's seat. "But I think it's cute."

Ellis finally found her phone and touched the message icon. She had to squint to read in the faint light.

"What's he say?" Julia asked, peering over her shoulder. "Oooh, is he sexting you?"

"Noooo," Ellis said, blinking, and rereading the message to be sure she hadn't misunderstood. "This isn't from Ty. It's from a woman I used to work with at the bank." Ellis looked up. "You guys, she's offering me a job!"

# 47

"It's my last night in the apartment," Ty told Ellis when she got back from dinner with the girls. "They're going to start tearing it down tomorrow, putting up the barn."

"Kind of sad, huh?" Ellis said.

He shrugged. "It's just a crappy garage apartment, I know. My grandfather built it with lumber from another house up the road that was blown down in a big storm. And later, my grandmother's maid used to live here with her kids. And the garage is literally so eaten up with termites, it could fall down before they tear it down. But I've kinda gotten used to living here."

They were sitting in the Adirondack chairs, out on the deck, staring out at the stars. The construction crews had finally packed up for the night and gone off to their motels, but they could hear the hum of the gas-powered generators set up to run the work lights.

"I think your place is adorable," Ellis said. "I love everything about it, except maybe the outdoor shower, and even that I wouldn't mind so much if it weren't so, uh, exposed."

That gave them both a laugh.

"I'd love to have seen the look on Kendra's face when she found out she wasn't going to get the chance to kick your white-trash ass to the curb," Ellis said.

"She's still trying to figure out where I got the money to stop the foreclosure proceedings," Ty said. "I've seen her drive past half a dozen times in the past two days, craning her neck, trying to see what's going on here."

"Ty," Ellis said, after a while. "What's going to happen when the movie people are gone and the money runs out? Do you think you'll still be able to hang on to Ebbtide?"

"Good question," Ty said, crossing and uncrossing his legs. "The movie money will buy me some time. And now that I'm paid up with the bank again, I'm going to see about getting the mortgage refinanced. Interest rates have dropped nearly three hundred basic points since my uncle sold it to me, so I'll save a bundle that way. After that, I honestly don't know."

Ellis was quiet. Suddenly, the generators shut down. Now they could hear the waves rolling in on the beach below. Fireflies blinked amongst the tall strands of beach grass, and a few yards down the beach, a group of college kids huddled around a bonfire. Ty and Ellis heard drifts of music from their iPods, saw two of the kids wandering away from the others, into the dunes, hand in hand.

"School starts back up pretty soon," Ellis said, watching them go. "I'll bet this is their last big party before everybody heads back to their real lives."

Ty's fingertips brushed against Ellis's.

"I don't want you to go," he said, staring straight ahead.

She smiled to herself. "I was hoping you'd ask me to stay tonight. The last night of the old crib. Maybe we'll even have one last shower out here for old time's sake—as long as it's before daylight."

"Not just tonight," Ty said. "I don't want you to go. Period. I don't want to stand here and watch you drive away on Saturday."

"Ty . . ." Ellis started.

He caught her hand in his. "Stay. Please?"

She sighed. "I wish I could. I've thought about it all week. Before that, even. Who wouldn't want to live at the beach year round and play house? With you?"

Ty kissed the back of her hand. "Good. Then it's settled."

"Ty, I've had a job offer." She blurted it out.

He dropped her hand. "What? When did this happen?"

"Just a little while ago. It was totally out of the blue. Dana, this woman I used to work with at the bank, texted me the offer, like, fifteen minutes ago. The thing is, it's my dream job. Dana's been hired to head up this new project at Pacific Trust, and she wants me to come with her. The money is fabulous, great benefits, they've even got a relocation package. They'll sell my town house! Nobody does that anymore."

"Pacific Bank? What? You'd be in their East Coast office?"

"No. The job's in Seattle."

He turned to look at her. "You're not seriously considering taking it, right?"

"I'd be an idiot not to. In this economy? Nobody's hiring. I haven't had a single response to any of the résumés I sent out last month. Not one! But this—this is amazing. Dana says I'd come onboard as an assistant veep. And I'd report direct to her. It'd be a huge promotion for me."

Ty hunched forward, his head in his hands.

"Say something, please?" Ellis whispered.

"Like what? Congratulations?"

"That would be a nice start."

He turned and stared at Ellis. "Have you heard anything I've been telling you tonight? I want you to stay. Right here, with me. In Nags Head."

"And do what?" the old, practical Ellis asked. "How would I make a living?"

"We could live on love," Ty said, trying to sound like he meant to be funny, but she could tell he was serious.

"And do what when it comes time to pay the bills?" Ellis asked. She swung her legs around and pressed her knees up against Ty's. "Your life here is a beautiful dream. You know how to make it work. You live by your wits, day trading, picking up shifts as a bartender, renting out the house in the season. And that works great for you. But it's not me, Ty. I've always had a nine-to-five job. Not the most exciting or glamorous life, but it works for me. I'm a list-maker, a rule-follower."

"You could find a job here," Ty said, but he knew as soon as the words were out of his mouth that it was a lie. "Maybe not making as much money, but you could find one."

"Or you could move to Seattle with me and find a job." Ellis gave him a crooked smile. "It's a different ocean, but it's still the coast. Kinda."

"I could give it a try," Ty said. "If you wanted me to."

"What was that you told me on that first awful dinner date? About never having another job in an office?"

"Yeah, well, I was just blowing off steam. I could do it, Ellis, if I had to."

"That's the point, Ty. I don't want you to think you have to. You'd be miserable in an office job. And then I'd be miserable. Did you ever see any of those old Tarzan movies when you were a kid?"

"Huh? How many drinks did you guys have at dinner?"

"No, listen. When I was a little girl, my brother Baylor was obsessed with Tarzan. He read all the Edgar Rice Burroughs books, got my dad to go buy him the videos of the movies—these old black-and-white films from the early forties. We'd watch them Friday nights, which was my parent's date night. Baylor's favorite Tarzan was Buster Crabbe, he was a silent movie star. But I loved Johnny Weissmuller. Oh my God, he had a body, running around in that loincloth. I think he'd been an Olympic swimmer. And Jane was Maureen O'Sullivan, so glamorous. My favorite one of those movies was called *Tarzan's New York Adventure.* I don't remember all the details, but Boy gets kidnapped and taken to New York, and Tarzan and Jane get on a plane and go after him. And Jane has to civilize Tarzan, you know, to get him prepared for the big city. They go to a tailor and have him fitted for a suit, and he has to ride in a cab, and all this other stuff. And Tarzan, who is this action hero, is just so sad, so out of place in the city. . . ."

"And you're saying if I were to move to Seattle to be with you, that I'd be like Tarzan—lost in New York? Ellis, this is Nags Head, North Carolina, not deepest, darkest Africa. And I'm no jungle savage. I have a college degree, two years of law school. I may not enjoy wearing a coat and tie, but I do wear shoes on a semiregular basis . . ."

Ellis pushed a strand of hair from her forehead. "You know that's not what I'm getting at. I'm just saying you've figured out how you want to live your life, and you're doing that. And me dragging you off to Seattle, making you wear a tie . . ."

"Instead of a loincloth?"

She laughed in spite of herself. "I wouldn't mind seeing you in a loincloth, now that you mention it. But I just don't see how we could make it work. I've tried it before, with a man who was totally different. It was a disaster. You and I don't even want the same things."

"How do you know it would be a disaster this time?" Ty asked. "How do you know what I want? Or what you really want? Are you telling me you want to go back to a job in banking, like you had before?"

"No," Ellis said. "Not exactly."

"And Seattle? That's the city of your dreams?"

"No!" Ellis said. "I've never even been to Seattle. But I've got to be practical. This job offer means something to me, Ty. It means I haven't been wasting the last fifteen years of my life. It means somebody values what I do. I'll have a profession, and a title at the bank. And yes, a paycheck and benefits and all those boring middle-class trappings you hate. So yes, I admit, I might have to compromise, move to a new city, go back into banking."

"You'll compromise for a crappy job you don't even really want, but not on taking a chance that we could make things work together?" Ty pushed his chair back and away from hers.

"I've known you for less than a month," Ellis said, her voice pleading. He stood at the deck railing, staring off at the water.

"A month is enough for me to know how I feel about you," Ty said, his back to her. "A week was enough. You were such a pain in the ass with those e-mails of yours, pestering me to get into this house. And then I saw you come bopping up the driveway, in your little pink shorts . . . I knew I was a goner."

She got up and stood beside him. The wind had picked up, and it was whipping her hair into her face. "I could come back out here, weekends, like that. Banks have lots of holidays. Columbus Day is what, six weeks away? You could come out there and visit. A long-distance relationship isn't ideal, but lots of people do it. Look at Booker and Julia."

"Booker and Julia are getting married. She's moving to DC to be with him, isn't that what you told me?"

Ellis bit her lip and wished she hadn't brought it up. "They've been together for years and years. It's different with us, Ty. You know it is."

He looked at her steadily, at her dark hair blowing in the wind. She kept trying to brush it away from her face, control it. Maybe she was right, maybe he didn't have any right to ask her to believe in him, to believe in them. But shouldn't she believe in them too?

"Time's got nothing to do with it," he said finally. "Kendra and me? We'd known each other since grade school. Started dating in eighth grade. I thought I knew everything about her. She sure as hell knew everything about me, or so she thought."

The wind had picked up more, he turned his back to the railing, and now he was looking at the apartment, thinking about his last night here, and how he wanted it to be. Through the kitchen window, he could see the bottle of wine he'd bought, sitting on the counter. And he was thinking about how he'd been planning this evening ever since Joe broke the news that they'd tear the place down come morning. Things were not going according to plan.

"Kendra and I were together, from the time we were, like, fourteen, 'til we split up in law school," Ty said. "This apartment? I shouldn't tell you this, but for some reason, I feel like I have to. We'd sneak over here in high school, you know, late at night. It was never locked."

He saw the look of mild shock on Ellis's face. "We were kids, still in high school. Kendra loved breaking the rules, loved the idea of pushing her daddy's buttons. He'd have had me arrested if he knew what we were up to over here."

"I don't want to hear this," Ellis said, stony faced. "I realize it was a long time ago, but I don't want to hear about you sleeping with your girlfriend in the same place where we've been sleeping."

"Not the same bed," Ty said hastily. "God no. There wasn't even a bed here, back then. Just an air mattress."

"Why are you telling me this?" Ellis demanded. "You want to hurt me, because I'm being realistic? Because I won't just throw my life away and move in down here with you? Move in where? You won't even have a place to live after tomorrow."

"I've got a little cottage rented less than half a mile down the Beach Road," Ty said. "Pelican Cottage. It sits right on the dunes. It's rustic, but you'd love it. And then, when the movie people are gone, we could come right back to Ebbtide."

"Not the point," Ellis said.

"I'm telling you all this," Ty said, "because I have a point to make. And that point is, it doesn't matter how long you've known somebody. People change. Or you don't really know them as well as you thought you did in the first place. You told me you made a huge mistake marrying a man you'd only known a short time. Well, I made a huge mistake too. Only I'd known Kendra most of my life. And it didn't make any difference, because we ended up just as miserable as you were. We were kids back then, young and dumb. Not like now."

Ellis was looking at the apartment too. It was tiny, cramped, barely two rooms. She'd fantasized about staying here with Ty, waking up with him, about moonlight showers and beach walks at sunrise. But it wasn't until this moment that she realized all her fantasies were based on the one sun-splashed idyllic summer month they'd spent together. Summer.

September was a handful of days away. And then summer would be gone.

"You're right," she told Ty. "We're not kids anymore. We're old enough to recognize that some things are just . . . of the moment. Ephemeral. Like the shells you pick up at the beach. They're so shiny and perfect and pearlescent when you pick them up, and then when you get them back home, they're all bleached out and lifeless. I'm afraid that's what we'd be like. Three months from now, six months from now, wondering what we saw in each other . . ."

Ty's expression darkened. "Really, Ellis? That's what I am to you? Just some hot guy you picked up at the beach? A fling?"

"No!" Ellis cried. "You know that's not what I meant."

"Sure you did," Ty said quietly.

"You're making this harder than it has to be," Ellis pleaded.

He looked at her calmly. "Do you love me?"

"Yes! But that's not the point."

"Do you want to be with me?"

"You know I do. But it's just not that simple."

"It's not that hard," Ty said. "Not to me. I want to be with you, so I'll do whatever it takes to make that happen. Apparently you don't feel the same way."

Ellis took a step backwards. Ty's face was cold, impassive. If he could be that calm, so could she. She took a deep breath, and then another, willing herself not to cry or slobber or, God forbid, beg. "Where does that leave us?" she asked finally.

"I think it leaves me living here and you on your way to Seattle," Ty said. "Alone."

# 48

Ellis stared moodily down at her coffee cup. No truths there. Just inky, lukewarm, bitter blackness.

For once, she was glad to have the kitchen all to herself. If she were truthful, she'd have to admit that after a month together, much as she and Dorie and Julia loved one another, they were all probably getting on each other's nerves.

Madison was wiser than any of them. It was time, Ellis thought, to go home. She was already devising a game plan for packing up: stripping all the beds, running a last load of laundry, disposing of the refrigerator's contents, loading the car. What she would not think about, under any circumstances, was what she would be leaving behind.

She heard the low rumble of a diesel motor coming from the front of the house and ran to see what it was. A flatbed trailer was parked in the driveway, and a handful of men were waving and directing as a bright yellow bulldozer inched its way down a steel loading ramp.

When the operator had maneuvered the dozer off the ramp, a man in an orange safety vest and a hard hat ran over, jumped into the cab, and conferred with the driver. A moment later, the hard hat guy was back in the driveway, waving and pointing at the garage—and Ty's apartment. But there was no sign of Ty. His Bronco was gone, and the garage was empty.

Now Ellis noticed a huge jumble of stuff piled off to the side of the garage—its former contents: a three-legged ping-pong table; a stack of bald tires; a rusty barbecue grill; the skeletons of aluminum lawn chairs; even a small, wooden skiff with a rotted-out hull. And a surfboard. A faded yellow surfboard.

As she watched, the bulldozer lumbered purposefully towards the garage, aiming at the support beam that separated the two parking bays. She closed her eyes, and a moment later, she heard the sickening sound of boards snapping, beams tumbling to the ground, the garage sliding easily, effortlessly to the ground, with a thud she felt as well as heard.

She heard whistles and applause, and when she opened her eyes, a cloud of dust and sand still swirled in the air around the demolished garage.

Ellis felt a hand on her shoulder. She turned and saw Madison standing beside her.

"I saw the trucks coming from my bedroom window," Madison said. "I came down because I had half an idea you might still be up there," she jerked her head in the direction of where the apartment had stood, "with Ty."

They heard the screen door open and slap shut behind them. Julia and Dorie joined them on the porch, barefoot, in their pajamas.

"Jesus, Mary, and Joseph!" Julia exclaimed, gaping at the remains of the garage. "I heard that crash and I thought somebody'd dropped a bomb on the place."

"Wow," Dorie said. "That didn't take long."

"Where's Ty?" Julia asked. "How was your last night together in the love shack?"

Ellis stuck her hands in the pockets of her shorts. "I don't know where Ty's gone. I didn't spend the night. We . . . had a fight. Not a fight, per se, but . . ."

"Oh Jesus," Julia groaned. "Don't tell me you guys broke up. Don't tell me you actually want to take that stupid job at that stupid bank in Seattle."

"I told Dana I'd get back to her Monday," Ellis said. "You wouldn't understand, but this is just too good an offer to pass up. Ty doesn't understand either. So probably we just weren't meant to be."

Dorie gave her a hug. "Oh, Ellie-Belly. I'm so sorry. What happened?"

"Nothing," Ellis said. "He wants me to stay here, to live on love and peanut-butter-and-jelly sandwiches. It's sweet, but it won't work. One of us has to have a job, and benefits . . . and common sense."

"Let me guess," Julia drawled. "That someone would be you."

"Don't start," Ellis warned. "I am not in the mood for relationship advice."

By noon, the remains of the old garage had been scraped up and loaded onto a dump truck headed for the landfill. More lumber trucks and pickup trucks arrived, and even from the beach, the women could hear the whine of power saws and the sharp bursts of nail guns.

"One more day," Julia said under her breath, glancing over at Ellis, who'd deliberately set up her beach chair and umbrella several yards away from Dorie, Julia, and Madison. "Our last full day at the beach, and she manages to screw it up for all of us."

"I can't believe she's just going to walk away and leave Ty," Dorie said, keeping her voice low. "He's the best thing that's ever happened to her, and tomorrow she's just going to get in her car and drive back to Philly—and then pick up and move across the country?"

Madison sat cross-legged on her blanket, sipping from a cold bottle of water. "Maybe she's just not ready for a relationship. To commit."

"Hah!" Julia chortled. "You don't know Ellis. Nobody was ever more ready for a relationship than Ellis. Before Ty, she hadn't been with a man in, like, dog years."

"Ellis got married right out of college to this totally inappropriate guy," Dorie said, filling Madison in.

"The marriage was over before she got the wedding dress back from the dry cleaner's," Julia added. "Literally. Right, Dorie?"

"She was devastated," Dorie agreed. "It stunted her emotionally. For years."

"She buried herself in work at that damned bank, never took a vacation, and then, poof! They go and downsize her. She wakes up and realizes she's thirty-five, single, with no prospects in sight. And then garage guy walks in, and sweeps her right out of those damned sensible shoes of hers. But because Ty doesn't have a 401(k) and he doesn't fit into her game plan, she refuses to consider how right they are for each other," Julia said, glancing furtively at Ellis to make sure she couldn't hear her life being dissected.

"Look at her, poor thing," Dorie whispered, nodding towards Ellis, who had dozed off, facedown on her chair. "She was probably up all night crying after their big fight."

"It's sad," Madison observed.

"Ellis never talks about it, but I know she's always wanted a family," Dorie said. "That's what's so heartbreaking. She could have that with Ty. I mean, he's perfect for her."

"And hot. Smokin' hot," Julia pointed out.

"They did seem pretty sweet together," Madison said. "But she's a grown-up, right? And she knows what will and won't work for her."

"Not this time," Dorie said. She looked at Julia. "We've got to do something. And quick."

Julia jumped to her feet, tiptoed over to the sleeping Ellis, grabbed her beach tote, and brought it over to her own chair. She rummaged around inside the bag, setting aside sunblock, lipblock, paperback novel, and a notepad containing Ellis's to-do list. Finally, jubilantly, she held up Ellis's cell phone. "Don't worry," she told the others. "I'm on it."

The tiny print on the computer screen seemed to swim before his eyes. The agribusiness start-up he'd been following was announcing its IPO. He glanced over at the notes he'd made. The research was more than promising. The opening stock price was ridiculously low—four dollars a share? Two months ago, he'd have taken the plunge, gone all in. He had a little cushion now, with the cash from the movie people, so why couldn't he make himself place the stock order?

Ty shook his head, got up from the wooden table he'd moved over to his new cottage, and walked out to the screened porch. The sky was crystal blue, cloudless, a slight breeze coming off the beach. He stretched and rotated his shoulders. He'd been at the computer most of the morning, deliberately avoiding Ebbtide.

He hadn't actually planned to move over to Pelican until later in the day, but after the breakup with Ellis the night before, he hadn't seen any point in staying in the apartment another night. He'd sat at the kitchen table, drinking half the bottle of wine, then dumping the rest down the sink before he loaded his stuff in the Bronco and moved it over to Pelican Cottage sometime after midnight.

Instead of making him sleepy, the wine had made him annoyingly hyper. So he'd spent the early morning hours burying himself in the minutiae of day trading.

It was nearly eleven now, and he knew the garage was gone, because Joe had e-mailed him a photo taken at the precise moment the rotted wooden structure collapsed into the sand. Ty had glanced at the photo and deleted it. Not a moment he wanted to celebrate.

He should have been at the house by now. He'd hired the frame carpenters and laborers needed to start the barn raising, but somehow, he just couldn't make himself take the half-mile trip down the road to Ebbtide. He wondered if Ellis had watched the garage being torn down. She'd probably applauded its demise. Why the hell had he told her about his idiotic teenage trysts there with Kendra?

Ty went back inside the cottage and began shutting down his computer. His cell phone dinged, signaling he had a text message.

DEAR MR. CULPEPPER: WE NEED 2 TALK. MEET ME @ BEACH, MIDNIGHT, 2NITE. YR. FRIEND, ELLIS SULLIVAN.

He stared down at the text block. She wanted to talk? About what? As far as he was concerned, she'd done all the talking that was necessary the night before.

The hell with her, he told himself, typing rapidly.

NOTHING LEFT 2 SAY.

. . .

"Shit!" Julia exclaimed, staring down at Ty's text. "He's as stubborn as she is."

"Now what?" Dorie asked, keeping an eye on the slumbering Ellis.

Julia flexed her fingers and looked towards the sky for inspiration, but found only a flock of seagulls circling overhead.

"We just have to get them together," she muttered. "He's crazy about her. She's crazy about him. What's so hard about this?"

"Talk about crazy, you two are insane if you think this is going to work," Madison said. "We're talking about two adults here, not a couple of sitcom characters."

"Let's analyze," Dorie said. "What is it that's keeping them apart?"

"Money," Madison said quickly. "Lack of it."

"Not really," Dorie said.

"Ellis is the least materialistic person I know," Julia agreed. "But she's so friggin' practical."

"And rigid," Dorie threw in. "If she can't list it, chart it, or graph it, Ellis doesn't get it. She craves security."

"Security," Madison with a snort. "I thought I was getting that when I married Don, and look where it got me."

"If she knew Ty had some kind of a job, and if she had a job—one that would allow her to live here with him—I think Ellis would stay," Julia said.

"Well, let's get them jobs," Dorie said, as though it were the simplest thing in the world.

"Doing what?" Madison asked, flopping back down to the sand. "This is hopeless."

Julia scowled at Madison. "We can do this. I know we can. We just need to think outside the box."

"You said she worked at a bank," Madison said, trying to regain favor. "What kind of work did she do there?"

"Marketing," Julia said.

"Couldn't she do that down here?"

"If there were any really big banks here, sure, but Ellis did corporate marketing," Dorie said kindly. "And those jobs are in big cities, like Philly or Charlotte, where she worked before, or Seattle, where she's going to move if we don't stop her."

"Couldn't she telecommute?" Madison asked. "I mean, these days, if you have a computer, a BlackBerry, and a headset, you can do just about any kind of work, anywhere."

"No," Julia said peevishly. "It doesn't work like that."

Dorie looked quizzically at Julia. "Why couldn't it work that way? One of our math teachers at school, her husband does IT work for a company out of Boston. He flies up there one week out of every month, but the rest of the time he works from home, right there in Savannah."

"See?" Madison said smugly. "Telecommuting. That's the answer."

"It could be," Julia said slowly. "But Ellis has a job offer. You heard her. It's the total package: pay, promotion, benefits. You know how the economy is. There just aren't that many jobs out there."

"Because she's really only applied for jobs in bank marketing and on the East Coast," Dorie pointed out. "Maybe if she sorta branched out, you know, widened her target, with the idea of telecommuting, she'd have a better shot."

"Maybe," Julia said. "It's worth thinking about. Ellis is terrific at what she does, nobody's harder working, or more creative or talented, that's for sure."

"And what about Ty?" Dorie said. "That's a tough one. Ellis told us Ty said he never wants another office job, never wants to have to put on a tie or sit in a cubicle again."

"I don't know, I don't know," Julia moaned. "This is hurting my head."

Dorie was still watching Ellis, who'd stirred, just the slightest bit, throwing an arm over her eyes to block out the sun. "Let's get back to business," she whispered. "Before Ellis wakes up and catches us with her phone. What are we going to say to Ty to get him to meet her on the beach at midnight?"

"Even if you get *him* here, how are you going to get Ellis here?" Madison asked.

"First things first," Julia said, typing again.

. . .

Ty read the text once, and then again, to make sure he'd read it right.

IF YOU LOVE ME, YOU'LL COME.

He typed rapidly, without thinking.

SEE YOU @ MIDNIGHT.

As soon as the "sent" icon lit up, he closed the phone and slipped it in the pocket of his shorts. He opened his computer, rebooted, and went to his account page. The IPO offer for the agribiz seemed to be going well. Share prices were up to $4.25. He hit the "buy" button, nodded, and shut the computer down again.

He went outside, unlocked his beach cruiser, and pedaled quickly up the road to Ebbtide. It was going to be an interesting day, no matter what.

"Oh my God!" Dorie squealed, when Julia handed her Ellis's phone. "It worked. It totally worked. He's coming." She held her hand over her heart and sighed deeply. "This is so romantic, I could die."

"You *will* die, because Ellis will probably kill you two when she finds out what you've been up to," Madison said. "Now, tell me, geniuses, how are you going to get Ellis down to the beach at midnight?"

"We'll get her there," Julia said, "doing what we do best: lying and trickery. All we have to do now is keep Ellis away from Ty until their midnight meeting. Just in case he happens to mention getting those texts."

"That won't be hard," Dorie predicted. "Ellis hates confrontation. If she even sees Ty, I bet she'll run the other way."

"Even so, I don't want to take any chances," Julia said. She took the cell phone back from Dorie, and carefully cleared the texts to Ty from the memory. Then she tucked it back in the beach bag, and tiptoed over to where Ellis was just beginning to stir.

Julia plopped down onto the sand beside Ellis, at the same time dropping the bag casually beside her chair.

"Hey," Ellis said, shading her eyes from the sun's glare. "What are you up to?"

"Nothing," Julia said innocently. "Just wanted to tell you to turn over. Your face is getting too much sun."

"Thanks," Ellis said, yawning. "You're the best."

"You don't even know," Julia said, handing Ellis a bottle of sunblock. "Listen, Booker left this morning, and I still need to return all that stuff I bought to HomeGoods. Dorie's got a farewell lunch date with Connor, and Madison . . . well, you know Madison. Anyway, I was wondering if you'd go with me to help load and unload the stuff. Dorie says we can take the van."

Ellis frowned. "I was kinda thinking I'd start cleaning out the fridge and packing this afternoon."

"Madison volunteered to clean the fridge," Julia lied. "And you'll have plenty of time to pack this afternoon, before we head out for karaoke tonight."

"Yeah," Ellis said slowly. "About karaoke. I know it's your birthday and all, but I really don't think I'm gonna be up for a lot of partying tonight. I'll go to dinner, but after that, I think I'll just have a last quiet night at Ebbtide. I want to get an early start in the morning."

"Nuh-uh," Julia said. "You're not weaseling out of karaoke. It's our last night together, not to mention my birthday. Don't make me play the guilt card, Ellis. Either we all go, or nobody goes." She crossed her arms and glared defiantly at her friend.

"Does it have to be karaoke at Caddie's?"

"Yes, it does," Julia said. "Anyway, it's Friday. Even if Ty is working tonight, he'll be too busy slinging margaritas to see what you're up to."

"This isn't about Ty," Ellis started.

"Sure it is," Julia said. She stood up and offered a hand to Ellis. "Now let's get moving. I'm pretty sure you've drawn up a new Kaper chart back at the house, telling all of us what we've got to do before checkout tomorrow."

# 49

"Ty," Angie said, "I'm at my wit's end here. Patricia's a no-show again. It's our last college night of the summer, and the place is already packed to the rafters. I'm begging you. Just come in 'til midnight. I'll get Nella to close, but if I don't get somebody behind the bar, like, right now, I may have to kill myself."

Ty pushed his chair away from the computer. He walked out of the cottage and stared out at the sky. It was past eight and the last orange streaks of sunset were barely visible over the dunes that separated Pelican Cottage from the beach. The view wasn't nearly as good as his own view back at the garage apartment at Ebbtide had been. He was going to miss that view, but there would be other sunsets, and in ninety days, give or take a few, he would be back home at the old house, this time for good.

"Sorry, Angie, can't do it," Ty said. "I've got something else tonight."

"What?" she demanded. "Look, I told you I'm desperate. Just tell me what it'll take to get you here, right now, and I'll pay it."

He considered Angie's offer. She was over a barrel, and he knew it.

"A hundred bucks an hour," he said promptly. "Cash. Plus tip out."

"Shit!" Angie groaned. "I could get five bartenders for that."

"So get 'em."

"No, damn it. I need you and you know it. Get over here now."

"Sure," he said. "But there's just one more thing. I can't stay 'til midnight. I gotta be out of there by eleven thirty. Sharp."

"Okay, fine, whatever," she said.

"I mean it, Angie. I don't care if every damn college kid on the Outer Banks is in there tonight. I'm walking at eleven thirty. No matter what. Understand?"

"Just get here," Angie snapped.

Julia sauntered into Ellis's room just as she was zipping herself into the pink Lilly Pulitzer sundress.

"Don't start," Ellis warned, when she saw Julia's disapproving frown. "I've already packed everything else except what I'm wearing in the morning. And I am not borrowing any more of your clothes tonight. This is who I am. I'm not Julia Capelli. I don't wear spike heels or black lace bras as tops. I am Ellis Sullivan. Boring, predictable, safe Ellis Sullivan. So deal with it!"

"I was just gonna ask if I could borrow your silver hoop earrings," Julia said, seating herself on the edge of the bed. "But if you're gonna go all postal on me, never mind."

"Earrings? That's all you want?"

"Yeah. What did you think I wanted?"

Ellis reached into the pink satin jewelry roll that sat on top of her dresser and fished out the silver hoops. "You didn't come in here to try and get me all skanked up tonight before we go to Caddie's?"

"Nope," Julia said.

"And you're not gonna try and talk me out of leaving tomorrow? Instead of staying here, with Ty?"

"Nope," Julia said. She held out her hand. "Just a pair of earrings. That's all I need. Oh yeah, Dorie asked me to come up here and tell you she needs you down in the laundry room. She can't figure out which towels are yours and which ones stay in the house."

"The fugly gray and maroon towels stay here," Ellis said, turning back to the mirror.

"Yeah, but she said there's some other laundry, she can't figure out who it belongs to. Extra sheets and pillowcases. You know Dorie, she gets flustered by the least little thing."

"Oh all right," Ellis said, running a brush through her dark hair. "I'll go."

"Great."

Julia followed Ellis to the stairway. She waited until Ellis was halfway down the stairs before she darted back to her room. She picked up Ellis's purse, fished out her cell phone and car keys and pocketed them quickly, before heading back to her own bedroom.

He had his back to the bar while he poured tequila into the blender, but Ellis knew that muscled back. She knew those wide shoulders, the narrow hips. She caught her breath and took a step backwards, but Dorie grabbed her arm.

"Come on, Ellis," Dorie said. "You don't even have to talk to him. We'll find a table in the far corner."

"You guys," Ellis pleaded. "Don't make me do this."

"Do what?" Madison said, hooking her hand through Ellis's elbow. "Come on, Ellis. It's ladies' night. Our last night. You don't want to spoil Julia's birthday, do you?"

"Anyway, this place is jammed," Julia pointed out as they maneuvered through the crowd. "He'll never even know you're here."

"I'll know," Ellis said darkly, but she allowed herself to be towed to a table near the tiny stage, and then, reluctantly, to be talked into a lemontini. And then another. The music got louder, and then the karaoke mistress stood up and began taking requests.

First up were a pair of leather-clad biker dudes, one short and round, the other a foot taller, with an impressive beer belly and an even more impressive handlebar mustache.

"'Hotel California,'" Julia predicted. "I guarantee." And when the two launched into the Eagles classic, the women shared high-fives all around.

A pudgy brunette in too-tight white jeans, her breasts spilling out of a white tube top, clambered to the stage next, and shocked the crowd by singing a rendition of "Crazy" so pitch perfect, the women all swore she was Patsy Cline come back to life.

While they all stood, giving the Patsy wannabe a standing ovation, Ellis glanced over at the bar. Ty was clapping, whistling. In a split second, his eyes caught hers. He nodded, smiled, as though nothing had happened. Ellis felt her face flush, and she looked away.

Two songs later, Dorie stood and announced, "I'm taking a potty break. Anybody need anything?"

"Potty break and a Connor break, right?" Julia teased. "You think we didn't see you watching the door to see if he was working tonight?"

"I have to pee every thirty minutes," Dorie said. "Can I help it if the ladies' room is right by the bouncer's booth?"

Twenty minutes later, she was back, a tray of drinks in hand, with the karaoke catalog tucked under her arm.

"Ty sent these over," she announced, distributing the cups. "He saw me talking to Connor, and insisted that he wanted to buy us all a round of drinks since tomorrow's our last day. He says we're the best tenants he's ever had. Isn't that so sweet?"

"Adorable!" Julia said, staring at Ellis, who nodded mutely, and then knocked her drink back in one long guzzle.

Dorie and Julia exchanged a worried glance.

"Hey, slow it down," Julia said. "You don't wanna be driving with a hangover tomorrow, do you?"

Ellis tossed her hair. "I think I know what I'm doing."

"So. What are we gonna sing?" Dorie asked, flipping the catalog open.

"We? There is no we," Madison said.

"I thought we'd do a group number," Dorie said, looking around at the others. "What'll it be?"

"How 'bout 'It's Raining Men'?" Julia asked.

"Or what about 'Love Shack,' you know, since the B-52s are from Georgia, like us," Dorie suggested. "What do you think, Madison?"

Madison glanced down at the book, turned the page. "I don't do karaoke, as I think I mentioned previously," she said. "But if I did, I'd have to say we should do 'I Will Survive.'"

"Oooh, good one," Ellis had to admit. "I think that could be the theme song for all of us, right?"

Dorie nodded absentmindedly, still turning the pages of the book. "No. I got it. This is it. The one." She pointed at Julia, Ellis, and Madison. "And we are all gonna sing it. Together. Every single one of us. Because it's Julia's birthday. Right, Julia?"

Julia craned her neck to see what song Dorie had chosen. "Right. I'm the birthday princess and you all have to do what I say. So, what are we singing?"

"You'll see," Dorie said, slamming the book shut. "When it's our turn."

He'd found the house with little difficulty, thanks to the faded EBBTIDE sign by the mailbox. He'd cruised past half a dozen times during the day, but there was a surprising amount of activity, some kind of construction project going on, with cars and trucks coming and going. At one point, he'd even ventured down the driveway, simply following a caravan of pickup trucks full of workers. He'd spotted Maryn's Volvo, parked off to the side of the house, and smiled to himself. She was still here.

After six, when the workers left for the day, it was easy to pull into the lot next door, and hide his vehicle behind the foundation of a burnt-out old house.

It had been ungodly hot, waiting, but finally, darkness fell, and he could see silhouettes of the women moving around inside the house. So far, he hadn't spotted Maryn, but it didn't matter. She was there, he knew that. And he could afford to be patient.

Finally, close to nine o'clock, he saw the lights in the house being switched off, one by one. He got out of his vehicle, crept to the edge of the stack of lumber that had been unloaded only hours earlier, and watched while the women filed out of the decrepit old house and piled into a red van. The other three women were dressed stylishly, as if for a night out, but not her. He smiled, seeing Maryn dressed incongruously in cheap jeans and an oversized T-shirt, with her hair tucked up beneath a long-billed baseball cap. As though that would make her unrecognizable to anybody who knew the real Maryn.

Ebbtide was a ramshackle old wreck of a house, with thick beams, walls of cedar planks, and solid wooden doors. The locks, however, were a different matter. He'd easily jimmied the rusted lock on the kitchen door at the back of the house. Once inside, he'd quickly moved through all the bedrooms to ascertain which one was Maryn's. He'd cursed silently when he discovered that she, alone among the women, had locked her bedroom door. Not that it had slowed him down much. He'd seen the open window from the beach side of the house, and the old-fashioned catwalk that led to it from another third-floor door. It had been easy enough to find the door to the attic, and the corresponding window. And somebody, it appeared, had recently taken that same route to Maryn's room, judging by the fresh-looking splinters on the attic access door.

And how convenient, he marveled, that he'd been provided such a neat and convenient escape route—the steel spiral staircase leading directly from Maryn's room to the ground floor, and the burnt-out skeleton of the house next to Ebbtide, where his vehicle awaited, behind a clump of shrubbery.

From the looks of things, his timing was impeccable. Their departure was imminent. Maryn's duffle bag was packed. It took him only a moment to find the laptop case, shoved to the back of the shelf in the closet. He sat down on the room's only chair to wait. He had all the time in the world.

Eleven o'clock came and went. Julia caught Dorie's eye and glanced meaningfully at her watch. "Hey, Dorie," she said. "How much longer before our number comes up?"

"Oh," Dorie said, catching the meaning. "Uh, well, there were a bunch of requests in front of mine."

Ellis picked up Julia's drink and took a sip. "What's the hurry? The party's just getting started."

Julia reached over and put her hand to Ellis's forehead. "Are you hallucinating? I can't believe you're not champing at the bit to get home and finish packing. You didn't even want to come tonight."

Ellis pushed her hand away. "I changed my mind. Is that a crime?" She turned to Dorie. "Hey, pass me that karaoke thing."

Dorie rolled her eyes. "Really? You? You're going to do karaoke? By yourself?"

But Ellis was flipping through the pages of the catalog, pausing only when she came to the next to the last page. She looked up and glanced over at the bar, and she was sure Ty looked away.

"Yep, this is the one," she said, getting to her feet. She grabbed a wad of bills from her pocketbook and pushed her way through the crowd towards the karaoke mistress.

"Is she drunk?" Madison asked, looking from Dorie to Julia.

"Drunk or in love. Either way, this ain't the Ellis we know," Julia said grimly, and Dorie nodded in agreement.

When Ellis got back to the table, she had another drink. As soon as she wasn't looking, Julia dumped most of the contents of Ellis's cup into her own.

Two songs later, the emcee called out, "Ellis. Ellis, baby, where you at?"

A moment later, an Ellis they'd never seen before was prancing around the vest-pocket-sized stage, doing her best to channel Cyndi Lauper singing the anthem that had been theirs in parochial school, when they'd prance around Julia's princess pink bedroom in their Our Lady of Angels Peter Pan blouses and blue-plaid jumpers, pretend microphones in hand, warbling about how "Girls Just Wanna Have Fun."

Despite dissolving into a fit of nervous hysterical laughter halfway through the first verse when she forgot the words, Ellis's enthusiasm and confidence grew with every beat, so that by the end of the song, seemingly every woman in the club was on her feet, snaking around the dance floor in an impromptu conga line, chanting over and over, "they just wanna, they just wanna-uh-uh-uh . . ."

Stuck behind the bar, Ty had to scramble on top of an empty bar stool to catch a glimpse of her. When he did, the slow grin spread across his face again. "Attagirl," he said softly, to nobody in particular.

When Ellis made it back to their table, pink faced and sweat drenched, the three women stood and applauded. Ellis collapsed into her chair. "I did it!"

"You sure did," Julia agreed, glancing at her watch. "Now we really probably need to get you home."

"No!" Dorie cried. "We are not leaving here tonight until we all do our group number." She gave Julia an accusatory look. "You promised."

"Fine," Julia said. She plucked a ten-dollar bill from her pocketbook and strode towards the karaoke mistress.

"Think you could move Dorie and friends in the lineup?" she asked, cupping her hands to the woman's ear. "One of the girls is pregnant, and we need to get her home pretty soon. And it's our last night at the beach. Our swan song, you might say."

The karaoke mistress palmed the bill. "No problem," she said. "One more song, and you guys are on."

Julia nodded her thanks and went back to the table, nonchalantly glancing in the direction of the bar. To her satisfaction, she saw Ty, deep in conversation with an older, blond woman. He was gesturing angrily at his watch. She was shaking her head, but a moment later, Julia saw Ty head for the front door.

"We're next," Julia announced.

But Ellis wasn't listening. She'd been surreptitiously watching the bar, wondering if Ty would approach the table, maybe try to catch her attention, or even draw her outside to talk. Now though, she saw him scurrying for the front door, and her heart sank. He hadn't come anywhere near the house all day. As far as Ty was concerned, she thought bitterly, they'd already said their good-byes.

She picked up her neglected drink and knocked back half its watery contents, then turned her attention back to the stage, where a gaggle of drunken chicks were inexpertly grinding away at The Pussycat Dolls' "Don't Cha."

And then the karaoke mistress was calling. "Dorie and friends! All the way from Savannah, Georgia. Come on up here, girls, and show 'em how it's done!"

Madison crossed her arms defiantly over her chest. But Julia Capelli was having none of it.

"Let's go," she said, jerking Madison's chair backwards. "Showtime!"

Ellis looked at Madison and shrugged. "Come on," she said. "It's our last night. Might as well get it over with."

Dorie herded them all onstage, and they heard the distinctive introductory bass thumps. "Okay," she said, taking charge. "Julia and I will do the Travolta part. Ellis, you and Madison do Olivia Newton-John."

And the next moment, the four of them were sashaying across the stage, warbling "Summer Nights" from *Grease*. And when it came to the part about how summer flings don't mean a thing, Ellis Sullivan sang that verse with newfound wisdom.

# 50

That was awesome!" Dorie cried, throwing her arms around her friends at the end of the song.

"Yeah, we totally rocked it," Julia agreed, herding the women in the direction of the table. "But you guys, I think the birthday princess needs to go home now, before she turns into a pumpkin."

"Sounds good to me," Madison said readily.

They piled into the red van, with Dorie behind the wheel, and were almost home when Julia, trying to sound casual, pulled out her cell phone and groaned.

"Oh, no. My battery's dead. And I promised Booker I'd call him before midnight. Damn!"

"I'd let you use mine," Dorie offered, "but I've used up all my minutes for the month."

"Here," Ellis said, rummaging in her purse. "Just call him on mine."

"Okay," Julia said, holding out her hand.

"Well, hell," Ellis said, sounding puzzled. "It's not in here." She dumped the contents of the purse onto her lap, and pawed through the lipsticks, pens, billfold, Kleenex packets, and a notebook of lists.

Julia turned around from the front passenger seat. "Are you sure it's not there?"

"Positive," Ellis said. "And my keys are missing too. Dorie," she cried, "turn around. We've got to go back to Caddie's. I think maybe my phone and keys fell out of my purse back there."

"What?" Julia said, sounding panicky. It was ten minutes before midnight. "I didn't see your phone and keys on the table. And I was sitting right beside you all night."

"They've gotta be there," Ellis insisted. "Dorie, please go back. You guys can stay in the van, I'll just run inside and check the table and be right back."

"It can't be there," Julia countered. "Right, Dorie?"

"When was the last time you remember seeing your phone?" Dorie asked. "Think back."

"I don't know," Ellis said. "I've been running around all day, between the house and the beach, and packing, and cleaning, and starting to load the car."

"The beach!" Dorie cried. "Oh my God, of course. Ellis, it completely slipped my mind. When I was picking up my chair and towel this afternoon, I noticed your phone and keys on your beach chair. I meant to say something, but I just figured you were planning to go back down there later in the afternoon."

"Dorie!" Ellis said, annoyed. "Why didn't you say something sooner? Or just pick it up and bring it to me?"

"I'm an idiot," Dorie wailed. "It was so hot out there today, and then Willa called me on my cell to yell at me some more, and I just forgot."

"For Pete's sake," Ellis grumped. "That means my phone and keys have been out on the beach for hours. Somebody probably already walked off with them."

"Maybe not," Madison said helpfully.

"Look," Julia said, "we're almost home. You can just hop out of the van as soon as we get back to Ebbtide, and go check. I'm sure they're still there."

"Not likely," Ellis said gloomily.

. . .

Ty's hair was still wet, but he'd managed to shower and change out of his work clothes in ten minutes flat and walk down the beach from his new cottage to the stretch in front of Ebbtide. Now, at exactly five minutes 'til midnight, he stood on the beach, wondering if coming back here tonight was a mistake.

He glanced up at the spot where the garage, and his apartment, had been only twenty-four hours earlier, and looked quickly away. He'd done the right thing, what needed to be done, but he'd miss the old rattrap.

Somebody had left a folding beach chair in the middle of the spot where the Ebbtide girls had pitched their camp for the past month. A pink-and-orange striped beach towel was tossed across the back of the chair, and as he looked closer, he saw a cell phone and set of keys under the edge of the towel. He picked up the phone, pushed the on button, and seeing the call log, realized it belonged to Ellis.

Ty sat down on the chair to wait.

He was waiting, sitting quietly in the dark, on the chair by the window—the same window Madison looked out countless times, every morning and night, searching for any sign of trouble. A bead of sweat trickled down his back as he sat in the stifling closet-sized room. He'd considered turning on the rusty air conditioner stuck halfway into the window by the bed, but then decided to do so would alert her that somebody had been in the room.

He glanced down at the LED display of his wristwatch. Nearly midnight. Had she met another man? His eye twitched at the thought of Maryn with somebody else. Then he shook his head. Impossible. He'd seen the red van roll away from the house hours ago with the four women inside. Girls' night out. Completely harmless.

Not that it mattered. He patted the laptop case on the floor, its sides bulging with the cash he'd easily discovered hidden on the top shelf of the armoire. His cash. He'd earned it. He meant to have it, and he would have it, just as soon as he dealt with Maryn. He'd had time to count it, waiting for her, stacking the bills in rows that completely covered the bed. And it was all there, save for one hundred dollars. That surprised him, that Maryn hadn't spent the money, hadn't fled the country as soon as she figured out what she had. Maryn had never struck him as a particularly noble type. She was a hard-edged realist, just like he was. Which was why he'd been attracted to her.

He saw the play of lights on the opposite wall of the darkened room and stood up to look out the window. The red van was bumping down the drive-way at a fast clip. It didn't stop until it was directly in front of the porch. Then the engine switched off, and a petite redhead jumped from the driver's seat and raced for the front porch. A moment later, the back doors of the van opened, and he watched, his pulse quickening, as Maryn climbed out, stretched, and said something to the lanky blonde who got out the other side of the car. The two of them looked up at the house, and he stepped back, quickly, even knowing that there was no way she could see him up here, in the dark. Still . . .

Getting up and walking softly to the door, he opened it just far enough to hear the front door opening below. Lights clicked on, and there were more voices. This time he was certain he heard Maryn, and one of the other women, giggling conspiratorially. He closed the door and took up a position just to the side of it.

Minutes passed. He heard steps coming up the stairs. "G'night, y'all," an unfamiliar woman's voice called gaily. The steps stopped at the second floor, and he heard a door close, water running, and then the flush of a toilet, the sound of the bathroom door opening, and moments later, another door closing.

He resumed his wait, slumped against the wall, listening to his own even breathing. He heard more footsteps on the stairs, and tensed. His hands were slick with sweat. He dried them on his jeans, stood, moving towards the door, his hand on the pistol shoved into his waistband. The footsteps paused at the second-floor landing. Maybe it was one of the other women, Maryn's house-mates? But then the footsteps resumed, slowly climbing the stairs to the third floor.

It was serendipity, really, that she'd chosen this room, isolated on the top floor of the house. Not a surprise though. Maryn didn't trust anybody, especially other women. The big surprise was that she'd moved in with these strangers at all. Didn't matter why she'd choosen this room, all that mattered was that it was perfect for his needs.

The footsteps were coming closer now. And she was humming. What was it? "They just wanna," she crooned, "they just wanna-uh-uh." Cyndi Lauper? Maryn? He'd never known her to hum, let alone sing. Was she drunk or high? The footsteps paused in front of the door, and he held his breath as she fumbled to fit the key into the lock.

The door opened slowly. "They just wanna, they just wanna-uh-uh." She stepped inside, her hand searching for the light switch.

He waited until the light was on, then he stepped forward, throwing his forearm across her throat, dragging her into the room, closing the door quietly behind them.

Her eyes widened in terror, and before she could scream he clamped his hand over her mouth. "Welcome home," he whispered in her ear.

Ellis grabbed a flashlight from beneath the kitchen sink and hurried out the door towards the walkway over the dunes. How on earth, she wondered, had she managed to leave her phone and keys at the beach? She could have sworn she'd seen them in her beach bag once she'd gotten back to the house, but the day had been so busy, maybe she'd just imagined it.

She kicked her sandals off at the landing on top of the dunes, and pointing the flashlight at the steps, gingerly climbed down, holding tight to the railing. It seemed especially dark tonight, she thought. Glancing up, she saw that dense banks of purple-edged clouds obscured the moon. The temperature had dropped, and the wind had picked up. Heat lightning crackled over the water, and she heard the low rumble of thunder. She prayed it wouldn't start raining until after she'd found her phone.

When she reached the beach, she played the flashlight back and forth until she spotted the forgotten beach chair, with her towel still draped over it. And Ty Bazemore seated in it. She inhaled sharply and grabbed the stair rail, her instincts telling her to turn and run back towards the house.

But before she could move, Ty was standing up, and he was looking at her, and, wait . . . Was he smiling? At her? Anyway, it was too late to run now.

She made herself walk towards him, like it was the most natural thing in the world. But her mind could not form a sentence that wouldn't sound idiotic. In the end she settled for, "I think I left my phone and keys down here today."

Ty held up the phone. "You did," he said. "They were right here on the chair." But he made no move to give them to her.

"I wasn't sure you'd really come tonight," he said. "Hell, I wasn't sure I'd come. But I'm glad you asked me to. I don't want things to end like this, Ellis."

"What are you talking about?" she asked, coming to a dead stop inches from the chair. "Asked you to do what?"

"Come on, Ellis," Ty said, feeling his face grow hot. "This was your idea, not mine. Don't do this."

"Ty," Ellis said. "I really have no idea what you are talking about. What are you doing here? Why did you come out here tonight?"

He reached out and brushed a strand of her hair, tucking it behind her ear. "I came because you texted me and asked me to. I came because you said if I loved you, I would come. I do love you. I'm here. I'll meet you more than halfway, if you'll just give me a chance."

"I texted you?"

He frowned. "What is this? Some kind of sick joke?"

She took her phone from him, checked the log of text messages. It was empty. She held it up for him to see. "I did not text you today. I swear."

"You did, by God," Ty said. He pulled his own phone from the pocket of his cargo shorts, pulled up the screen, and showed her. "See! Why would I make up something like that?"

Ellis read the messages, glancing up at Ty, whose face had gone stony. Her own face was beet red.

Suddenly, she knew. "Julia!" she cried. "And Dorie! They did this. They stole my phone while I was asleep on the beach this afternoon, and they sent these texts to you. I woke up, and Julia was fiddling with my beach bag. I thought she was getting my sunblock out, but she must have just been putting the phone back. And then sometime later, she must have stolen it again, and planted it out here."

"And why would they pull a juvenile stunt like that?" Ty demanded. "They're your friends. Why would they punk you like that? Or me?"

Ellis wanted to die. She wanted to sink into the sand and disappear from the humiliation.

"Because," she said, biting back tears, "my idiot, deranged, meddling friends have this stupid idea that we belong together. They feel sorry for me, because they know I'm a loser, that I have no life outside my job. They know you're the first man I've been with in eleven years, and they probably have this stupid idea that we're in love. . . ."

"Hey," Ty said softly, catching her hand in his. "That's not so stupid."

She looked up at him, tears streaming down her face. "It's not stupid for them to send you fake texts from my phone to lure you down here?"

He chuckled. "That part was totally stupid. But it worked, didn't it? Here I am. And here you are."

She sniffed loudly. "Because they stole my phone and my car keys. I thought I'd left them back at Caddie's, but Julia forbid Dorie to drive back there so I could look. Dorie had this lame-ass story about how she'd seen them down here when she was leaving the beach this afternoon. I should have known. She's the world's worst liar."

"They wanted you here at midnight," Ty pointed out. "Because they knew that I'd damn sure be here, especially after that last text of yours."

Ellis blinked back a fresh set of tears. "Which one was that?"

He put his arms around her waist and pulled her close. "The one that said 'If you love me, you'll come.' I do. I did. So what should we do now?"

It started to rain. Fat, seemingly random drops full of August heat. Ellis rested her cheek against Ty's chest. Right here, in this moment, safe in the arms of a man who would do anything to make her happy. She had the answer. And all she had to do, she realized, was let him love her. Let go and let love happen. She felt the sand swirling around their ankles, the wind tearing at their clothes, the rain, coming down harder now, and above it all, she heard the crash of the surf.

She leaned her head back to look up at him, and his hair was already plastered to his head. "I think we better run for it," she said.

Ty grabbed her hand, and the two of them raced up the steps over the dunes. Ellis stopped at the top of the stairs to catch her breath, and her eyes drifted past the boardwalk, to Ebbtide, a shadowy gray hulk. The lights were on in the top-floor bedroom, Madison's room, and silhouetted there, she realized, were two figures. And one was a man.

"Ty," she said, pointing. "Up at the house. That's Madison's room. There's a man in there with her."

"Good for her," Ty said, tugging at her hand, pulling her towards the house.

"No," she said, stopping dead in her tracks. "It's got to be Adam. The man she worked with in New Jersey. She was expecting him a couple of days ago, but he never showed. We all thought there was something fishy about him, but Madison insisted he's harmless."

"I still don't see a problem," Ty said. "Look, can we have this discussion inside?"

"How did he get in the house? We lock the place up tight every time we leave. Madison locks her bedroom door, even if she's just going to the bathroom. Ty, he knows she has all that money. A hundred thousand dollars. She told him. He must have broken in while we were gone tonight."

# 51

"You still haven't asked me why I came down here," Don said, leaning back in the chair to enjoy the sight of the usually cool and composed Maryn fighting the panic he knew she must be feeling. Her face was pale and beaded with sweat.

"I know why you're here," she said, jerking her head in the direction of the briefcase. "You came to get your money back. It's all there. So take it and get out, why don't you?"

"What?" he said in mock disbelief. "My adoring wife doesn't enjoy spending time with her adoring husband?"

"Adoring?" Maryn hooted. "You never adored *me*. You adored owning me, bossing me around, showing me off to your friends. But I was just a thing to you. Nothing more, nothing less."

"And you didn't adore spending my money, living in the home I gave you, flashing that big diamond engagement ring, honeymooning in Bermuda?"

"Believe it or not, Don," Maryn said, grimacing, "I fell in love with you. The nice things were . . . nice, but for a while there—until I figured out who you were, and what you'd made me—I did love you."

"About that ring," Don said. He lifted one hip and reached for his pocket.

Maryn flinched. He's got a gun, she thought. He's got a gun, and he's going to shoot me.

Instead, Don brought out the black velvet ring box. He opened it, and thrust it towards Maryn.

"It hurts my feelings that you're not wearing your engagement ring," he said. "Put it on, why don't you? As a token of your affection."

"Fuck you," Maryn said, batting his hand and the ring box away. "It hurts *my* feelings that you've been screwing around with Tara Powers. Did you think I wouldn't find out? Taking her to the same restaurants you took me when we were dating? The same freakin' motels, afterwards? You've got the ring. Give it to your little whore Tara. Let her wear it."

Ty and Ellis stood, riveted, watching the shadow man reach out and slap the woman in the top-floor bedroom. "We've got to do something," Ellis said.

"First we've got to get out of this rain," Ty said, and hand-in-hand, they went splashing up the boardwalk towards the back porch. When they were safely under the shelter of the porch roof, Ellis remembered the cell phone she'd stuck in the pocket of her dress only a few minutes earlier.

"I'm calling the cops," she said. "Dorie and Julia are inside the house. What if he tries to hurt them?"

"Nine-one-one," a recorded woman's voice said. "You've reached Dare County Emergency Services. This line is to be used exclusively for life-threatening situations. If you are calling to report a nonemergency or inquire about county services, hang up and dial the number listed in your telephone directory. If you have a bona fide emergency, please stay on the line until an operator can assist you."

A faint hum came on the line.

"I'm on hold!" Ellis said, listening to a series of beeps. "Damn it, I have a real emergency. Come on, come on."

Ty pulled his own phone from his pocket and started punching numbers. "I'm calling Connor," he said. "He's still at the bar, but if he picks up, he's only ten minutes away." He waited, listened, and frowned. "It went to voice mail," he reported. "He probably can't even hear the damn thing ringing." He waited a moment. "Con, it's Ty. Look, we've got an intruder at Ebbtide, and I think he's holding one of these women hostage, in the top-floor bedroom. We've tried calling 911, but we're on hold. If you get this, haul your ass over here, right now."

"We can't wait," Ellis said. "The girls are alone inside the house. I've gotta get them out of there." She started for the kitchen door. "I'm gonna sneak upstairs and let them know what's going on, and get them out as quietly as I can."

"Fine," Ty nodded. "I'll stay here and watch the back staircase, in case he tries to take Madison out of there. Stay on the line for the cops. And be careful, okay?"

"Okay." Ellis eased the kitchen door open just far enough to slip inside.

Ellis tiptoed up the stairs, praying her bare feet would avoid the creaking boards, that she'd make it to the second floor undetected.

She heard water running in the bathroom, saw a flash of light from under Julia's bedroom door. She pushed into the room without knocking, finding Julia pulling a pink sleep camisole over her head.

"Julia!" Ellis whispered. "He's here."

"Who?" Julia said, stepping into her yoga pants. "Ty?"

"Not Ty! I mean, yes, Ty's downstairs, watching the back staircase. It's that Adam guy. He's upstairs, in Madison's room."

"How do you know?" Julia asked, alarmed.

"We were coming in off the beach because it started raining, and I happened to look up at the window. There are two people in Madison's room, and one of them is a man. It's got to be Adam!"

"How the hell . . . ?" Julia exclaimed. "How did he get in here? How'd he find the house?"

"I don't know, but he did," Ellis said. "We've got to do something."

"What?"

"I don't know," Ellis said. "I'm on hold for 911, and Ty left a message for Connor, asking him to get over here right away. But in the meantime, he's up there with Madison. We saw him slap her!"

"Where's Dorie?" Julia asked. "It would be just like her to go tripping up-stairs to have one last gabfest with Madison."

They heard the sound of running water coming from down the hall. They tiptoed towards the bathroom. Julia tapped lightly, but there was no answer.

"Dorie," she whispered. "Open up."

"I'm not done yet," Dorie called, her voice echoing on the tile walls. "For God's sake, if you have to go that bad, use the downstairs bathroom."

"Let me in, damn it," Julia whispered hoarsely. "And shut the hell up."

Dorie opened the door looking peeved. Her hair was gathered in a purple scrunchy on top of her head, and she was wrapped in a damp towel. "What do you want?"

"Shut up!" Julia exclaimed. "You'll get us all killed." She grabbed Dorie's arm and yanked her out of the bathroom, herding her down the hall to her own bedroom. When they were inside the room, with the door locked, Ellis pointed upwards with her index finger.

"He's here!" she said. "Adam! In Madison's bedroom. He must have broken into the house while we were at karaoke. Ty and I were coming in off the beach, and we saw him."

"Call the cops, for God's sake," Dorie said.

"I have," Ellis exclaimed. "I've been on hold for, like, forever."

"Are you really on hold?" Julia asked. "Can they do that, put you on hold for 911?"

"I'm waiting for the next operator," Ellis said. "What should we do?"

"I know what I'm gonna do," Dorie said, heading for the door. "I'm gonna go put on some underwear. I can't handle an emergency naked."

"Wait for me," Julia said. "Come on, Ellis. We need to stay together."

Don Shackleford crossed his legs and sat back in the chair, regarding Maryn with a sardonic smile.

"You see," he said, shaking his head. "When you go nosing around in other people's business, you might find out stuff you regret. You shouldn't worry about Tara. She was just . . . convenient."

"The same way I was convenient when you met me?" Maryn asked. She let her right arm drift casually to the side of the bed, inching it down until her right hand rested loosely on the edge of the box spring.

"Not the same thing at all," Don said. "I married you, didn't I?"

"Eventually," Maryn agreed. "Although you conveniently forgot to mention that you were already married when we met."

"Separated, technically," Don said. "But you never asked if I was married, did you?"

"You also conveniently forgot to mention your vasectomy," Maryn said bitterly. "When were you going to tell me about that, Don?"

He sighed. "You've been speaking to Amy, I guess. Such a vindictive bitch. You'd think the fact that I never miss a child-support payment would soften her attitude, wouldn't you? Anyway, you don't really want to have a baby, Maryn. You're too self-involved to be a good mother. And God knows, I've been a less than stellar parent to the two brats I did father. No, I won't be reversing the vasectomy."

Maryn inched her fingertips between the mattress and the box spring, silently praying that she'd feel the comfort of the cool, blue steel at any moment.

"Look, Don," she said. "You've got your money. That's what you came down here for, right? Take it and go. I'm not going back to Jersey. As soon as I get settled and get a job, I'll hire a lawyer and we'll get a nice quiet divorce. You and Tara can sail happily off into the sunset. Just leave me the hell alone."

"A divorce?" Don tsk-tsked, mockingly placing a hand over the breast pocket of his crisply pressed, pale yellow dress shirt. "Why would I want a divorce? Why can't we just happy-ever-after?"

"I'm done," Maryn said, her fingers searching between the layers of foam and batting. She felt crumbs, and was that a dead fly? Where the hell was the revolver? "I'm not going back. I don't care what you did back there. The money, whatever went on with Prescott's? None of my business. I don't want to know it. I don't know anything. Not really."

Don sighed. "Oh, Maryn, I'm really disappointed in you. Never bullshit a bullshitter, okay?"

. . .

Voices wafted from beneath the door of Dorie's closet.

"The air shaft!" she whispered, pointing to the door. She tiptoed over and opened the closet door while Ellis closed and locked the bedroom door.

They heard Madison's voice.

"What happened to Adam?" she asked. "He's coming down here, you know. He knows I'm here. And he knows you threatened me. If anything happens to me, he'll go to the police."

"Don?" Julia whispered. "She's talking to Don? The husband?" She turned to Ellis. "I thought you said it was Adam up there with her."

"It was a guy, that's all I could tell," Ellis said, cupping her hand over the cell phone. "We were worried about Adam. How the hell did the husband figure out where she is?"

"Oh, bad news," Don said. "Adam won't be able to make it, I'm afraid. But he sends his regrets."

Maryn felt the hairs on her neck prickle. "I talked to him on the phone. What did you do to him?"

"Me? What about what he did to me? Blackmail is a crime, you know. Did you realize your boyfriend was a filthy little blackmailer?"

"Adam is not my boyfriend," Maryn said through gritted teeth. "I know somebody as promiscuous as you might not believe it, but I never cheated on you. Not with Adam, or anybody else."

"So you say. But he was under the impression that you were going to cheat on me. And that you were going to run off with him, just as soon as he got this money." Don patted the briefcase.

"Adam didn't know about the money," Maryn lied. "I deliberately didn't tell him about it."

"He knew all about it," Don corrected her. "It was supposed to be his. Do you mean you hadn't figured that out?"

"I don't believe you," Maryn said, but a sickening feeling in the pit of her stomach told her Don was telling the truth.

"It was only supposed to be twenty-five thousand dollars, in the beginning," Don said. "Adam isn't nearly as smart as he thinks he is, but he was just smart enough to go poking his nose where it didn't belong. He came to me with his suspicions, and although I didn't admit anything, I did agree to a payoff. It was supposed to be twenty-five thousand dollars. He was supposed to keep his mouth shut, but the greedy little bastard just couldn't do it. He had to keep pushing. And then . . . well, you know what happened then."

"Adam called in the auditors?" Maryn asked, confused. "Why would he do that?"

Don shrugged. "He was squeezing me for more money, and I really didn't believe his threats. I guess he decided to show me who had the upper hand. Rookie move."

"But why tell me?" Maryn asked.

"He probably thought you'd leave me and run away with him," Don said, chuckling. "Not that it matters now. I've got five million dollars stashed away. And Adam? Well, poor Adam won't be making any more idle threats."

Dorie looked wide-eyed at Ellis, who still had the cell phone pressed to her ear. "Are you still on hold?"

Ellis nodded.

"We've got to do something," Dorie said. She grabbed a pair of shorts and a T-shirt and started dressing. "This guy is a maniac. Do you hear how calm he is? Discussing bribery and embezzlement? And murder? He'll kill Madison, I know he will. What can we do?"

"What are you saying?" Maryn asked, horrified. "What have you done to Adam?"

She kept fumbling around with the mattress, trying to keep her expression calm, impassive. Had Don found the pistol and confiscated it? He had to remember he'd given it to her, even showed her how to fire it.

"Adam wanted another hundred thousand dollars after he called the auditors. And you. He said if I didn't come up with the money, he'd make an anonymous phone call to the state attorney general's office. They were already sniffing around by then, and so I agreed to the little bastard's demands. And that," Don said, patting the briefcase, "is how the hundred thousand dollars came to be in my laptop case."

"Adam was blackmailing you? I don't believe it," Maryn said, stalling, because now, actually, she really could believe Adam was capable of blackmail.

"I don't give a rat's ass what you believe," Don said. "But since we're having this chat, you should know that I was going to meet *him* that morning, the morning you made the unfortunate decision to go snooping around my office."

"Why? Why would he do that?" Maryn had her hand completely under the mattress, but the pistol definitely was not where she'd put it. Don? No, wouldn't he have shown her the gun first thing? Slowly, it dawned on her. Julia! She was the only other person who'd been alone in this room. She'd found the money easily enough. Had she found the gun and swiped it? Damn her!

"You can imagine how desperate Adam got when he realized his plan backfired," Don said. "And that you'd absconded with all his money. Not that I ever really intended to give him a cent," Don added.

He looked at Maryn with interest. "What are you fiddling with over there?" He stood abruptly and jerked Maryn off the bed.

She cried out in pain as her head hit the sharp edge of the nightstand, and the lamp fell to the floor, its glass base smashing to bits.

Maryn was sobbing softly.

One floor down, Dorie, Ellis, and Julia were riveted to the spot.

"He's hurting her," Dorie exclaimed. "Ellis, are you still on hold? Hang up and redial, for God's sake."

"What?" they heard Don say, with a low chuckle. "Were you looking for that pistol I gave you? I already looked. It's not there, is it?"

"The pistol," Julia whispered. "My God, I forgot to put it back under her mattress." She sprinted from the room and came back with her beach tote, holding the gun out with a look of horror and fascination.

"What should we do?" Dorie asked. "Y'all, we can't wait for the cops."

Ellis clicked the disconnect button. "I'm calling Ty," she whispered. "He's out back. He needs to know things are getting hairy in here."

"Where'd you put the gun, Maryn?" they heard Don ask, and when she kept crying, they heard the sickening sound of a slap, and then Maryn crying harder.

"Do something," Dorie implored. "He'll kill her."

Ellis's fingers were shaking as she tapped his name on her cell phone. The phone rang twice, three times, no answer. "Come on, Ty," Ellis breathed. "Pick up. Please, please, pick up." A moment later, she got his voice mail. "Hi, it's Ty," his voice said. "Leave a number and I'll hit you back."

"Ty, it's me," she said, cupping her hand over the phone, her lips close to the receiver. "The man in Madison's room is her husband. He's beating the crap out of her. I still can't get through to 911. Get your friend, get the cops, get somebody over here now. And hurry."

"Maryn?" Don's voice was threatening.

"The gun's not here," she cried. "It was stolen from my car the first week I was here. I haven't had time to get another one. That's why I put the locks on the door."

"You're sure it's not in your purse?" Don asked, and they heard the clink of change and metal on the wooden floor.

"I told you it was stolen," Maryn whimpered. "Why would I lie?"

"All right," he relented. "Maybe you're telling the truth. Doesn't matter, does it? Come on, get up. And be quiet." He slung the briefcase over his shoulder.

Maryn was crying again.

"I said get up, damn it," Don growled, pulling his own pistol from his waistband.

Maryn gave another cry of pain, and they heard footsteps on the wooden floor.

"Where are you taking me?" she asked, her voice quivering.

"You wanted to see Adam Kuykendall, I'm taking you to see him," Don said. "Let's go."

"I'm not alone here, Don," Maryn said. "My friends—they've probably already figured out you're here. They'll call the cops. They won't let you . . ."

He slapped her so hard her ears rang.

"Friends?" he sneered. "You don't have friends, Maryn. Those women let you live here—why? Because you paid them? Nobody's coming to save you, Maryn. It's just you and me. That's the way it's always been. The way it always will be. Now move, God damn it."

When they heard the sound of the heavy door opening, the slide of the dead bolt, all three of the women knew what was happening.

"Come on," Ellis said, racing for Dorie's door. "He's taking her down the back staircase. Ty's down there, somewhere. Julia, is that thing loaded? Do you know how to shoot it?"

"It's loaded now," Julia said, her voice grim. "I haven't fired a gun since Daddy showed me how when I was fourteen, but it'll come back to me."

"Wait for me," Dorie said, sliding her feet into a pair of flip-flops.

"Stay here," Julia ordered.

"The hell I will," Dorie said fiercely, and the three of them sprinted down the stairs as fast as they could go.

When they reached the living room, Ellis made a detour towards the fireplace. "What are you doing?" Julia whispered.

Ellis raised aloft the heavy wrought-iron poker, and Julia nodded approval.

"Wait a sec," Dorie ordered, peeling off towards the kitchen. When she came back, she was brandishing a meat cleaver and a butcher knife. "Now we're set," she said.

Crouched under the rear stairwell, Ty heard the rusty door hinges squeak, and finally heard the heavy old door swing open. Shit! He felt the vibration of footsteps on the old steel stairway.

Madison was crying. "Don, no. Please, no. I won't tell anybody. Please . . ."

"Shut up!" The man's voice was hoarse, and Ty heard the sickening sound of a slap, flesh against flesh, and Madison cried out again. "Go on, move," the man ordered. "Move or I'll, by God, throw you down these stairs."

Ty looked around for something, anything, to use as a weapon, but the only thing handy was a scrap two-by-four left behind by the construction crew. He looked longingly at the shovels and rakes lying around by the construction site, but that was thirty yards away in the open, and it was too late now to risk making a run. He'd be seen for sure if he tried to move. The staircase shuddered under the weight of the footsteps descending it.

"Move, God damn it," came Shackleford's hoarse whisper.

# 52

The women crept onto the front porch, huddling together in a knot. "I wonder where Ty is?" Ellis worried. She peered out at the driveway. The rain had gotten steadier, and mist rose eerily from the construction equipment and debris scattered around Ebbtide's weedy yard. "How'd Don get here?" she whispered. "There's no car in the driveway."

"Maybe he parked somewhere down the block," Dorie suggested.

"No good, because then he'd have to drag, or carry, Madison to his car," Julia said.

"Wait," Ellis said. She ran across the driveway, veering around the remains of the old garage, towards the lot next door, the one where she'd parked what seemed like months ago to get her first sneak peek at Ebbtide. A moment later she was back, panting and out of breath.

"There's a black Escalade parked over there, behind that burnt-out foundation," she told them. "That's got to be Don's. Dorie, do you think you can make it over there to the car, like, fast?"

"Of course," Dorie snorted indignantly. "I'm not a cripple, for God's sake."

"Okay," Ellis said, gesturing to the knives Dorie wielded in each hand.

"Get over there and slash his tires. If he does manage to get Madison past all of us, that should slow him down. And then get the hell away from there."

"Be right back," Dorie promised. "Don't do anything without me."

When she was gone, Ellis and Julia crouched down and crab walked towards the edge of the front porch.

"What's the plan?" Julia asked, her voice unaccustomedly shaky. "Ellis, even if I could pull this trigger, I've only ever shot at hay bales, in broad daylight, with Daddy right beside me. I've got no idea whether or not I could actually hit anything, especially in the dark like this."

Ty felt the footsteps coming closer. He crouched into a fetal position, willing himself to fade into invisibility. Rain trickled down his head and into his ears, it dripped off the tip of his nose. He blinked and shook his head just slightly, with sudden understanding of the efficiency of Chinese water torture.

"God damn it, move your ass," Shackleford rasped. "Or I swear I'll kill you right here."

"My ankle," Madison moaned. "I think I twisted it."

Ty looked up and saw Shackleford shove Madison down the last few steps of the staircase. He saw the gun, too. She cried out, landing in a heap on the matted grass. The man stepped over her and jerked her to her feet. He had a briefcase on his shoulder.

"This way," he growled hoarsely, shoving her in the direction of the driveway.

Now or never, Ty thought grimly. He stood and launched himself into a flying tackle, fueled more with testosterone than skill, remembering his high school coach's mantra: "Square up and drive, son." Ty slammed into the back of Shackleford's thighs, sending him sprawling headfirst onto the ground. *BOOM!*

The gunshot was so close and so loud, for a fleeting moment, Ty wondered if he'd been shot. Madison fell too, and now the three of them were flopping around in the rain and the mud, arms and legs hopelessly entangled.

"What the . . . ?" Shackleford rolled onto his back. Ty slapped awkwardly at Shackleford's gun hand, managing only a grazing blow, and Shackleford retaliated with a vicious backward kick to Ty's gut. Now he was pointing the gun directly at Ty, who was scuttling backwards in the mud, trying desperately to get out of firing range.

Madison somehow managed to scramble to her feet. "No!" she screeched. "No!" She darted forward and managed to land one good kick in her husband's ribs before he caught her foot and jerked her off balance. She screamed in pain, screamed in fear, screamed until she thought her lungs would catch fire. Senseless with rage, she kicked out at Shackleford, who grabbed her ankle with his left hand and flipped her to the ground.

Seizing the moment, Ty spied a piece of scrap two-by-four, grabbed it, and was advancing on Shackleford. But the other man saw him coming, raised up on his elbows, aimed, and fired.

*BOOM!*

This time he didn't have to wonder. Ty felt a searing pain in this thigh.

Ellis and Julia startled at the screams coming from the back of Ebbtide. "He's killing her!" Julia whispered, peering around the corner of the garage. "We've gotta do something."

"Wait!" Ellis said, clutching the hem of Julia's shirt. But the gunshots coming from the back of the house canceled the women's sense of caution.

"My God," Ellis gasped. "He's got a gun. And Ty's back there. He'll kill them both!"

Before Julia could stop her, or argue for a reasonable plan of action, Ellis was sprinting towards the rear of the house, with Julia close behind. Ellis's legs felt like concrete. Her lungs, calves, and thighs burned as though she'd set fire to them. But Ty was back there, and that bastard Don Shackleford had a gun. For once in her life, she didn't have a plan. All she had was adrenaline.

Rounding the corner of the house, in the dim yellow of a single porch light, Ellis saw Madison, her face streaked with blood, flailing around on the ground, screeching and kicking out at the man Ellis knew must be her husband.

Standing over Don Shackleford was a mud-covered Ty Bazemore, with a crazed look in his eye and what appeared to be a two-by-four raised menacingly above Don Shackleford's head.

In the moonlight, they saw the gun clutched in Shackleford's hand, pointed directly at Ty's chest. For a nanosecond, time seemed to stand still. And then Ellis heard her own voice, at a decibel level she didn't know she possessed. She burst out of the shadows, with Julia right beside her, the two of them screaming like banshees.

Instinctively, the friends split up, with Julia running in one direction towards Shackleford, and Ellis in another.

Julia stopped five yards away, held the pistol out, elbows locked, the gun clutched in both hands, the way she'd seen Clint Eastwood do in all those *Dirty Harry* movies Booker loved so much. "Stop, or I'll shoot!" Unlike Clint Eastwood, her voice cracked and the words came out more of a squeak than a roar. Also unlike Clint, her hands shook like a drunk with a bad case of the DTs.

Shackleford's expression was more of bemusement than terror. He shoved Madison aside and stood easily.

"I'll shoot your ass," Julia screeched, planting her feet and assuming the position.

"Sure you will," Shackleford said, laughing. He raised his own pistol and pointed it at Julia, but at just that moment, they heard an earsplitting burst of siren: *Whee-OO, whee-OO, whee-OO.* Startled, Shackleford turned his head, just for a second.

*Whee-OO, whee-OO.*

It was all the distraction Ty needed. He slammed the two-by-four across the top of Don Shackleford's skull, at precisely the same moment that Ellis, crouched behind Shackleford, circled around, leapt into the air, and with an unearthly howl which Julia later described as "half Karate Kid, half feral dog," made a direct hit to Shackleford's groin with the fireplace poker.

At which point, the bad guy, Julia said in subsequent retellings, "folded like a Kmart lawn chair."

# 53

Ty dropped the two-by-four and limped over to Ellis, gathering her into his arms, deliberately turning her away from the sight of Don Shackleford crumpled on the ground with a gaping gouge across the top of his head.

Julia stared down at Shackleford, who was motionless. Wordlessly, she dropped the pistol, and went to comfort Madison, who had retreated to the cover of the back porch, and was now weeping softly, clinging to the handrail of the iron staircase.

"It's all right," Julia said, hugging Madison. "You're all right. He can't hurt you anymore. Not anymore. Not ever." Her voice was soothing, singsongy. Madison shuddered, and Julia petted her, as she would a frightened kitten. "I swear, he'll never touch you again."

"You guys!" they heard a voice call. Looking up, Ellis and Julia saw Dorie loping towards them, through the mist. "I heard gunshots. Are you all right?"

"Dorie!" Ellis cried. "We're okay. We're all okay. Ty . . ." Her voice was as shaky as her legs, which now felt like they might collapse under the weight of her. "Ty saved us."

"You saved yourselves," Ty corrected her, wincing. Now Ellis saw the blood oozing from his left thigh. "You're hurt," she exclaimed. "Oh my God, he shot you." She looked wildly around. "Ty's been shot. We've got to get an ambulance."

"I'm fine," Ty said wanly, clamping his hand over his thigh. "Just a flesh wound. Like on TV."

Ellis fumbled in her pocket for her cell phone, but now they heard a different set of sirens, and looking up, saw a procession of blue and red flashing lights: three Dare County sheriff's cruisers, a K-9 drug enforcement unit, and an ambulance.

"Thank God," Ellis murmured.

Everything happened at once then. Cops with dogs swarmed out of the cruisers, weapons drawn. Connor Terry pulled up in his Jeep a moment later, and rushed to Dorie's side. The EMTs strapped Shackleford to a gurney and shoved him into the ambulance.

"Come on, buddy," said another technician, trying to herd Ty towards the same ambulance.

"Nothin' doin'," Ty said through gritted teeth. "I'm not getting in the same buggy as the asshole who just tried to kill us all."

Madison, despite her own vehement protests, was told that her head injury, and a shoulder that was likely dislocated, meant a direct ticket to the emergency room. Red lights flashing, the ambulance left, bearing both Madison and her unconscious husband to the emergency room.

Ty was still arguing with the EMTs when the pretty black paramedic who'd just finished applying a butterfly bandage to Madison's forehead came walking up. "Aw, Bazemore, don't be such a hardhead," she called.

"Kalilah, you know this guy?"

"Sure," she replied. "You know him too. He works the bar at Caddie's."

"Hey, Kalilah," Ty said. "I'm was just trying to tell your friend here it's no big thing."

"Lemme see," Kalilah said, pushing him gently onto the bumper of the nearest cruiser. Donning a fresh pair of latex gloves, and illuminated by the headlights of another cruiser, she gently probed the wound. "You are one charmed sumbitch," she told him, swabbing the wound with disinfectant. "Looks like that bullet only grazed you. Couple inches to the right, and it would've hit your femoral artery. You would've bled out before we got here."

"Yeah," added the first EMT, "and another inch to the right of that and you'd be singing soprano."

"My lucky day," Ty said, wincing.

Kalilah was an efficient worker, and a moment later she had his thigh cleaned and dressed. "Now," she ordered with a grin. "I need you to drop those pants so I can hit you with some antibiotics. Which one of those cheeks is the prettiest?"

Ty shrugged, and unflinchingly dropped his rain-sodden shorts to offer up his left buttock. Before he could stop her, she jabbed him with a second needle. "A lil' something for the pain," she said. "You're gonna sleep good tonight, my friend."

Thunder growled in the distance, and a streak of lightning tore through the night. But the rain had slacked off to a gentle drizzle, and finally, after what seemed like an eternity, after all the witnesses had been questioned and statements taken, the police cruisers made their bumpy exit down the Ebbtide driveway. The group stood, huddled under a green-and-white striped golf umbrella, watching them go.

"Hey," Ellis said suddenly. "It just struck me. That first siren we heard. Right when Don Shackleford was going to shoot Ty. Where the hell did that come from?"

Dorie laughed. "My bad." She reached in the pocket of Connor Terry's borrowed, bright yellow Dare County Sheriff rain slicker and brandished her weapon of choice. "You ever try to slash a steel-belted radial Michelin with the equivalent of a butter knife?" She gave Ty a reproachful head shake. "Dude, you gotta get some decent equipment in that kitchen of yours. I was still sawing away on that first tire when the Escalade's car alarm went off. I thought for sure he'd kill all of y'all."

"Actually, that car alarm probably saved my life," Ty told her. "Shackleford had a dead bead drawn on me. He'd have shot me for sure. So it looks like you're the real hero here."

"She did great," Ellis said, looking around at all their haggard, mud-splattered faces. "But I think we all did pretty good. We make a decent team, don't you think?"

"Awesome," Julia said. "But I'd just as soon not ever go through anything like that again. Ever."

Ty nodded his agreement, but his eyelids were drooping, and it was clear he was in pain. "Come on," Ellis said finally, draping Ty's arm around her shoulder. "I'm taking you home."

He looked off at the spot where his garage and apartment had been, and yawned. "Got no home anymore," he said drowsily.

"Sure you do," Ellis told him, nudging him gently towards the weather-beaten gray house. "Ebbtide's still here. It's not going anywhere. And neither am I."

# Epilogue

Julia burst through the kitchen door. "Ellis," she exclaimed. "I just got back from my run and noticed that Madison's car is gone! I called the hospital and they told me she got herself discharged early this morning, AMA—that means 'against medical advice.'"

Ellis finished wrapping the last pink-and-green-flowered dinner plate with a sheet of newspaper and nestled it tenderly in a box with the other dishes from the now-empty cupboard. "Madison's gone," she said calmly.

Julia opened the refrigerator door and stood there, letting the chill spread over her sweat-soaked body. "You don't sound too surprised."

Ellis gestured towards the kitchen table, where the high-heeled Christian Louboutin sandals rested atop a scap of paper. "I was originally. But I guess it's not really all that shocking that she would leave like this. Not when you think about it."

"Okay if I read it?" Julia asked, craning her neck to look over at the note.

"Of course," Ellis said. "It's addressed to all of us."

Dorie came wandering into the kitchen then, barefoot and dressed in a navy blue Dare County Police Academy T-shirt over her shorty-pajama bottoms. She yawned and ran her fingers through her tousled strawberry blond locks. "What's addressed to us?"

"This," Julia said, holding the note. "It's from Madison."

"Madison?" Dorie scrunched up her face in confusion. "Isn't Madison in the hospital?"

"Not anymore," Ellis said. "Read the note, Julia."

*Dear Ellis, Dorie, and Julia: I'm no good at good-byes, so this will have to do. The ER docs say I don't have a concussion, and they managed to stitch up my head and pop my shoulder back in place, so aside from some cuts and bruises, I'm good as new. Which means it's time to hit the road. I want to thank the three of you for giving me something I've never had before—friends. Real, true girlfriends. I know I'm not easy to warm up to—hah!—understatement, right, Julia? The three of you—and Ty— saved my life this summer, not to mention last night, literally. Now it's time for me to start over. Not sure where I'll end up, or what I'll do next, but I do know I'll try hard not to screw up this time around. You guys take care. Your friend, Madison.*

*P.S. The nurses at the hospital tell me Don has a fractured skull— and something they call "blunt force trauma" to the testicles. Bravo, Ellis! P.P.S. Dorie, your friend Connor is a nice guy. He called the police in Jersey and found out that the cops in Camden discovered Adam's body Friday morning. It was stuffed in the trunk of his car, parked in a mall. I would have been in that trunk too, if it hadn't been for you guys. So, thanks again. -M-*

"Aww," Dorie said, sniffing and blotting her eyes with the tail of her T-shirt. "Where'd you find this, Ellis?"

"On the front porch," Ellis said. "I woke up around six thirty, because I thought I heard a car door. After everything else that happened last night, I guess I was still on edge. I ran downstairs and looked out the living room window, just in time to see a taxi pulling away. Madison's Volvo was right behind it. She left the note and those shoes."

"Wow," Dorie said, sinking down into a chair. "Poor Madison. First she finds out the only person she trusted betrayed her, and then she finds out he's dead. That's a lot to handle."

Julia plucked a peach from a bowl on the kitchen counter, and sank her teeth into it. For a moment, she chewed busily, letting the pink juice dribble down her chin. "I know it's awful, but I'm not gonna waste any time feeling bad for that guy. I'm guessing Adam's the one who told Don where he could find Madison. He sold her out!"

"I don't guess we'll ever know the truth about that," Ellis said. "I suppose there'll be a trial, either here or up in New Jersey. Wonder if Madison will show up to testify? Or if she'll just disappear all over again."

"I bet she'll testify," Dorie said loyally. "She cared about Adam, even after she was pretty sure he'd turned on her. She's a good person at heart. I mean, she could have taken off with all that money, if she'd been a crook. But she didn't, did she?"

"About that money," Julia said slowly. "What happens with that? A hundred thousand dollars is nothing to sneeze at."

"I saw one of the cops putting the laptop bag in the back of his cruiser," Dorie volunteered. "Maybe they'll give it back to the company Shackleford stole it from? I'll ask Connor."

"And when are you seeing your new *boyfriend* again?" Julia teased.

"He's coming over this morning to pick up the rain slicker I borrowed last night, and to help me pack the van," Dorie admitted. "But you've got to stop calling him my boyfriend. He's just a friend. . . ."

"Who happens to be a boy, who has a major crush on you," Ellis pointed out. "What's he think about you heading home to Savannah today?"

Dorie sighed. "He wanted to help me drive home, since Julia's not coming back with me, but I told him I didn't think that was a good idea. I've got so much to do when I get home, getting the house packed up, meetings at school, and classes start next week. Not to mention, I've got to have a long talk with my mother. Oh yeah, and meet with my divorce lawyer! Connor's got a week of vacation in October, and he wants to visit then."

"Have you decided where you're going to live?" Ellis asked.

Dorie's face brightened. "Willa—bless her interfering heart—managed to work that out for me. I think she must have laid a major guilt trip on Phyllis. Can you believe it? Mama called this morning and told me she wants me to move into my nana's house in Ardsley Park! Rent-free! She says my brother is fine with it."

"Of course Nash is fine with it," Julia said. "He's probably thrilled at the idea of you living there and cooking and cleaning for him."

Dorie shook her head. "Nuh-uh. Nash will have another think coming if he thinks I'm gonna be his personal housekeeper. I am done being Dorie the Doormat," she declared.

"What do you hear from Stephen?" Julia asked.

"He wants to see me as soon as I get home," Dorie said. "And he asked if he can come to my next OB appointment. He wants to be there for the ultrasound I've got scheduled."

"So, give him a printout," Julia snapped.

"I told him I'm fine with him coming," Dorie said. "He's the baby's father. I've seen Phyllis struggle with being a single mom. And I've been the kid whose dad never came to back-to-school night. I don't want that for this baby. No matter how I feel about the decisions Stephen's made, he's not a monster. He's a good man. And I want him in my child's life."

"You are such an adult," Julia said, shaking her head in admiration. "Really, Dorie. You amaze me."

Dorie dipped a curtsy. "Thanks. Sometimes I amaze me too. We'll see. How 'bout you, Julia? What time are you expecting Booker?"

"With Booker, you never know," Julia laughed. "He's driving down in the new car he bought me. I haven't owned my own car in years, but Book insists I'll need one, working here and living part-time in Atlanta. Thank God I kept up my Georgia driver's license." Julia glanced at her watch. "Which reminds me, I've got a production meeting at Joe's hotel in fifteen minutes. I know you need to get your car loaded, Ellis, but do you think Ty would mind loaning me his Bronco? Just for an hour or so?"

"What's this about taking my car?" The three women turned their heads in unison as Ty walked, stiff legged, into the kitchen. He was unshaven, and dressed in a threadbare blue terry cloth bathrobe, but otherwise looked remarkably fit for a man who'd been shot only hours before.

"Well," Julia started, "I just need to run up to Kitty Hawk for our production meeting, and I know Ellis probably wants to get on the road, so I thought maybe . . ."

Ellis and Ty's eyes met. Ty raised one eyebrow, and Ellis gave a barely perceptible nod. "Ellis," he said succinctly, "isn't going anywhere." He wound an arm around Ellis's waist, and dropped a kiss on her cheek. "Right? You wanna tell them, or should I?"

Ellis rubbed her face against Ty's day-old beard, reveling in the casual intimacy.

"That's not exactly accurate," she corrected. She turned to Julia and said apologetically, "Actually, I do need to get my car loaded this morning. But I'm sure you can borrow Ty's Bronco."

"What?" Ty looked taken aback. "We agreed. You said last night . . ."

Ellis shrugged. "I changed my mind."

Ty's eyes darkened. "Ellis, don't do this . . ."

She caught him by the belt of his robe and drew him back towards her, as though she were reeling in a particularly cooperative fish. "You," she pointed out, "took a bullet in your thigh last night. You can hardly walk. You don't need to be going up and down these stairs all morning. I can easily load my stuff myself, and move it down to Pelican Cottage. I loaded it in here by myself, and I can load it out by myself."

"Now wait," Ty started.

"You mean it?" Dorie squealed. "You're not going back to Philly? At all? You're gonna stay here? With Ty?"

"Well, not here at Ebbtide," Ellis said, trying hard to suppress a smile. "We'll be shacked up in that little hovel he rented just down the beach. For at least the next three months. Give or take."

"Give or take?" Julia said with a hoot. "Who are you, Ellis Sullivan? And what about that cushy job in Seattle? I thought you couldn't live without a job and a 401(k) and a parking pass. And a Kaper chart. What's the plan, Ellis?"

"There is no plan," Ellis said blissfully. "I guess I finally figured that out . . . last night. There's nothing I need or want in Seattle." She glanced at Ty, whose arm was around her shoulder. "I've got what I want. Right here."

"Happy ever after, that's the plan," Ty said. "I'm going to teach her how to surf."

"And I'm going to teach him how to read a spreadsheet."

"If you need us, we'll be at Pelican Cottage," Ty broke in. "And it's not a hovel. It's oceanfront, and it's quaint. . . ."

"It's a dump," Ellis said, shushing him. "Just like Ebbtide is. Was. But we can fix that. Fortunately for you, *Mister Culpepper*, I happen to have a weird fondness for dumps. And their landlords."

"Ellis Sullivan," Ty retorted, determined to have the last word. "You are a major pain in my ass. Promise me you'll be a pain in my ass forever and ever." He gathered her into his arms as Dorie and Julia danced around them, providing loud, inappropriate, immature smacking, smooching sound effects.

Ellis nodded, and allowed herself to be kissed, right on the lips, and right in front of her best friends. "Yes," she said solemnly. "I promise. I do. I will."

1. Each of the four characters comes to Ebbtide with a major problem. How would you characterize each problem?

2. Which of the characters' dilemmas did you find the easiest to relate to? Which one felt the least identifiable to you, and why?

3. There is a famous saying that "money is only something you need in case you don't die tomorrow." Do you feel that money could have solved each one of these characters' problems, including Ty Bazemore? Why or why not?

4. Maryn Shackleford leaves her life behind to create a new identity. If you were in her position would you have done the same? Would it be easy to leave your life behind? Have you ever been tempted to do so?

5. Does the idea of a monthlong rental with a group of girl-friends appeal to you? Where would be your dream place to go? What problems could you foresee occurring?

6. Do you think it's possible to be married to someone and not realize he's gay? If Dorie's situation happened to you, what would you do?

7. For someone who has devoted her entire life to her career, being fired is the ultimate devastation. Can you relate to Ellis's situation? Do you understand why this threw her so much? Do you think being fired can actually end up being the best thing that ever happened to you?

8. Julia fights against the physical realities of growing old. What do you really think she's worried about? Do you embrace the concept of aging with humor, acceptance, or dread?

9. Ty and Ellis could not be more opposite. But did you see any ways in which they are similar? Can you see their relationship working in the long term?

10. What is your go-to karaoke song?

11. If you were to create a sound track to go along with this book, what would be on the playlist?

*For more reading group suggestions,*
*visit www.readinggroupgold.com*

St. Martin's
Griffin

Turn the page for a sneak peek at
Mary Kay Andrews's new novel

# Spring Fever

Available June 2012

# 1

From her seat in the sanctuary of the Church of the Good Shepherd, Annajane Hudgens wondered if there had ever been a more flawless day for a wedding.

Spring had arrived spectacularly early in Passcoe, North Carolina. Only the first week in April, yet the dogwoods and azaleas were already burst into bloom, and the weeping cherry trees lining the walkway to the church trailed fingertips of pale pink onto a blue and white carpet of violets and alyssum.

It was as if the bride, the equally flawless Celia Wakefield, had somehow managed to *will* perfect weather. Or perhaps she'd specified blue skies and color-coordinated bursts of blooms in one of her famously precise memos. If anybody could do that, Annajane mused, it would be Celia.

Could there be a more beautiful setting? Baylesses had been getting married at the Church of the Good Shepherd for nearly two hundred years. Not in this grand sanctuary, of course. The original church was a quaint, stoop-shouldered gray granite affair, with uneven oak floors, a single Gothic-arched leaded-glass window above the altar, and two rows of ten primitively wrought pine pews built by black laborers from the casket factory in Moore County, twenty minutes down the road.

Annajane could remember sitting beside her best friend, Pokey, in the Bayless family pew after countless Saturday-night sleepovers, back when they were both still in pigtails. By then, Pokey's grandmother had already started her slow descent into senility, although Annajane had not known that. Miss Pauline, for whom Pokey had been named, seldom spoke, but she was content to sit in church on Sunday mornings and smile and nod to the hymns, dabbing at her cataract-clouded blue eyes with her ever-present handkerchief and patting Annajane's hand. "She thinks you're me," Pokey would whisper, giggling at her grandmother's confusion and grimacing and holding her nose when Miss Pauline passed gas, which she did frequently.

When the "new" Church of the Good Shepherd was built in the early '90s, with reproduction Tiffany stained-glass windows, solid cherry pews, and a custom-built German pipe organ, the old church was renamed the Woodrow Memorial Chapel in memory of Pauline Woodrow, who died in her sleep the year Pokey and Annajane turned fourteen.

Annajane's own wedding had been held in the chapel, the one concession her new in-laws made to what they considered Annajane's "quaint" ideas. Since she'd paid for the wedding herself, she'd insisted on having an intimate affair, just family and close friends, fewer than forty people, with Pokey as her only attendant. It had rained the November evening of her nuptials, and at the time she'd considered it wildly romantic that the loud thrum of the rain on the church's tin roof threatened to drown out the wedding march played on the chapel's original wheezy pump organ.

Had it been only seven years ago? Sometimes she wasn't sure any of it had really happened at all, that it wasn't something she'd just remembered from a long-ago dream.

Today's affair was nothing like Annajane's modest wedding. The sanctuary was at capacity—beyond capacity, if you went by the county fire code, which said the church could hold five hundred people. It seemed to Annajane that every living person who had ever known or done business with the Bayless family, or even just sipped a bottle of their Quixie cherry soft drink, had crammed themselves into one of the polished wooden pews beneath the soaring exposed rafters of the imposing Episcopal church.

Annajane felt her eyelids droop now. It was too warm in the church, and the scent of the lilies and roses banking everything that didn't move was overpowering. She'd had almost no sleep the night before, and not much more sleep the night before that. And, yes, she'd had herself a good stiff drink, Quixie and bourbon on the rocks, back at the house, after she'd finished dressing and before she'd left for the church. She closed her eyes, just for a moment, felt her chin droop to her chest, and the next moment, she felt a sharp elbow dig into her ribs.

Pokey had managed to wedge herself into the pew. "Wake up and slide over!" she ordered.

Annajane's eyes flew open, and she looked up, just in time to see Sallie Bayless, seated in the front row, two pews ahead of them, turn and shoot Pokey a stern look of warning. Sallie's gleaming auburn hair shone in the candlelit church. She was sixty-four, but still had the dewy complexion, sparkling brown eyes, and slender figure of a woman twenty years younger. Now, those eyes narrowed as they took in Pokey's tardy and disheveled appearance.

Pokey gave her mother a grin and a finger wave, and Sallie's head swiveled back around, eyes front, head held high, the Bayless pearls, a double strand, clasped firmly around her neck.

Annajane offered an apologetic smile to the elderly woman to her right. The woman frowned, but begrudgingly inched aside to allow the new arrival to be seated.

As usual, Pokey Bayless Riggs took no notice of the stir she'd caused. She'd been causing a stir nearly every day of her thirty-five years, and today, her brother's wedding day, was no different.

The boatneck collar of Pokey's expensive new red silk jacket had slipped off her right shoulder, exposing a leopard-print bra strap and an unseemly amount of cleavage. Little Clayton was two years old, but Pokey was still struggling to lose her baby weight. She'd managed to pop one of the jacket's rhinestone buttons, and the tight silk skirt had somehow twisted around so that the zipper was now in the front, rather than on the side. She was bare-legged, which was a scandal in and of itself, but now Annajane noticed that her best friend had ditched the Sallie-mandated sedate dyed-silk slingback pumps in favor of a pair of blinged-out silver flip flops.

Pokey's thin, poker-straight blond hair had already lost its beauty-salon bounce, and now hung limply on either side of her full pink cheeks. Her lipstick was smeared. But her eyes, her amazing cornflower-blue eyes, glinted with mischief.

"Busted!" Annajane whispered, not daring to look at her best friend.

"Christ!" Pokey muttered. "This is so not my fault. I couldn't find a parking spot! The church lot's full and the whole block is lined with cars on both sides of the street. I had to leave the Land Rover clear down the block in front of the gas station and run all the way here."

"Aren't you supposed to be up there with your mom and everybody else in the family?" Annajane asked. "I mean, you *are* the groom's only sister."

"Screw that," Pokey said swiftly. "I refuse to make nice with that woman. Mason knows I don't like her. Mama knows it too. I'm taking a moral stand here."

"Who the hell are all these people anyway?" she asked, glancing around at the packed church and zeroing in on the bride's side of the aisle. "Not family, right? Since poor lil' Celia is an orphan, and the only family she could produce is that elderly great aunt staying over at Mama's house. Did Celia charter a bus or something?"

Annajane shrugged. "You're apparently the only person in Passcoe who *doesn't* think that Celia Wakefield is the best thing since flush toilets and sliced store-bought bread."

"Don't give me that. You hate her as much as I do," Pokey said under her breath.

"Not at all," Annajane replied. "I'm happy for them."

"Yippy-fuckin'-skippy," Pokey drawled. "Happy, happy, happy. It's fine for you. In less than a week, you'll pack up your U-Haul and head for Atlanta and your nice new life without even a glance in the rearview mirror. New man, new job, new address. But where does that leave me? Stuck here in stinkin' Passcoe, with my mama, my evil brother Davis, and good ole Mason and his new bride, Cruella de Vil."

"Poor, poor Pokey," Annajane mocked her right back. "Richest girl in town, married to the second richest man in town."

"Third richest," Pokey corrected. "Or maybe fourth. Davis and Mason have way more money than Pete, especially since people quit buying furniture made in America."

"Speaking of, where is Pete?" Annajane asked, craning her neck to look for him. Instead of spotting Pokey's tall redheaded husband, Pete, her eyes rested on another tardy couple, Bonnie and Matthew Kelsey, hurrying up the right-side aisle of the church.

Bonnie Kelsey's eyes met Annajane's. She blushed, and looked away quickly, clutching Matthew's arm and steering him into a pew as far away from Anna-jane's as she could manage in the overcrowded church.

Pokey saw the maneuver for what it was. "Bitch," she said.

"It's all right," Annajane said smoothly. "I mean, what do you expect? Matt and Mason play golf every week. From what I hear, Bonnie and Celia get along like a house afire. Best friends forever! Anyway, Bonnie's not the only one to sign up for Team Celia. Every woman in this room has been staring daggers at me since I walked into this church. I knew when I agreed to come today that it would be awkward."

"Awkward?" Pokey laughed bitterly. "It's freakish, is what it is. Who else but you would agree to show up at her ex-husband's wedding?"